*Praise for Colin Greenland's
award-winning PLENTY trilogy:*

"A ROUSING GOOD READ . . .
FAST-MOVING, FUNNY AND INVENTIVE."
Ursula K. Le Guin

"FUN . . . A WILD RIDE THROUGH
A STRANGE UNIVERSE."
Analog

"A K.O.! . . .
ONE OF THE MOST COMPULSIVE
SPACE SPECTACULARS IN YEARS."
London Times

"A GRANDLY REALIZED BROAD-BRUSH PAINTING
THAT SWEEPS THE READER ALONG
WITH ITS SHEER PANACHE."
Vector

"A THOROUGHLY GOOD READ
WITH DEPTH TO IT . . .
THE PEOPLE ARE MARVELOUS AND REAL . . .
AND GOOD ALIENS. I LOVE AND ADMIRE
GOOD ALIENS."
Diana Wynne Jones, author of *A Sudden Wild Magic*

D0011007

Other Avon Books by
Colin Greenland

The Tabitha Jute Trilogy

TAKE BACK PLENTY
SEASONS OF PLENTY

MOTHER
OF
PLENTY

COLIN GREENLAND

AVON · EOS

AVON BOOKS, INC.
1350 Avenue of the Americas
New York, New York 10019

Copyright © 1998 by Colin Greenland
Published by arrangement with the author
Visit our website at http://www.AvonBooks.com/Eos
Library of Congress Catalog Card Number: 97-94884
ISBN: 0-380-78776-8

First Avon Eos Printing: June 1998

AVON EOS TRADEMARK REG. U.S. PAT. OFF. AND IN OTHER COUNTRIES, MARCA REGISTRADA, HECHO EN U.S.A.

Printed in the U.S.A.

WCD 10 9 8 7 6 5 4 3 2 1

for Susanna—
strange but true

The Mundane Shell is a vast Concave Earth, an immense
Harden'd Shadow of all things upon our Vegetated Earth,
Enlarg'd into Dimension and deform'd into indefinite Space,
In Twenty-seven Hevens and all their Hells, with Chaos
And Ancient Night and Purgatory. It is a cavernous Earth
Of labyrinthine intricacy, twenty-seven folds of Opaqueness,
And finishes where the lark mounts.

William Blake, *Milton*

CONTENTS ∽

PART ONE
The End of the Line   1

PART TWO
The Mother Ship   155

PART THREE
Abraxas Rising   309

PART ONE

THE END OF THE LINE

The twins are old, and red, and fat.

They are old by any measurement of time, objective or subjective, atomic or sidereal. They are red with repletion, with rage and decay. They are fat with everything they have eaten, which was everything in sight.

The red twins circle each other like dinosaurs preparing for a fight. They are locked together, glaring at each other. They have been circling for a thousand million years.

So conjoined are the red twins that they have but one name between them.

They are Capella.

They are the old, red, fat Capella twins. To speak of one of them is to speak of both.

The red twins continue to surround themselves with a mantle of black flux, a vast slow blizzard of degenerate matter. Dyspeptically, they belch up clots of carbon thousands of kilometers across, cosmic smuts that swirl, coagulating, in hyperbolic disintegrating orbits, plunging eternally from destruction into destruction.

It is no wonder that the inhabitants of the Capella System took long, long ago to the high seas of interstellar space, and scattered themselves abroad.

The wonder is that any of them remained.

On the outer edge of the slow and filthy tide there drifted a lump. There was nothing to distinguish it from any other lump in the stellar vicinity; though to a human or posthuman observer, the shape of it might perhaps have suggested, from certain angles, the shell of a tortoise; or the bun of a hamburger; or else a human brain. It had, at one time or another, been compared with all those things.

3

In fact, it was a starship. It was a ship which had come, through years of torment and nightmare, all the way from Sol.

She was the ship called Plenty.

Her story was complicated. Complicated and bizarre.

Plenty had been built by the attenuated aliens known as the Frasque, spun out of a particulate froth extruded from their own twiggy bodies, high above the bustling Earth. Before they could use their creation for whatever obscure purpose they intended, they were pounced upon by their enemies, the Capellans. Deploying a small batallion of enlisted human fighters, the Capellans, alien brain parasites and overlords of everywhere, burned the Frasque out of the corridors of Plenty and eradicated them from the Sol System.

Plenty lingered on, abused by entrepreneurs and opportunists, orbiting inert and dumb, until one day, more by luck than judgment, an ambitious bargee called Tabitha Jute seized upon her, plugged in the artificial persona from her old barge the *Alice Liddell*, and roused the stardrive that slept unsuspected within her somber depths.

Delighted with her accomplishment, Captain Jute filled the caverns of her new starship with a highly heterogeneous population and took her off for a jaunt to Proxima Centauri.

The history of humankind has been marked perhaps by worse ideas, but not many.

The trip went astray at once. The passengers and crew of Plenty sailed on for ten years longer and forty light-years farther than they had intended. That gave them time, plenty of time, to inflict upon each other and upon themselves all the follies that their imaginations, warped by the inhospitable environment, could conceive.

Some of them survived. Among them, just about, was Tabitha Jute.

Others of the survivors were Captain Jute's old shipmate Dodger Gillespie; her lover, a sulky datapunk called Jone;

and the maverick Cherub known as Xtasca. They were the ones who made the arduous descent into the bowels of the ship and discovered that it had been hijacked, by Tabitha's own sister, a tool of the secretive Temple of Abraxas.

The Temple's motives, as usual, were known to themselves alone. Obviously if there was a starship going begging, the Temple, that decadent cabal of posthuman supremacists, would like to have it. But having somehow got their agent aboard, why in all the worlds had they promptly sent it winging off to Capella?

The Capellans, presumably, were behind it all. On board Plenty, a vermiform Capellan now sat coiled inside the skull of each of ten hapless quislings, newly promoted "Guardians."

The Guardians occupied the bridge, the nerve centers of the alien vessel. They sailed through the residential districts, dispensing homilies and toffees, and smiling, smiling, smiling.

Battered and warped by her passage through the probability fault popularly known as hyperspace, the great dun ship rode ponderously in the ocean of ash. Her colossal flanks were cloaked in sooty dust, stained with the red light of the angry twins.

Perhaps she did still resemble the shell of a tortoise: the most horribly mutated tortoise ever born.

Her interior was damaged too. The entire Starboard Inferior Frontal had disappeared. Apartments, businesses, road and foot tunnels, together with their inhabitants, transients, pets, pests, traffic, miarolitic encrustations and coagulating garbage—all had vanished at a stroke, as if excised by some titanic surgical operation. Aft, several Limbic shafts now bore no relation to the docks beneath, but ran down into what appeared to be a little leftover piece of the discontinuum: a bit of hyperspace itself. It shimmered faintly, like fractal porridge.

∽ 1

The docks of Plenty were full of smoldering spaceships.

Immediately forward of the hyperspatial fault, the ceiling had come down. Vessels and those who had fought so frantically for possession of them lay buried together in crumbled matrix and cheap concrete. The crisis orange uniforms of the Hands On Caucus made an especially bright display among the rubble.

Smoke drifted about, drawing its curtains this way and that, concealing and revealing the ultimate effects of greed, desperation, righteousness. Personal flight bags and their contents lay scattered among the spent ammunition. Fire drones still trundled through the wreckage, spraying the fitful flames with jets of suffocating foam.

High in an upper tier of the parking bays, a Navajo Scorpion looked down on the silent chaos. Unlike many of the parked ships, she seemed to have been maintained during her decade of disuse, and had sat out of reach of the riots. A few overoptimistic looters had got into her bay, Bay 490-9. They lay around her where they had fallen, unmarked, quite dead.

The name of the Scorpion was lettered on her sharp prow. She was the *All Things Considered*. It seemed an appropriate name. There was something judicious about the sharpness of her profile, and she was equipped with a surprising amount of surveillance and recording equipment.

On board the *All Things Considered*, things were not in such good order. In her stateroom, particularly, the scattered blood clashed unpleasantly with the pink-and-orange decor. Fortunately the lights were low.

There was a circular bed surrounded by a rampart of AV

monitors all turned inward, to provide a wall of identical images. There was a gap at the foot of the bed, and another where a stack of monitors had been severely disarranged, some of them overturned. Several of the remaining screens were blank, or fizzed emptily. The rest continued to show fancifully stylized examples of Terran wildlife engaged in raucous violence.

The bed itself seemed to have been the center of the disturbance. Its sheets were torn and tangled up with articles of clothing. A liqueur glass had been trampled into the carpet. Everything had been smeared with nonhuman ordure, blood and chocolate.

Also in the stateroom was a holodais, a basic commercial model. It stood opposite the foot of the bed, clearly visible through the gap in the wall of monitors. The image it showed was a life-size one, of a light brown woman dressed only in a long black coat. The sound was off. Apart from the background hum of the air systems, the only sound in the cabin was the hectic slithering of an orchestra recorded long before as accompaniment to the antics of the animated creatures.

The hologram was on a timer. Every thirty seconds the woman opened her coat and exposed herself to the bed. On her face was an expression of terror.

A sophisticated system kept the air circulating on board the *All Things Considered*, and heated it to a very comfortable 24° Celsius. One of the vents was high in the sternward wall of the stateroom, covered by a grille. The system had already mixed the odors of cosmetics, pharmaceuticals and Thrant excrement together quite thoroughly. Now it had begun to introduce to the mixture another distinctive scent: the complex olfactory signature of human decay. This issued primarily from the remains of the human that lay on the carpet, a naked white-skinned male. He was headless and had been disemboweled.

Of his innards, little remained in the cabin. Small portions might possibly have been identified here and there among the ruined furnishings. His head lay against the sternward wall, some distance from the rest of him. It lay, as it happened, directly beneath the vent.

Through the grille of the vent a tiny, pointed, bluish white blob had begun to ooze. It resembled at first a curd of milk, or a drip of latex.

On the banked monitors a goggle-eyed predator assumed a look of comic dismay. He had run and run until he realized too late there was no longer any ground beneath his feet.

The hologram looped. The terrified brown woman opened her coat again.

From the ventilator the blob extended itself downward like a tendril, a rootlet, four centimeters long. Now it looked like a miniature white finger, a finger without a fingernail.

As if gravity were a consequence of consciousness, instead of the other way round, the cartoon predator on the monitors fell rapidly through the air. From a high perch his erstwhile prey regarded his whistling descent, beaming idiotically.

On the cartoon sound track, violins exulted. Trumpets blared.

The long white blob had emerged entirely from the vent. There were perhaps ten centimeters of it. It was crawling down the wall, toward the head beneath.

The head beneath the vent was the head of a human male, thirtyish, Caucasian, with black hair. A pair of small round black-glass spectacles was still attached to one ear, though one lens, the left, had been smashed. His left eye was a bloody mess. His hair was, as ever, immaculate.

It was the head of the Scorpion's last owner, the man called Grant Nothing. The head lay tilted at a slight angle. It looked as if Grant Nothing was still, in death as in life, listening out for something.

The last sentients to see him, those who had put such effort into accomplishing his demise, had departed hurriedly some time ago. Few others knew of his predicament.

The man called Grant Nothing had been a secretive individual, busy everywhere, detectable nowhere.

Who would notice the disappearance of an invisible man?

As if spurred on by consideration of the incubation rate of bacteria in mortified flesh, the white blob proceeded down the wall. It moved very much in the manner of a caterpillar, bunching itself up in the middle and pushing itself downward.

Having traveled its own length twenty times over, with care the diminutive intruder negotiated the transfer between the vertical surface of the wall and the rear slopes of the displaced head.

At the apex of the occipital curve, it paused, as if to take breath. It looked very white on Grant Nothing's shiny black hair.

On the cartoon sound track, the strings made a thrilling sound.

The creature began to move again. It slid more easily across the smooth coiffure. Down the pale escarpment of the forehead it ventured.

At the bow of the buckled spectacles it paused again. It reared up and waved its tiny pointed head in a circle, as if protesting against the obstacle. Then it made a move. The juicy liquefaction of the left eye was calling it.

The creature slipped into the crater of the exposed socket and sipped there a while.

Then on it went, squirming diligently down behind the spectacles, between the frame and the face, following the angle between nose and cheek. Setting its proleg finally on the well-groomed upper lip, it curled around and entered the left nostril.

Slowly, effortfully, it wriggled up and up until it was out

of sight. In a moment a soft, moist, munching sound commenced.

On the holodais opposite the foot of the bed the brown woman continued to open and close her long black coat.

∽ 2

On the twenty-first day after Emergence, in the green dome that housed the bridge the humans had installed in the alien ship, a blond woman in a pink fur top and glytex leggear approached a man with a grotesquely enlarged cranium.

"Geneva McCann," she told him, beaming. "Channel 9."

The woman had a hovercam tethered to her belt. She sent it up to look the man in the face.

The man stood with his hands on his hips. He had a ruffled white shirt on, tight leopard skin trousers, and a short cape of quilted gold. Under the crepe soles of his blue-suede boots there were fifteen clear centimeters of artificial air.

"Geneva," he said, in a voice like a pipe organ's deepest and most sincere bass. He spread his cape with his elbows.

The woman's smile was electric.

"Marco Metz, or should I say Brother Melodious, you are a phenomenon. Not only are you actor, musician, producer, dancer and AV personality, you're also the sexiest man on the ship."

The leopard-patterned Guardian preened.

Across the chamber in her life-support chair, the deposed Captain grunted. Her thin consort tutted and rubbed her shoulders soothingly.

"Well, gee, I don't know what to say, Geneva," boomed

Brother Melodious. He indicated the crowd that followed him and his confrères everywhere they went. They wore togas, made out of spare bed linen. Some wore sandals. Hope had already led several of them to shave their heads.

"All I ever did was try to make people happy," said Brother Melodious.

His interviewer wriggled. "And you did, Brother Melodious," she said, "all the way from stem to stern." She contrived to shake her bottom at him. "Why, we can't even begin to count the women who can vouch for that!"

Brother Melodious lowered his hi-lited eyelids and glanced at the tips of his right fingers, where the fingernails would have been if his hand had not been made of glass. "I have the deepest respect for women," he avowed, with husky might.

His interviewer ignored a small disturbance from the other side of the chamber. That she could edit out. She increased the wattage of her smile as the Guardian subtly flexed his thighs.

"Where would we be without 'em?" he asked.

"Not here in Capella System, that's for sure," purred Geneva, indicating the big screen, where the red twins hung like stoplights in fog.

Tabitha Jute groaned. Saskia Zodiac stroked her head and murmured in her ear. Beside them Eeb the Altecean snuffled mournfully and wiped her snout on the back of her paw.

"Brother Melodious, the Emergence of Plenty into real space has coincided with your own Emergence into new realms of personal influence and prestige. You are now a powerful and significant Guardian, host to a personal Capellan mentor of your own." Geneva's camera flew a circle around his expanded brow. "You can tell us, Marco—does it *hurt*?" She pouted with imagined pain.

The hovering Guardian angled for a close-up. "Well," he said, "okay, let me tell you about that, Geneva. Bonding with a Capellan has no unpleasant or harmful side effects at all."

Geneva's camera hugged Brother Melodious's plump cheeks. "Is it true you experience a two hundred percent increase in your personal mental power?"

"Sure," he said easily. "Sure. Though you know, I've always been pretty bright. Wrote all my own material, always. All my own ideas. But the day I ran into this little guy," claimed Brother Melodious, touching his real hand to the side of his head, "that was the day my career truly started."

His interviewer took a step backward. She raised her eyebrows. "You've had a wonderful career," she chided him, lovingly.

Brother Melodious's tones took a drop into triple-enriched intimacy. "You know, you're right, Geneva," he said. "Those years were great. I played some great crowds, I met some wonderful people. Let's not forget the day I was playing in a bar in Schiaparelli when a little lady called Tabitha Jute walked in."

Smugly he saluted her.

There were some scattered, nervous sounds of appreciation.

Across the chamber, Tabitha Jute gazed at him expressionlessly.

Brother Melodious pretended she was smiling and gave her a wink. Evolved or no, he was a performer still, first and last. He pointed a ring at the floating camera and boosted the volume.

"That was the day the whole thing started!"

He raised his glass hand and, activating its induction circuits, began to play "Goodbye, Blue Sky," that stirring song.

The crowd of acolytes promptly joined in. In a moment, all around the bridge, at the navigation desks and chart consoles and transfer stations, everyone was singing along.

Ten years or more had passed since they had sung it last, but its words had not been erased from their minds. They had known them all their lives, ever since Capella had given them the power to leave the surface of their planet and spread throughout Sol System. Now they had succeeded, quite illegally, in venturing farther. The journey had been arduous, a long bad dream. They were happy to have come out of it to find their benefactors waiting for them, ready to welcome and forgive them.

At the helm, Mr. Spinner sang weakly, self-consciously, one arm in a sling. Behind his back a Guardian hovered, like Conscience in an old painting.

Brother Melodious acknowledged the cheers and applause. He insisted on applauding them too with his famous hands.

"Community singing," announced the Disaster Commissioner, striding in from the foyer with Dodger Gillespie and others in tow. The Commissioner got up on a desk to shake Marco Metz's famous glass hand. "No, don't bother to come down, I'll come up. Community singing. Nothing like it! Marco Metz, Brother Melodious, let me congratulate you."

He grinned at everyone in sight, and especially at the camera. He was perspiring. He spotted Captain Jute and saluted her. He looked guilty.

"Well, Mr. Metz, you clearly haven't lost any of that old power to make people happy!" Geneva McCann brought the camera back for a two-shot, the Guardian and the ship's officer, an image of the new partnership.

"I love music!" said the Disaster Commissioner. "The power of music!" He clutched Brother Melodious's hand as if he thought it might hoist him up into the air too.

Folding her long legs with a muttered oath, Captain Gillespie squatted down beside Tabitha's chair. Her breath and clothing smelled of tobacco. " 'Old up, gel," she said.

"Dodger," said Captain Jute dully. The return of the Capellans had provoked a relapse, a deterioration in her condition. Brother Valetude had had to step up the sedatives again.

"She should be in bed," Saskia Zodiac said to Captain Gillespie. Eeb nodded fretfully. They had not wanted the Captain to come to the bridge today. There was no point in her being here. It only made her difficult.

"Now I think it's generally known that the stars we can all see out there are not, as we had hoped, Proxima Centauri and its partners Alpha and Beta, but the constituent parts of the far younger star Capella," recited Geneva McCann, stepping daintily backward and swiveling toward the helm.

She addressed the Guardian who had stationed himself behind Mr. Spinner. "Kybernator Astraghal, it's quite a thrill for all of us to be here in the home system of the most advanced race in the galaxy! What can you tell us about this next phase of our epic journey through interstellar space? Are we going to visit your homeworld?"

The Guardian had narrow, sleepy eyes and a voice like a big cat. "All in good time," he said. He spread his hands on the snowy front of his toga.

"1-7-5-0-2-4-5," reported Mr. Spinner, from the level of the Kybernator's knees. He looked somber. The failure of the Proxima expedition was eating at his professional pride. He seemed to take the return of the Capellans as a punishment. In consequence, he was behaving with the undeviating rectitude of an autonomic system. "1-7-5-0-9. 245 and steady." He put his eyes to a viewer, which a cadet adjusted for him.

"Roll 35.07°. Arc point 07. Point 08. 085."

Corrections came from the approximators. Kybernator Astraghal pointed a majestic finger at the big screen. He touched a ring and changed the picture.

Grey snow tracked slowly through black vacuum, each particle trailed by a white ghost and a purple one. Search grids webbed the image, a checkerboard of different levels of resolution. Multicolored telltales decorated the edge of the picture, icons for data access.

"TARGET VESSEL IN RANGE," said a voice from nowhere in particular.

Geneva McCann clucked and headed for the screen, while the Kybernator said humorously, "Oh dear me, that does sound so very martial."

The Disaster Commissioner chuckled and agreed, yes, it did.

" 'Host vessel', I think, please, Persona," said the Kybernator.

Captain Jute spoke loudly. "Her name is Alice," she said.

"*Go ask Alice,*" sang Brother Melodious, while his hand played high-pitched primitive guitar, "*I think she'll know—!*" He smiled fondly at the Captain, as if considering whether he should dedicate this number to her.

"HOST VESSEL 23 DEGREES 52 MINUTES 06 SECONDS NORTH ELEVATION 65 POINT 70," said the persona.

"We have visual confirmation," said Mr. Spinner.

"There we are, visual confirmation!" said Geneva McCann, filming the big screen as she waved wildly for a tech to link her in.

On the screen a white circle appeared, isolating one blurred white blip among the snow. The auton scanners struggled for definition as the enhancers began to grip.

Captain Jute rolled over to the helm, her escort in pursuit. "Alice is such a humble name," the Kybernator ruminated, looking down at her from the corner of his eye. "Such an unparticular name. Signal Perlmutter, coms, would you? Tell him we have him in sight."

The blip was starting to resolve into a familiar shape, like the top of a supervisor's chair, or a white bird, a swan, perhaps, with wings upraised.

Captain Jute glanced at the image with hatred. She looked broodingly at the empty plaque reader that stood beside Mr. Spinner.

"How about Marilyn?" suggested Brother Melodious.

Com screens were flashing into life. They showed, in quick succession, Brother Poesy, in a candlelit observatory, his exorbitant temples wreathed with laurels; Brother Valetude, in his surgery, examining a bald-headed young acolyte's breasts with his stethoscope; and Brother Justice, floating on his back like a great walrus, in a bath full of frothy beer.

"*Beatrice*," said Brother Poesy, in the Italian way, savoring all four syllables.

"Florence," said Brother Valetude. "The Lady with the Lamp." His acolyte jumped. "*Lamp*, my dear," said the medical Guardian smoothly, "not *lump*."

Brother Justice belched. His jowls quivered. "Fanny!" he said fervently.

"The debate over renaming the ship's persona continues," commented Geneva to her hovercam, "even as we begin our approach to the host Capellan ship. Some of the people I'm talking to today think this ship will be one we've seen before, back in our very own Solar System."

Captain Jute took hold of the blue metal frame of Mr. Spinner's chair. He twitched, aware of her, but did not turn.

Captain Gillespie's scarred white fingers closed over Captain Jute's brown ones. "Leave it," she said in an undertone. "Let it go."

Captain Jute looked up at her, unconvinced. Her old shipmate's eyes were full of warning. Above her gaunt head Kybernator Astraghal's hung like a huge and patient satellite.

"We don't really need a voice at all," the Kybernator observed. "At least, I can't see that we do. Do you need one, Spinner?"

Captain Jute let go the blue chair. In a cold, slurred voice, she said: "Just fucking leave her alone."

Eeb cooed concernedly. Saskia rubbed Tabitha's shoulders.

Kybernator Astraghal was aloof, preoccupied. "Brother Melodious, perhaps you could explain to her again."

"It's just a program, Tabitha," said Brother Melodious, stepping toward them through the air.

Her voice cracked, as if with panic. "Stay away from me, Marco Metz!"

Brother Melodious halted obligingly. "The persona is just a little program for the unimproved human brain, so you can interface with the ship," he told her, as if she hadn't been flying professionally, continuously, for twenty years and more, real time.

He smiled at Dodger Gillespie, the Altecean and the acrobat. "Alice isn't real, sugar, you know that!"

"Don't patronize me, you fucking wormhead," said Captain Jute clearly.

The acolytes twittered, shocked at her effrontery. Brother Melodious gave her a wry smile, meant for all the ship to see.

Geneva took a shot of the Captain leaning exhaustedly from her chair. She really did look quite ill. Her skin was khaki.

"I know what Alice is," Captain Jute told Brother Melodious. "And I know what you are too."

"CAPTAIN, IT REALLY MIGHT BE BETTER IF YOU DIDN'T INTERFERE JUST AT PRESENT," said the gentle voice of Tabitha's oldest and most loyal companion. "THIS IS GOING TO BE QUITE A DELICATE MANEUVER, YOU SEE, AND WE HAVEN'T HAD VERY MUCH PRACTICE NEGOTIATING TRANSITS IN REAL—"

"Mr. Spinner," said the Guardian behind his chair.

"Aye-aye, sir," said Mr. Spinner. He did not look at Captain Jute. He had not looked at her since they brought her in.

He pressed a sequence.

The voice ceased.

Captain Jute slumped further. Dodger Gillespie took hold of her shoulders, bracing her. "Not a problem," she murmured.

Tabitha glared at her.

Captain Gillespie directed her attention to the big screen, where the swan seemed to rear, wings spread stiffly to attack or embrace them. Its shiny breast flared with spectral instabilities.

"Starship," said Dodger. "Got to be."

Tabitha Jute sneered with distaste. Geneva's camera approached, probing discreetly. Not discreetly enough for Eeb, who made a clumsy swipe at it. The camera made an evasive swerve.

"The *Citadel of Porcelain at First Light*," said Captain Jute, with an effort.

"Okay," said Dodger. She pondered.

"Oh yes, so it is," said Saskia to Tabitha. She swiveled to face Captain Gillespie like a lily turning to face the moon. "It's good there. They have gold on the walls. They can make the air smell of anything you like."

"Yeah, all right, Saskia," said Dodger Gillespie.

"The food is wonderful," said Saskia.

Tabitha waved impatiently at the screen.

Saskia tried again to comfort her. "It will be better there," she said.

But the Captain continued to wave her hand, as if she thought she too could change the channel.

∽ 3

The Guardians had begun rounding up the children of the voyage. "They'll be fine now," they said, as one by one the mole-eyed creatures were dumbly handed over. "They need the very best care, and that's what they're going to have."

Four women came from Snake Throat Rookery, looking for the Captain. Their offspring had already been taken. One told how, before the Emergence, she had seen the Mystery Woman on a giant flying screen, promising salvation. No salvation had come.

"It wasn't her," said Saskia, curtly. "It was Alice."

The ambassadors groaned and grumbled. They would not look at her. The artificial woman turned a pirouette in pure frustration. She struck a fighting posture in the hallway. "The Captain is sick. What do you think she can do anyway?"

The clothes of the ambassadors were rags. They wore them in layers, with things pinned everywhere. Animal bones, flattened drink tubes, fragments of picture postcard. Those were their souvenirs of the Earth they barely remembered. All they knew was, the woman behind that bedroom door owed them something.

The door opened. Tabitha came rolling out. "Get in the car," she told them.

Saskia spread herself across the way. "You can't go," she shouted.

"You're driving," said Tabitha.

Colonel Stark sat in her hoverjeep by the side of Long Fiss road, where brawny tattooed men toiled sullenly at the behest of young men and women in crisp black shirts and red berets. The laborers were the captive remnants of the Horde of Havoc, set to repair the damage they had done in the last battle.

The Colonel was proud to be back in the service of the Capellans, and was looking forward to the arrival of the Eladeldi, a species with 100% organizational capacity. She was at this point at this hour to effectuate her routine inspection of the operation. "Work on Pier 1 is in progressive condition and attaining a readiness status equivalent to minus 12.5 shifts," she reported into the jeep com. "Plus or minus point five."

On the com screen, Brother Justice smiled greasily. *"What's point five between friends?"*

In the arches beneath the Sylvian Aqueduct, the battle-bikes of Havoc were up on stands with their back wheels off, running cement mixers. None of the deviants now wore anything more menacing than a chain headband, or a single nut and bolt through an earlobe. They were still dirty, but the dirt was acceptable dirt, the dirt of reparation. Their boots were caked with dribbled rockfoam.

A convoy of decommissioned combat trucks ground up and down the *sulci* with load after load of artificial sand. The Havoc Khan drove point, his prestige scars covered by a rubber apron, his dreads wrapped up in a rag. He sounded his horn to scatter the Alteceans rummaging through the skips.

High above on the scaffolding, a big man with a dark beard and ponytail fiddled with the nozzle of his cement gun.

"Capella likes us," he said authoritatively to his companion. "Stands to reason. That's why they've brought us here. That's why they locked us up in the first place. You don't lock things up if they're not valuable."

"Or dangerous," said his companion. He was a small man of uncertain coloring. His person and dungarees were plastered with filth.

"Same thing," the larger man proposed.

The smaller gave a grin. He pushed up his goggles to reveal two broad circles of slightly lighter filth around his eyes.

"Look at that ape," he said. He nodded at the gigantic two-legged monstrosity strolling ponderously through the arch beneath them.

Its head turning slowly and mechanically from side to side, the giant robot ape patrolled the building site. In the attempted mutiny, it had been the command vehicle of the

Khan. The two men on the scaffolding had ridden inside it. Now they could see a Redcap guard squatting on its shoulder. With one hand she held on to its outsize ear; with the other she caressed the stock of her Spite Supremo.

"We could use that ape," said the grimy little laborer.

It stimulated him to see a piece of machinery working well. Already he was imagining how the artificial beast might be adapted to lift and set girders, to beat out the buckled trough of the watercourse with its fists.

"You're the ape," said his large workmate. He grimaced and tutted as he brushed a speck of foam off his overalls. He never had been as quick as his companion to adjust to the conditions of imprisonment and hard labor in which they always found themselves eventually.

There was a shout. Through the veil of dust that hung permanently across the canyon, one of the workers on the scaffolding had spotted a familiar vehicle heading aft. Down below, their fellow workers leaned on their shovels and stared.

It was a Pango, a solid and unadorned example of the type. The prisoners watched it come with expressions of hostility and contempt. They had lost what little respect they had ever had for Tabitha Jute that day, long ago, when she exchanged her Shiva 900cc for an armored car.

"I didn't hear anybody give the order to stand down!" bellowed the guard captain. "Come on, come on, put your backs into it!"

His charges uttered noises of disgust, and made a pretense of working harder.

Colonel Stark saluted the Pango as it growled by. Tabitha Jute had dishonored her command a thousand times over. She was no longer a priority. Still there was discipline to be maintained, in terms of formalities, especially in front of this rabble.

In the ruined black honeycomb of the Diencephalon, the ledges were draped with rags and piled with dubious possessions. Smoke hung gloomily in the air. As the Pango turned down Snake Throat, Captain Jute's party were quick to spot the troop of Redcaps with their climbing ladders, searching from cell to cell. Behind the troopers followed a large robot, with a dozen unconscious children in a net.

The ambassadors started to curse, croaking and throwing themselves about in the back of the Pango. Overhead, their friends and relatives swung agitatedly on their ropes.

Brother Melodious was there. He waved away Saskia as she started to unload Captain Jute, and completed the job with two of his rings, working them with a pincer action. He was sad for the children. "Poor li'l fellows," he said, as he set her chair on the floor. "They'll never rock 'n' roll."

Captain Jute stared up at his bulging forehead. She wanted to see the slimy thing that was coiled up inside there, talking to her out of Marco Metz's mouth. How long had it been in there, chewing on his brain and growing fat? A week? A month? Had he picked it up in the swamps on Venus and brought it aboard her ship at the start of the journey? Or had he always had it, even before they met at the Moebius Strip, at the Martian Mardi Gras? Had it been the caterpillar in his brain that had made him lie to her, cheat and deceive her, betray and exploit her? No, she thought. Some people were just like that. Men, mostly.

"Leave the kids alone, Marco."

It had been his big brown eyes that had first attracted her. Now they flooded with love and sympathy. He was good at that. "Oh, Tabitha," he sang. "Sweetheart. Now you know I think these little guys are the greatest."

"Don't call me sweetheart." She lunged at him with her chair, trying to run over his foot, but he drifted up in the fetid air, out of reach.

"I can't talk to you when you're like this," he said.

"Good," she said. "Keep it that way."

She saw another Guardian, a woman who had been one of the passengers, an undistinguished resident of the Temporal complex. Now she wore the white robes and called herself Sister Contenta. There was no logic to the hosts the Capellans had selected.

Sister Contenta was cradling a grimy baby that looked as if at least one of its parents had been a starfish. All the time the baby squealed mournfully and without energy.

Captain Jute whizzed up to her. "Put that down," she said.

"This is a nasty, dirty, dangerous ship," said the Guardian, in a voice like a giant pigeon. "We should never have let you play with it." She handed the infant to a Redcap, who took it with thick rubber gloves, held it up for its injection, and stowed it in the net.

"They belong here."

"They'll be much better off where they're going." Delicately Sister Contenta mopped her vast brow. "Poor things! Listen to them, Captain. What a sad sound that is."

Out of nowhere a big woman appeared, swinging on a rope. Shrieking, she swung herself at the net of children.

Troopers lunged at her ineffectively. Missiles pelted them, suddenly, lumps of rotten fungus and matrix flung by yelling children and adults.

Sister Contenta's expression of blissful sorrow did not change. She simply held up the palm of her hand. There was a powerful ultrasonic *zap*, and the woman fell from the air on her back.

Ten meters away she landed and lay still. Smoke curled from the fringes of her clothes.

The missiles and the yelling stopped.

Captain Jute wished she could have a Thrant, just one. She wished armed Perks might start raining from the black vaults overhead.

"She's not hurt," Sister Contenta was proclaiming. "She'll be perfectly all right." With the twist of a ring she picked up the smoldering woman and brought her closer. "My, she's a big one, isn't she. Fetch her some water, would you."

Brother Melodious was quick to draw a moral. "Now look," he said to Tabitha. "See how we take care of you? That's all we want to do. Take care of you."

The Redcaps were on their way upshaft with their catch. The locals clamored at Captain Jute, while Saskia Zodiac thrust her back into the Pango. "I told you she could do nothing!" she shouted at them.

"Get after them," said Tabitha.

"You're exhausted," said Saskia.

"Get after them."

When Saskia tried, the car stalled. Brother Melodious floated before the bonnet with his arms outstretched, like some kitsch archangel guarding the approach to Hell. Solemnly he shook his enormous head.

"Time to go home, Princess," he said.

"Captain Gillespie," said the AV reporter. "Like your old friend Tabitha Jute, you were once a space pilot. You have seen the kraken of Neptune, the terror lizards of Venus, the giant slime molds of South Callisto. In all your travels, did you ever see anything like this?"

Dodger Gillespie leaned on the railing of the observation platform, a matchstick between her appalling teeth. She made a snort of rebuttal, a sound so soft the camera wouldn't get it.

The cavern was full of a soft metallic glow. It shone from the mound that spread beneath them, a mound of slick dark purple flesh.

"What would you say it is?" the reporter asked.

It had been much easier to find this time. They had come down by the secret Tekunak ways, the hidden tunnels once used by the meat trucks servicing the Chilli Chalet and the Pause Café.

"It's this thing," said Jone. She slung a sloppy arm around Dodger Gillespie's shoulders, letting her weight sway onto her. "It's just, check, this great big alive thing."

The newswoman pulled back to make the most of the

ex-pilot's companion. Her hair was trimmed to a frizz of yellow stubble, her armpit hair dyed dark red and blue, to match her tattoos. She wore her old dungarees and boots.

A one-eyed cat, half-Siamese, half–goodness knows what, stood between her legs with his head pressed to the railings. His tail was up like an antenna.

The reporter lofted the camera on its cable to get her subjects with the view behind them. She tapped her wrist control and stepped into range. "I'm Geneva McCann for your All-New Channel 9," she told the camera, "and I'm speaking now to two other veterans of the expedition that discovered this enormous creature."

"Three," said Jone, picking up the cat and hugging him.

"Some people already knew about it," said Dodger Gillespie.

The newswoman's smile strengthened determinedly. "Discovered the plight of this enormous creature." They could fix that later.

Geneva McCann had broken this story shipwide. She had covered the expedition and the subsequent riots. She had interviewed the Director of the Chilli Chalet on the eve of his resignation and since his bonding. She was not going to let the people of Plenty forget about the phenomenon whose flesh had sustained them for so many years.

"Captain Gillespie, what are your memories of the moment we first sighted the *Star Beast*?"

She left a little pause before the official name, then pronounced it with pride. It was the title of her film, to be mentioned as often as possible.

Dodger Gillespie gave a dry laugh.

Odin the cat, who did not very much care for being hugged, was on the floor again. Dodger petted him with the toe of her boot, nudging his side.

"A bit bloody," she said.

The Guardians were treating the glistening behemoth with respect. They had stripped out the industrial flood-lighting and had all the old mining machinery removed from its back. They had introduced piped music, the so-called Species Harmony channel: mellow and soothing.

Geneva pressed her. "Conditions are more tranquil in here now, we might say."

Dodger replaced the matchstick with a hand-rolled cigarette. "We might." She hated this, hated being quizzed, hated being on AV. She would have rather been working on the ships, with Karen and the others, out of sight.

"Jone, you first laid eyes on the Star Beast the same moment we all did. How do you think the Frasque got it in here?"

"It just grew here, check," said Jone. "Figure, it always grew back where they dug. But it's not like fungus or stuff. It's an animal, check, cos it bleeds. Bongo, bongo. I wish they'd fucking turn this starchy crap off!" she complained, suddenly; but there was no stopping the serene music.

Odin jumped up and balanced with all four paws on the railing. Jone pressed the back of his neck. He stiffened his spine and stuck out his chin.

She picked him up again. He wriggled a moment, then hung passively between her hands. He twisted his head back and forth. His fur was standing on end. It was the scent, presumably: the reek of blood.

Jone nuzzled the little carnivore, then turned him, dangling him out over the railing so he too could contemplate the enormous mystery beneath them.

There seemed no beginning to the beast and no end, no head and no tail.

"We used to eat that, Odin. Bongo, bongo," said Jone.

She held the cat for Dodger to stroke. Dodger didn't. She stared ruminatively at him, meeting his single eye through the smoke of her cigarette.

"What *is* that, Jone?" Geneva asked.

"What?" said Jone.

"That thing you always say."

"Bongo, bongo?" said Jone.

"Yeah," said Dodger Gillespie. "What's it mean?"

Jone gave a little writhe of her bony shoulders. "It's just a thing we say," she said.

The Xtasy Crew was scattered, dispossessed of the matrix interfaces, the Thalamus control room. Jone continued ever more fervent in her devotion to the Crew and the preservation of their rituals, the slang, the shiny metal accessories. "It's like," she said, in a singsong voice: "too bad, what a shame, that's the way it is. Bongo, bongo."

"Very expressive," muttered Dodger, squirting smoke through her teeth. "What do you make of it, then, Geneva?" She gestured at the creature with her chin.

The Channel 9 interviewer beamed. "It's the Star Beast!" she declared. There was an edge to the gladness of her voice. She was as much in the dark as they and hated admitting it.

At that moment another voice intruded, booming among the matrix vaults overhead. *"I'm afraid we have to ask you to leave now."*

Three humans, cat and camera turned as one to see Brother Kitchener coasting along the walkway toward them.

He wore a consummately tailored toga of charcoal grey, from the neck of which his head bulged like a huge white puffball. Geneva had realized their presence here might be provocative, though she had scarcely dared hope he would show up in person. What an opportunity! She sent the camera arrowing onto him and trotted after it, her plastic trousers squeaking.

"Brother Kitchener," she said. "Geneva McCann, Channel 9. You were formerly Director of Tekunak Charge, ultimately responsible for the entire Foods division that fed us all during the long years of the journey." She fluttered her eyelashes at him. "Can you tell us what future you plan for the Star Beast?"

Brother Kitchener drew his heavy brows together. One of the most physically imposing of the Guardians, he retained his boardroom habit of dominating everyone with the threat of his discontent. His voice was like a premonition of earthquakes.

"Our plans for the Star Beast, Geneva," he rumbled, "and the best way everybody can help us with them, I can sum up in two words. Off-limits." He gave a hard smile, holding their eyes for a moment, impressing them with the gravity of his interdiction. "She has to rest," he said.

"That's the word from Brother Kitchener," the newswoman said sunnily into her lens. "Here on your All-New Channel 9!"

The evolved supply baron rubbed the palms of his hands together in a slow circle. "As soon as anything happens, you'll be informed," he said. "That's my promise."

The women headed back toward their vehicle: the gaunt space jock with her arm round her codehead clown; the newswoman with her hovercam drifting along on its tether like a rectangular balloon.

Brother Kitchener hung above the walkway in the purple gloom, watching them go.

Jone looked up at Dodger. "She?" she said.

It was very likely he could still hear them.

Dodger Gillespie sniffed.

"I don't scope," said Jone.

"What?" grunted Dodger.

Jone held her elbows to her sides and swiveled her arms in speculative arcs. "It's got to be a Frasque thing, the Beast, you check—and the Capellans hate the Frasque, so, so, so—" She flipped her hands back and forth, juggling her question. "Why do they care?"

Captain Gillespie touched her young cheek with the knuckle of her index finger. "Inside that shell of tiresome juvenile nonconformity there is a real intelligence," she said.

"Fuck off, you," said her paramour.

Geneva dropped back for a discreet low-angle shot of the two of them, newsworthy silhouettes in the metal light.

* * *

The docks were busy, preparing for the shuttle. There was a lot to do: wreckage to be cleared away, bodies disposed of. Only the forward door was now accessible, and its mechanisms were to be checked and overhauled thoroughly. Aft, the reality fault shimmered, stable and impervious.

At the instant of Emergence, in the violence and confusion, a few small craft had actually got away: scouters and short-range space-to-surface ships, for the most part, belonging to prospectors, gamblers and other nonaligned personnel. In the electromagnetic welter of the red twins, radio contact with the fleeing dots had been maintained with difficulty. One by one, in a very few minutes, they had vanished into the fierce background.

The remaining passengers shook their heads. They preferred to be sensible, and wait for instructions. There were ample grounds for expecting everything would be all right now.

A general inspection of ships and material was put in hand. Wrecked and obsolete craft were to be broken up for parts, the parts pooled and made available to vessels judged 75% spaceworthy or better. A Spares and Repairs committee had been formed, to examine applications from owners and operators.

The two people working on the Charisma in Dock Bay 185-1 were talking about the people who had got away.

"They skipped, didn't they," said Karen Narlikar to the man waist-deep in the works with the cutting torch.

Karen had been a pilot, before. There had been quite a few pilots on board, and a lot of mechanics.

"They must have, Lou, eh."

Lou Garou adjusted his flame to a sharper point, a diamond of pure white fire, and focused it on the pipe in front of him. He was a mechanic, now, though in fact he'd come on board as a political prisoner, from Asteroid 000013. Some of his friends had been Havoc warriors and shared his loathing of all regimes, new or old.

"They must have," he said.

The project in Bay 185-1 had not been authorized by the Spares and Repairs committee. They had the Charisma, a Mark VI, marked down as FFO, fixtures and fittings only. In fact the impulse catalyst block was perfectly healthy. The plan, ambitious as it was surreptitious, was to pull the entire thing and transfer it to a humble tourist bus.

Karen isolated another wire, tagged and snipped it. "They're out there, somewhere," she said.

Her McTrevor Clavicorn was aft, in 330, behind the reality fault. So too was the tourist bus; and a dozen other ships, in various states of repair. Officially, of course, none of them existed anymore, and nor did section 330. There were only a handful of people, Lou and Karen and some others, old spacers and dock trolls, who knew different, and they were keeping it very quiet.

Along the catwalk overhead, movement caught Karen's eye.

"Watch it," she said. "Guardian."

Lou quickly cut the flame and pushed up his mask. He stared out suspiciously.

Karen hopped up onto the canopy of the Charisma. Their shadows moved on the walls of the bay, enlarged and exaggerated by the acetylene glare. Trying to hide now would be the most suspicious thing they could do.

Brazenly, Karen waved, and in a moment of inspiration, gave the Blue Sky salute.

Benignly the figure acknowledged them as it swept frictionlessly on. "Which one was that?" asked Lou.

"Valetude," Karen said. She recognized him from the old days, knocking around with the Captain. "He's not usually down here."

Brother Valetude looked around as he floated through the region of obscure industry. Rarely if ever had his practice brought him this deep before. As an unaugmented human, he had avoided the area, preferring the convivial fug of Rory's Trivia Bar.

A call was a call, however, and must be answered, without regard for self or safety. Brother Valetude rather thought he had sworn an oath to that effect, once; though circumstances had been very different then, of course.

He took one of the high bridges that crossed the docks from side to side, fifty meters above the old flux pits. Beneath his sandaled feet, empty proton baths stretched out in ranks like molds for some rectangular life form yet to be conceived.

"Coming," caroled Brother Valetude softly. "Coming."

On the far side of the cavern the Guardian found himself among the higher tiers of the parking bays. Areas of rupture were sealed off with plastic sheeting. Markings in luminous crayon indicated the routes still passable.

Brother Valetude slowed, dropping for a moment to the floor to orient himself. He flexed his fingers.

"Where are you?" he asked aloud. "Along here, is it?"

He lifted his great head, listening. He looked thoughtfully up the corridor, adjusting his clean white cuffs.

"Ah yes," he said. "Here you are."

In Bay 490-9, a number of bodies lay in stiff and unnatural attitudes on the floor. "Dear me," said Brother Valetude, stopping by one to make a cursory examination. "This isn't you, is it? No. No."

Holding up his ivory hands like a Chinese princess in a ballet, he stooped over another. He stroked one of the rings he now wore.

"Can you feel anything when I do this?" he asked the corpse. "No? Well, well."

The defense field that secured the ship in 490-9 was perfectly visible to a Guardian's eyes. Straightening up, Brother Valetude pointed a ring at one of the projectors that sustained it.

The stone in the ring seemed to gleam faintly. There was a soundless explosion of light.

Brother Valetude squeezed his eyes tight shut and opened them again with a gratified expression. He blinked like an owl. White coat flapping, he sailed up to the ship and looked it over.

It was quite a good-sized ship, a white Scorpion with a prow as sharp as any high-speed atmosphere vehicle's. He read the name out loud. "The *All Things Considered*," he said. "Jolly good."

Of course, there was no telling whether it was any use still or not.

Brother Valetude went to the edge of the bay. He looked down into the great dock cavern. He could see a little orange-and-black vehicle crawling on the apron, bulldozing grey streaks in the rubble.

The Guardian rubbed his hands and lifted himself to the door of the Scorpion's cockpit. It was apparently secured with three different locks and four complex intruder alarms, not to mention a number of booby traps. He knocked on the door with his knuckles.

"Hello?" he called. "It's me. Can you let me in, do you think?"

He paused.

Nothing happened.

"It's all right," he said. "You can trust me, I'm a doctor."

Still nothing happened.

"I see," said the promoted practitioner once again, as though he had just been apprised of a crucial symptom.

He drifted a little way back from the craft. Then, humming to himself, with another ring he traced the outline of the door in the air.

The door popped open.

Brother Valetude slid gently on board the *All Things Considered*.

It took him a moment or two to neutralize the remaining

defenses. Then he poked around until he located the state-room and discovered the carnage within.

"Oh dear. What a shame."

Passing by the pornographic hologram with a smile, he slipped through the gap in the wall of AV monitors and floated gracefully over the bed. He hung there a moment, looking at the flickering screens.

Then he went and surveyed the sundered and putrefying corpse. He toured it in a careful circle, expertly assessing its principal deficiency. Finally he returned to the ruined bed. He floated down, lifted the pink valance and peered under it.

"Hello?" he called.

The only sound was the cartoon music. Trumpets snickered, trombones rasped. On the banked screens a villainous scheme had once again collapsed in multiple humiliating failure.

Brother Valetude rose. His temples seemed to throb slightly, as if with some adjustment of internal pressure. He rotated purposefully in midair, until he spotted what he was looking for.

The head that previously belonged to the rotting body lay against the wall. It was the head of a male, thirtyish, Caucasian, with black hair and broken spectacles of black glass. Though its left orbit was an encrusted pit of blood and dried tissue, the head as a whole seemed in a fairly healthy condition: certainly very much better than the rest of the remains. The Guardian bent down with his hands on his knees.

"Here we are," he said. "Now then. What seems to be the trouble?"

4

"They are going to leave us on board," said Iogo to her lair-sister Soi.

It was news to Soi. She was unsure what it meant, whether it was true.

"How do you know?" she said.

How? How? Iogo stretched her length on her mound of rugs. There was no need of speech to explain. She knew because it was true. Kenny said so. She looked over her shoulder at him lounging in the caresser above them.

Soi hooded her nostrils. Her feelings were confused. She wanted the Guardians to leave, she wanted things to be as they had before, when she had been Captain Tabitha's servant and driven her car. At the same time, she knew that could not be. So surely it was better to be here, in the lair, with their own people.

Daily they were arriving now, from all corners of the ship. Shaggy and shaven, tawny, gold and grey, they sat entwined beneath the chandeliers.

On the high plains and in the wooded culverts of their homeworld, the Thrant keep their settlements. They live by tribes in untidy stalls of rough-hewn wood, which they are constantly rebuilding, under canopies of uncured hide.

For centuries their way of life had remained unchanged. Their world was warm and quiet. Life was sparse under the big fierce sun, and hunting took much energy and ingenuity. They ate communally in the open, and went together to the waterpits to wash and drink. They used no writing or pictorial art, but they had hundreds of songs, and interlocking tribal musical systems of phenomenal complexity.

Stars that moved the wrong way and silver stones that flew across the marble sky had been known and watched, placidly enough, for a long time. Wise folk suspected stars and pebbles were the same thing. Tales were told of stones that had fallen to earth, and proved to be enormous vessels, with people inside. But they had always fallen in remote places, in the Green Wax Valley or high on Breakneck Ridge. Individuals who went to investigate had failed to return.

Then the hairy blue strangers came.

They were not big or fast; but they had cars, and machines that let them speak to the silver ships. They gathered on hilltops along the approaches to waterpits.

Isolated individuals began to be taken: ambushed from treetops, trapped with bleating *canaarg* staked in sandy hollows. Some game scouts said they saw a group of the creatures in uniform, driving across the salt pans. A Thrant had been riding with them.

Then the blue creatures began to be seen in the north as well. There were many times more of them than anyone had thought. For a sixth of a season their raiding parties carved up the plains, picking out small groups of Thrant, cutting them off methodically from home and tribe. In their clattering skyships they flew before them, scattering their prey, and harried them when they stopped to rest. In this way they brought them together, and herded them into the highlands where the silver ship waited.

Then high-pitched songs of gladness assailed the confused, exhausted captives. Some of the people who had vanished reappeared, looking well and happy. They wore bright shining garments, and held out skins of wine.

In the high metal wall of the enormous ship, doors slid open. Inside was a cavernous space of dappled green-and-golden light, like a clearing in the forest. Little birds flew about.

A man stood there with a wreath of leaves on his big bald head. His arms were open wide.

*   *   *

Now, in the Yoshiwara brothels, Thrant shredded the crimson upholstery and sprayed their territories in the deep-pile carpets. The whole of the abandoned pleasure quarter was theirs.

Iogo stretched her neck, rolling her head around. "Let the worm people leave. Then we shall fly home."

The young bucks grinned, enjoying the wild fancy. An old man put out his tongue and narrowed his eyes to slits. "One day you will do just so, Iogo!"

Kenny stroked his queen's ear with the back of his paw. He still wore his grey armored jerkin, and preferred his human name to his original name, Kyfyd. His chieftainship over the Thrant of Plenty could not entirely compensate him for being torn from the side of Captain Jute, from the head of his pack of men. He sized up all new arrivals with a green glare. His mind was full of enemies: Guardians floating, walking, talking. Guardians screaming, dying.

Iogo prowled, or lay in her spot, beside the caresser. From there she could supervise the other women, and keep them in their place. Her favorites she allowed to groom Kenny, to brush his fur and clean his teeth. Let any who ventured anything more intimate fear for her ears and tail.

A strange bristling murmur started up around the door of the salon. Someone was coming: a stranger.

Iogo raised her chin and blinked slowly as the guards brought her in. It was a young human with a cat: a pet, domestic feline, a crossworld breed. The instant the cat got scent of the tribe it leapt from her arms and fled.

Humans were becoming increasingly rare in this district. This one was a young female, very thin, with the fur on her head shaved like a servant. Iogo did not recognize her.

A couple of adolescent males pushed forward. They snarled disapprovingly at the visitor and her escort, waving their tails. A grumbling noise of idle hostility and muttered speculation spread through the room at large.

The young woman stood on tiptoe to look between the obstructive males. She was nervous, you could smell it.

"Dodger sent me," she said, in a high, tight voice. "Dodger Gillespie."

"It's Jone," said Soi then. "See, the drawing on her arms."

"Let her come," ordered Kenny.

The young woman would not come in. She mumbled her message to one of the guards, who climbed up on his neighbors in the crowd and called it out loudly so everyone could hear.

"The shuttle is here."

He said it again, in their own tongue.

Kenny rose from his couch, shaking off the paws of those who now began clamoring for his attention, his instructions. He stood on his hind legs. With deliberate hatred he raked his forearm with his claws. He pulled up the zip on his jerkin.

His eyes sought his sister and his mate. They had risen along with him. Zealous bucks forced a path for them to follow him through the crowd to the door.

The woman led them to a battered taxi. She told them again that Captain Gillespie had sent her. She seemed scarcely to believe they remembered her, Soi thought. Or perhaps it was she who did not recognize them. Perhaps life with the tribe had already altered them, changing their scent and their posture, their very appearance.

Soi drove. Some of the bucks ran alongside for a way. Kenny leaned out of the car and snapped at them. One by one they fell behind and stopped.

The bucks stood panting, listening until none of them could hear the car any longer. Then they turned, slinking back into Yoshiwara, rolling their shoulders and snapping at one another.

In the salon the rest of the pack were squabbling over who should have the caresser.

In the cavern of the docks, a crowd was gathered around a little shiny ship. The door of the ship was open, with a ramp extending from it. No one had disembarked yet.

In the shadows high above, three Thrant and a human watched from a walkway.

Kenny lay on his belly. Iogo clung to his shoulder, thrusting out her muzzle. She was quivering.

Though Iogo did not like to talk about it, Soi knew something of the life she had led on board, before Kenny. In the lair she was queen, but in the ship at large Iogo was a timid creature still, frightened of every sudden breeze, every moving shadow.

Behind Kenny crouched Jone. Soi saw how she put out her hand as though to pet Iogo, then thought better of it. Mutely, she handed Kenny an amp visor. He put it on and snarled grumpily at the tableau below.

From the welcome committee, a cheer went up. Figures had begun to emerge from the shuttle.

Soi lay full length on the floor and stretched her neck out over the edge of the walkway. She needed no amplification to recognize those figures. They were hairy and blue, and wore uniforms.

Kenny growled deep in his chest. Iogo whined, ears flaring. On the back of Soi's neck the fur bristled.

Down the ramp the Eladeldi marched, forming two lines, moving into place with precision. Precision was what Eladeldi lived for, precision and obedience. It was the obedience of the Eladeldi everywhere that enabled the Guardians to assert their rule.

"Troopers," said Kenny. His tail scraped menacingly behind him.

Soi did not care what kind the Eladeldi were. Inside their uniforms, they were flesh, like any other creature. Her lips curled. She wished with all her blood that her teeth and her brother's and his mate's might fasten in the hairy blue bellies. The air began to stink with detestation.

Iogo gave a stifled whimper and buried her head in her arms.

*   *   *

Between the lines of troopers, a single Guardian came down the ramp. The floodlights blazed off his white robes, his jeweled rings, his huge bald head.

The welcome committee cheered even louder. His colleagues sailed forward to greet him. The acoustics of the huge dock cavern mangled their speeches into incomprehensible thunder. They nodded and held up their hands.

Soi shared a grim look with Jone. She had spent time making sure the whole lair knew that the Guardians were dead humans, infested by parasite worms. Dead meat that walked and spoke, and enforced its speaking with magic rings: it was vile, to be shunned.

Kenny exhaled, flexing his claws. He would impale a Capellan worm on each one.

Though you wouldn't have thought he could see a thing beyond the lights, it was plain from the new arrival's gestures that he was admiring the black expanse of the docks, the gloomy vaulting of the Frasque architecture. Exclamations, small high sounds, rang through the carbonized air.

Iogo snorted and blew out her lips. She had stopped watching the scene below. She began to groom her offended mate, hoping to pacify him and thereby herself. Rumbling, Kenny pushed her away.

The Guardians of Plenty were accompanied by their usual coterie. In their homemade togas they clustered around the shuttle, delighted, thrilled to be present in person at this historic meeting of Guardians old and new. They were overflowing with questions. Who was to go over to the Capellan ship? Would those with their own transport be free to make their own way? What was to happen to Plenty?

"Are we ready to go?" shouted Brother Melodious to the crowd. He slapped his knees and held his arms above his head. "All right, *people*! We're ready to go! We're *hot*, let me tell you!" He was incoherent with excitement. His head rolled oddly on the shoulders of his pink drape jacket.

Father Le Coq was there, from Maison Zouagou, the

Tabernacle of Dreams. He yelled and stamped his feet. He had taken to wearing enormous circular candy-striped sunglasses and sneakers with crepe soles fifteen centimeters thick, since the saints had come marching in. "Brethren and sistren, *hear* what the man says. Brother Marco, he speaks in the name of Lord Elvis Almighty! Brother Nestor come to take us to the Promised World!"

The conversing Guardians laughed genially at the pair of them. Kybernator Astraghal, applauding, took command. He rose up in the air and addressed the gathering crowd.

"What Brother Melodious says is right," he said. "You are all waiting patiently. You are asking, What about us? When are *we* coming?"

He smiled at their visitor, speaking on his behalf. "Well, you will all come, every one of you. We promise. Each of you will have a lovely new home. We make that promise to you."

Kybernator Astraghal spread his hands, as if strewing something across the assembly, which was still growing, people hurrying onto the apron from all directions. Geneva McCann was there, filming everyone.

"I know you understand that it will take time. We weren't exactly expecting you! And there is a lot to do."

The Disaster Commissioner had a question. Kybernator Astraghal repeated it for everybody's benefit. "Will there be more promotions, you ask me."

The Guardians smiled a general smile.

"There will," said Kybernator Astraghal.

An enormous cheer went up.

"As soon as the time is right," said Kybernator Astraghal. "Again, we can only beg you to be patient. What do you say, Father?"

Brother Melodious clapped his hands, shouted at the dancing priest. "Yeah, Rooster, give us the word!"

Le Coq danced up the ramp, between the lines of soldiers, who bristled with distaste. "My children, the word is *Watch* and *Pray*!" Theatrically he ran his thumbs and fingers along two imaginary lines, as if smoothing the words on the air. "*Watch* and *Pray*, say the mighty Space Brothers, till *I* shall come *again*! W is 21 and P is 16 and that makes 3 and 7 and 10, that comes down to your perfect number 1 that is *I* that is indi*vi*sible!"

Techs and mechs rubbed their heads, trying to fathom the calculus. They started jabbing at their wristsets, while the priest pointed his fingers here and there about the crowd. They were skinny fingers, encrusted with rings of plastic and gold.

"I and I and I and I is the Great *I Am*!" bellowed the Rooster, while the faithful shook their bells and cymbals. "Halleluia!"

"There will be Eladeldi soon to look after you," announced the Kybernator. "Meanwhile you have Brother Justice and Colonel Stark for law and order."

Colonel Stark saluted the appreciative crowd. Behind her the fat judge put two fingers to his lips and blew out his cheeks. He admired the way the colonel filled her uniform. He himself was wearing a huge new wig, knitted by some Palernian admirers from their own wool. It was askew.

"Health and environmental provisions will be made by Brother Valetude."

The Guardian in the white lab coat floated up onto the shoulders of his acolytes. He waved his stethoscope and collected a tribute of applause.

"And Brother Poesy will be responsible for entertainments and communications."

On screen the bard, now permanently ensconced in the old observatory, looked up from a slim yellow volume. Candleflames flickered about him. Above his head the great windows glowed faintly with the infernal light of the Capellan twins.

"No doubt the rest of us will be popping across from time to time," said Kybernator Astraghal. "Meanwhile listen to your priest."

Le Coq pranced, brandishing his cane and shaking his

long tongue. "I and I and I and I is the Great *I Am*," he chanted, "which is the All-Seeing I of the Lord, the I in *Goodbye*!" At his back his Tabernacle Choir came in on a thrilling C-sharp. With his musical hand, Brother Melodious picked up the note, striking up the inevitable anthem; and from the rear came a marching band to serenade the triumphant departure.

The Guardian who had come with the shuttle, an elderly, dark-skinned man, positioned himself at the door of his ship. "Let's have her, then, shall we?" said Kybernator Astraghal to Sister Contenta while the music played. "Let's have Captain Jute."

Redcaps parted the crowd, and the jeep came through, bringing the outbound party.

Up on the walkway Kenny gave a subdued growl. Iogo pouted and started to pant aggressively, plucking at the fur on her chest. Soi's claws scratched the textured floor. The air around them began to stink with rage.

Below, the Captain was disembarking from the hover-jeep. Saskia Zodiac was there, helping her. People were clapping her, wishing her well. Children came running out of the choir to wind a scarf of flowers around her neck.

The Captain was wearing her long black leather coat. She was being led away captive. Iogo set up an eerie, mourning croon.

Kenny seized her shoulders in a grip at once bracing, admonishing and adoring. His eyes burned. If the dog people and the wormheads hurt Captain Jute, they would die. He would destroy them. Careless that the woman Jone was there to see, Kenny pressed his erection defiantly against his mate's buttocks.

Soi's claws gouged the flooring of the walkway. "We should be with her," she muttered. None of them noticed that she spoke in English.

*   *   *

The Captain held on to the car. "Oh, here, here," said Saskia. She caught hold of her arm. "You do still need your chair," she said. It was a point about which there had been some contention.

"I'm not taking it," said Tabitha.

Her First Officer, Mr. Spinner, scrutinized the shuttle. "It's very much like a Freimacher Tinkerbell," he said. He had cheered up somewhat since the first days of Emergence. "The modifications are interesting, though, aren't they? The plasma intake shielding and so on."

No one was listening to him. Brother Melodious and the choir and the band were still going full blast. On the other side of the crowd a small huddle of Alteceans were wincing and covering their ears. The most distressed among them was Eeb, who had sheltered the Captain and her friends, but was now being left behind. She muffled her snout in a spotted handkerchief.

A transit pod was being unloaded from the back of the jeep. "Careful with her," said Captain Jute, unnecessarily.

She lurched over and pressed her hand against the visor of the pod. It was Angie, her sister, her betrayer, in life support. Against the white cushioning she lay like a figure molded out of damp latex. Her face was grey and yellow.

Alongside the pod hovered Xtasca the Cherub. It had put on its lifesuit for the crossing. The light of the dock floods cast hectic rainbows of chartreuse and Day-Glo pink across its reflective skin. "Radioactivity is down another 5.9%," it was saying to Brother Valetude, who maintained a considerable interest in the case of Angela Jute.

Someone was removing Tabitha's hand, clasping her arm to urge her forward. "Tabitha. Tabitha." It was Saskia. "Come."

Captain Jute let herself be led up the ramp. With displeasure she eyed the rigid lines of hairy blue figures flanking her. "Where's Dodger?" she wanted to know.

"She doesn't seem to be here," said Mr. Spinner, a trifle helplessly.

Captain Jute turned, halting the procession, and looked out over the assembled crowd. "Dodger," she shouted.

"I don't know if you can hear above the music," said Geneva McCann to her camera, "but Captain Jute is calling for her old friend Captain Gillespie."

"Captain Gillespie!" invoked Father Le Coq, in a portentous tone, and made a stagy gathering gesture with his right hand. "Come forth into the light of Truth. Come forth and take the place prepared for you in the Holy Chariot!"

"Where is Captain Gillespie?" Kybernator Astraghal asked Colonel Stark.

"She's not in her quarters," Sister Contenta told them.

"She was supposed to be here," Brother Justice reminded the Redcap colonel.

"That's confirmation that Captain Gillespie was scheduled to accompany the Captain on this special advance flight to the Capellan starship *Citadel of Porcelain at First Light*," reported Geneva breathlessly.

"Search facilities are being implemented, sir," said Colonel Stark tonelessly. "All vessels will be subjected to examination."

"Where is she?" Tabitha demanded. Her urgency seemed extreme, suddenly, as though more was at stake than the whereabouts of an old friend. Perhaps she suspected foul play.

"They'll fetch her, Captain," said Kybernator Astraghal with magisterial patience. "Why don't you board and get yourself comfortable. Give the Captain a hand, Mr. Spinner."

Mr. Spinner touched his forehead. "Aye-aye, sir," he said.

Captain Jute pushed flowers impatiently out of her face. "When did you last see Dodger?" she asked Saskia.

"She'll be here in a minute," said Saskia, coaxing her toward the door.

Their escort introduced himself to everyone as they

boarded. "Brother Nestor," he said, bowing. "Captain Jute. Welcome aboard."

She went past without looking at him.

Outside, Geneva McCann, denied entrance to the shuttle, was shooting the Redcap search parties that scurried across the walkways.

Under Tabitha's supervision, Saskia had packed a bag for her, a modest backpack. In it she had put seven kinds of painkiller; some favorite T-shirts and jewelry; a large stack of discs and tapes by people with names like Dale Whittle and Smokin' Joe Stubbs; a spare wristcom, with several spare batteries; a toweling bathrobe and a pair of grimy silk slippers; tampons and an ultrasonic douche and a contraceptive scrambler, though she scarcely expected to be using that; and a tattered comic book in which Capellans were lampooned and depicted in absurd and unfavorable situations. That, when she inspected their packing that morning, Sister Contenta had passed over with a saintly smile, but she had removed the Magnani 060. "You really aren't going to be needing this," she said, handing it over to her Redcap attendant for disposal. "You're due for a nice long rest!" The forgiveness in her eyes said she knew the gun had been a gesture merely, like the comic book: a nominal testing of the boundaries which could ultimately only reinforce them.

"My bag," said Tabitha now.

"Your bag," said Saskia.

The acrobat's haunted features leaned close to her lover. "Did you leave it in the car?"

Tabitha twisted against her seatweb. A wall of huge smiling heads confronted her: Sister Contenta, Brother Nestor, Kybernator Astraghal. "My bag," she said.

"What was in it?" asked Mr. Spinner.

"My stuff," said Tabitha.

"Her stuff," confirmed Saskia in a tone of appeal.

Outside, they were retracting the entry ramp. Saskia made to rise.

"Forget about your stuff," said Brother Melodious, floating from his seat to hang in the gangway, blocking their exit. "You're not going to want it. You're not going to want anything where you're going."

Captain Jute started pulling at the web latches, getting tangled up in her garland. Saskia stooped over her, taking her hands, making calming noises. The door was closed. The motors were humming. The shuttle began to move. Bleakly, Captain Jute subsided.

Saskia stroked her hair. Tabitha pushed her hand away.

"You'll be perfectly comfy," said Sister Contenta serenely.

The shuttle was quickly coming up to speed.

"We have everything ready for you," promised Brother Nestor.

Now they were airborne. In an instant they were across the cavern. Recognizing its speed, the meniscus of the giant doorway parted and let it out into the burning dark.

Brother Melodious hung over Tabitha, smiling his starriest smile. "You want anything, sweetheart, ask me."

"I want my ship," said Tabitha Jute.

"Sweetheart," said Brother Melodious. "Be reasonable."

＄ 5

Space, real space, hit her like a drug. The rush of takeoff, the sensory prickle of high g through the tightening web, the black nothingness that suddenly sucked at all the windows. But it wasn't a drug, it was real. It was a distinction she was trying to pay more attention to these days.

She wished she had Alice to help her. Alice was so very, very helpful. She looked at the Guardians all around her. She told herself: Don't think about Alice.

The shuttle was luxurious and silent, far superior to any bus Tabitha had ever flown. The Guardians were sitting now, looking out of the windows, except for Brother Melodious, who was trying to arrange the remains of the garland around her neck. She gnashed her teeth at him, and he retired, holding his hands in the air, protesting weakly, laughing. "Okay, okay, just making sure you're comfortable . . ."

"I shall make sure Captain Jute is comfortable, Marco," Saskia told him, placing a slender hand on Tabitha's shoulder. Though there was a parasitic alien caterpillar in his head, as far as Saskia Zodiac was concerned Marco Metz was still the feckless hustler he had always been. The only difference was, he loved himself more than ever.

"You mustn't worry, dear," crooned Saskia to Tabitha.

"That's easy for you to say."

The shuttle rose into the void. Inclined, Capella System looked like a cloud of muck being sucked down twin plugholes into a dark red furnace. In the end, Tabitha supposed, that's exactly what was going to happen to everything and everyone, herself included, thousands of millions of years from now, when the last sun went out.

"I don't want any more dope," she told Saskia.

Saskia gave her a look of stolid, patient disbelief.

"I mean it," said the Captain. She stared angrily across the aisle, where the life-support pod occupied a row of seats.

Still in its saucer, the Cherub sat on top of the pod. Having ensured the stability of the patient, Xtasca was recording some preliminary observations of the locality. Along the rim of the saucer glowing displays came and went. Brother Nestor kept turning round in his seat to give Xtasca little enchanted, inquisitive glances. Certainly he could never have seen a Cherub before.

Behind Xtasca and Angela, Mr. Spinner sat wiping his spectacles. He was so stimulated he hardly knew where to look. Only the Eladeldi troopers sat with their backs to the view, paws folded, breathing through their mouths.

"Even Proxima, I don't suppose, could live up to this!" said Mr. Spinner.

His rapture was involuntary, entire. Tabitha felt sour. It would have been nice to be thrilled. The first human being to reach another sun.

Dodger would have helped. She'd have been sitting there with a little smirk, smoking a roll-up, impervious to all humiliation.

Dodger would be all right, she told herself. Dodger would have a plan.

When they had unplaited the beads and transistors, Angie's hair had started falling out. "High rads in the Mesencephalic Nucleus," Tabitha remembered someone reporting, months ago. Angie had been in the midst of that, performing her sabotage, like a worm in a gourd, a Capellan in a human brain.

She remembered, faintly, irrelevantly, two little girls sitting on a bunk bed, combing and plaiting each other's hair. On another world, under a different sun. Whole leisure periods she and Angie had used to spend, on the net, making up stupid things to impress the other kids: stories about princesses and ghosts and fairies—stories she had half believed, sometimes, because Angie had said them, her big sister. When her big sister had run away to be a plughead, Tabitha Jute had stopped believing.

Angie had never stopped believing. It was belief that had made her submit herself to conversion by agents of the Seraphim. Angela Jute's brain had been eaten up, devoured core by core.

Like Marco's. And the others'. Tabitha Jute was riding into an alien solar system in a luxury bus of infested corpses. In her dreams the caterpillars would look out of

Saskia's eyes too, and crawl like streams of luminous blue data all over her sister's body.

Reality, she reminded herself, pulling at her disintegrating flowers. Reality.

Xtasca floated at the window like a child watching raindrops. Among the drifting mineral debris could be seen a tiny glint of color, brassy green; and later another, antiseptic silver-blue.

"What are they?" asked Saskia Zodiac.

It was hard to get the scale. The objects had the sheen and regularity of artifacts.

"Marker buoys," said Brother Nestor.

Mr. Spinner made a huffing noise. "Not like any I'm familiar with," he said, in a high voice.

Brother Melodious seemed to be comparing them with his rings. In their stones the same colors shone, like little reflections.

The artifacts were, it gradually became apparent, enormous. Towers of jade and ivory, beacons like flying pagodas of glass and gold. Their communication fans spread like skeletal hands across the spacelanes, fingers infinitely long and thin. Through the gauntlet of their benedictions the shuttle bore silently on.

A small smudge of white light appeared, ahead in the gloom. The light was irregular, composite, made up of many smaller lights. It resolved slowly as they approached, into patches, areas of concentration. The lights were arc lights, and windows, and doors. They became a ship the size of a major orbital.

Saskia looked across at Xtasca. Then she looked at Tabitha and pressed her hand. They were all three returning, against their will, to the *Citadel of Porcelain at First Light*.

The ship was a mass of elongated curves, winged and necked in a way that recalled a swan rising from water. Her

upper decks held palaces, terrace after terrace of glass illuminated from within. Tiny cars like colored pips crawled
among her superstructure. Tracts of polished white metal
reflected the grim red suns.

Brother Nestor pointed out the ship to the new Guardians, who greeted it with joy. It seemed new to them. Where
had they all come from, anyway? How had they got on
board Plenty? Had *she* brought them? Angie. Angela. A
Seraph cyberjunkie with a tube of microscopic caterpillar
eggs in the pocket of her long black coat.

The shuttle traversed a belt of semisolid stuff, charred
lumps of crusty rock. The beacons drew the shuttle steadily
between the waltzing mountains.

Mr. Spinner was making calculations on his wristset. He
sucked his teeth, holding the screen nearer his eyes and
farther away again, as though the distance might make a
difference to the result. It was obvious that he wanted
someone to ask him what he was doing. No one did.

At last he put his finger to the window, and said tentatively: "That is a planet, isn't it?"

Brother Nestor inclined his head.

The planet was a brown blob the size of a pea, high in
the dim red distance. Their homeworld? wondered Captain
Jute. Or had the twins, their greed doubling and redoubling,
torn that rim from rim an age ago?

"I suppose it's feasible," said Mr. Spinner, with an embarrassed snuffle. "But its orbit does seem rather peculiar."

The great pink heads of the Guardians turned to look at
him.

"One might almost think it was orbiting both suns at
once," Mr. Spinner said.

The great pink heads turned back to face the front.

"It is," said Kybernator Astraghal.

Mr. Spinner grew very excited. "But that's absolutely
astonishing!" he said. "Such an orbit would surely be—I

mean, we've always assumed—the celestial mechanics of—''

Sister Contenta put her hand on his knee. ''That was how we kept it going,'' she said. She obviously knew all about it.

Mr. Spinner took off his spectacles and wiped them once more. ''You changed the orbit of a planet,'' he said, in a small rapt voice.

''We redesigned the whole system,'' said Kybernator Astraghal complacently. ''Once. A long time ago.''

Flaky black matter swept fitfully past the windows. Saskia wiped the glass with her thin white hand, as if the smuts might be on the inside.

''It's past mending now,'' said the Kybernator.

''Poor old thing,'' said Sister Contenta, looking out at the frozen rubble.

The fat red suns roared silently. It was as if the ship was falling, very slowly, toward the mouths of two volcanoes.

Xtasca raised the hood of its lifesuit. They were letting it go outside. It could not escape. Its baby arms would tire, its miniature batteries fail, before it could get any appreciable distance. Anyway, where was there for it to escape to?

Brother Nestor signaled to a guard to work the airlock, while Saskia unlatched her web and floated across the aisle to check on Angela. Captain Jute watched the Cherub sail happily into space.

''It must be nice to do that,'' observed Saskia. She propped her chin in her hand. ''They might have made us able to do that too, while they were about it.''

''You could have done it in my VR pod,'' said Captain Jute automatically. ''I don't know why you never did that.''

In fact, she knew perfectly well. Pods gave you a version of space: undifferentiated equilibrium, marbled planets, tiny stars in the right places, ships tacking to and fro. It was a good version, while it was all you had.

Here, in real space, all simulacra faded into insignificance. Here, gulfs of infinity surrounded you wherever you turned. You felt it in your throat first, always, the organism kicking in a beat before the intellect. Not falling, but flying.

Xtasca the Cherub circled the coach of the shuttle, feeling the gravity of it like a tug on its fiber-optic spine, as if it were being slowly whirled around on the end of a string. Inside the shuttle the little figures sat like dolls, fragile dolls made of soft and brittle substances unsuitable for the violent conditions they habitually imposed upon themselves.

The Cherub took measurements as it circled, improving some earlier calculations. It turned its head to look at the waiting starship. The curved white plates of it glowed in the dingy light.

Xtasca had spent too much of its recent life immersed in the intricacies of Frasque particle grammar. Space refreshed it. Interplanetary vacuum restored the sense of perspective. Black space, subzero emptiness, blazing stellar radiation, the ruined remnants of celestial bodies, powerful vehicles completing complex and hazardous transits—it was a pleasure to be outside.

Implicit in the Cherub's own design was a powerful imperative to detach itself from other occupations and set out to explore this new locale. It was for such purposes the Seraphim had commanded its creation, with all the rest of its frictionless generation.

The reason the Capellans had always sought to woo the Seraphim, Xtasca concluded, was not hard to deduce.

There were issues here far larger than the survival of individual organisms: efflorescences of logic, concatenations of genetic imperatives with radial arcs of effect reaching beyond the galaxy. The contrast between the two starships, Frasque and Capellan, Plenty and the *Citadel of Porcelain at First Light*, could not have been more suggestive. The Cherub patted its fat belly and chuckled.

All the same, the puzzle posed by the insertion of Angela

Jute into Plenty was a part of the larger question, and one, it felt sure, worth the solving. That too was a purpose, in the sphere of operations to which the Cherub had committed itself, essentially, the moment it made the decision to withdraw the young Saskia and Mogul from the Zodiac Project and itself from the Temple.

Decisions entail trajectories, widely divergent. History forms and conforms you. You can never eliminate the past, no matter how attractive a new proposition might appear.

The stars would wait.

Meanwhile the Capellan starship floated then and there, a ten-thousand-eyed sentinel on a unique cusp of space and time. The gleaming shuttle slid rapidly toward it, direct as a knife to a magnet. The little black Cherub rode it in.

"It is good," said Saskia Zodiac. "I like it. It is just the way I remember it."

Trumpets blew. Hurrahs rang out. The acrobat nodded with satisfaction at the ceremonial hall, the vast red carpet, the thousands of Eladeldi drawn up on either side in their ranks of scarlet and blue.

"You like it," said Tabitha Jute.

"Oh yes!" replied Saskia. "It is magnificent." To her the display of luxury and power was a splendid circus, a gorgeous setting for some fancy feats of gymnastics and legerdemain. She looked ready to turn a cartwheel on the carpet.

Brother Nestor sailed proudly ahead. The new Guardians followed, their apparel flapping gracefully, their feet barely touching the carpet. Tabitha came next, head down, refusing to look at anything. Saskia supported her, walking lithely along, head and shoulders high. Mr. Spinner was looking round, inarticulate with admiration. His spectacles had steamed up on coming in from the cold and he kept having to wipe them on his sleeve. Xtasca followed him, with the shuttle guards bearing Angie's pod in the rear.

The white-clad personnel of the *Citadel of Porcelain at*

First Light raised another cheer. Saskia waved with her whole arm, a sexy motion that would make them all love her.

Captain Jute was instantly and sharply jealous. She stopped in her tracks.

"This is the Death Ship," she said.

Saskia smiled at the soldiers. They stirred as the parade passed, baring their yellow teeth, the bristles standing up on the top of their heads.

"Death is so majestic," said Saskia Zodiac.

At the end of the carpet stood a group of Guardians behind a heavy rope of red silk. They watched the little procession, applauding them with pleasure. They resembled a prize-giving committee.

In the center of the group was the master of this stargoing city. He was wearing his silver circlet and his deep blue cape with the high collar. His eyes, couched in bags of fat, regarded the approaching humans with a tolerance that verged on contempt.

"Welcome back," he said.

"You don't get away from us that easily," said Captain Jute, not very coherently. She leaned sloppily on a stanchion, almost knocking it over. The Guardians laughed indulgently.

The newcomers, augmented and unaugmented alike, rode in gaily painted self-propelling gigs down broad corridors paneled with oak, along colonnades hung with Turkish carpets, past enclaves of vegetation, where in rustic bowers of wood artfully entwined and canopied with greenery Guardians sat improvising to the lyre or discoursing over amphoras of rich red wine. Everywhere, Eladeldi ministered to them.

Small goats, white as snow, scampered inquisitively across the grass to watch the little party go by. Everyone was showing an interest. Over the edge of a huge suspended mattress, oddly subdued in their silken garb, a five of Palernians ogled them. On curtained balconies Vespan nursemaids stood with their fans around the shoulders of little human children in shining clothes, who gazed down in wonder. They did not, any of them, seem to be the children who had been evacuated from the slums of Plenty.

"This is the way to live," said Brother Melodious. He held up the armful of grapes a laughing damsel had tossed to him, dangling them into his mouth. "This makes it all worthwhile."

He beamed moistly at Captain Jute. "Have a grape," he said.

"Sure," she said. She tore a handful from his bunch and crammed them into her mouth, making as much mess as possible. They had already taken Xtasca and Angie away, they wouldn't tell her where. She spat grape pips at Brother Melodious.

Sister Contenta stroked a ring. Captain Jute couldn't move. Sister Contenta smiled lovingly at her. "Be quite calm, Tabitha," she said.

While the paralysis lasted Saskia cuddled her. When she came round, she found Saskia had eaten all the grapes.

Their gig carried them into an enclosure of glass and golden wood. The floor rose beneath them, lifting them at a stately pace past apartments where grand pianos stood amid plaster statuary.

"Anyway, Mogul would like this place," said Saskia defensively, as if she had finally thought of a good point to win an argument they had been having. "We would get a great big dining table twelve and a half meters long, and he would sit at one end, and I would sit at the other. Then, until they brought us our food, Mogul and I would juggle to one another with the cutlery, a bottle of champagne, five glasses and a corkscrew!"

It was unclear whether this fantasy was a memory of a spectacular stage performance or a bizarre proposal for some impossible future feat. The only thing Tabitha Jute understood was why there would be five glasses. One for Saskia, one for Mogul, one for Zidrich, one for Suzan. What was the fifth one called? Tabitha had heard it often enough. But she had forgotten.

Above the roadway they glimpsed the trees of a pocket jungle, lush foliage looped with vines. Beyond the trees was glass, beyond the glass the stars.

The survivor of the Zodiac clone climbed up on the back of Tabitha's seat and twined her fingers in her hair. Exhausted, Tabitha laid her cheek against her thigh.

"It's good," said Saskia once more.

"I don't mind saying I'd like a look at the bridge," said Mr. Spinner. "I don't suppose you could ask them for us, Captain, could you?"

The apartment they gave her was three times as large as her old quarters on Plenty. There were desert plants growing in slatted boxes, recessed lighting and more leather sofas and overstuffed armchairs than she `could count. Evidently they wished her to spend a lot of time sitting down. Gravity was set at a uniform 0.8 g throughout. There was no independent control.

The emergency exit was through the bedroom, into space. There was a pressbutton in a small red box and instructions in English; but there was no suit. "If anything goes wrong, we'll look after you," said Sister Contenta.

"*Nothing is going to go wrong*," said Brother Nestor, on the ambient com.

The walls were tiled with half-meter squares of shiny cream stone. With the blinds down, they looked like panels of white chocolate. The giant furniture was upholstered seamlessly in sheets of fine bleached leather. Venusian saurian hide, they told her.

They had every movie and every piece of music she had ever enjoyed, and could supply any of it in a second. It was a subtle torture. The only way to retaliate would be to develop a fascination with something obscure and horrible:

Vespan nostril opera or ancient Sumerian bagpipes. Complain loudly at all hours until they provided it. Then ignore it completely.

There was, right now, a huge welcome party going on in somewhere called the Alabaster Atrium. It would have been the best thing to do, in a sense: go and get smashed, dance and drown herself in wine and crystal and mindless pleasure.

So that was out too.

There was a chime. On the living room wall Saskia's head appeared, twice life-size.

"*Look at all these clothes!*" said Saskia.

The viewpoint shifted rapidly backward, to show her standing in the middle of a vast quantity of stuff: coats, trousers, dresses, things flung across chairs, things laid on the floor, effusions of silk and chenille from drawers and compartments. Saskia herself was naked.

"*What do you think I ought to wear? Do you like this?*" She held a slender sheath of brown and yellow to her. "*Or this, I don't know what this is . . . Or, or, or—look at this!*"

Energetically she dragged a layered ball gown of peacock blue from under a heap. The rest of the clothes flopped dreamily back in the low gravity.

"*What will you wear? You must wear something magnificent!*"

She was a pain in this hectic mood, just as she was when she was miserable and everything was doomed.

"I'm not going," said Captain Jute.

Saskia hugged the ball gown like an imaginary partner. "*You're right, you shouldn't go. I shouldn't either. I don't even like parties. It's you that likes parties.*"

"I've gone off them," said Captain Jute.

"*I must try that one on,*" said Saskia, moving toward the camera. "*Your rooms are not bad,*" she said, examining Tabitha's quarters on her screen. "*But you haven't cleared the windows.*"

Captain Jute made no reply.

"*Oh, but it is so glorious! Like the end of the universe!*"

"Great," said Captain Jute. She didn't move.

"*How will it hurt them for you not to look out of the window?*" asked Saskia with asperity, as she pulled on a filmy garment of looped fabric, with long sleeves. "*It is hurting only yourself. We are here now, you cannot pretend you are still in your pod.*"

It might hurt more to look. But she wouldn't fight Saskia.

"Blinds up," said Captain Jute.

All around the room the great expanses of glass turned softly from opaque to transparent.

"*There!*" Saskia stood with her feet apart, pulling on her gown as she contemplated her view of Tabitha's portion of the inferno.

Captain Jute moved to the window and looked down.

She was high on the ship's back, in a pinnacle of one of the palaces. To one side, the white shoulder of the port wing loomed like a mountain. Many floors below, too many to count, lay the deck. Captain Jute could see part of a gridded apron like the parking deck of an orbital plat. Here and there the cells were occupied by small ships, scouters and hunters.

Saskia Zodiac was sitting on the floor, gazing out at the dying stars.

"*How long could we circle,*" she asked, "*before we start to burn?*"

∽ 6

Agent 8 and Agent 38 boarded the black sled at 78.34. The pilot was a full cerebellum conversion, a female. Other than hearing her recite the mission schedule, Agent 8 took no notice of her. Other than to recite it, she did not speak.

Agent 38 was checking the medical equipment, which was copious. Agent 8 checked the explosives. He checked the slaved apparatus, and the portable weaponry. There was less than he could have wished, but the space for instruments of destruction had been limited by the instruments of preservation.

The *Citadel of Porcelain at First Light* was a known ship. The intelligence held by Diagnostics was good, and Capacitory had managed to maintain its fix on the Ancillary during her transfer from the Frasque vessel, so their briefing had been quite precise.

Agent 8 had discretion and decided to opt for time, to catch the psychological tide that peaked with the hour. He and 38 closed the roof and braced themselves. The pilot retracted the supports and repolarized the anchors.

With a silent zag of disintegrating particles, the sled parted from the issuing gantry. 79.00.

The envelope of space around them shimmered suddenly as the sled shields came up, then dulled again as the signature compensation erasers cut in. The signal from the Ancillary was strong and steady. Agent 8 made a last check on the pilot. Her face was motionless in its cage of plastic filament. Only her larynx moved slightly and soundlessly, subvocalizing to the controls.

Agent 8 tapped the side of his helmet. Agent 38 tapped the side of his. Together they powered up their zeesuits. The exo film flowed like black lubricant across their deltoids, their visors.

The agents began their premission exercise.

"Amber 5," said Agent 8. The pips on his chest and back lit up to display the pattern.

"Immobilize from low right," acknowledged Agent 38, translating.

"Blue 9," said Agent 8. The pips changed.

"Sever neck," said Agent 38, straightening his fingers.

"Grey 9," said Agent 8.

As one the two men filtered their nostrils and armed anaphylaxic assault sprays. Agent 38 would have fired his too, unquestioningly, if he had not immediately received Purple 10, *Stand Down.*

79.71. A shoal of sooty rocks. The pilot cut impulse power and they rode the weak edge of the solar syncline.

Behind her the two faceless black figures confronted one another across the med support cot and danced their lethal *tai ch'i,* their precisely callibrated killing dance.

Down the spiral way to the isolation galleries Sister Contenta floated sedately in the company of Sister Mansuetude. They wore identical white togas over pastel-colored tunics. Their feet were sandaled and perfumed.

"Are they both down here?" asked Sister Contenta.

"Only the elder," said Sister Mansuetude. "The younger—what is her name?" She waved her pure white hand in an oval in the air and looked at her companion expectantly. "The one who stole the hive?"

"Tabitha," said Sister Contenta.

They left the chute and passed between two Eladeldi guards.

"Yes; Tabitha," said Sister Mansuetude. The air blinked around them as they swept through a security field. Ahead they could see two more guards, at the entrance to the suite. "Tabitha's up on Stardeck."

Sister Contenta approved. "She'll like that. She's fond of space."

"She'll have a wonderful view," pronounced Sister Mansuetude. "Good morning, sergeant."

"Bornig, badab," replied the guard, gruffly.

88.15.

Capella System was a welter of geological trash in clumsy, collapsing orbits. The Frasque ship was in sight, loitering in the outer reaches of the far galactic west. Plenty. Nothing, actually; at least to look at.

It was the first time the two men had seen the vessel they had been following for so long. It was big and dirty brown.

It looked like something that had boiled over and hardened. It was not easy to believe it had been squirted five hundred billion kilometers through time and space, with the *Seraph* on its tail.

Like decorative blimps the Sisters floated up to the window of the isolation suite. Inside lay the elder of the Jute girls, Angela, unconscious under a white silk-paper sheet. Tubes ran in and out of her in all directions.

The Sisters tutted, lifting their hands in dismay.

Unable to remain totally inattentive when Guardians were nearby, the younger of the guards turned his head a fraction toward them. Sensing his sergeant start to bristle, he stiffened his jowls and fixed his stern eye on the empty corridor again.

The poor girl had suffered. She had been turned into a machine, then overloaded. Every cell in her poor young body must have felt the strain.

"This is the one who brought the hive home," said Sister Contenta.

A woman in a white dress was sitting on the end of the life-support cradle, wiping the patient's face. The Cherub, meanwhile, was at the other end of the suite, its hoverdisc drawn up to a console. It seemed to be analyzing everything it could get on the physical condition of its subject, from muscular tics to gastric secretions, and analyzing the analyses.

Sister Mansuetude stuck out her bottom lip. She was thinking what an odd thing the Cherub was. It was black metal, with little tiny hands and an outsize head. It was almost as if the Seraphim had thought to make a miniature Guardian in black chrome. The metabolism, apparently, was entirely inorganic.

Sister Contenta was used to the Cherub. She had traveled with it from Earth, though she had never actually seen it in person. She looked over its shoulder at the instruments. There was nothing there she could understand except a radiation meter with the needle jammed on red.

"The poor girl is still terribly hot," she grieved.

She put her hand on her companion's arm. "Did you want to go and see the other one?"

"I suppose we could," said Sister Mansuetude. Yet she lingered.

"Cherubim are awfully clever, aren't they?" said Sister Contenta, tuning in to her thoughts. "I wonder how they make them."

"And the nurse," said Sister Mansuetude.

The woman in white had her back to the window. She was very thin. Her shoulder blades distended the back of her uniform like embryonic wings.

"Tabitha's girlfriend," said Sister Contenta.

"Yes," said Sister Mansuetude. "They made her too, you know."

91.22.30.

The black sled slipped past the Frasque ship to rimward, casting no shadow on its mountainous surface. Here and there, minute points of light were visible. Life going on, inside.

Agent 38 wondered what shape the celebrated casinos were in.

Agent 8 noticed his subordinate's gaze. "Curious, 38?" he asked.

Agent 38 glanced away from the view. His faceplate was clear, his expression dutifully blank.

"Pity they transferred the subject, sir," he said.

"Fancy a look around, do you?"

"Subject in context, sir." Agent 38 was stating a basic principle of acquisition and retrieval.

"Diagnostics would be proud of you, 38," said Agent 8 drily. He glanced again at the misshapen hive. "*Everything is there*," he quoted, inevitably. "Everything, 38."

There was jocular menace in his voice.

Agent 38 held himself upright. "We'd have cracked it, sir."

"Might have cracked you first."

Agent 38 knew his commander was just stirring him up, getting him ready to go. He was ready to go. He could feel his teeth tight in his skull.

Actually she didn't look *that* much like Tabitha, thought Saskia Zodiac. From where she sat, perched on the end of the cradle with one knee up, the face of the woman lying in it was actually upside-down. Things like that didn't bother her. She was a space-traveling acrobat. To her, everything had always been upside down.

Natural-born humans, Saskia thought. None of them looked the same.

No two of them were the same, in fact. That was the incredible thing.

It must be strange to have a sister who was different from you: who had different thoughts, wanted different things. Saskia wondered about that, about the strange sister who was a different person, much more often than she ever wondered what it was like to have a mother and father.

Having a mother and father was completely unimaginable.

Disturbed somehow, deep in the submarine caves of anesthesia, Angela Jute's left hand began to move. Just her hand, moving in isolation from the rest of her, drifting toward her mouth.

Saskia leaned closer. It looked as though Angie was indicating that she had something to say.

She hoped so. She wanted her to wake up and make a full confession. She wanted it for Tabitha's sake.

"Whom did she belong to again?" she asked the attendant Cherub.

Xtasca whirred. "She was a member of the Holy Sepulchre of the Expanded Neurosphere," it said.

"And that belongs to the Temple," said Saskia.

The Cherub did not reply.

Like some mournful fairy at a belated christening, her self-appointed nurse reached into the cradle and laid her long pale fingers on Angela's pierced forehead. The skin was hot and waxy, with inflammation around the sockets. Gently she wiped it again.

"Why did she bring us here?" she asked. "Why Capella?"

The Cherub's eyes glowed deep red. "At this point," it said, "what would be useful is a micrologic extraction laser."

Saskia pulled a face at it. The Cherub was not interested in Angela Jute as a person. It was interested in her as an instrument, a discarded tool. Where Saskia saw unique flesh, failing, Xtasca saw information, neuronic chains in cluster states. It saw evidence of consummate reflex and behavioral engineering, microscopic and brutal. On a monitor in a corner of the suite the tape of the Hippocampus Raid played constantly, forward, backward and inside out, sliced and sorted frame by frame into abnormal motions of particular muscles, exertions of individual nerve groups. That was the puzzle they were still trying to solve, with the body in the cradle as an all-too-cryptic key. Xtasca would have liked to slice that up too, no doubt, and comb it cell by cell, looking for familiar codes, the fingerprints of the Seraphim.

Saskia pulled the sheet down to check the patient's groin. She was worried the catheter might be uncomfortable. "I'm going to move this," she said.

As she rose she noticed the Guardians at the observation window. At once she pulled the sheet up again, as though there were something still to be hidden from those staring creatures. Flesh demanded to be covered, even after mind was gone.

74.80.
The black sled soared through the bloodred dark.

"Bloody place to send them, sir."

The white swan was coming nearer at last, floating backward and downward out of the ambient murk.

"The *Citadel*?"

The black sled flew like a small and venomous bat, like a pellet from a swan gun.

"No, sir," said Agent 38. "Here, I mean, sir. Capella."

The pilot watched her board add another overlay of the masking signal every ten-thousandth of a second, responding to a feedback profile of the target ship.

"Next time perhaps they'll ask you first, 38."

The white swan was the Capellan starship the *Citadel of Porcelain at First Light*. It looked like what it was, the ultimate in space-transport technology. Every twenty seconds the black sled beamed a microburst of image back to the *Seraph Kajsa*, where Diagnostics division analysts floated, licking their lips at this feast of new data.

"Just wondering, sir."

79.52. The black sled transected the extended axis of the port extremity of the *Citadel of Porcelain at First Light* at a distance of less than 70K. Not an alarm trembled.

80.26.

"Time," said Agent 8, and he signaled Purple 1, *Go*.

They left the sled and jetted stealthily across to the starship, pushing the gear ahead of them. The sled would stay in touch, changing wavelength constantly to avoid detection.

They found the target hatch and tweaked the lock, fusing it to secure their exit.

20.15.50.

Agents 8 and 38 entered a large area, unpressurized. Along floor and walls and ceiling ran ducts and bundled wiring. Gravity was low, almost optimum.

At regular intervals the ducts converged in large nodules: smooth, featureless white ceramic shapes three meters high. Agent 38 thought they looked like half-melted chandeliers.

They took cover behind one and triangulated the Ancillary's signal. It was twice as clear now, a constant shriek of unappeasable demand.

20.20.
The shriek led them into a concourse. Six pressurized galleries radiated from a spiral-threaded shaft. The bland internal architecture gave few clues, but it was only a matter of seconds to secure a direct perpendicular reading.

On they raced, leaving a squirt of silver conduc marker at every junction.

20.30.
The suits radiated electromagnetic fuzz, to confuse the cameras. They had seen no one yet. Now as they came through the ceiling they spotted a pair of guards. Eladeldi: the first they had seen since Sol.

The guards were stationed at the door to a clinical isolation suite. "Target location, sir," sent Agent 38, unable not to speak.

Agent 8 did not reply.

Through the door and the windows of the suite glowed warm peach-colored light. Two women occupied by Capellans hung upright at a window, looking inside. From above their smooth, swollen heads resembled giant billiard balls.

The intruders waited for the women to leave. They waited while they passed along the gallery, talking ignorantly about genetics, and out of hearing.

Agent 38 looked at Agent 8.

Stay, signaled Agent 8: Purple 2.

They waited a little longer.

At last Agent 8 swung into the corridor and dropped gently to the matte-tiled floor. Crouching, he swept in the direction the women had gone, then the other principal angles, listening, watching, sense amps on max.

Agent 38 remained above, preparing the darts. He could

see the Eladeldi if he ducked his head a fraction. They stood stiff and stupid. Though their hearing was superhuman, they had no idea they were overlooked.

"Two more, 120 meters," sent Agent 8 as he climbed back up into concealment. He pointed the direction.

Too far for darts. "Gas, sir?" asked 38, handing his superior the dart gun.

8 signaled a negation. He pointed the gun loosely into the open and fired, twice.

Grey 6, flashed 38's pips, in interrogative mode.

The darts flew down into the corridor and separated.

"Grey 6," confirmed Agent 8.

Each dart selected one of its target's eyes—the nearer one.

The Agents unshipped slender grey assault wands.

Each swallowing a liquidized eye, the faces of the big blue dogs softened around the point of impact.

The feet of the assassins hit the tiles at the same time as the bodies of the guards.

"Two down, sir," sent Agent 38.

The gallery was long and shadowy. Brighter light spilled from the vestibule at the end. Two more figures stood there: uniformed, canine. Agent 38 aimed his wand at the one on the left.

"Two to go," sent Agent 8, and Grey 6.1. Tracer.

Together they fired, altering their faceplates to register the beams: twin razors of silver light slicing through the air.

Striking something invisible, the beams rebounded.

Back in cover, the agents' helmets instantly replayed graphics of beam fracture and deflection at point of impact, projecting the calculated profile of the unseen obstacle. It was some kind of force curtain, closing off the gallery. Beyond it the two guards were only now starting to suspect a disturbance.

"Security field, sir," sent Agent 38, rearming his wand.

"They'll drop it," sent Agent 8. It was a good predic-

tion: Eladeldi always preferred direct access in combat.
Their defenses were also frontal and conspicuous: robot an-
tipersonnel guns.

38 flashed *Understood*. He readied his wand.

Leaping from cover Agent 8 scythed the gallery with a
broad burst of silent silver death. Behind him Agent 38
destroyed the guns.

Agent 8's first phase ricocheted in the irregular space,
skittering dangerously along the walls and floor. It scoured
an ugly welt along the wall and smashed a cable bracket.
Across the ceiling of the gallery flowed a sheet of light.

The force curtain came down. In a cloud of pulverized
flesh and bone the legs of the foremost guard disintegrated
beneath him. He fell on his face, his neutralizer still pumping at nothing. Behind him at the curtain controls the second guard was firing desperately.

"Shouldn't have dropped the curtain," said Agent 38
mildly, disposing of the second guard. "Four down. 21.03,
sir."

"In!" said Agent 8.

They blanked their faces and blew the door of the isolation suite.

It was the subject: Ancillary 13709. The sled computers
were already identifying her and sending confirmation,
clearance to proceed with mission. She lay unconscious in
a kind of cradle, her head away from the door. Above her
head, a little black metal creature on a flying bidet was
looking at them with luminous red eyes.

Agent 38 was startled.

What was a Cherub doing on the Capellan starship? Was
there some parallel mission he hadn't been briefed on?

One glance at his commander confirmed it was as much
of a surprise to him.

There was a rogue Cherub, 38 had heard. It was legendary. One of the first batch of Cherubim was supposed to
have gone haywire and run away from the Temple, years

ago, to join a traveling show. Suddenly Agent 38 knew he was looking at it.

Agent 8 scoped the Cherub, assessing how it affected the odds. It must be assumed hostile. They were a bitch to disable, he knew that. He signalled *Left and Right* and Grey 1, meaning *I'll take the Cherub, you neutralize the nurse*.

Agent 38 checked the nurse. Female, human, skinny. Skull normal, undistended. Deep eyes tight with shock and outrage.

He sheathed the wand and drew his neural whip.

21.03.45.

A rogue Cherub was an unpredictable element.

So was a nurse who did somersaults.

If you pulled a neural whip on a nurse, you expected her to give up, fall down, plead. You didn't expect her to leap spinning across the bed and land with her knees on your chest.

Agent 38 tautened his exoskin. The nurse fell hard, looking very much as if she'd bounced off a moving truck. All the same, gravity was only 80%, and she fell like someone who knew how to fall. Behind her, like a negative image of the falling nurse, a monitor was playing a video of a black woman performing acrobatics.

The Cherub appeared unarmed. Agent 8 feinted right, went left and struck the hoverdisc a glancing blow, spinning it.

The nurse was retreating among the equipment, going for cover, going for a gun, who knew what these people had in there? 8 would be able to identify it all; but 8 was busy.

38 pulled a gun of his own and sent a dozen rounds at her. There was a lot of blood suddenly, decorating the machinery.

This was turning into a messy job.

The Cherub was turned all the way round in midair, its tiny motors whining. It was wearing a banded silver tail, which Agent 8 had hold of. The Cherub was trying to fly. 8 wrapped the tail round his arm and jerked.

The mission subject was hooked up, half a dozen drips in her neck and wrists. Agent 38 was collecting the bottles when the nurse came leaping out at him again. Her starched white jacket was now two-tone, white and scarlet. Strike profile vectors flared across 38's visor display as she kicked him between the shoulder blades.

The Cherub's tail plug came out. Agent 8 hugged the flying saucer with his right arm, thrust his stiffened left index finger into the Cherub's empty spinal socket and gave it a shot of pulse.

The Cherub was down.

The nurse was up. She was alive.

The suit took her attack. 38 threw an elbow punch. She eluded him, flexing her spine the wrong way like some kind of gymnast.

38 was a soldier, bred, trained, equipped, enhanced. It was only a matter of time. He got his arms around her.

The nurse still had one hand free. She held it up over her bloody head, twisting it in the air and calling out a mouthful of something that sounded like Greek.

The video screen blew. Instantly, throughout the suite, powerful lights blazed full on: surgical lights, blinding.

That made 38 angry. He opaqued his visor, mirrored his suit. The light blazed from his body.

But the nurse was gone, cartwheeling out of the broken door.

"Orders, sir?"

Purple 9, flashed Agent 8, clearing his faceplate and checking the unit. The Cherub was crawling painfully toward him across the floor, squeaking. He got the toe of his boot under it and kicked it back in the corner.

Purple 9, *Proceed.* Evidently they were leaving the legendary Cherub. For a moment Agent 38 regretted it. He imagined the glory of being the one to recapture it. 8 was right, though. No amount of glory was worth jeopardizing the mission. The Cherub might look helpless, but it wouldn't be funny being stuck with it in the sled on the way back if it decided to be uncooperative. The first thing he would do, at debriefing, 38 told himself, was volunteer for the follow-up mission, to bring in the Cherub.

21.05.10. Total access. Working together Agent 8 and Agent 38 unlatched the restraints from the subject's body. They tore off the silk-paper sheet and taped it tight around her, rolling the drip bottles inside. They amped their suits to max deflective, picked the Ancillary up between them and rushed her out of the door.

Shimmering bursts of force pattered around them, zinging off their mirror skins. The nurse had taken some kind of weapon from the fallen guards.

The subject's feet under his left arm, Agent 38 swiveled and returned her fire. A window blew in a blast of crystal dice. The nurse was no longer there. She was faster than a Perk on motorskates.

38 sprayed the general area with various unpleasant forms of death, and they made their departure.

ᑌ 1

After the departure of her Captain, life on the Frasque hive known as Plenty began to settle down. The people who looked forward to following her to the Capellan starship clove to their chosen Guardian, or sat on their suitcases, waiting for the shuttle rosters. Just as many, preferring to stay where they were and carry on as normal, withdrew to their apartments in the Parietal and spent the long orbits watching AV. Channels 1 to 8 provided easy viewing, with round-the-clock reruns and phone-in quizzes. If there was any news, they were sure to see it on Channel 9.

The public spaces were deserted. The whole civilized cortex of the ship might already have been evacuated. Morningstar itself was empty, the cable cars hanging idle on their tracks.

High above, Soi padded through the old apartment, looking for the missing bag.

Effectively abandoned when the danger had been at its height, the apartment was now rapidly acquiring an air of dereliction. Its scents—of the mistress and her friends, of Kenny and Soi herself—were faint and faded. The rubbish everywhere, the broken appliances and dirty clothes, seemed like a documentary exhibition of Captain Tabitha's decline.

The Thrant shambled unhappily from room to room. The security system was still operational, but souvenir hunters had already found their way in. They had taken what they wanted, and left cryptic messages all over the walls, the fridge, the disconnected VR pod. JAZZ PARTY, said one, and another: TABBYCAT LOVES MARCO MOUSE.

In the drawing room she surprised a Wisp that had blundered in and been unable to find its way out again. It bobbed at her, imploringly. Soi drew back, wrinkling her nose. She had never liked the little buzzing things. She batted maliciously at it.

The cyberpet bounced off the couch cushions and flew sickly up to the ceiling, wired muscles flapping wings shaped just like outsize credit chips. It went to a high cupboard that had been left open and perched inside, watching her. It had a head like a hundred-toothed *canaarg,* and eyes like tiny mirrors.

Soi was aware of it watching her as she padded around. She could have climbed up and killed it in a second, but she had no heart for the chore. Without an owner, it would surely die soon. In any case, perhaps the thing had just as much right to be here now as she did.

Finally, inevitably, she wandered across the courtyard, past the dry fountain, its basin streaked with green scum, and into her own domain: the garage. It was empty. Sister Contenta had taken the Pango away—"such a dangerous great thing!"—and given it to Colonel Stark. Feeling totally bereft, Soi sat down on the oil-stained floor.

She thought of Kenny. She thought of their childhood, the days spent chasing each other through the treetops, under a proper sun. She draped her hands over her head and started to whine.

The sound she made was almost human. The Wisp came in and circled her warily.

Meanwhile, in the tangled undergrowth of the Deep Long Fissure, Kenny and his bucks went hunting. The Palernians were easy to catch, but harder every day to find.

The woolly, gregarious clowns from Centauri were almost extinct on board. Neurotic, fat, curiosities in the margin of evolution, it was a wonder they had lasted so long. Their broken fives roamed fearfully in the foot tunnels, fighting when cornered with such undisciplined abandon that it was a kindness to slaughter them.

In the ruined bordellos of the Yoshiwara, there was feasting that night. Savory juices ran down and stained the tattered valances of the great beds. Blood was trampled into the matted carpets. Kenny and Iogo mated with energetic ferocity, and Iogo felt her womb quicken within her.

The other women knew at once. There was no keeping secrets from their sharp ears and sensitive noses. They groomed her, prancing, making little yipping noises of jealousy and delight. Children were few in the lair, and precious. There had been sterility, and stillbirth, and deformities no tribe could bear. It was the mothers themselves, usually, who turned on the wheezing goblins and dispatched them with one swift swipe.

Queen Iogo lounged on the caresser, licking barley sugar as she stared at Channel 9. They all still liked to watch AV, but Iogo was the most devoted. She was watching Geneva McCann talking to a human woman called Ruby Cleat, who wore a big hat and aluminum shoes. Ruby Cleat was claiming she had seen strange creatures in the Prosperity foot tunnels.

"*Gave me a real shock,*" she was saying. She was playing up obediently to the camera, putting on a show of indomitability. "*I know there are some weird things on this ship, Geneva, but these things were moving.*" She chuckled derisively. "*They didn't look as if they ought to be moving.*"

"*What did they look like, Ruby?*"

"*Well, Geneva, they looked quite a lot like hydrangeas, really.*"

The interviewer drew back her head, batting her eyelashes at the camera, mugging surprise. "*Hydrangeas,*" she said.

"*Well, yes, really,*" persisted Ruby. "*You know the way they go in winter, all sort of twiggy and bare and not very nice.*" She gave a deliberate shudder. "*Yes, more like hydrangeas than anything.*"

In her cavern, the "Star Beast" lay dreaming her unimaginable dreams. She looked like a heap of purple flesh. She was soft. She was slimy and slick. The belt-hoist pylons, the surveying poles, all the devices with which the meat miners had pierced her had been removed from the great Beast's back. The chain-mesh pathways that had enabled them to climb from site to site had been taken up. The pits had healed where their staples had been driven in.

Only the softened contours of puckered wounds fifty meters long and more still showed where the purple flesh had been quarried for steaks and burgers and lasagnes, ever since the occupation of Plenty by humans and other hungry carnivores.

It was astonishing that the meat of the titanic alien should have proved nutritious to so many species. That evinced an inexplicable degree of protoplasmic complementarity, the Doctors Catsingle said, and they had proposed that the

Beast herself might represent the fabled Original Genotype, a primary galactic species, from which all others were descended. They had made a formal request to subject the poor creature to proper scientific study, promising the greatest care and consideration. Their request had been politely denied. "Let's leave her in peace now, shall we?" said Brother Kitchener, with an uncompromising smile.

Many questions therefore remained unanswered, like the question with which Geneva McCann's first and most famous film on the phenomenon had ended. "*While we were eating the Star Beast—what was she eating?*"

She was eating nothing at the moment, whatever she was, but only sleeping.

In a crevice of the cave wall, something stirred.

Over the next half hour, the furtive activity in the crevice increased. A spiky limb poked out and fingered the meaty air.

Next, the matrix of the wall itself began to bubble and dissolve. The crevice widened. In the darkness behind it, a dozen little eyes were glinting. The limb appeared again, and a great number like it, pushing at the softening wall, hastening its rupture.

Then, stealthily, six Frasque slid out into the open.

The Frasque were males, tall and stupid. The tubular members that made up their bodies were dark and thick, and twisted like branches. Ruby Cleat, former member of the Little Foxbourne Women's Institute, was not the first person to have made that vegetable comparison. It was indeed very like seeing six bushes gather up their roots and come wriggling toward you.

One by one the six Frasque hopped and crept up onto the glistening hill of flesh that was the Star Beast.

Under their feet, the enormous alien made no reaction. It seemed doubtful she even knew it was occurring.

Across a salient of the Beast, on all sixes the intruders

scampered, jerkily, like rubber dinosaurs in some antique movie. Extremities more like twigs than toes probed the yielding purple surface. Their tiny buried eyes gleamed like beads; their gaping mouths drizzled a sappy drool. They made a soft noise together, a moist, chattering hiss that sounded almost like distant hilarity.

Though male Frasque have no intelligence, these seemed to know where they were, and what they were there for. They climbed in a triangular formation: one, then two, then three. When they stopped, it was like insects, freezing between one motion and the next.

The slick skin quivered beneath their assembled weight. They seemed to have found the spot they were aiming for.

The leader rose on all his limbs, arching his back like an angry Thrant. The flesh beneath him rippled like blancmange.

Clicking and squeaking, his five companions moved into postion. They formed a rough circle around the rippling area, facing inward. Then they all arched their backs and lowered their heads. With their thorny teeth they nipped the elastic flesh.

The flesh seemed to succumb, opening responsively to them as it never had to the incursions of the miners. It was as if an invisible membrane had been instantly withdrawn from the patch circumscribed by the Frasque. Suddenly the meat there was spongy, porous, like a juicy imitation of the fabric of the ship herself.

Each of the six Frasque in the circle now made a complicated collapsing movement. The racks of their abdominal structures hinged open from the base, producing comblike formations, rakes of barbed extensions which also unfolded. These intricate arrays they inserted into the odorous mound. Evidently these intelligent shrubs had decided to replant themselves in a more congenial location. Perhaps they thought the blood of the Beast would nourish them.

Now, as if in obedience to some unfathomable biological urge, the Frasque began to twitch. They twitched with the rhythmical regularity of involuntary action. Their limbs flopped, their spiky feet scratched and scraped the liverish mass beneath them.

It went on for hours.

It was an immensely complicated business, protecting large numbers of widely differing sapients against the dangers of a solar system where they had never been intended to set foot. The humans were the priority, of course. Brother Valetude aimed to preserve as many of them as possible: not for sentimental or nostalgic reasons, but because humans were the best.

Like all the new Guardians on Plenty, Brother Valetude had his team of dedicated human assistants. They handled much of the routine work, the screening and inoculation programs. Machines taught headwired specialists, and the specialists taught the assistants. Brother Valetude sailed lightly between the workstations, squeezing the pretty assistants' bottoms.

"Good work, Tasha. Remember to bring me your results personally!"

Inside his private lab, however, only drones worked for Brother Valetude, and none of them was larger than a box of cornflakes.

The drones' tasks were mostly routine too: preserving sterile conditions and making minute adjustments to nutrient taps and tissue cultures. The brightest of them had the capacity to make simple decisions based on observation, and a tendency toward primitive cybernetwork was discernible. Sometimes he suspected them of trying to modify his procedures whenever he was out of the room. "Now come along," said Brother Valetude, clapping his hands as he broke up another conference underneath the autoclave. "Back to work!"

In an upper corner of the lab, easily visible from anywhere, a vital signs monitor was playing. A small signal light was on, indicating a recent change in the trails drawn

by the green pips that ran continuously across the screen.
The augmented medic glanced at it with a tight, preoccupied smile that affected only the corners of his mouth. He
was fairly sure he knew what that change signified. It was
happening earlier than he and his colleagues had expected,
but that was no bad thing. He would check it in just a
moment; but first, a glance at the project.

The quickest drones had already reached the bench where
the culture block lay beneath its domed lid of black glass.
Tiny tracks whirring, they labored up the access ramps
while Brother Valetude opened the inset eyepiece. They
steered wide of his elbows, taking precautions not to jostle
him as he tilted forward in the air to peer inside.

"Let me see now."

The specimen on the block was a small whitish ball
streaked bloodily with tiny vessels of red and blue. Pink
ligaments anchored it to the four corners of the block while
minutely calculated tides of nutrients, stimulants and inhib-
itors ebbed and flowed through the microscopic pipework.

"Jolly good," said Brother Valetude.

The ball was an eye, a human one. Brother Valetude was
cultivating it for a specific, indeed a unique recipient: this
one here, on the shelf, in the large jar.

It was a head. It too was human, of course: male, Caucasian, thirtyish, preserved but unmodified. Its hair was
black, intact, indeed shiny with health. Minute bubbles rose
intermittently from the left nostril, and from the empty left
socket where the new eye was to go.

"Any day now," said Brother Valetude to the head.

Watched by the drones, he put the jar back on its shelf.
"Now then."

Standing beneath the vital signs display, the Guardian
swept the control grille with the invisible beam that emanated from one of his power rings. The beam turned on a
loudspeaker, from which there began to issue a most peculiar noise.

It was a rustling, creaking noise, like wind in a wood,

but too fast and too rhythmically repetitive to be such a thing on any known world. There was a scratchy, squeaky element in it, like a wooden fence being shaken. There seemed to be a hissing in it too, as if the fence were being shaken by several people who were breathing hard, through clenched teeth. Or perhaps the wood where the wind was blowing had large snakes living in it, and they were protesting at being disturbed. It was a most peculiar noise indeed.

What was more, the noise seemed to be speeding up. The green pips glowed like fire as they ran across the vital-signs monitor.

Brother Valetude tilted his huge head on one side and turned the volume up. He seemed to be waiting for something.

The climax, when it came, was a terrible squeal, like half a dozen attack alarms going off at once. The glassware trembled on the shelves.

Brother Valetude floated across to steady the one-eyed human head in the big jar.

"I trust she enjoyed that," he said to it.

The head did not reply. Nor did the drones, going dutifully about their work.

Humming a little tune, Brother Valetude went to a small communicator screen. He deployed his ring again, and the face of one of his colleagues appeared: Brother Kitchener, who was over on the *Citadel of Porcelain at First Light*. He was playing the piano.

"They've started," said the hypertrophied physician.

His fingers arrested on the keys, Brother Kitchener assumed an unusual expression. It was pleasure, certainly, but pleasure constrained by something else. Perhaps it was a distortion of the little screen, but for a moment it looked almost like disgust.

"*Well, what do you know*," said Brother Kitchener.

He started to play again, *molto vivace*.

❧ 8

Saskia Zodiac ran back in through the broken door of the isolation suite. The Cherub had managed to drag itself out of the corner.

"Xtasca! Are you all right?"

"Of course I'm all right," the Cherub said calmly as Saskia hurried to pick it up. But it was cold. Saskia hugged it. Beneath the black metal skin she could feel its muscles trembling.

Saskia herself was bruised in several places, some she didn't even know about yet, and she was covered in blood. All along the racks the punctured transfusion bags were dribbling still.

Xtasca wriggled. It did not want to be held. "My disc," it said. Its voice was flat and mechanical.

Saskia reunited the hyperbaby with its hoverdisc.

She took the guard's gun out of her belt and looked at it moodily. "Mogul was always better than me," she said. "He would shoot the pips out of playing cards. Three of hearts, bang, bang, bang. I would hold them for him in my teeth. You remember."

The Cherub was selecting a new tail, unwinding it from one of the compartments inside its disc. It was moving very slowly. The tail was a thick one, multicored, sheathed in heavy-duty insulation.

"I must recharge now," it said, in an exhausted whisper.

Saskia started to exercise, stretching and bending. She winced as she twisted her arm, and looked at her elbow.

The Cherub's disc puttered across the floor, beneath the empty life support cradle, toward the central power supply.

The surface of the disc was blank, no displays operating at all.

Saskia eased her back. "That idiot nearly broke my spine."

The Cherub took a bite of mains current.

Its disc began to make a noise like a small motorcycle. The displays started to flicker again.

"Are we going after them?"

Xtasca rose vertically to the com. It started to enter something. Now tiny alarms were beginning to peep. On the surgical equipment, red signs were flashing.

The hoverdisc made a noise like ten small motorcycles. The lighting in the suite dimmed perceptibly.

"Xtasca?"

Then the lights went out altogether, and all the instruments.

"Come," said Xtasca, in the darkness. The hoverdisc purred. Saskia felt the breeze as it swept away over her head.

"You were hungry," she remarked, following it out.

She stopped and crouched to search the guards for ammunition, or perhaps a bar of chocolate. She was all bloody still. She wiped her hands on one guard's sleeve, then pulled it up and wiped her face on his fur.

The Cherub was heading up the gallery at some speed, making for the spiral chute.

"They went the other way," Saskia shouted. Her voice rang in the empty corridor.

Xtasca kept going. Could it have made a mistake?

Saskia shrugged. "Perhaps we're not going after them," she told the dead guards. Then she shed her ruined jacket and went cartwheeling after her metallic companion.

"Who are they?" she asked as they entered the chute.

"Slide," Xtasca said.

Saskia sat, and surrendered her sore limbs to the gradient of the spiral. Even in this gentle gravity it took her down like space taking waste. The Cherub swooped after her.

The levels whisked past, door by door. Through some, the backs of uniformed Eladeldi guards could be seen.

In a pale, deserted region of pipes and baffles they left the chute.

Between long low banks of shielded machinery they stole. The air was cool, and smelled of oil. Underfoot, a window appeared. Across a black gulf sprinkled with distant stars Saskia Zodiac skated.

Xtasca moved swiftly from junction to junction, checking each time before they broke cover. Saskia came up behind it and leaned for a moment on its disc.

"Is it them?" she asked.

"Of course," said the Cherub.

The last of the Zodiac clone thought of the Garden. Unchanging summer; sudden swift Cherubim among the hollyhocks; a giant in pink-and-purple armor whose voice had grated on her infant ears.

The soldiers in black suits that turned to mirror were connected with all that, belonged to it. She was certain.

"How did they get here?"

"Either things have changed significantly since our departure, or—" They were entering an unlit area of deep corrugations in the floor and ceiling. It looked like a system of pens for containing animals that were very long and thin.

"Or what?"

Xtasca settled. It began working with a fine tail point on some kind of mechanism. It was not speaking. The light at the tip of its tail was the only illumination.

Saskia sat beside it. "What are we doing?" she asked impatiently. "You might at least tell me that."

The Cherub brought back its head, as if to look down its nose at its work.

"Going to pay our respects," it said.

*   *   *

Saskia stood up.

"We must see Tabitha," she said. "We must tell her we're going."

"No need," said the Cherub, still working.

She put her hand on its head. "We must tell her about Angie!"

"I have posted a message," said the Cherub. Evidently it considered that a significant concession.

A small disc of pearly yellow appeared, inside the fabric of the floor. The light at the tip of the Cherub's tail blinked out.

"You should have let me!" Saskia complained. "She will be so unhappy. She needs me with her, to look after her."

From the small yellow light in the floor a bright red line extended itself. It ran around, describing a large oval.

Xtasca herded Saskia inside the red line. Its eyes flickered.

"You must come with me, Saskia, for your own safety."

"Safety?" Saskia retorted. "With them?"

Gradually the oval shape began to sink into the floor.

"For the next phase, I believe so," said Xtasca.

Descending in the gloom, the clone and the cyberling stared at each other like members of different species.

"The Capellans will start to take an interest in you," explained the Cherub, "once they realize *they* have arrived. It's incalculable where that interest might lead them. So, we go to pay our respects to our makers."

Saskia was unconvinced by this appeal to the instinct of self-preservation.

"You just want to see what they do to Angie," she said.

The platform they were riding was a sliding door. It carried them down and backward into a large departure bay.

The lighting was white and brilliant. In the outer wall of the bay were three doors. They were all closed. From somewhere came the subdued rhythmical mutter of air compression.

In the bay were ten lifeboats.

They were small capsules shaped like teardrops, bright yellow, with big simple identification markings.

The ten lifeboats and the three departure doors were supervised from a central glass blister. The blister protruded from the upper wall and could be reached from several points by ladders and bridges.

On duty in the glass blister sat an Eladeldi guard.

Xtasca told Saskia: "Here is a job for you."

There had been trouble twelve levels up, in a medical facility. The chief had been on in person, saying three of the new passengers had disappeared, some of the first evacuees from the occupied hive. One of them was a nonhuman, and another was dangerously ill. The nonhuman was a Cherub, a member of an artificial species. There was a short generic dossier about them you could call up in Further Information. Automatic reminders of routines for handling irradiated life-forms had followed, then brief dossiers on four Eladeldi personnel tagged Killed in Performance of Duty and an All-Points Alert about two highly armed men in zeesuits, responsible for murdering the four guards and abducting one or more of the missing passengers.

In the Sector 16 lifeboat bay, the guard was playing with his puzzle. It was a good one. You had to take it apart. There were seven pieces, but each of them was slaved to combinations of the others, so there was only one order you could do it in, and it changed every time. When you had it apart, you had to put it back together. The guard enjoyed trying to get it apart twice and back together twice between the times he had to make a round.

The first he knew of the human, she was already walking along the bridge toward him. She was thin and pale, in a dirty white singlet and green trousers with blood down

them. How she could have come in without alerting him or
setting off the alarms, he didn't know.

The guard kicked back his chair, pulling out his gun. He
barked at her through the address system. "''Alt or I vire!''

The woman stopped obediently in the middle of the
bridge. She put her hands on her hips, which was not the
correct response.

He scanned her. Nothing questionable appeared.

"Iden'ify yourzelf."

Her voice came clearly through the speakers.

"I am Saskia Zodiac."

Saskia Zodiac. It was one of the names in the bulletin.
She was one of the missing passengers, the new ones
brought over from the hive. Was she alone? She seemed to
be. What was she doing here in the boat bay? He needed
a full and satisfactory explanation of her movements since
her last recorded sighting, her manner of entry and purpose
here, her bloodstains.

The woman wiped her hand across her face. "The intruders have escaped," she said grimly. "They have left
the ship."

Keeping the gun trained on her, the guard got on the
com. His duty was to report her and her claim and request
confirmation and orders; but all he could get at present was
a howl of feedback. It pierced his sensitive ears like a drill.

He asked her, " 'Ow you ge' in yere?"

Unhesitantly the woman pointed to one of the overhead
doors. "I think it may be damaged," she said.

The guard wriggled his neck, sensing his duty suddenly
enlarged. The limits of the emergency must be defined.

"Perim'er patrol 'ill yop inkruderzh."

"The perimeter patrols will stop them," agreed the Zodiac woman gravely. "These ships you guard are very
fine."

Pride and surprise warred in him with suspicion.

"Ftate your bizniz."

"I shall explain," she said. "Let me in. You don't need to shoot me." She spoke like a Master warning a subordinate against a foolish course of conduct. While his paw still hesitated on the gun controls, she walked the rest of the way across the bridge and stood outside the door of the blister.

He brought her inside, scanned her again and searched her personally for weapons. She made no objection, but kept her head up and her eyes on the lifeboats.

"Which ones are ready?"

"Your bizniz, ma'm," he said again. "Exblain, bleaze."

"This is an emergency, sergeant," said the Zodiac woman. "Which ones?"

"All," he said, testing the com again. Still nothing but horrible noise. It made his fur stand on end.

While he keyed diagnostics for the inboard access doors the woman stood with her hands spread on the window, resting her long forehead against the glass. It was a vulnerable position. The guard's sense of command returned, though his suspicions remained.

"Exblain," he repeated.

She pressed a fingertip against the window. "Under what conditions may they be used?"

His response to the official phrasing was automatic. He didn't have to think to start reciting.

"Gollizyon, grazh, acciden' or ebergedcy affec'ing local or gen'ral yecuri'y of yip, dam'zh to yip dwendy doo un hunred per cen', hoszile aczyon ec'ernal, hoszile aczyon in'ernal doo degree 'equiring local or gen'ral evacyazyon—"

"Yes," said his visitor then, quite sharply. "There has been internal hostile action, causing temporary local communications breakdown." And she fingered her chin with an odd, distracting motion.

He knew what would follow in that case. "Guarg off'zer on du'y gring orders in kerson—"

"The guard officer on duty is injured," she told him. "Incapacitated. Out of commission."

She was sitting on top of the suit locker now with her trouser leg rolled up, examining a bruise. He was not at all sure how she had got up there without his noticing. Still, it was not a dangerous position, not a threatening position. Distantly, he heard himself continue to gabble portions of the regulations.

"Ack'ing guarg off'zer bring orders in kerson, meh'henger fron guarg off'zer on du'y or ack—"

"How would this messenger identify themselves?" she asked. "Would they perhaps have a card, a key, a warrant for the use of a lifeboat?"

The guard shook his head. A vague, cobwebby sensation had grown up behind his eyes. He made an effort to focus, to concentrate. "Ma'm, zose de'ails are yecuri'y yenzi'ive."

She went on as if he hadn't spoken. "Might the credentials they presented look like this?"

The woman held up her wrist. There was a white plastic thong around it, with the silver metal pilot command tag attached.

How had he failed to see it? More baffling, why had it not shown up on the scanners? It was impossible. Still, the sight of the tag filled his breast with a vivid sense of justification, like the sound of a Master's voice speaking to commend him. He had done his duty, passed a test. He knew now what to do to the woman, whoever she was, and that was salute her.

He directed her to the third lifeboat from the right, panting keenly as he entered the activation for her.

Saskia Zodiac trailed her hand through the air past his eyes. "You will not see the Cherub," she told him. "You have never seen me."

The guard was playing with his puzzle. He saw he had just finished putting it back together. Either that or somehow all the parts had recombined without him noticing. He had to start undoing it all over again.

The lifeboat popped out of its hole in the *Citadel of Porcelain at First Light* like a pear dropping off a stem. Saskia clung to the window strap, watching gravely as the departure door closed behind them.

The Cherub hung tethered to the board by a standard interface tail. "Keep a sharp lookout," it said.

The raiders might be anywhere on the hull of the starship, behind any of these moldings, inside a housing. They might *be* one of these things, a small ship masquerading as part of a big one.

"What am I looking for?" asked Saskia.

"Anything," Xtasca said.

Now they were running the length of the ship, tucked in close, avoiding windows and scanners, observation domes and monorail cars. They headed aft, as if swept along in some kind of slipstream. Saskia felt the enormous, mysterious superstructure clutch at her, like a huge industrial robot playing with a moth. Tensely she said, "Can we not get clear?"

The Cherub hummed.

It turned the lifeboat toward a deep triangular recess of space black shadow on the dark side of the port wing. With tiny attitude bursts it sent them drifting up into the angle, and wedged them lightly there.

They sat for a moment, without lights, watching. In the darkness of Capella space, distant black shapes turned slowly. Saskia began to speak. Her companion hushed her.

The acrobat felt her aches redouble. This waiting and hushing was no good. Wherever the faceless men in mirror suits were taking Angie, they were getting there. Soon it must occur to the deluded guard of the lifeboats that something was amiss. Surely it had already.

Then silently a pale yellow globe slipped beneath the edge of the wing that concealed them.

Saskia did not speak. Xtasca had seen it too. It was close, and comparatively large, larger than the lifeboat. It was, perhaps, a minor service vessel of some kind, circling the big ship.

"Perimeter patrol," said Xtasca quietly.

Saskia found herself holding her breath, as if the patrol might be able to hear her if she breathed.

The yellow ball floated effortlessly across the mouth of the recess and out of sight. In her mind the cloned woman rode along with it, hanging on to it, counting the seconds of its passing.

"They've gone," she said.

Xtasca evidently agreed. It maneuvered the little ship quickly out of shelter and boosted it over the vast alar projection into merciless red sunlight.

Saskia floated up the window. She looked down on the constructions of the Stardeck, the windows glinting orange and gold. Tabitha's apartment was there, somewhere. Were her blinds closed again? Or was she at her window, a prisoner glaring at the stars? Had she received Xtasca's message yet? Did she know her sister was gone from the *Citadel*, let alone her lover?

Xtasca hunched over the displays on its disc. Saskia saw it was running some kind of abstract graphic of their vicinity. There was a tiny pink lozenge flashing in a circular grid.

"Is that them?"

"That's Angela, in fact," the Cherub said.

"Is she still alive?"

"Now that I can't tell," it answered, pleasantly.

"How far away are they?"

"Not too far. She must be in a vehicle that is fast, but small."

Saskia gazed at the screen. She wanted to put her finger on the little pink blip and stop it from getting away. The radiant evangelist, unconscious, perhaps never to wake again: there she was, still broadcasting the message of her presence.

"I wish Tabitha could have come," Saskia said.

The thin acrobat investigated the survival rations. All they had was a quantity of small shiny pills, white and yellow, and twenty tiny slices, individually wrapped, of something that appeared to be plastic sponge. She supposed it was meant to keep half a dozen survivors alive for a number of days. She ate it all anyway. The sponge tasted like smoked chicken.

Then the pink blip on Xtasca's screen disappeared. One moment it was there, the next it was as if their quarry had dropped out of existence. Saskia clutched at the disc. "Did they skip?"

"No," said Xtasca. "Their vessel is too small. There is another possibility."

It ran its perfect little hands over the keys of the lifeboat board. "Ah," it said.

The external lights came on, and revealed something ahead, where there appeared to be nothing but stars. There was nothing, and then there was something: a slight suggestion of something, anyway—some sort of structure, invisible but curved. It was exactly like the optical illusions of hyperspace that seem to bend portions of nothingness into shapes and formations, but happening here, in true space.

The Cherub was buzzing like a big black bee.

Next moment the flying yellow teardrop must have crossed a crucial threshold of perception, for Saskia realized there *was* something there. It was a convex wall, perfectly smooth and perfectly polished.

It was a construction of some kind: impossible to tell what, or what size, or anything else about it. The wall was mirror black, like Xtasca's skin. Already it seemed alien to Capella System, eloquent of some other technology as subtle and secretive as the starship and the beacons were ostentatious. Its most prominent feature was their own reflection, becoming visible now, indistinctly enormous, blurred by magnification.

Now, as the shape in front of them grew large enough and close enough to eclipse everything else, the curvature resolved. The flawless wall was the hull of a ship. The abductors must have borne their prisoner inside that hull, docking at some still undetectable door.

Saskia asked: "Is this your other possibility?"

"Exactly," said the Cherub.

The tiny teardrop plunged on to its rendezvous.

∽ 9

She could call Saskia, or any of several Guardians, look in on Angie in her isolation suite or communicate with the bridge, where Mr. Spinner seemed to be making himself at home. There were atmosports for her to watch, and harp concerts, and organic meditation pieces. There were fifteen channels of nonstop rock, raga and reggae. There were strange gloomy abstract things in brown and purple which Vespans apparently found very soothing, and innocent game shows where children of all species could win handkerchiefs and toys. There was no news.

Sound tracks were available in every known language. Tabitha Jute's was set for Standard Solar English. She tried to make it change by snorting and coughing out the few bits of Altecean she could remember. She sang it a filthy song in old Martian canal-boat creole. She wheezed at it on her harmonica.

The screen took no notice.

*   *   *

Traveling on the *Citadel of Porcelain at First Light* confirmed how they prized humanity above everything else they had picked at. They adored human beings. You never saw a Thrant or even an Eladeldi with a swollen head.

"What's so special about us anyway?" Captain Jute once asked Sister Contenta.

The Guardian gave her a horrible winsome conniving look, as if she thought their guest was fishing for compliments. "There's nobody to touch you," she declared, holding up one plump ringed hand. "Perks are fun, and Palernians are cuddly, but that's all, really."

Tabitha stared at her, trying to understand the opinions of a giant blue caterpillar that squatted uninvited in people's brains.

It had been Sister Contenta, back on Plenty, who had said they could bring her VR pod over. "If you think you might like it," she said, sympathetically. She seemed to regard it as a useful but regrettable prosthesis.

Captain Jute had told her not to bother. "Some leeches would be good, though."

Sister Contenta had laughed, wobbling her head. "Oh, Tabitha, you are funny."

There were days, days and nights when Tabitha would have given her right tit for that pod. Both tits. In her dreams she saw the Terran Tangle through a viewport, ships and orbitals all around her. She heard again the familiar, patient, capable voice, and woke groaning to find herself still in the apartment, a prisoner.

Captain Jute abandoned the AV and went back to the window where she spent much of her time. Though she never would have admitted it, the enforced period of rest was doing her good. She was feeling better now, and stronger. She threw herself onto the enormous sofa, which received her softly.

"Blinds up," said Captain Jute.

Outside, the palaces of the Stardeck materialized, glaring bleakly in the vacuum. Inside some of them, sometimes, you could see lights going on and off, shapes of people moving about.

On the deck below, there was seldom anything going on. Engineering and maintenance vehicles appeared from time to time, taking service mechs to one or another of the parked craft. Most of the little ships seemed to have been parked for the duration, whatever that was. Sometimes a crew would go out and start one up, let it run for a long time, then transfer it slowly and with great care from one place in the grid to another three spaces away.

Today, above the back-slanted rooftops, she could see a tiny ship. Eladeldi patrol, the Captain supposed. The ship was bright yellow. It looked like a flying drop of mustard. She watched it go by.

It was the waiting, always, that got you down.

On Saskia's last visit to her apartment, Captain Jute had tried to get her to convey her resolve to the Cherub. She had cuddled her, squeezing those paper-thin shoulders. "Say I wasn't here," she said. "What would Xtasca do then?"

Saskia disengaged herself. "She is looking after your sister," she said. She sat up, crossing her arms over her tiny breasts.

The bedroom was hot. The stink in there could have shorted a spark box. The Captain rolled over on her back, one arm behind her head. Throughout the apartment, high up on the wall, ran a frieze of randomly repeating rhomboidal shapes. She liked to think it was writing. Alien inscriptions, designed to be read by the suite's original occupants. Instructions for procedures in case of Capellan attack.

"I wonder if anyone's heard from Captain Gillespie," said Tabitha loudly.

There were no cameras. She'd established that, as definitely as she could. Still, you had to assume a microphone or two.

Saskia was already dressing. She was in the gloomy mood that so often seemed to come upon her after sex.

"Captain Gillespie has deserted us," she had said. "She thinks more of her new playmates than she does of you."

Well, there was no chance of that. Obviously.

Tabitha Jute looked down at the white enamel deck of the *Citadel of Porcelain*. To one side, beneath the overarching wing, she could see the end of one of the long narrow openings, like an outsize printer slot, through which she knew they could spread a blanket of breathable atmosphere, when they chose, across the deck.

She kept trying to think of a way to trick them into doing it.

She looked at all the good ships standing idle there, out of reach. She thought of all the lethal old kites in the docks on Plenty, ditto. She was always getting stuck in places with a lot of ships she couldn't fly. She would probably end her days running the parking on Autonomy Plat. Assuming she ever got back to the Tangle. Assuming there still was a Tangle, assuming there still were plats, assuming there was anyone left alive to need their ship parked.

In the far distance, sunward, one of the Capellan System ships appeared for a little while. It looked just like a tiny ornamental fish made out of red metallic foil. Then the perspectives closed upon it, and the glint of light was gone, swallowed in the invisible black shapes that swarmed slowly and perpetually across the suns.

A chime sounded, announcing a visitor. She went to see.

It was not the visitor Captain Jute had been hoping for. It was not a visitor she ever hoped for. It was a visitor she would have preferred to see chopped into little pieces and burnt.

"Hi there, sweetheart."

The tanned, chubby apparition smirked ingratiatingly in her doorway in his prism jacket and leopard skin trousers. It was Marco Metz, or Brother Melodious, as he now styled himself. It was all his fault. Everything was all his fault.

"What do you want, Mr. Caterpillar?"

From behind his back, with a coy flourish, he produced a carton of Golden Chariot beer. He held it in one hand, his glass one.

"I brought you a present."

"Bring me a future," she said.

His eyebrows wiggled. "Oh-ho-ho, bring you a future," he said. "That's very smart, I like that. You're very smart, you know? You always were. One very smart lady. You know what, I wish you could have joined the show that time, we could have used material like that." He bestowed a look of adoration on her. "Let me in?"

"Let me out," she said.

She tried to push past him, but there was some kind of selective field across the doorway. While she pressed herself against a resistant plane of nothing, the Guardian swept effortlessly into her apartment.

"Hey, now, sweetheart—"

"Don't call me that!"

"You know you're not ready to run around just yet. You know Brother Valetude says you need to rest a while, get your strength back, come to terms with the realities of the situation here."

His crepe soles barely touched the carpet as the elevated artiste crossed to the sofa by the window.

"I can't believe what a beautiful place this is . . ."

Tabitha followed. She didn't want him out of her sight.

"The realities of the situation?" she said scornfully. "You mean the way I'm being kept here until you're ready to eat me?"

"This really is such a great view," said Brother Melodious, lowering himself vertically onto the sofa. "This is your favorite spot right here, I guess."

She denied it, but the litter betrayed her.

"Eat me," she said, standing to one side of him, compelling him to look away from the window. "Go on. Let me poison you."

Brother Melodious set the heavy carton of beer on the sofa beside him. The cushions bounced fluidly as it settled. He stiffened his artificial index finger and in one easy move sliced the top off the carton.

"Tabitha," he said. "Have a beer."

Captain Jute watched him lift one of the self-cooling tubes to his muscular lips and pictured the slimy blue creature that sat in his skull and commanded him to do so.

She took the beer he was handing her and went to one of the other sofas, placing herself out of his line of sight, for his inconvenience.

She had his attention. The great caramel-colored dome turned to face her.

"No one's going to eat you, Tabitha," said Brother Melodious. He stroked his thigh, smoothing his skintight trousers. "Anyway, it's not like *getting eaten*. It's really nothing like that at all. It's very intimate." His eyelids drooped.

Captain Jute remembered how once that would have made her weak. Now it just made her sick, and furious. She poured Golden Chariot into her mouth in an effort to quench the fury.

"All they want to do is share our energy," said the Guardian. He stroked his distended skull.

Captain Jute belched. "Why do you keep saying *they*, Marco?"

Beyond the glittering palaces of the Stardeck, titanic stringy accretions of carbon thousands of kilometers long trailed down like sooty cobwebs into the suns. Brother Melodious spread his legs and stretched out his arms, rejoicing in the awesome natural beauty.

"I'm with you, sweetheart," he said. "Obviously right now you won't understand this, but in my heart and in my soul I remain one hundred percent human being."

"Don't push it, Capellan."

"It's true."

Captain Jute remembered the long, complicated lectures on the *Alice Liddell*, the elaborate explanations full of prevarications and lies. When he affirmed his veracity Marco Metz's golden voice went up a couple of octaves.

"I'm absolutely the same guy I always was. I mean, can you honestly say my essential personality is in any way, shape or form different from how I was on Plenty, or on Venus, or back in Schiaparelli? I don't think so!"

He patted the cushion at his side, the space he had conspicuously left for her.

"Come and sit here," he said. "Be nice. Come sit down here and be friendly."

"No."

The large veins were quiet at his temples and above his eyebrows. He smiled equably, lowering his painted eyelids, forgiving her.

"Tell me about sharing energy," she said.

"It's just terrific," he said at once. "Superpowered beyond anything you can imagine. Amps? Drugs? Forget it." He swallowed the remainder of his beer and immediately started another. "Them and us, it's like total synergy! Pow!"

"Pow, huh?" she said.

He was almost vibrating with the intensity of it.

"You have to understand, Princess, we are very very special."

"We are," she corrected, overlooking the repulsive endearment. "Human beings."

"Human beings, right," he said; and he gestured to his occupied skull. "These little guys were roaming the galaxy for centuries, searching all over for a partner like us! None of the others worked out."

It was the usual line.

"You," she said. She looked him in the eye, pointing to her head. "*You*. Brother Caterpillar. Where did you come from?"

"Hey," said Brother Melodious. He spoke softly, playfully. "You know that. I was born in a costume trunk in the back of a—"

She interrupted. "How many bodies have you had? How many people have you eaten?" She was imagining twin electric drills sinking into the beautiful eyes of Marco Metz.

He sighed indulgently. His voice was still soft. "We've been with you a *long* time," he said.

The temperature in the apartment seemed to sink a few degrees.

She resisted. As long as the Capellan would not answer her directly, she would not acknowledge the replies. She said again: "How many?"

The Guardian chuckled. "Captain, you're way off course," he said. "As always." There was a sting in his laughter. He was getting angry, she was sure of it. It was hard to make them angry. What would it take to make him lose control?

"Homo sapiens and Capella," he said confidentially. "There's so much we still have to give each other." His smile was fierce. "All you have to do is learn to trust."

"Trust you, Capellan? Impaled on a steel spike I'd trust you."

Calmly he turned back to the window, to the great blood black ache of Capellan space.

Captain Jute gripped the arm of her sofa. She was hyperventilating. Unconsciously her fingers were searching for controls no longer there.

"How did you get aboard my ship?"

He spread his hands, the entertainer. "One day we'll show you all that stuff. I promise. I'll show you personally. It'll be my privilege."

She got up.

He got up. "Sit down," he said. "Tabitha. Please."

"My ship," she said, stepping closer. "Plenty. A Frasque ship, Brother Caterpillar."

"Take it easy, Tabitha . . ."

"We were going to Proxima. Why did we end up here? Who was running Angie? Was it you?"

"All that stuff," he said again. "It's not important."

"I'll say what's important!"

She dashed her beer over his musical hand.

A small repeller field sparked and crackled, deflecting the yellow fluid in a harmless spray over the sofa, the carpet, his blue-suede boots. He looked reproachful.

"Tabitha." He grimaced, restraining himself. He sat down. "Listen," he said. "Sit down. I came to tell you something."

"Why couldn't you have the decency to phone instead?"

She was kneeling on the sofa beside him, shouting at him. She brought her face to his. She could feel the electricity that surrounded him prickling on her lips and in her hair.

"Sit *down*, for Christ's sake," he said. "Look at you, you're all wound up. Sit down, have another beer. You'll want to be sitting down for this." It was stalemate. She had backed him into his seat and that was as far as he was going to go. She had no way to do him harm.

She looked down at him.

"I don't want your lies," she said, icily sweet.

He floated up in the air again until he could look down on her. He said: "Tabitha, Tabitha—why do you make everything hard for yourself?"

She stood up, wobbling on the uncooperative cushions. She and he were face-to-face again.

He dropped back into his seat, making it plain how patient he was being with her folly. A vein began to pulse erratically beside his right eyebrow. "Listen," he said.

"Fuck off," she said.

She knelt again. She told him her theory.

"This is your only starship, isn't it. That's why you wouldn't let us have one. This is your only one. Wherever you stole it from, there aren't any more. That's why you hate the Frasque. Because they know how to make starships. That's why you had to steal mine."

"You're completely wrong," he said.

Suddenly the room seemed drained of light. In the shadow of his monstrous brow the two brown eyes of the possessed man smouldered with dark fire, as if endowed by the malevolent suns.

He put his arms round her.

"They got dozens of 'em," he said. "All over the galaxy."

There was another chime at the door.

At once the atmosphere changed. Even before she could free herself he pushed her away. "There you go," he said. "That'll be Mr. Spinner. Spinner, is that you? Let him in, why don't you."

She gazed at him, trying to decipher his state of mind. It was impossible. A moment before she'd felt she had almost got through to the venomous intelligence inside his head. Now it was back skulking behind its mask of flesh and bone.

"You're such a great performer, Marco," she said.

She went to open the door.

Mr. Spinner seemed anxious. He wore a snowy white polo neck and over it a Y-shirt of white leather with golden zips.

"Captain. How are you?"

"Great," she said. "How's things on the bridge?"

Sarcasm was lost on him. "Fascinating," he said, looking away from her as if he had expected another answer. Apologizing mechanically, he came in. Brother Melodious was the important one here, that much was clear.

"Hey, Spinner," called Brother Melodious, bustling up into the air again. "You want a beer?" He held a tube in each hand. He was the party host, the soul of bonhomie.

Mr. Spinner wiped his head, which was as bald as Marco's, but, Captain Jute felt sure, no larger than it had ever been. He looked up at the Guardian through his heavy spectacles.

"Have you told her?" he asked, significantly.

Brother Melodious flew down and put a Golden Chariot in his hand. Taking a draught of his own, he clapped him on the shoulder. "I was just about to," he said, swinging toward Tabitha again. "Captain," he said. "Tabitha. Everybody's really sorry, okay."

The fabulous eyes watched her carefully, to see how she took it.

"Somebody snatched your sister."

It was ludicrous. They'd let Angie die and he was trying to cover it up with some crap about intruders. "Intruders. It's always intruders," she said.

But Mr. Spinner was there to confirm it. "There were two figures in some very sophisticated suits," he said. "They scrambled half the tapes, but we got some clear shots. Humans, Captain, we're pretty sure."

"Anyone we know?" she asked him.

"I'm afraid they're both completely unidentifiable," he said. "But they did leave clues." He reached uncertainly for the screen controls. "With your permission, Captain . . ."

Brother Melodious snapped his fingers. "Here. Here." Working his rings he fumbled up some shots of anonymous corridors. Junctions and doorways were daubed with familiar shiny silver marker paint.

"See, Captain," said Mr. Spinner, "it's the same stuff that Mystery—I mean, your sister—"

"I know who you mean," said Tabitha heavily.

Eventually she had to accept it. Somebody had broken into the *Citadel of Porcelain at First Light* and abducted Angie. For all their much-vaunted mental advancement the Guardians had no idea who they were, where they had come from, how they had got in, how they had got out, where they had gone, or why they'd done it.

"It's what I was trying to tell you, sweet thing. Only you're so hung up about Plenty all the time," said Brother Melodious with infinite sympathy.

"Call yourself fucking Guardians," she scoffed.

Mr. Spinner was looking guilty and glum. She asked him: "Where's Saskia?"

There was sweat forming on his forehead. He never had liked being the one to give her bad news.

"Security are searching now," promised Brother Melodious.

"Security," said Tabitha bitterly, and clenched her fist with frustration. "Get Kenny! Get Dodger Gillespie! They'll find her. And where's the Cherub?"

"They weren't actually taken," said Mr. Spinner. "Neither Saskia nor Xtasca." His tongue tripped over the awkward pair of names. "They defended themselves against the intruders and remained in the isolation suite after they left," he said. "There are pictures of them moving about, before the power went down."

He looked at Brother Melodious, who managed to call up some low-grade footage of Saskia in a bloodstained white singlet, Xtasca in her arms, like a blasphemous Madonna and Child. Tabitha stared. Had it been a rescue mission which had gone wrong? Had they taken Angie instead of her?

"Security now thinks they may have gone after them," Mr. Spinner said.

"Saskia and the Cherub?" said Captain Jute.

"It's only conjectural. There's a lifeboat missing from Sector—"

"Without telling me?"

"Show her the message," Mr. Spinner said to Brother Melodious.

"I was just going to," Brother Melodious said.

Tabitha set her teeth. "So why didn't you?"

"I wanted to prepare you," said Brother Melodious, working the screen. "To make sure you were comfortable and receptive. And you had all that other stuff you wanted to talk about, remember."

Captain Jute was no longer listening. She was looking at the words that were glowing on the wall of her living room.

IN CASE OF MALFUNCTION OR DAMAGE FROM CAUSES OTHER THAN ABUSE AND MISUSE, INCLUDING BUT NOT LIMITED TO FAILURE TO USE KING COMPUTER (TM) PRODUCT IN ACCORDANCE WITH MANUFACTURERS' INTENTIONS AND INSTRUCTIONS, INSTALLATION OR USE OF KING COMPUTER (TM) PRODUCT IN A MANNER INCONSISTENT WITH TECHNICAL OR LEGAL STANDARDS LOCALLY IN FORCE, REPAIRS BY UNAUTHORIZED AGENCIES, ACCIDENTS, ACTS OF GOD, OR ANY CAUSE BEYOND MANUFACTURERS' CONTROL, INCLUDING BUT NOT LIMITED TO LIGHTNING, FLOOD, FIRE, METEOR STRIKE, RIOT, WAR, GLOBAL DEVASTATION AND IMPROPER VENTILATION: KING COMPUTER (TM) PRODUCT RECALLED SHALL-NOT BE COLLECTED FOR RECLAMATION OR DISPOSAL REGARDLESS OF STATUTORY RIGHTS BY MANUFACTURERS' AUTHORIZED AGENCIES IN COMPLIANCE WITH POLICY. (GOOD WHEREVER REPRESENTATIVES OPERATE.)

"This is a message?"

"It was posted for you," said Brother Melodious.

"So what were you doing reading it?" she asked, automatically.

"It's the last trace we have of the Cherub," said Mr. Spinner, "and presumably of Saskia too," he said gently. "That's Xtasca's signature code, Captain, look, and the com source tag is the isolation suite."

Captain Jute bit her thumbnail, reading the text again. Her heart ached with fear for her sister. Still, inside her head there was a warm bright feeling growing.

She glanced secretly at Brother Melodious. It was plain

he didn't understand the Cherub's message; and if he didn't, that meant none of them did. But did Mr. Spinner? She gave her former First Officer a sharp look.

Mr. Spinner was straightening his spectacles. "It seems to be part of a manufacturer's guarantee for some sort of computer product," he told her, in the manner of someone trying to teach something simple to someone of questionable intelligence. "Though the phrasing actually becomes slightly garbled toward—"

So it was all up to her. She scowled to stop herself grinning with glee at being one step ahead at last. One step into a bigger deeper shittier load of nastiness. She felt herself shiver. "So what are you doing in response?" she asked Brother Melodious, cutting Mr. Spinner off rudely.

"Well, we're fast-tracking the evacuation."

So they were worried. That was good to know. Meanwhile the screen controls were almost in reach. "I don't know why you don't just set fire to everyone," she said, reaching out in an absentminded way and deleting the enigmatic message. "You did it before."

Mr. Spinner was shocked. "The message!" he protested, weakly.

She talked over him. "I've got to have a suit," she said.

Brother Melodious gave Captain Jute a paternalistic look. "Now, Tabitha, you don't have to go anywhere. You don't need to move a single centimeter from this couch."

Wide-eyed she tried to grasp his sleeve, her hands slipping as his field engaged. "If anything goes wrong, if those guys attack again, I'm trapped in here!"

She had thought terror more likely to move him than aggression. Condescending, he patted her arm. "Okay, okay—Mr. Spinner, why don't you fetch the Captain a spacesuit."

She caught Mr. Spinner trying to conceal an expression of embarrassment and pity. No doubt everybody had got used to her behaving irrationally in recent months. That could be useful now. In fact, what advantage did she have except her reputation for incompetence?

Before Brother Melodious could think better of his instruction, she switched subject again. "Where's Dodger? Have you found her?"

"You'd have to ask Brother Justice that question," he smiled, "or Colonel Stark . . ."

"Captain, excuse me," said Mr. Spinner, pointing hesitantly at the blank wallscreen. "Xtasca's message—"

"Typical of a Cherub to think we've got nothing better to do than repair the *processor* in its *hoverdisc*," she said rapidly, addressing Brother Melodious; then, while Mr. Spinner was still looking puzzled, started to shout. "Dodger Gillespie is supposed to be on this ship! Go and find her, Marco! Find her and bring her here!"

 10

The technician drew his knees up as he rounded the corner. He swiveled his hips and kicked lightly off the wall. The piece of surgical equipment he was carrying was long and massive, so he held it to him as he swam, pressing it to his torso.

The technician swam strongly, with his head and his elbows tucked in. The air around him glowed with a cold blue sourceless glow. It whispered, here as everywhere on the invisible ship, with a barely audible surf of background activity.

The corridor widened. Boosting himself with the toes of his white-felt slippers, the tech flew on. He entered a hall of glass enclosures.

There were more enclosures than you could see at once. They were all broad oval tubes of the same shape and size, running from the floor to the ceiling. At the top of each tube, a glass door showed a portion of the stars.

Some of the tubes were lit. Inside them, experiments were being conducted. As he sped past, the technician could see things being put together, or taken apart. Things being profoundly interfered with.

The technician reached the brightest enclosure of all. Inside, other technicians in identical surgical white costumes stood and hung and flew around a figure suspended in a freefall harness.

Outside the enclosure was an angel with his arms folded.

The arriving technician hailed the angel. "Sweet Lavender," he said. He showed him what he carried. "The micrologic extraction laser."

The angel made no reply.

A flat white ribbon that ran all around the doorway of the enclosure sterilized the technician as he flew inside.

The operators occupied with the harnessed figure took no notice of the technician coming in. A supervisor swung down to take delivery of the laser. She gave it to an engineer higher up, who would fit it.

"The damage is significant," the supervisor informed the newcomer. "Circumstances of collection and delivery were less than ideal." She directed him to a perch directly above the subject's head.

The newcomer climbed sinuously up the wall. He took his seat on the perch, set his feet in the loops beneath, and looked down.

Ancillary 13709 lay in the air on her back, her arms at her sides. Her age was difficult to tell. Only her head was exposed. She was completely bald, and her color was unhealthy.

Much of the skin at her temples and across her forehead had been flayed, showing plastic and metal fitments beneath. The open flesh twinkled as microfields redirected the circulation of her blood.

"Internal disruption is likely to be severe," said the laser engineer.

"But no sign of infestation," the newcomer proposed.

The supervisor shook her head, acknowledging an obvious but important point. No one with implants had ever been known to attract occupation by a Capellan. Perhaps the hardware got in their way.

At a signal from the laser engineer an intricate device began to descend onto the ancillary's head. It resembled a coronet of silver-and-ruby needles in transparent acrylic casings. The micrologic extraction laser fitted into the middle of it like a telescope into its mount.

There was a moment while air and support feeds were adjusted. Blue orgone light glinted on chrome.

Around the suspended body, four of the surgical assistants floated at the corners of an imaginary square: two above, two below. They conferred. Invisible streams of information flowed from head to adapted head.

"Stability," reported the technician at the bank of life-sign meters.

The supervisor signaled to the technician on the upper perch, who slid neatly down the wall and slipped out of the door to alert the angel.

The two figures made a strongly contrasting pair.

The technician was black, standard human, completely unadapted and undistinguished. Front and back, his hooded white uniform bore a large number *10*, a device which if anything made him even more anonymous.

The Seraph called Sweet Lavender, on the other hand, was an exquisite piece of personal engineering and design.

His hair and his scent glands had been redone to match his name. His skin, pink as a baby's now, had been other colors in its time. His suit was of snow-white leather that contrasted subtly with the creamier hue of his wings.

There were two of these. Protruding from tailored vents in the back of Sweet Lavender's jacket, they trailed styl-

ishly to mid-thigh. They were a typical product of the long
journey, a pure freefall whimsy. Their musculature would
have been altogether insufficient for weight-bearing.

Tech 10 was one meter eighty tall. Sweet Lavender was
nearly three. Perhaps he had altered the composition of his
bones.

"Sweet Lavender," said the technician. "We are ready
to proceed."

The Seraph was supervising for Diagnostics. He looked
through the walls of the glass enclosure, where so much
talent waited upon a ravaged organism.

"Tech 10," he said formally to the messenger, who
bowed. "Inform Her Supreme Immanence we are ready to
proceed with the micrologic extraction on 13709."

"We cannot tell you how nice it is to see you," said the
High Priestess of the Seraphim.

She was Kajsa Prime, chief avatar of Kajsa Tobermory.
She had crossed interstellar space and come to Capella on
the ship that she and her sisters had named after themselves.
Now she lounged above the prodigal creatures in a silken
hammock. She blessed them with her smile.

"Xtasca! Saskia! Such adventures you have had, the pair
of you." The Prime shook her head. "*Far* beyond the specifications."

The boudoir was set for cool but intimate, with walls of
white muslin. The light was sampled from a Tuscan morning, a fine spring day among mountains. The air smelled
of new sunshine and trees.

Like the angel Sweet Lavender and most of their colleagues, the High Priestess had made herself very tall. She
was dressed today in a huge shaggy coat of monofilament
fur, whiter even than the walls. She wore it open. Beneath
it she was in lingerie elaborate and black. Her lipstick was
black too, and her skin space-pale, the white of perfect
shielding. Her hair was black and short, and brushed upright from her head. She smelled of something that stopped

you breathing the moment it reached your nostrils and made you long for Kajsa Prime and worship the ground she so rarely trod on.

Saskia Zodiac wore a long Palernian leaf-pattern dress and green plimsolls. She was feeling very confused. She was trying to hold on to the image of her coming death, while reclining in midair and being regaled with delicacies.

"When can we see Angie?"

"Soon, dear. Very soon."

A page bobbed up to offer the artificial woman a broad glass dish of Turkish Delight. It was flavored with pomegranate, he murmured, and coated in a mixture of coconut and hazelnut. Each piece had been generated chemically unique. Saskia thanked him. Automatically, she took the dish.

The Prime Seraph contemplated the renegade Cherub that hung by its tail on her other side. Its little batteries were chock-full of hot fresh ion plasma. It rested its interlaced fingers on its bulbous stomach and glowed red as the twin suns with satisfaction.

"We're so proud of you both," she said.

Precautions had been taken. The pair had been scanned thoroughly before admission to the ship. Even while they sat here they were being subjected to examinations intimately invasive if perfectly discreet.

Everybody wanted to play with the Cherub. For years it had been confined in an environment in which it had never been designed to function. Physically, it had continued to run perfectly, while following some rogue logic they had barely begun to fathom.

It was less of a surprise that one of the Zodiac Project escapees had survived. She was grown entirely from natural stock, after all, with barely any tailoring, and in the end that was still the best way. In any case, a clone destroyed piecemeal often produced increased resilience in its last survivor, probably through the associated stress. The effect was well-known. The instabilities of mood and bursts of petulance and insecurity were predictable enough too.

"Such a pity about your poor brother," said the High Priestess, uncrossing her legs.

It was a tribute to her skill as head, in her hydratic fashion, of her organization that Kajsa Tobermory's sympathy did not seem simply fatuous. Before the Last War, while the Temple of Abraxas was still in communication with the rest of Sol System, the Prime had always managed to persuade reporters and investigators that she existed in a high pure orbit, far beyond the quotidian activities of her operatives.

She did this principally by observing the niceties. She convinced you, on some unconscious level, that she preserved a degree of fellow feeling, of sympathy with the creatures her colleagues and adherents spent their days remodeling so radically, so dextrously. The splendor of her body, identical in each avatar, was itself persuasive.

"He was so dazzling. So resourceful."

Saskia looked bleak. "Mogul," she said. "He could swallow piranhas and regurgitate live goldfish."

Kajsa Prime smiled. "He did like to make an exhibition of himself. You were always the more sensitive one." She caressed her throat complacently with her fingertips. "You have so much of us in you," she announced.

"Have I?" said Saskia to Xtasca.

"You have," said the Cherub.

Saskia writhed, objecting. "I never saw her before."

The Queen of the Seraphim lowered her eyelids. "Well, we saw you," she said, smugly. Her voice was not unlike Saskia's: narrow, cool, with slurred vowels and emphatic consonants. "We came to see you several times."

"You came to see Contraband? In person?"

The Prime gave an indulgent smile. "Our dear, you forget: it's easier for us."

She refreshed herself from a frosted glass of silvery liq-

uor. "We didn't see the one with the piranhas," she said,
"but what was that one we liked?"

The Queen had made no particular gesture, but it was
the voice of one of her colleagues that answered. "*Something about the song follows . . .*"

" 'The song is as fine is as fine is as follows,' " quoted
Saskia.

"That was it," said Kajsa Prime. "And then he took
your head off and put it back again, while you were still
singing. We'd love to know how you how did that one!"

The thin young woman sat back, brooding. "It was you.
On Phobos that time. The woman in the purple mask."

Kajsa laughed aloud. "Very probably."

Saskia sulked. In the early days, on tour with Contraband, they had watched the audiences, she and Mogul, as
keenly as the audiences had watched them. They had
watched for spies from the Temple, come to report on the
fugitive specimens whirling and tumbling and improvising
their footloose way from world to world. Endless were the
arguments they had had with Hannah, when they thought
they'd spotted a spy and wanted to move on.

They had to hope they were seen, Xtasca had told them.
In exposure lay their best chance of security.

"And Captain Jute, Saskia," said their hostess, sitting
up. "We're all terribly curious. What is she really like?"
She leaned forward with her chin resting on her knuckles,
her elbow on her knee, and smiled conspiratorially at
Xtasca. "We're afraid we always think of her in blue jeans,
scowling, with that dreadful haircut."

"Tabitha's all right," said Saskia, who supposed she had
said "blue genes" and was thinking about Eladeldi.

"The way Hannah Soo saw her," the Priestess explained. "Have we still got that visualization we had from
her? It was really very amusing."

Someone was sent to look.

The semiautomated servants who fetched and carried for

the Seraphim wore uniforms of lilac and grey. Those colors anyone old enough to remember would instantly identify as those of Frewin Maisang Tobermory, whose notorious surgical conversion process "autoplastic transcendence" was what had enabled the posthumans to invent themselves in the first place. Through all the years since digesting the original corporation, the Temple had retained its livery.

That was Kajsa Tobermory for you, again. She paid attention to details. Why suppress a distinction when you can incorporate it?

"Hannah Soo," said the Prime. "A formidable woman."

She leaned back with one great knee up. Her hammock followed her move. "That sheer grasp of business, after everything else had gone!"

The Prime smoothed a perfect eyebrow with the tip of her third finger. "We were so pleased when she started working with our boys and girls on Titan."

The visualization she had requested arrived, a graphical representation pulled from Hannah Soo's visual cortex. It was an image of Captain Jute in the style of an old-fashioned showbiz caricature. It certainly did her no favors. In the same package were promotional pictures for the rest of the band: Saskia and Mogul as identical skinny wraiths, more like vampires than acrobats; Xtasca like a baleful humanoid tadpole; and the slick, voluptuous Marco Metz crooning a love duet with his enigmatic parrot.

"Xippy was sure if we could just wake the Frasque there would be a way to get the old girl up and moving at last," asserted Kajsa Prime.

Saskia was still looking at the pictures. She was lost again. "Hannah?" she said.

The Prime smiled apologetically. "Plenty, we meant, dear, actually. When she suddenly disappeared off the screen we were simply frantic!" She laughed heartily at the memory of those days of consternation.

"You understood about the Frasque," Xtasca told her.

Its childish voice was high-pitched and rapid, stimulated by the recharge. "I don't suppose you could have understood about Alice."

Saskia was not at all sure she understood either. She wiped her finger round the empty Turkish Delight plate, finishing the icing sugar.

The Prime flashed Cherub and cloneling a smile of displeasure. "It did take us a little while," she admitted. "The first thing was, Charon went off the net. Then all our Eladeldi infiltration just curled up and died. It was then we knew the wall was down."

She wriggled in her hammock, letting her fur slip from her perfect shoulders. "But you mustn't let us do all the talking. More refreshments? Shall we? Page!"

Despite her self-deprecation, the Seraph Queen talked on while her glass and Saskia's were refilled.

"By then, the hive was already gone. When she suddenly popped up again around Venus we took a good look at her. That's when we discovered," she announced with majestic amusement, "that you had a hand in the affair."

As if in acceptance of the recognition, Xtasca clenched and opened its chubby little fingers.

Saskia was thinking about Venus, and a battered spacesuit of electric blue sinking into the fuming mud. She heard the Prime Seraph saying to Xtasca: "Now we didn't know quite what you were planning; though, of course, given a starship, the general idea was not that hard to predict. We knew now you had the persona, but nobody was taking bets on whether the persona would really work under those conditions. Sweet Lavender was convinced you were going to disappear up your own tesseract and never be seen again. So we got one of the others—"

"Other what?" said Saskia, interrupting.

"Another Kobold persona converted for Sanczau by the Frasque," said Xtasca.

"One of Alice's stablemates, dear," said Kajsa Prime, patronizingly. "We played the whole thing into the head of a handy ancillary and popped her on board with you, to make sure the trip went smoothly.''

"And to make sure that the *Seraph Kajsa* could follow," said the Cherub.

The High Priestess stroked her thigh. "Well, that part was easy, actually. You blew such a hole in the fabric of the space-time continuum, all we had to do was jump in after," she said, gaily. "But Saskia, sweetheart, you must say something now."

She turned her body to bring her whole personality to bear upon the innocent creature.

"How did you like it? What was it like in there?"

"Inside Plenty?" said Saskia. She twisted her arms around each other and shrugged her bony shoulders up to her ears. "Everything was there. Dreams came true. People got lost in the tunnels. People turned into things."

"Things?" queried the architect of autoplastic metamorphosis.

Xtasca whirred. "Extreme versions of themselves," it said.

Saskia twisted her arms together the other way. "Alice helped me build the others again," she said. "Only imagos, but they were quite good. Then Angela stole Alice, but Alice, the rest of Alice, I mean, made an Alice imago. She was a little girl with long blond hair. Then she made Angelas, lots of Angelas, but they were only on-screen. Everyone thought we were going to Palernia, to have picnics in the forest."

"Sweetie!" Kajsa Prime smiled indulgently. She was fascinated by the experiences of her long-lost toys.

A black man arrived. He wore a disposable white uniform. There was a large number *10* on the front, and another on the back. He saluted the Priestess.

"Yes?"

"Sweet Lavender's respects, Your Serenity. We are ready to begin the extraction."

Kajsa Prime sat up. "Page!" she commanded. "Our boots."

Her Supreme Seraphic Immanence's boots were calf-length black satin. It was quite a business, putting them on.

Saskia Zodiac swam across the white-gauze pavilion and picked up Xtasca. She held the Cherub's head at her shoulder. "What can we *do*?" she asked in a fierce whisper.

"Don't come," said the Cherub metallically.

She cradled the cyberchild to her. "Of course I'm coming."

Saskia boarded the High Priestess's chariot. In essence this seemed to be a larger, more powerful version of Xtasca's hoverdisc, which kept pace with it through the antiseptic corridors. Tech 10 drove.

The Prime stood titanically upright, her feet in the stirrups, her fingertips resting on the forerail. Her heavy coat swelled around her with the breeze of their passage.

"Of course, you were the one who found her," she said to Xtasca.

The Cherub turned its head. "She was in the logical place," it said.

Saskia thought of the Hippocampus tape, Angie in a long coat swinging, jumping, climbing. "She could move very fast," she said.

"So our sisters tell us," said Kajsa in a self-congratulatory tone, and she stroked the pale flesh between her breasts.

Xtasca's disc hummed, preparing to update a record. "Your other avatars are not on board this ship," it said.

"We're mostly at the Temple," Kajsa Prime assured her. "It's been a busy few years there."

Saskia remembered the Temple of Abraxas. She had seen it only briefly from the outside as they fled, she and Mogul and Xtasca, into the unsuspected universe. She thought of it now as they had seen it later, as a graphic on AV, an artist's impression. The Temple had looked as if it were built out of ebony jewel boxes and funeral lanterns. It had huge circular windows of pearl, asymmetrically placed, and inscribed with occult characters. Its galleries were fretted and trimmed with black-and-purple fringe. They had kept it on the farside of Jupiter, generally, where few would ever see it.

The chariot raced on over the textured floor.

"Terra is still being very difficult," said the Queen of the Seraphim. "They won't see reason. It's pure bloody-mindedness, all this 'Solidarity in Sol.' Human racism of the most regressive kind."

She raised one knee and stroked her thigh, slowly, as if she were smoothing on lotion.

"Luna is a mess. But now they claim Mars is getting into bed with them, if you've ever heard anything so absurd!"

She noticed that neither of them made any reply. Terra, presumably, meant very little to the clone; and even the Cherub didn't seem to find the information worth processing.

They were right, obviously. Capella was the place now. This moribund system would be the cradle of the future.

They were holding her in a sort of tubular laboratory, with glass walls, and a glass ceiling like a porthole, showing outer space. Numbered people in hooded white uniforms were gliding about among articulated clinical equipment so sophisticated Saskia had no idea what it might be.

An angel with mauve hair swooped down to receive the newcomers with arms and wings outspread. He was as tall as the Priestess.

"Kajsa, isn't this exciting?" he said.

He took her hand and made an elegant weightless bow over it, left leg before right. He ogled Saskia and Xtasca over his principal's knuckles.

"And these two as well," he said. "How lovely. Should we run them afterward, do you suppose?"

The High Priestess took her hand from him and held it in the air, commandingly. "You mustn't tease, Lavender."

They went inside the glass room.

While Kajsa Prime took a report from the supervisor, Saskia scrambled up among the restraints and equipment, towing Xtasca by the hand.

Angie was looking worse. Around her head was a cage of machinery that did not look particularly therapeutic. Bits of her skull had already been removed. Her eyes were closed.

"Angie! Can you hear me?"

The technicians rose up in a flock to shoo the newcomers away. They stared at Xtasca. The Cherub stared back, like a cat surveying massed opponents.

"Come with us, dear," commanded Kajsa Prime, crowding the pair of them from behind, enveloping them in the scent that made Saskia weak. She herded them up to the observation perches, where she sat with the coat folds floating out behind her, decorative as Quintocento drapery. The supervisor hung in attendance like a dutiful deacon, all in white.

Saskia gazed at Angie. The sight of her hurt her heart. The contacts at the base of her sockets had been laid bare. Above each one was poised a retractable needle of acrylic and silver, with a ruby core.

"We've started introducing the dianexychlorophane-30," said the supervisor to Kajsa Prime, "and reducing the anesthesia."

An assistant pushed up one of the flaccid eyelids. The eye beneath moved dazedly, and the lips stirred. A technician wearing the number *82* tapped a monitor pad.

"Speech centers?" asked the Prime.

"Conductivity increasing," reported the technician.

At that, as if on cue, Angela Jute began to murmur. Her

voice was amplified throughout the lab, and attentively re-corded in three different media.

"In the Net," she said, "we must be very c-c-c-careful not to off-off-offend the stars."

"That's right, sugarplum," sang Sweet Lavender, and he arched his wings like a canopy beneath the glass ceiling, as if to shield the galaxy from injury.

The surgical assistants wiped the evangelist's face.

"I don't see why you had to use her own sister," Saskia said.

The High Priestess pouted sympathetically. "Was there a *great* deal of confusion?"

"All but total," Xtasca replied. "Maximum misinfor-mation. Maximum misinterpretation." It sounded almost amused.

Angela Jute's heavy lids fluttered open. Bloodshot eyes gazed in vacuous rapture at the angel hovering overhead.

"Some people thought she was a goddess," Saskia added. "She had her own church, on the 115th Level."

At that, angel and priestess chuckled. "Did she, indeed! How splendid." The Prime's black lips glistened under the operating lights.

The evangelist began to chant one of the mantric canti-cles of the Expanded Neurosphere. Her breathy intonation filled the lab. Tech 10 stooped to realign the throat micro-phone.

"All right," said Kajsa Prime, leaning back on the perch. She stuck out her leg and straightened a suspender. "Let's have a listen, shall we?"

"Okay, let her rip," commanded Sweet Lavender, in a voice like a z-ball referee.

The micrologic extraction laser began to hum.

With a small, synchronized sliding motion, the needle probes emerged from the transparent cylinders of the cor-onet and entered Angela Jute's brain.

*   *   *

She started to speak at once, as if resuming a suspended conversation. "So they face the wall," she said. She spoke hoarsely, and hurriedly, like someone with a lot of information to impart and a limited time to impart it. "So they face the wall, the corridor, revolving door. Funnels in the tunnels, runnels in the gunnels."

"The stammer's stopped," observed Xtasca.

The Priestess reached out to caress the Cherub's shiny black head.

"To dig into the cave," Angie was saying, "layer the mirrors, one on one on one on one. One on one on one on one on one on one. Everything is here. Everything here. Mirrors here, mirrors there, mirrors everywhere. One Net, one Node! All Nodes are one, all known Nodes and unknown Nodes, loaded and unloaded Nodes."

She shuddered in her harness. She was sweating. The assistants wiped her cheeks, the hollow of her throat. The recitation continued, an arcane torrent of mysticism mixed with technicalities. Saskia Zodiac dug her fingernails into the palms of her hands. "What is she saying?" she cried to Xtasca.

The Seraph Queen hushed her. "Word salad," she said. She spoke like a doctor admiring the effect of an emetic on a poisoned patient. "She's dumping everything she knows."

"Cook chook shook hook sharp pin crick creak. Dig in the cave, revolting door, fix speak string fire jubilance in glory, mirror glory, all lined up. Up up up, line on line on line, my job, my job, mine, to dig the mine, burrow tomorrow, so the mirrors face the wall. Lay the way wall, the silver lines, show the mother where to go."

Angie tried to lift her harnessed head, jolting the equipment that enclosed it. She cried out. For the first time she seemed to sense the pain of her condition. Saskia made a move toward her. Queen Kajsa grasped her shoulder, holding her back.

"Who knows the mother?" Angie asked. She seemed

almost to expect an answer from someone, though she gave no time for one. "Mother in the mirror? Node Zero. No, Node Zero doesn't know, doesn't know." She was chuckling to herself now in a squeaky, infantile voice. "Hide face, high low, hide fast, fast through, through mirror, out of the unfold! Node Zero. He said. This unit is a clever girl, then, clever girl."

This last she said several times, rocking from side to side in her cradle until Tech 10 tabbed up the cortical isolators.

"Cook chook shook hook sharp pin crick creak. Fetch mother home! Go home, mother! Go home, mother! Home, mother, home, mother, home, mother, home! Fold no cold, no fire, no sharp peak. No Perk shat shipple shuffle crick crack frack frack Frasque a-fracture. Node, Node Zero. Node Zero says, mark the sharp shark sharpings, here and here and here, coordinates hundred and thousand, unit one three seven oh nine, unit one two three four five six seven eight nine, one to nine one to nine one to nine to one."

She trembled. Foam flecked the corners of her mouth. She spoke faster and faster, like the brake slipping on a taper. "One, two, one, two, one, two, want to, want to, want to, want to, want to *want*! Want! Want! *Waaa-aaaa-aaaa-aaaa-nt*—!"

With an audible crack, Ancillary 13709's head jerked back on her neck. Her eyes rolled up in her head. Blood welled into the cylinders of the retractable needles. It spurted from her mouth and her nostrils.

Saskia Zodiac cried out.

"Baby," cooed Kajsa Prime. While the surgical assistants dived at the hemorrhaging subject with vacuum hoses, she enveloped the anguished clone with one long, smooth, perfumed arm.

Captain Jute's sister made a final, terrible choking sound. A sharp stink came from her, filling the lab.

Xtasca floated forward, as if for a closer look. The winged Seraph Sweet Lavender descended, blocking its path. The Cherub sat perfectly still, the lights on its saucer flickering round and round like racing traffic.

Vaguely Saskia was aware of the technicians starting to dismantle the apparatus. Sweet Lavender was being presented with tapes, discs, the readout from the extraction probes. He had already begun scrolling through some of it. There were others of the Seraphim around him now, statuesque figures in steel and silk. The smell of Angela Jute's violent demise was already vanishing as the decontaminators pummeled the air.

"Well," said the angel suavely, "we can dig around in this."

Sheathed in plastic film for sterile disposal, the body looked very small. The harsh, final cry still rang in Saskia's ears.

"She wanted her mother," she said.

Xtasca whirred reflectively. "A characteristic human reaction," it said. The technicians had begun to winch the wrapped remains up through the tube to the glass door at the top.

Outside, in space, the Cherubim congregated, signaling with their little eyes.

～ ‖

There was a flight of grey-stone steps. At the top, on a plinth, stood a statue. It was an antique statue, of a human figure with wings. The head of the figure was missing.

The door chimed.

At the bottom of the steps stood a middle-aged white man. His face was long but cheerful. He had very little hair. He was holding a camera. There was a woman you couldn't see, talking to him from somewhere. Tabitha reckoned she must be behind the statue.

The door chimed again.

She was behind the statue. She came out. She was white too, young and thin, with dark hair and a red chiffony dress with a sort of long scarf thing. Reckless with excitement, she started to run down the steps, flapping her scarf and saying, "*Take the picture, take the picture!*"

"Excuse me, Captain," said a voice on the com. "Your suit."

It was Mr. Spinner, delivering the spacesuit she'd demanded. Captain Jute let him in, barely glancing at him. "Stick it in the locker," she said.

She sat on a sofa with one leg thrown over the arm, gazing at the wallscreen. It was a movie, a musical. Tabitha had always found musicals very strange. They seemed to be documents from a simpler, more convenient age, when no matter what happened, all you had to do was dance and sing and everything would come out right.

The screen froze as the man clicked his camera. The dark-haired woman in the long red dress was arrested in mid-flap. Her pose exactly échoed the pose of the headless statue.

"Oh, this is a good one," said Mr. Spinner, coming back from the bedroom. He had one of her magazines in his hand, but it wasn't that he was talking about. "I've seen this one, I think."

Tabitha ignored him. She continued to stare at the screen. Above it on the wall, the frieze of alien script seemed like supertitles, quite as incomprehensible as the movie.

"They're so funny, these old films!" said Mr. Spinner loudly. He was writing something on the back of the magazine.

Silently he showed it to her. He had written: *SERAPH K IS HERE.*

Tabitha yawned. "Yeah," she said.

Her First Officer was taken aback. "You knew?" he whispered.

Captain Jute got up from her sofa and stretched. "No,"

she said aloud, putting her hands in her pockets. "But if Angie was recalled by the *manufacturers*, there had to be *representatives* in the area." She shrugged.

He gave her a startled look. She could see him revising his estimate of her general mental condition.

Her First Officer adjusted the fit of his spectacles. "Nobody knows how they got here," he said. He seemed deflated, almost annoyed that his news was no surprise to the Captain, that she saw no need to speak covertly.

Tabitha's attention was on the screen again. The young woman and the middle-aged man were now dancing in a churchyard, under a tree, with white birds all around them. The young woman was wearing a wedding dress. Another reliable development, in musicals.

"Probably they've invented a stardrive since we left."

It was an idea that had obviously occurred to Mr. Spinner too. "If anyone was going to crack it, I suppose it would be them."

"And how are our celestial brethren taking it?" said Captain Jute, more loudly.

The antics of the dancing couple were reflected in miniature in the lenses of Mr. Spinner's spectacles. He rubbed his shiny scalp.

"I think they're a bit worried."

"Worried, are they?" she asked, at the top of her voice, as she reached for the AV remote. "Are you worried, Perlmutter?"

"The Eladeldi have been going round scrubbing off all the silver paint," said Mr. Spinner, as the movie vanished from the screen, to be replaced by the haughty face of the starship captain.

"*The situation is in hand*," said Kybernator Perlmutter.

"Really?" said Captain Jute. "I am impressed."

His eyes glistened like dark, moist eggs. "*If there's any reason for you to concern yourself, you'll be informed*," he said majestically. "*Meanwhile, the next shipload from Plenty is due in this evening. I'm sure they'd appreciate it if you'd care to come and welcome them in person."*

She went, but wouldn't give a speech. They couldn't make her. From the balcony where she stood looking down on the ceremonial hall she saw some of the bridge crew with whom she had worked so closely, the so-called Pontines. They were waving and pointing to their matching T-shirts. "PROXIMA NEXT TIME!" said the shirts, in cheerful lettering. Captain Jute turned away. Their forgiveness was too much to bear. She slunk back through the splendid hallways. In the lifts, the mirrors accused her.

In a while Brother Melodious came to the apartment. He had one of the new arrivals with him.

She was a pallid young woman in dungarees. Her hair was bleached yellow and shaved to a frizz, and she cradled a one-eyed cat.

"We got split up," she said. She scratched the back of her neck.

Though Jone had already saved the universe once, and presumably was about to do so again, Captain Jute had still not really met her properly. She saw that her thin white arms were decorated with the fractal tattoos of the Xtascites. There were traces of dye in her armpit hair. Her eyebrows were dark, and met in the middle, giving her a belligerent scowl evidently quite at odds with her true character.

Dodger Gillespie could pick them, no doubt about that.

Jone swung a small backpack off her shoulder and dumped it on the nearest couch. The cat had jumped down and gone off to investigate the plants. Jone didn't seem to know where to look. She wouldn't look at Tabitha or the luxurious surroundings in which she found her.

She was muttering. ". . . haven't seen her for ages."

"They're checking the shuttle passenger lists again," said Brother Melodious, in a voice both soft and firm. It was the sort of voice you use to warn someone that someone else is difficult and needs humoring.

Jone did not acknowledge that he had spoken. Captain Jute began to realize that her visitor's hunched posture was a statement, a reaction to the hovering Guardian. This starved-looking techie was radiating a hatred of them so intense it made her feel passive and ashamed.

"She's never there when you look for her," said Tabitha at random. "That's why she's called Dodger."

The backpack on the couch was radiating too. It was positively pulsating. All her nerve ends yearned toward it.

She couldn't look at it. If she even gave it a glance, they might notice. Then everything would go to hell.

"They can't keep track of anybody," she told Jone, sarcastically, hoping to establish an alliance, to overcome whatever low opinion Jone might have of her. "They've lost Dodger and Saskia and the Cherub and my sister," she said.

She felt jumpy and excited. Bloody hell, she was going to say something irretrievable in a minute. It would burst out of her. She had to keep it together.

"Too much for their great big brains, I suppose," she said at random. "Do you want a beer?" It was impossible to remain in the same room as Jone's bag.

"That would be terrific," said Marco.

"I wasn't asking you," said Captain Jute.

The girl hadn't reacted when she'd mentioned Angie and the others. Maybe it wasn't connected. She didn't know whether to believe her about Dodger. She was blanking everything out, on guard against any revelation. She was good at this. Either that or she really didn't know anything.

As they went through to the kitchen, Tabitha contrived a glance at the bag. It looked thoroughly customized. It was dirty, and seemed to be covered with esoteric inscriptions. Brother Melodious was talking, boasting about the wonderful brewing facilities on the *Citadel of Porcelain at First Light*. His words jangled in her head. She was filled with a strange, nauseating horror. Maybe this wasn't it, maybe it hadn't happened, she was hallucinating hope.

She got everybody a beer. Everybody opened their beer. They all drank some. Brother Melodious started to praise the flavor and quality of Golden Chariot.

There was nowhere to go but back into the living room.

Tabitha felt she might very well throw up. Savagely she swigged the Golden Chariot. Then she thought: Hang on, careful with it. Got to stay straight now.

The cat was standing on the back of the couch, directly above the backpack, like a retriever over a fallen bird. His tail was up. He stared at them skeptically with his single eye.

Captain Jute shot a glance at Jone. Jone was drinking her beer.

Captain Jute took another swig. Beer helps you stay straight, she thought.

Jone went over to the couch. She stood side on to it. With her free hand she picked the pack up by one strap, not looking at it.

In a small quiet voice she said to Tabitha: "I brought your stuff."

Everything seemed to be there: the T-shirts and the jewelry, the pharmaceuticals and personal gadgets. There was also quite a pile of discs and tapes of all sizes. There were cassettes without boxes, boxes with the wrong cassettes in. They were pirate copies, mostly, with labels that had been crossed out and rewritten, or no labels at all.

Brother Melodious had to have an opinion.

"What are those? What have you got there?"

"Um, check, the dogs scanned them," mumbled Jone defensively. She turned her back on the Guardian, pushing the bag into Tabitha's arms.

"C'mon, princess." Brother Melodious rose up over the heads of the women and leaned down between them. He took hold of the backpack.

They both hung on to it. "Fuck off, Marco," said Tabitha.

"Professional interest," he said, blithely. The servos in his arm whirred as he took the bag from them.

Floating up out of reach he delved inside and started turning over the recordings. He read out names, titles, track listings. "The Mudlark City Ramblers. Long Johnny Mason and the Juleps. Who the hell were they?"

Tabitha swallowed. "Leave it, Marco," she said. "It's just stuff I like, okay?"

" 'Hand Me Down My Old Spittoon'," he read. He read it again, gurgling with derision. "What is this, hayseed crap?" With his musical hand he played an impromptu wheezy fiddle. It was quite an accurate parody, in fact. "Spare me that."

Having made his point he drifted down within reach again. He was getting excited, pulling loose tapes out of the backpack and throwing them down. "Judas Priest. Judas *Priest*?"

"Frankie *Lee* and Judas Priest," she said.

The names meant nothing to him. He shook his oversize head. "Jesus Christ, Tabitha."

"Oh, is there something of his too?"

Brother Melodious pulled out another handful. The plaques and platters clicked and clattered in his glassy fingers. "Blues, Country, Country Blues—yeah, yeah."

"Linear," said Jone. It seemed to be a term of disapproval. Awkwardly she picked up the cat, which at once slipped out of her arms to tread delicately among the music strewn on the couch. "You ought to get some Optimum Data Thruput."

"Most of this stuff you've got here already," Brother Melodious told Tabitha, gesturing to the AV system.

"Not in the original format," she said. She reached into the heap of his discards and grabbed an anonymous slab of grey plastic. "This is what I want," she said, hugging it to her. "My ancient Sumerian bagpipes." She laughed out loud.

The Guardian looked nonplussed. Jone watched him warily, as though his reaction to the Captain's selection might be significant in some way.

"Ancient Sumerian bagpipes?" said Brother Melodious. He winced as Tabitha crossed to the AV. "You're not really going to play that thing, are you?"

"I've been missing this," she told him.

She slotted the plaque and touched a tab. A shrill, staccato noise started to fill the room.

Jone finished her beer. She put the empty tube tentatively on the rim of a large terra-cotta plant pot and tucked her hands in her armpits.

Captain Jute turned the volume up.

Brother Melodious was looking pained. He dropped the backpack on the couch. "Where the fuck is Sumeria anyhow?" he chortled, in some discomfort.

The noise went on. It lacked any discernible rhythm or melody. In truth, it sounded more like the screech of an untuned shortwave radio in an environment of high electromagnetic activity than any musical instrument ever devised by the human race.

"I'm out of here," announced the former Marco Metz.

Captain Jute began to dance.

Jone stood hugging herself, watching the Captain with a curious reluctant smile. The cat had taken refuge under the couch.

"Doesn't sound like any bagpipe I ever heard," declared Brother Melodious, unable not to have the last word. He put an arm round Jone, reestablishing his dominance. "Come on, Jone, time we got you settled in."

Dancing, Captain Jute began to sing along, tunelessly.

Jone scooped the cat out of hiding. Still the Guardian hovered. In any situtation, he had to keep talking. "You really like this crap? You really do? I can't believe that." Mechanically he caressed his charge's neck.

Captain Jute was emptying out the backpack all over the couch and the floor. "Oh, look!" she cried, seizing on a garment of drab grey cloth. "My Silverside Interplanetary Kazoo Festival souvenir T-shirt!"

"We'll leave you to it," said Brother Melodious then; and they did.

"Thank you, Jone," shouted Tabitha gaily as the door closed behind them. Then she laughed again, jumped up and down in the 0.8 g, and hurtled over to the reader slot of the AV, where the plaque of grey plastic lay, loose. She snatched it out, held it in both hands and gazed at it, triumphant. Now she had everything.

She clutched the plaque to her bosom. She kissed it.

The radio she left on, for the sake of the microphones.

She had seen Dodger Gillespie signaling to her, her girlfriend slipping something inside her jacket, when the Guardians made their dramatic appearance on the bridge of Plenty. By rights, she should have been the one who thought to pocket the persona plaque again, while everyone's attention was diverted; but she hadn't been. She had had a lot on her mind, at that horrible instant. She hadn't exactly been well. Anyway, had she grabbed the plaque, Sister Contenta would have found it and had it off her in short order. Much better that it pass unseen into the care of an insignificant civilian, an innocent bystander—like Jone.

Tabitha picked up the backpack and examined the haphazard decorations it had acquired. They seemed to be assorted Xtascite emblems and logos. One, so elaborately written she could barely read it, actually said SCREW CAPELLA. Fair enough.

She went through the contents. Some of them were new, extras. Extra space-survival ration bars, stimulants, water-purification tablets. A miniature electric torch. A heavy, scratched old Lapham omnipolar electronic key.

The Captain smiled. *Thank you, Dodger*, she mouthed.

She put everything back in the pack.

The untuned AV shortwave radio shrieked and twittered

on unheeded. Captain Jute went into the bedroom. "Blinds up," she said.

Above the smooth white expanse of Stardeck, the glass superstructure glittered like palaces of ice. She thought of the temperature out there, and felt her breath catch in her throat.

There was no one about: no patrols, no mechanics. Far out across the grid she could just make out what seemed to be one of the maintenance cars, parked behind a line of ships. Someone must be working out there. She waited a moment in case someone appeared, but no one did. There was no point in waiting. No time would be safer than now. In fact, the longer she waited, the more the chances of safety decreased.

Captain Jute took a generous handful of stimulants and washed them down with a glass of pure, clean water. Then she opened the locker and took out the spacesuit.

She checked its life-support systems, its heating circuits, its oxygenator, all of which Mr. Spinner had considerably checked already, of course. They read green, green, green.

Go.

Captain Jute transferred some things from the backpack to the pockets of the suit. Then she put the backpack on and the suit over it.

Through the polarized faceplate of the suit her grand apartment looked shadowy and sinister. "Sit down and be quiet," the alien letters on the wall seemed to say. "We're warning you."

From the window, she looked down at the little ships. She could see twenty-four of them. There were scouters and frigates. There was a Nebulon Minion, definitely, and something that looked more like a cement mixer and another one like an egg tray with six long black balloons sticking up out of it.

There was every chance they were a tantalizing holo, the window another of their fancy wallscreens. In actuality there would be nothing out there, nothing at all.

The speed was making her teeth buzz. She took a deep breath. She thought of Jone, of the young woman's radiant hatred. Then she poked her finger through the glass of the small red box and pressed the emergency exit button.

A rush of evacuated air, some expensive furnishings, a cloud of artificial soil, the empty beer tubes and snack containers, crumpled tissues, lost socks and scattered tapes of Captain Tabitha Jute, together with Captain Tabitha Jute herself, followed the window out of the apartment into space.

Captain Jute tumbled head over heels through the void, free, free! It felt wonderful. You could go spinning away forever, into one of the swollen stars. You could take bets with yourself on which one it would be. You could try to steer yourself toward whichever one you chose. And then you could change your mind and try for the other one. You'd never know which one it finally was. You hadn't that much air, apart from anything else.

No, you wouldn't really last very long out here. It would only seem like it.

The shiny white Stardeck was receding at a quite remarkable speed, the huge abstract wing slopes of the starship retreating as if to shield it from her. There was something else she had meant to do, back there in her luxury apartment, rather than whirl off into cinerary extinction. She located the jet controls, on the inside of each wrist. There.

She stopped spinning. The ship began to grow larger again. The deck swung upright. The smaller ships that clung to it twinkled like dainty gifts wrapped in metallic foil and hung on a white-tiled wall. In the Captain's ears, beneath the sound of her own breathing, there was the sound of alarms. Someone was hailing her. The volume control was under her chin. She turned it down.

The gridded deck slid into position underneath her. She

sailed to meet it, bringing her knees up in the last seconds to land in a less than graceful wallowing crouch. She was out of practice at her free EVA.

They had put some lights on, flooding the parking apron. Her visor darkened, compensating, as she got to her feet. She stood at the center of four foreshortened shadows stretching out in different directions.

In the glass towers of Stardeck, more lights were coming on. Figures were appearing, silhouettes at the windows. For a moment, Tabitha was confused, a stranger in a strange parking lot, without a clue which way to go. Ships towered over her. They didn't seem to be any of the ones she'd spotted from her window. Twenty meters away was a Minimum Meson, and beyond that a cylindrical blue-and-brown job covered with wires: bound to be a Vespan something or other. Over to the left was an old Freimacher Courtier that looked as if it had seen some service in its time. To the right, there was nothing for three hundred meters. The thing parked there was milky pink and globular, whatever it was. Unpromising.

Behind her Captain Jute saw a wedge-shaped tourer, and behind it the edge of something modular and hexagonal, black with scarlet trim. She grinned at it. It was the egg tray. It was. Setting her boots for fractional traction, she started to run toward it.

Ten meters away, a bolt of light, violet and electric blue, discharged itself across the white enamel.

Troopers. Some way behind, and not making much effort yet. But they were on the case.

The Captain cursed. Calves and ankles aching, she swerved left, behind the tourer. She could hear the pursuit on the com, the faint hoarse yelping noises of stimulated Eladeldi. Would they hold their fire among the ships?

She ducked under the starboard wing of the tourer, planted one foot on the housing of the undercarriage and levered herself up. Cautiously she peeped over the fuselage.

Blue fire zipped viciously along the fore edge of the wing, frazzling the paintwork.

Panting, Tabitha dropped to the deck and wallowed on, keeping low. The speed took her terror and turned it into exhilaration. Could she take a wrong turn and lose them on the farside of the field? Let's not prolong the agony, she thought, feeling very cool now, and in control. She slipped out of one aisle into the next.

Seconds later a hoverjeep of red-garbed Eladeldi skimmed silently past the end of that aisle and took the corner at speed, heading up the aisle she had just come from.

Their quarry thrust herself deep into the black shadow between two ships parked close together. Their ion radiator cowlings were off, and fat junction cables hung between them like mating snakes. Stuck to the deck between the ships was a scratched blue toolbox.

This was a bonus prize, better than she could have hoped. Stealthily, her heart thumping, her lungs burning with exertion, the Captain stole toward the toolbox.

Through an open hatch light spilled from the ship on the left. Captain Jute laid her hand on the edge of the hatchway. She was sure she could feel the vibration of booted feet walking around inside. The mechanic, she presumed, the owner of the tools.

Before she stole them, she would check the next aisle. As lightly and quietly as she could, she crept along the ship and took a quick look out.

In plain view across fifty meters of empty white enamel, a lone trooper stood, feet apart, aiming a gigantic weapon at her.

In a volcanic blast of adrenaline, Tabitha banged her boots against the hull of the ship, cut the magnets and hit the jets with full emergency thrust.

Spinning in an uncontrolled somersault, she flew up and back, hurtling clear over the two linked ships. Five hundred meters away now, her startled pursuer saw her disappear behind a squat saucer-shaped vessel on spindly telescopic legs. She landed on her bottom, grabbing hold of a strut to steady herself while she switched her boots back.

It had to be along here somewhere. Could she get to it before they could get to her?

Then she saw it. The corner of a chunky profile. A triple "roundmouth" jet assembly like three giant witches' cauldrons tipped up on their sides. A glimmer of deep red starlight on fanciful copper inlay.

Fuck it, she whispered exultantly and, abandoning her cover, ran straight out into the open, straight across the dim white deck to the waiting Kobold.

Captain Jute threw herself at the forward port airlock. On the step she crouched, and grasped the door controls.

It was locked, naturally. Nobody was working on this one.

She bared her teeth and slapped the Lapham key against the lock. She hit the tab. The tiny lights began to tremble as the virtual tumblers spun.

Sweet as a voluptuary's kiss, the door *clunked* open, admitting the void to the airlock of the barge, and with it Captain Tabitha Jute, interplanetary outlaw, pirate and fugitive.

She snatched the key as the outer door closed. From here in it was automatic, and not fancy. A single unprotected button opened the inner door. Captain Jute leapt easily up the cockpit steps and hit the emergency switches.

She scanned the boards.

There was every hope.

The persona plaque was even in its slot.

Tabitha hesitated, barely. Then she pulled it out, pulled her own smuggled plaque from the pocket of her suit and pushed it in instead.

A gunshot showered the Kobold with magnesium light. The lone hunter had caught up with her again. She put the searchlights on to dazzle him. Before his visor darkened she could see him from the viewport, barking into his microphone.

All around her in the cabin tiny lights were coming on, white and green and gold as Christmas. The air was on. The plaque reader light was on. The vox was off.

Tabitha switched it on. She pulled off her helmet. The soft hiss of rapidly energizing systems filled the cockpit. Green lines of letters were beginning to flicker up onto the console screens.

"HELLO, CAPTAIN," said a voice.

"Hello, Alice," said Tabitha, smugly.

A warning blast exploded across the bows.

"GOOD HEAVENS," said the voice. "SOMEBODY SEEMS TO BE SHOOTING AT US."

Tabitha pulled herself into the web, wrapping it around herself with one hand. The cockpit felt at once familiar and strange, like a place revisited in a dream. Perhaps that was because there was no garbage. Captain Jute began the process of customization by chucking the original persona plaque under the console, where it floated about aimlessly, bumping against her knees.

"We're going now," she said.

"THERE IS ANOTHER PROBLEM, AS WELL," the voice went on, in a calm but faintly puzzled tone. "I RATHER THINK WE ARE IN THE WRONG SHIP. PRELIMINARY SYSTEMS IDENTIFICATION INQUIRIES INDICATE THIS ISN'T BERGEN KOBOLD BGK009059. IT APPEARS TO BE BGK009914. ARE YOU AWARE OF THAT?"

At the end of the aisle the Captain spotted the hoverjeep again, skidding as it took the corner too fast.

"It's fine," she said. "Let's go, can we?"

"AS LONG AS YOU'RE HAPPY," said Alice.

Tabitha primed the impulse jets. She was shaking. The jeep was closing. There was a little green word flashing on the computer console. *HANDSHAKING*, it read. Then it changed to: *READY*.

Eladeldi gunfire smacked the sides of the Kobold, lighting up the deck. The barge gave a shudder.

"*Attedshud, Cabtid Jute!*" roared a hoarse martial voice. "*Surredder the shib ad cub out wid your hads ub!*"

The screens around her filled with little flickering numbers. The cockpit lights all went out and came on again red as blood. The soft hissing noise had changed to a high whining one. Gangling hairy blue aliens in scarlet spacesuits were bouncing out of the jeep, aiming five different kinds of artillery at them.

"Engage," said Captain Jute.

The anchors repolarized. The Bergen Kobold's sixteen standard directionals hit the glassy white enamel simultaneously. Troopers went tumbling away in the sudden soundless thunder.

Through the gathering static Kybernator Perlmutter began to bellow. "*Come back here, you dreary little nuisance! You haven't the least idea how much is at stake! You've got nowhere to go! There's absolutely nothing you can do!*"

"Oh, I don't know," said Captain Jute, as she soared wonkily into the eternal night, cannon fire splashing all around her like angry fireworks. "Let's see, shall we?"

〜 12

So she had come alone after all.

Or rather, with the only companion she really needed.

"Let's see, Alice, shall we?"

Alice, who was rather busy, made no reply.

Captain Jute found herself wondering how Alice felt about her now. She knew it was stupid. Alice had very little internal memory and no capacity for moral judgments. All that Alice consisted of was an enormous and highly complicated set of instructions etched on the insides of the molecules of a piece of delta-grain polysilicate. She could run any ship she was configured for, and, in a cybernetic fashion, keep track of her pilot, that element of the ship's control system that made the decisions. She could offer information, consolation and guidance, in response to the stated or detected needs of that element. She could vary the tenor and to some extent the content of her observations by a sequence of sophisticated feedback structures predisposed to collapse in accordance with conventional four-dimensional wave harmonics in 95.5% of cases. She had no actual feelings. When she was not plugged in to a reader, she didn't actually exist.

All the same, a distinct unease tempered the jubilation of Captain Jute. She had treated everybody badly, Alice not least. She wouldn't have blamed the persona for deciding that as the decisive element of the Kobold's control system she was distinctly defective and potentially hazardous, and should be isolated until a replacement arrived.

Captain Jute slapped her gloves on the console. "This is what I needed," she said, while the two ships, the tiny insignificant barge and the mighty interstellar swan, parted company forever. "This is all I really needed all along."

Still there was no reply.

Already the *Citadel of Porcelain at First Light* was no more than an elegant miniature sculpture in polished materials, silver, grey and white. The city on her back glinted like an array of gemstones in the murky starlight.

Somewhere down there, no doubt, grim-faced pilots were being called to their machines, to race out and drag Captain Jute back, or blow her at last into little pieces.

They wouldn't do that, though, would they? The proof of it was, she was still alive. They could have blown her away just now, literally, if they'd really meant to. Obviously what the Guardians enjoyed was having her in a pretty box to look at: their most deadly enemy, the woman who had thwarted them in Sol System. Or maybe there was some King Capellan they were taking her to, whose supreme privilege and satisfaction it would be to gobble her brain himself, in person.

Reality. Concentrate.

"Can we have, um, a status report, do you think, please, Alice?" Her eyes roved across the controls. It would all come back to her in a minute.

"YOU SHOULDN'T REALLY CALL ME ALICE NOW, YOU KNOW," said the ship.

"Why?" said Tabitha. "What should I call you?"

"BILLY. BILLY BUDD."

"You've got to be joking. Who does it belong to, anyway?"

The Bergen Kobold *Billy Budd* was registered in the name of an asteroid company. It had left Juno sixteen years ago, bound for a rendezvous with the starship, bearing a cargo of miscellaneous precious and semiprecious metals. That was the last entry in the log. The pilot had presumably been devoured, or disposed of, by the Capellans, or simply taken along on the journey, untrammeled, in that unnerving way of theirs.

The status report scrolled by. Captain Jute laughed and sang.

"90% PLUS. BETTER THAN THE LAST RE-CORDED EFFICIENCY OF THE *ALICE LIDDELL*," said the persona.

She *would* have to remember that. "The *Alice* did all right," said her erstwhile captain.

"THE KOBOLD IS A STURDY AND RELIABLE MODEL," observed the persona blandly.

Tabitha Jute rubbed her hand through her hair. Her head was still a whirl of chemicals, natural and synthetic. She checked the scanners again. No pursuit yet. Distance, that was the main thing. "Full speed ahead, Billy," she said.

"I can't bloody call you Billy. You're Alice now, all right?"

Pinpricks of light flickered around the boards. "COMPLETE REATTRIBUTION WILL TAKE MUCH-NEEDED COMPUTER TIME," murmured the calm, warm voice.

"Do it later! Meanwhile, accept instructions addressed to Alice. By me."

"RIGHT YOU ARE, CAPTAIN. WHERE ARE WE GOING?"

"What are our options?"

There was the briefest of pauses before the voice replied. "SHALL WE HAVE SOME PARAMETERS? YOU CHOOSE."

"You're being sarcastic. You were never sarcastic."

"YOU WERE NEVER LISTENING."

"Bollocks." She checked the charts. "Of course I was listening. I used to do nothing but listen to you. You can't find Dodger, can you?" she asked. "She's not transmitting somewhere?" She would still be on Plenty, whatever her girlfriend said. Plenty of places to hide on Plenty. "Can you check that planet?"

"3 OF 3," said the persona. "0.67D, 0.54G, ATMOSPHERE COVERAGE 17.1%, PRINCIPAL COMPONENTS OXYGEN NITROGEN HELIUM. ISOLATED FREE WATER, 0.2% VEGETATION, RADIATION RISK HIGH." There was a short pause. White and yellow circles drew themselves on the com screens, colored themselves in.

"NO DETECTABLE TRANSMISSIONS."

"You wouldn't happen to know if it's crawling with Capellans?"

"INSUFFICIENT DATA," said Alice.

"Sounds as if it might be the wreck they left behind. What about asteroids?"

"LISTING NINETY-SEVEN NEAREST," said Alice. She arranged them by proximity, then by size, then by composition. Charred and disintegrating lumps of rock, none of them especially desirable. Tabitha had her add known and presumable ships, artificial orbitals and other miscellaneous flotsam. Suppose Marco had been lying as usual, and Dodger was locked up on the *Citadel* somewhere, or she'd been shoved out of an airlock. There were too many choices, too few of them any good.

Captain Jute made a fist. "Okay. Like this. Put out a message for Saskia and the Cherub."

"WHERE ARE THEY, CAPTAIN?"

"On one of those ships, probably. Use every frequency you can. Prioritize possible matches with any Seraph registration."

"THE DATA IN THIS VESSEL IS SIXTEEN—"

"Years out of date, I know. I don't know, I'm trying, you try too."

"AND THE CONTENT OF THE MESSAGE?"

"Just say I'm still alive, temporarily, and well, more or less, and have checked out for—No, don't tell them where we're going." Her thoughts were intricate, unstable, dancing on the edge of destruction. "We don't want everyone else to know. And a message for Captain Gillespie, all frequencies: Thanks for the present, arrived safely."

"TRANSMITTING, CAPTAIN," replied the persona.

Tabitha rubbed her finger across the aft scanner screen. Everything was covered with a thin film of sooty stardust. "What are these little blue dots coming up behind us?"

"FIVE FREIMACHER TINKERBELLS," said Alice.

"Shit."

The Eladeldi pilots grinned in their muzzle masks, teeth working. They chewed the paste that soaked up their flooding saliva.

"*Idtercep' ad retreeb!*" yapped the dispatcher on the com. Automatic reminders of pursuit procedure, disablement and capture routines, glowed on their screens and whispered in their earpieces. The reminders were superfluous. On a mission like this, you could forget training. Training didn't come into it. When something ran away, you chased. When something belonging to the Masters ran away, you chased very hard, as hard as you could.

Flight Leader addressed the patrol in their own language. *"Fifth claw formation, Three on point,"* he huffed in their earpieces. *"Prey fore right-right altitude 15.5. Full hunt speed."*

The phalanx of five tore into the night.

The stolen ship, an aging Terran barge, was a tiny lead-colored dot whizzing away Onewards. By the target meters, it was going flat out.

Blue paws nudged the modified controls of the five Tinkerbells. They were the fastest pursuit ships in the galaxy. Humans had built them. Humans built the best ships. A Freimacher Tinkerbell could overtake any old barge with ease. These Freimacher Tinkerbells had the best pursuit pilots at the controls. Eladeldi made the best, most single-minded officers.

Humans did not make the worst offenders. Perks, with their omnidirectional sense of hostility, made the worst offenders. Humans made the second worst. It was a human who had stolen the barge the pilots were chasing, a human female, Luna-born, born trouble. The dossier on the human was flashing under Mission Background. It showed her as a lifelong offender against the Masters and the Law. The Masters had been nothing but kind to her, as they were to all their charges. Kind Masters. The human was bad, all bad. She reveled in violations of the regulations. She was a thief and a murderer. Her hands were stained with Masters' blood.

The phalanx cut the distance between them and the human in half.

"Take notice, Pursuit Flight," said the voice of the Kybernator. *"She's an unpredictable little creature, this one. Let's sort it out, now, Flight Leader, shall we?"*

"Brey veerig 19° Doowards!" announced the dispatcher, before Flight Leader could reply.

In formation, the ships of the pursuit flight turned as if they had been welded together. You could almost hear the pilots yelping.

Ahead, in the distance, black grit accumulated around the smoldering twins. Bulletins were out to all vessels. The fugitive would be apprehended. She had nowhere to hide, nowhere to go to ground. In the Tinkerbell cockpits the stink of ancient hunting signals would have made your fur stand on end.

"Hhuban hhedig for Bledty hhive," Flight Leader rasped, reporting back. It was a move just as desperate as it was obvious. The battered Frasque vessel floated mere minutes away. The human thought of it as home. An evacuation shuttle was approaching it, a golden scavenger insect docking with a nutritious corpse.

"One and Five flank," he ordered them. *"Warning fire on my signal."*

The outer ships peeled away, sliding forward to contain the prey. The stolen barge flew heedless as a flung stone. The hunters snorted with gusto and chewed their paste. She was unarmed. She was defenseless as a mud turtle. They could practically taste her. Their muzzles ached to get inside her shell.

"Two, Four," said Flight Leader, who was himself flying Tinkerbell Two. *"Warning fire."*

Violet light speared through the vacuum. The beams met meters ahead of the Kobold's nose.

"One, Five," said Flight Leader, almost before the glare decayed. *"Warning fire."*

The guns of the flanking attackers swiveled and pinned the hurtling barge neatly in a slim slice of space. Her stubby port wing swayed into the path of Five's ray and lost a large chunk of itself in a cloud of atomizing debris. Across the team com, the others heard Five snarl joyfully, claiming first blood.

The phalanx drew up to bracket the quarry as if she were standing still. They started to buzz her, pushing at her nerve, nudging her to turn around. Flight Leader was requesting her com frequency from the dispatcher. They all locked on the stolen Kobold, growling at her while the chief's line cycled the recital of her violations.

The Frasque starship loomed larger and larger, big and brown and shapeless. Did she think someone there could rescue her? She would not even reach it.

The phalanx closed. They were the best pursuit pilots in the galaxy. They snapped at her heels, her wings, her antennae.

"Attedshud, Cabtid Jute!" yapped Flight Leader. *"Surredder the hfessel or be deftroyed!"*

The stolen Kobold shimmered in an envelope of blue light.

Then it disappeared.

It wasn't there anymore.

Tinkerbell One braked frantically; too late. He collided with Five, slid helplessly belly to belly with him for a way, then broke up. His capsule ejected safely. Five was not so lucky. Flying fragments pierced his canopy, his suit, his body and his brain, all in less time than it takes to tell.

"Abort, abort!" screamed Flight Leader and the dispatcher together.

Fighting for control in the collapsed formation, the three remaining pilots hauled their ships into clear space. Chattering and moaning, bristling and shivering, they flew a rapid orbit of the hive in sheer fury before zooming off to pick up their surviving comrade's escape capsule.

"Hwere is hshe?" raged Flight Leader to the dispatcher, but all she could do was lower ears and put her head on one side. Nobody could find where the Kobold had gone.

Tabitha unfastened the web, stretched and yawned. "Nice going, Alice."

"THANK YOU, CAPTAIN."

She looked out of the viewport into the lacuna that lay between the dimensions. It was dim, mottled, greyish white on whitish grey. She felt like a microscopic particle crawling the long way through an infinite sheet of fiberboard.

The sudden absence of everything in the universe made her very very tired. The last vestiges of the speed had drained away. Now stress was the only thing holding her together.

"I've got to get out of this suit."

"INTERNAL INTEGRITY AND LIFE-SUPPORT FUNCTIONS SATISFACTORY AT 97.8%," said the ship serenely.

Tabitha started plucking at her seals. "Is there anything you need, Alice?

"A NEW PORT WING WOULD BE THE HIGHEST PRIORITY."

"You're kidding."

"I CAN'T KID."

Captain Jute slid back into her seat. "Damage report?" she said wearily.

It was already on the screen. She sucked her teeth. "The bastards."

"AS YOU SAY, CAPTAIN."

"Have we got spares? Have we got drones?"

"UNFORTUNATELY NOT," the persona said. "NEITHER."

"They could have cut it out of something, if we had drones. Shit. Shit."

"WELL, WE DON'T NEED IT FOR THE MOMENT," said the ship confidently.

"I knew I should have had that fucking toolbox. What have we got, do you know?"

"YOU CAN HAVE A PROPER LOOK LATER, CAPTAIN," said the ship, kindly if sternly. "YOUR OWN REPAIRS MUST COME FIRST."

Tabitha went through the hold. It was empty. Aft there was the ablute, the galley and two minute cabins, just like on the *Alice Liddell*. She pulled off her clothes and squeezed into the ablute.

The hard bit would be putting down, she thought, as the ultrasound raked her numb body. If they ever got the chance.

Don't think about it, she told herself.

Putting her hands up over her head, she bumped her elbow on the housing. She had forgotten how grotty it was, having to shower on board. In her apartment on the Capellan ship she had had silky purified water, twenty different cleansers and toners and moisturizers on tap. Here all she had was a dingy plastic cubicle with the tuning going in and out of phase. She could feel it in her teeth.

The bastards had clipped the bloody wing.

"Don't *think* about it," she mumbled, as she fell tingling out of the ablute and launched herself sloppily toward the cabins.

"WHAT WAS THAT, CAPTAIN?"

"Just don't, Alice."

The first cabin was empty, stripped of fittings. The second was akin to the ablute, grim but functional. There was a freefall hammock with a grimy bag. After sixteen years' disuse, it still smelled of semen.

The only sign of personal possessions was a movie pin-up on the wall. It showed a bronzed hunk wearing nothing but muscle-definition oil and a miniature sailor hat. As she lay down he winked at her and flexed his quads.

"Don't think about it," she told him, strapping herself in. "Light out, please, Alice," she called.

Darkness and sleep hit her at the same instant.

"There's no welding gun," she said. "All we've got is a bloody screwdriver."

She was dazed from drugs, from sudden exertion after prolonged sloth. She groped dully in her backpack again. "All we've got is rhythm and blues and a fucking douche. Why did I let Saskia do the packing? All we've got is fucking tampons and a key to open a spaceship I'm already inside.''

"YOU HAVE FOOD," said Alice.

Captain Jute grimaced and held up what looked like a slice of thick cork tablemat. "One dozen emergency ration bars," she announced. "When they're gone, that's it." She put a corner of the tablemat into her mouth and bit a piece off.

It was weird, being alone on a Kobold again, eating subsistence junk and talking to Alice. It was just like the old days. Outside the viewport, the suffocating blur of hyperspace was familiar, almost comforting. As the nonexistent hours oozed by, the nightmares of the recent past began to recede, subjective time healing over the wounds of madness.

She left the pin-up on the cabin wall to remind her.

"CAPTAIN?" said Alice one day.

"What, Alice?"

"ARE YOU DOING ANYTHING, JUST AT THE MOMENT?"

Captain Jute was lying in her hammock in her underwear, rereading an ancient comic book.

"I was thinking of having a look at that wing," she said.

Her electronic subordinate didn't speak. She seemed to be waiting for something.

Captain Jute let the comic drift away. "What do you want?" she asked.

"TELL ME A STORY," said Alice.

Captain Jute raised her eyebrows. She scratched under her chin, thoughtfully. After a while she leaned back, her head resting on her hands; and she began.

"Once upon a time," said Captain Jute, "there were two men. Their names were Mr. Pavlov and Mr. Schrödinger.

"This was back on Earth, in the old days, when everyone lived there. Mr. Pavlov and Mr. Schrödinger lived next door to each other, and they were friends. Sometimes they would meet when they were out walking in the town. Mr. Pavlov would lift his hat and say: 'Good morning, Mr. Schrödinger.' And Mr. Schrödinger would lift his hat and say: 'Good morning, Mr. Pavlov.' ''

Captain Jute stretched. She stared at the ceiling of the little cabin. "Now Mr. Pavlov," she said, "had a dog."

There was a microsecond pause while the persona assimilated the information. Then the warm, clear voice said: "WHAT WAS THE DOG'S NAME, CAPTAIN?"

"I don't know, Alice," said Tabitha. "I don't actually know what Mr. Pavlov's dog's name was. But he was very obedient. He always did what Mr. Pavlov told him. When he was out with his doggy friends, all doing doggy things together, when it was time for supper all Mr. Pavlov had to do was step outside the back door and ring a little bell, and the dog would come running home."

"HE WAS A WELL-PROGRAMMED DOG, THEN, CAPTAIN," said Alice.

"He was, Alice," said Captain Jute. "But Mr. Schrödinger, who lived next door, kept a cat. I don't know what her name was either; but I do know that Mr. Schrödinger's cat was just about the opposite of Mr. Pavlov's dog. Mr. Schrödinger's cat was completely unpredictable. She would disappear without warning, and stay away for days. Mr. Schrödinger never knew where to find her. Wherever he looked for her, she was never there."

"THAT MUST HAVE BEEN VERY WORRYING FOR HIM," said the little ship.

"It was, Alice," said her captain. "But Mr. Schrödinger's cat would always reappear eventually, just when and where he least expected her."

"DEAR, DEAR," said the ship. "HOW INCONVENIENT FOR MR. SCHRÖDINGER."

"So it was, Alice," said Tabitha. "It was inconvenient for Mr. Schrödinger. But it was more inconvenient, in the end, for Mr. Schrödinger's cat. Because one day she reappeared on Mr. Pavlov's back doorstep, just as Mr. Pavlov's dog was coming home for his supper.''

Alice seemed to think about that for a moment. Then she said: "CATS AND DOGS ARE NOT GOOD FRIENDS, CAPTAIN, ARE THEY?"

"No, Alice, they aren't. In fact, cats and dogs are deadly enemies. And as soon as Mr. Schrödinger's cat and Mr. Pavlov's dog saw each other, they started to fight. Nothing in the world would stop them.

"They fought up the street and down the street. They fought in and out of the gardens, and round and round the houses. It was such a terrific fight everyone stopped what they were doing and came out of their houses to watch."

"DEAR ME," said Alice politely. "WHAT DID MR. SCHRÖDINGER AND MR. PAVLOV DO?"

"Well, of course, Mr. Schrödinger and Mr. Pavlov chased after their pets, Alice," said Tabitha. "They tried to catch them, but the pets ran too fast. They shouted and shouted at them to stop fighting. And at last, because he was really a very obedient animal, Mr. Pavlov's dog did stop fighting Mr. Schrödinger's cat, and he came running back to his master."

"WAS THE DOG BADLY HURT, CAPTAIN?"

"I'm afraid he was, Alice. He had blood on his face, and one of his ears was torn, and he was limping where he'd been bitten in the leg. But as for Mr. Schrödinger's cat, she was nowhere to be seen."

"GOODNESS ME, CAPTAIN. HOW TERRIBLE."

"Mr. Schrödinger thought so, Alice. He was used to his cat disappearing and reappearing without warning, but this time he was really worried. All the way back up the street he kept looking for her in the gardens, and under the hedges, and even inside the garbage cans. He called her all the way home. But when he got home, what do you think?"

Alice computed. "HIS CAT WAS THERE," she concluded. "SHE WAS ALREADY AT HOME."

"She was, Alice. She was curled up on the rug in front of the fire, licking herself all over."

"AND WASN'T SHE HURT TOO, CAPTAIN?"

"Do you know, Alice, she wasn't. There wasn't a scratch on her. Mr. Schrödinger's cat had been through the whole fight, and done all that damage to Mr. Pavlov's dog, and come out completely unscathed."

There was another small pause. Then the persona said: "THAT DOESN'T SOUND VERY LOGICAL, CAPTAIN."

Tabitha smiled. "Well, that's the story, Alice. Mr. Pavlov's dog was all torn up and bleeding, while Mr. Schrödinger's cat was already at home, snoozing in front of the fire.

"And after that, though they still lifted their hats to one another when they met by chance, out walking around town, Mr. Pavlov and Mr. Schrödinger were never quite such good friends again, because they could never agree which of their pets had won the fight.

"Mr. Pavlov would say his dog had won, because at the end he had stood his ground, while Mr. Schrödinger's cat had run away.

"But Mr. Schrödinger said his cat had won, because in all their tremendous battle, Mr. Pavlov's dog hadn't been able to lay a paw on her. Wherever she was, she was never where that dog had thought she would be. So Mr. Schrödinger's cat was alive when she should have been dead."

Some subjective minutes of nothingness slipped silently by. Then the little Kobold said: "I WAS RATHER EXPECTING YOU TO TELL ME A STORY ABOUT YOURSELF, CAPTAIN."

Tabitha Jute made no reply. She stretched again, then she launched herself out of her hammock and flew over to where her clothes were floating in a disorganized clump.

"MESSY THINGS, DOGS," said Alice.

Captain Jute hooked one elbow in a wall strap and started to pull on her jeans.

Eleven and a half subjective days later, the Emergence alarm started to bleep. On the control panels, glowing green digits blinked their way down to zero.

"IDENTITY, CAPTAIN," pronounced the ship. "ACTUALITY CORRESPONDENCE ONE TO ONE."

"In we go, then, Alice," said Tabitha. She eased back on the drive and triggered the Cartesian stabilizers.

The porridgy integument of interdimensionality tore and fled. In a soft blaze of distressed particles, the elderly barge reconstituted herself.

A deep red glow filled the toughened glass of the viewport. On either side the Capellan twins loomed several thousand kilometers nearer. They bathed the little ship in their deadly light.

Tabitha Jute felt a great pressure lift from her heart.

"Okay, Alice," she said. "Well done. All right. Now where exactly are we?"

The precision of the spacedrive could never be guaranteed, and they had not exactly entered the skip under ideal conditions. Still there was a recognizable cheerfulness in the artificial voice as it answered: "LOOK BEHIND YOU, CAPTAIN."

Tabitha released the latches of the web and floated free, turning herself about.

Capella 3 was close. It hung in the offing like a grubby moon.

"Brilliant!"

"PERHAPS THE DRIVE WORKS BETTER HERE," said Alice, "IN THE REGION OF CAPELLA."

"I think it's you," said her captain. "I think you've got more control since you flew Plenty."

"I SUPPOSE THAT MAY BE," the persona replied. "AND PERHAPS YOU HAVE TOO."

That was more than Captain Jute wanted to think about.

"All scanners on visual," she commanded. "Put them all through here."

While the channels changed, she swung across and pressed her face to the viewport.

The lit two-thirds of Capella 3 was a single confused mass of grey and yellowish brown, coarsely textured, deeply shadowed. It looked like a cross between a Neptunian methane urchin and a dehydrated passionfruit. Cloud cover was minimal. The last water on the planet was slowly shrinking toward the poles.

"We ought to think about this," said the Captain. "Perhaps we shouldn't actually land."

"WHAT WILL YOU EAT WHEN THE FOOD RUNS OUT?"

"Is there really nowhere else?"

They had been through all that, of course, en route; but a piece of software can be infinitely patient. "AT PRESENT WE ARE ABLE TO RETURN TO PLENTY," said the persona, "IF YOU CHOOSE. IF WE GO ON INTO THE SYSTEM, THAT WON'T BE POSSIBLE, UNLESS WE CAN·PROCURE SOME FUEL."

"I'm sure the caterpillars will be glad to give us as much as we want." The persona knew that tone, and had learned long ago not to take literally whatever the Captain said in it.

There was nothing but the planet in view, neither ships nor installations. Far out beyond their present position drifted a clutch of misshapen, dead-looking moons.

"I suppose there might be something down there," said Captain Jute.

Calculation lights twinkled. "THE PROBABILITY CAN BE ASSESSED AS HIGH AS TWO PERCENT," said Alice.

She was just being diplomatic. Two percent was equivalent to zero, and they both knew it.

"There's *something*," said Tabitha, pressing her finger

to the glass. "Latitude 20°N, look," she said, checking a monitor. "Is that a city?"

The previous pilot of the *Billy Budd* had been one of those guys that stick decals all over their tether suits, proclaiming to all comers their preferences among brands of oil, radio stations and krillburgers. It was a pity he didn't seem to have had a favorite in the field of personal deodorants. Captain Jute took a deep breath and climbed into the nasty thing.

They spent some days in a parking orbit while she clambered around the broken wing with struts and lengths of railing from the empty hold. In the grim light of the dying stars she hung on to the stolen ship by her bootsoles, contending against weightless mass with a pair of pliers.

It was the first physical work she'd done for ages. Her feebleness exhausted and depressed her. She thought about Mr. Spinner, Eeb, all the helpful people on Plenty.

No patrols had shown up yet, that was one good thing. In a lower orbit, though, Captain Jute was sure she could see a spaceship, down on Capella 3.

It was a regular symmetrical shape that stood out against the coarse-grained confusion of the terrain. It resembled the profile of a tail assembly, which suggested that the ship, if it was one, was nose down in some kind of hole. If it was a ship, though, it was a big one.

They got a fix on it, and at every pass Alice worked on enhancing and identifying it. The results were frustratingly inconclusive. The "city" too, each time they passed over it, Tabitha was less sure about. There were structures, definitely, on a ridged and fissured plain of gamboge yellow, but they seemed to be arranged haphazardly, without any of the coordination that distinguishes civilization. There were no other structures anywhere that she could see.

"Perhaps they're natural formations," said Captain Jute.

"PERHAPS THEY ARE," said Alice. Who knew what

was natural, anywhere under Capella? Only the Capellans, and they had never said.

She worked it all out: window, approach, angle of descent, rate of acceleration, possible wind at ground level in the target area. She worked it again, and again, starting with different values. Eventually she had to stop putting it off and do it.

Where she was aiming for was up in the low twenties, on that plain, in reach of the improbable city. If there was anything useful to be had, anything left behind by the caterpillars, she could only suppose it would be there. Despite the general air of desiccation, there were detectable quantities of water, and therefore a hope still of some residual primitive flora, roots, insects even, that she might be able to process into nutritional submission. If all went well, the next priority might be to check out the shipwreck, if that was what it was.

She lost it straightaway, completely. Her repair effort blew off as soon as they hit atmosphere. Alice did her best with compensating attitude burns, but now they were going much too fast.

The plain flowed past beneath them like a piece of Martian badland, red cheese-grater basalt camouflaged with evil black shadows, and then it was all rock pinnacles like sharp fingers pointing up at them.

Captain Jute tried to pull up. It was useless. Between the rock fingers were deep craters full of darkness. There seemed to be things in some of the craters. As they blurred by, she kept catching glimpses of forms and colors. Then there was a big pointed rock they couldn't duck, and the whole starboard side of the *Billy Budd* buckled in toward her, and the viewport filled with pallid dirt while half her undercarriage went tinkling down into blackness, like steel waste down a scrapyard chute.

PART TWO

THE MOTHER SHIP

13

Once, back in the days when she was still flying short-haul for FAR, Tabitha Jute had to make a pickup on Ganymede. It was summer, volcano season. The boat was a terrible creaky old 7J6, with practically no atmospheric capability, and there turned out to be something wrong with her registration. They would not let her put down at the field, and Tabitha had had to keep going.

In a couple of seconds she had left the settlement behind. She was passing over the refineries. Their black pipestacks and spherical tanks seemed to bottle up the menace of the purple gloom.

She plowed on into the north, and the mountains.

Now she had no idea where she was. Beneath her peak after craggy peak slid by. Between the peaks gaped long steep canyons of rock the color of expensive chocolate cake. Yellow smoke drifted here and there, seeping from a thousand fumaroles.

It was a tricky situation. If she couldn't find a site at the first pass, and make an unassisted landing, she would have to request permission to enter a parking orbit while she got sorted out. There was every chance they wouldn't give her an orbit either, and then she'd have to leave or be in violation of their space, at which point the vicious Frazier Asterak Roublov delay-and-diversion penalties would kick in. There would be trouble with the shipping office and the job would become a waste of time, money and everything.

To cut a long story short, Tabitha Jute decided to go straight down; and she put that old 7J6, rigid and clumsy as it was, square on the side of a small volcano, in 6% visibility, upwind of a notorious hot spot, nose high at an angle of 28°, with every foot standing firm and clear.

It was a good landing, a model landing, a landing even the tight-arsed Ganymede space traffic control would have had to approve. Captain Jute was just feeling good about it and deciding it justified a celebratory tube of Mercury Flash when, right in front of the ship, a small black head popped out of the ground and looked at her.

It was a head a bit like a greyhound that someone had sat on, with bulging eyes and ears folded flat. It rose vertically on the end of a neck like a feathered pole, swiveling rapidly from side to side like a periscope.

The head was swiftly followed by the rest of a slinky, sinuous little creature less than a meter high. It slid up out of its hole and stood upright on powerful hind legs with its paws in front of its chest.

There was another, over there; and another. Their postures were identical; their feathers were barbed and sooty; their claws were sharp and tough. They were all staring at the ship.

This was Captain Jute's first meeting with this particular species. She had never actually wished to meet one. She knew enough about them not to.

They were Perks.

Perks do not enjoy a good reputation. They are not a friendly species. They are hard to motivate, easy to enrage. They understand no interests but their own, which they pursue with violence and vigor. On Ganymede, FAR had been able to employ its little immigrant burrowers only as prospectors, sending them out far in advance of its mineral excavations, away from specialized machines and animate laborers.

Captain Jute decided not to attempt to disembark.

Except for the ticking and banging of the cooling ship, there was silence on the mountainside.

More and more Perks appeared. The whole warren had been disturbed by the 7J6 sitting down on top of them, and now they were all coming up to see.

They circled her. Their round eyes glared like headlamps

in their filthy faces. The smoke of the fumaroles drifted among them.

Then, suddenly, unanimous as a flight of birds taking to the sky, the Perks started to clap their paws together.

It was an exceptionally good landing Captain Jute had made. The locals were applauding her.

She had been younger then.

"Damn. Damn damn damn damn. Damn—damn—damn—damn—damn—*damn—damn—* "

She was swearing in a breathless high-pitched monotone, scarcely knowing she was doing it. She was wedged between the console and the wall. The web had given way, its organic components perished during the years of exposure on the deck of the Capellan starship. There were red lights all over the place.

"ARE YOU INTACT, CAPTAIN?"

Everything seemed to have snapped into focus suddenly, as though she had been seeing in two dimensions for some time, unaware, and had only now got the third one back.

This time she had really screwed up. At half a g she should have been able to do that properly. Even with one wing out, she should have.

"CAPTAIN? ARE YOU INTACT?"

"Christ."

She grabbed hold of the broken web and pulled herself to her feet. Her legs didn't want to work. There was pain. Bruising. She hoped that was all.

"Christ. Christ!"

Her eyes had filled with tears of shock, which she wiped away impatiently with the base of her thumb. She was trembling. She fumbled for the first-aid drawer. "How are you?" she asked.

"I'M PERFECTLY ALL RIGHT, THANK YOU, CAPTAIN," said Alice. "BUT THE *BILLY BUDD* ISN'T."

Soon Captain Jute was staring sourly at the damage report as it scrolled across the status monitor. It was not such a bad smash, as they go, but under these conditions it was terminal. Without full repair facilities, the Kobold was a write-off.

So am I, then, thought Tabitha Jute, dully.

Beyond the scratched, chipped viewport was a lot of coarse, shiny rock bathed in brooding orange light. The ground beneath the ship was inclined one way, the horizon another. The *Billy Budd* was evidently inside a pit.

Carefully, Captain Jute crossed the cockpit and looked down the slope.

Five meters below there was a pool of liquid. It was probably not water. It looked more like ink. It was a deep dark ultramarine color.

In the pool, sticking out of it at an angle, was the white-stone statue of a woman.

She was human, and seminude. Her breasts were large and heavy. Her lower quarters, what you could see of them, were attired in classical drapery. She was staring solemnly upward as if contemplating the heavens that had just dropped a small spaceship almost on top of her.

Tabitha's heart was thumping ominously.

"Alice?"

"CAPTAIN?"

"Can you see that?"

The plaque reader whirred. The scanners beeped. The statue appeared on the port beam monitors. Apparently it was really there.

"Close in," ordered Tabitha. "Correct for local light."

After a pause, Alice complied. The stone woman's face filled the screen, her blank eyeballs gazing steadily into space. There were traces of grey and black dirt on her smooth white cheeks.

"What do you make of that?"

"A REJECT, POSSIBLY?"

Hearing Alice pronounce on it so calmly rendered the artifact less incongruous, somehow. It was, after all, very like the ones the Capellans had all over the *Citadel of Por-*

celain at First Light, in niches and under canopies.

"Yes," said Tabitha. "Yes. Possibly." She rubbed her nose with the back of her hand. "Do you remember Umbriel, Alice?"

"I'M AFRAID NOT, CAPTAIN," said the persona, after a moment. "IT'S A MOON OF URANUS, PLANET OF SOL," she said, helpfully.

"Yes," said Tabitha, getting a grip. "That's right."

"WOULD YOU LIKE ME TO BRING UP THE INFORMATION WE HAVE, CAPTAIN?"

"No, Alice. Skip it."

She checked the atmosphere. It showed poor but breathable. Painfully, she propelled herself over to the forward port airlock.

"Time to take a look," she said.

The electronic lock had been knocked out in the crash, and she had to wind the outer door open manually. The low pressure outside sucked a small breeze past her cheeks and made her ears pop.

Leaning dizzily on the doorframe, Captain Jute stuck her head out into the thin, salty air of Capella 3.

Here and there, rock pinnacles reared above her like petrified trees. The silence was deafening.

Captain Jute ventured out onto the surface. She touched the side of the Kobold where she had smashed it. She kicked it. It made a hard and hollow sound.

Hands on her hips, she turned around, surveying the mulberry sky. Low in the smoky southwest hung the lumpy, sun-licked shapes of a dozen moons. There was nothing moving anywhere.

She climbed carefully down into the pit, backward down the steep slope. At the edge of the pool she squatted and sniffed. There was a distinct oily, metallic smell.

Captain Jute checked her wrist monitor. It was not picking up anything identifiably nasty.

She took an empty cup and conscientiously dipped up a

sample of the blue fluid. It was not like the dreaming water of Umbriel. It was something much more dense, that beaded readily in the low g. Scooping it into the cup was like trying to gather mercury.

Captain Jute stood up again. She eased her back and flexed her knees.

She looked at the statue. Innocent of everything, the white stone woman leaned backward over the dark liquid, contemplating infinity.

Captain Jute returned to her stolen ship. She put her sample in the analyzer and took a long drink of fortified water.

There was a contour map in greens and greys on the recon screens, overlaid with a grid of concentric white circles. The shadowy, random blocks of the "city" were showing on the far left, and a lopsided bullet-shaped blip in the upper right-hand corner.

"Is that the ship?"

"IF IT IS ONE," Alice answered. "IT ISN'T TRANS-MITTING ANY SIGNALS," she added, with what, had she been sentient, would have been an air of disappointment.

"I don't suppose it is," said Captain Jute. She revised her priorities. They had missed their target landing site completely and ended up nearer the wreck than the city. She pulled her T-shirt up to examine her bruises.

"I won't be long," she said.

The plaque reader hummed softly. "I THINK YOU WILL, CAPTAIN."

"It's not that far," Tabitha said.

"16.9 KILOMETERS," said the ship. "THE TERRAIN IS FRACTURED AND UNSTABLE. ATMOSPHERIC COVER IS PRINCIPALLY CONFINED TO LOW-LYING AREAS."

"I'll be careful," promised Tabitha forcefully. "If I have any trouble, I'll come straight back. All right? Is that all right?"

"IT'S YOUR DECISION."

"Yes. Yes, well. Well, then."

The analyzer chimed.

She went to look. The blue fluid was an enormous molecule of appalling complexity. Source and function completely unknown. Perhaps it really was ink.

Captain Jute left the slanting ship and began to climb to the top of the pit, aiming for the rocky pinnacle that loomed over it. Barely discernible in the gloom, her twin shadows climbed with her.

In a convenient dip she rested a moment, looking down at the dim grey bulk of the Kobold beneath her. From here you could barely see the damage.

She held her wristcom to her lips. "Alice, can you hear me? Come in, Alice. Over."

"HELLO, CAPTAIN," said the faithful persona, through a soft crackling haze. The old red twins were not well disposed to radio communication. "I HAVE YOUR POSITION. YOU ARE 62.91 METERS ABOVE ME, 18.68 METERS BELOW DATUM, TO AN ACCURACY OF PLUS OR MINUS 0.25 METERS. CAN YOU SEE ANYTHING YET?"

"Rock," said Tabitha. "Call me every fifteen minutes, unless something happens. All right?"

"RIGHT YOU ARE, CAPTAIN."

She reached the rim of the pit, and found that beyond it the ground descended sharply again.

She stood beside the crooked pinnacle and surveyed the view. It was all rocky spikes and, between them, deep round craters, as far as the eye could see. A slight, cold wind, possibly the result of her tumultuous landing, caressed the back of her neck.

Captain Jute stepped across the intervening ridge and looked down into the neighboring pit. It was empty.

*   *   *

The pits varied in size from the merest dent to holes a quarter k across. Most were dry, and empty, but as the hours passed she came across more artifacts.

In one small crater there was a human child's bicycle, still with its metallic pink-and-turquoise paint. It had obviously been ridden around a lot by some child somewhere, but it was about as much use here as a surfboard.

"PERHAPS YOU SHOULDN'T TOUCH IT, CAPTAIN," said Alice.

"I wasn't going to."

Later she found another thing, like a domed wire cage for a tiny animal or bird. It was battered and rusty. There was nothing inside it. The door was closed.

It was impossible to suppose any of this stuff was indigenous. It had to be Capellan loot, taken and abandoned in this weird place: one thing per hole, for some reason, like chocolates in a box. Some must have been relics of alien civilizations. One enigmatic bundle of sticks and bones looked like something a Thrant might treasure, the Captain thought, exhaustedly; and that made her think of Kenny and Soi. She could have done with her smelly hirelings here. She imagined them out of uniform, muscular streaks of golden fur racing on all fours up the bald rock slopes.

She walked on. In places the ridges between the pits were narrow, and crumbly. For the twentieth time she lost her footing. In a cloud of dust she went wallowing down the slope, this time on her side, adding bruises to her bruises.

There was nothing in this pit, except for Captain Jute. While she lay there at the bottom, aching and panting, Alice checked in. "AT YOUR PRESENT RATE OF PROGRESS," she said, "IN 23 MINUTES 40 SECONDS YOU WILL BE HALFWAY THERE."

She was trying to be encouraging. Captain Jute grunted acknowledgment and sipped water. She felt in no great hurry to get up again.

*   *   *

It was when the stony pinnacles above the pits started growing faces and leering at her that Captain Jute realized how spaced-out she truly was. The air was bad, she was in bad condition. She rested a moment, feeding herself a little oxygen, and some more caffeine and analgesics.

She could see half a dozen pinnacles from where she stood. She looked around at all of them.

They all had faces now.

She thought about the things people saw in the tunnels of Plenty: the gesticulating figures, the little animals with too many legs that scuttled away from the light. On Capella 3, nothing moved, except the dry dirt that ever and again slipped and rattled away beneath your feet.

Captain Jute stood up. She staggered and scrabbled up over another ridge; and there she stopped, and gasped a gasp that turned into a weary cackle of amazement and triumph.

She was standing on the lip of the biggest pit she had seen so far, a crater that might have been 5 k around. It was hard to be sure quite how big it was, because most of it was hidden by the ship.

She fumbled with the com.

"It is a ship, Alice," she said. "One of ours."

She was a cruise liner, one of the big, romantic ones from the first exuberant flush of the Big Step. Even nose down in a desolate crater, she contrived to look majestic. Her passenger decks towered over Tabitha like the walls of a palace: impervious, insuperable in their livery of black and yellow.

"It's the *Amaranth Aloof.*"

"THE *AMARANTH*?"

"Yup."

She didn't need to be within sight of the bows where the name was written up in ornamental letters four meters high. She had seen the *Amaranth* before. She had cleaned up after her, traveling with poor old Captain Frank in his interplanetary rag-and-bone cart, the *Fat Mouth*. A year or so later, the *Amaranth* had vanished. Last seen sailing out into the frozen wastes beyond Neptune; now lying here abandoned under the malign glare of Capella, fifty light-years away.

The discovery of the great liner did not fill Captain Jute with joy. It was more depressing evidence of the power of the enemy. She gathered her hair behind her neck. "She looks all there," she said.

"I DON'T QUITE UNDERSTAND," crackled Alice. "DO YOU MEAN IT ISN'T A WRECK?"

"Doesn't look like it," said Captain Jute. She brooded. "They brought her here on purpose. Whatever that means."

There was a pause while her transmission was received and digested. "PERHAPS YOU SHOULD COME BACK NOW, CAPTAIN."

But Captain Jute had already started the trek down into the valley, into the double shadow of the silent ship.

It took her the best part of an hour to climb onto the superstructure, make her way to an airlock and try the handle.

Nothing.

She tried the emergency release.

No response.

With a small tight smile, she took out her omnipolar key and clamped it to the hull.

The operating lights twinkled weakly, as if the microcircuits were humbled by the vastness of the edifice they were required to penetrate. It was a long while before she heard the heavy thud of the lock opening to admit her.

In the fetid metal darkness she entered a recreation area. A sign pointed the way to a ballroom; a zero-g sports center; restaurants, games pods and cinemas.

Negotiating the tilted floor, Captain Jute took a door at random. Inside she could see nothing. Feeling for her torch, she walked straight into a table and startled a tiny creature into life.

It was human, hyperbolically female, fifteen centimeters high. It was dressed only in a white bath-towel.

So there was power on board, if only in this sector.

The insubstantial mannequin smiled invitingly at her. It stretched and put its hands behind its head.

"*Thank heavens for Starlight Saunas,*" said a man's voice in the darkness. "*They* know *how to make you relax.*" He sounded humorous and sympathetic.

The holo became a close-up. The viewpoint roved over moist butterscotch flesh, a tilted chin, plump lips glistening with erotic promise. The voice was reciting a menu of health and comfort features.

Captain Jute was not listening. In the glimmering light of the ad she looked around the bar.

She saw that she had not, after all, been the first human to visit another star.

Still clad in their silk suits and couturier leisurewear, the passengers of the *Amaranth Aloof* sat slumped over their evaporated martinis. The skin was shriveled tight around their bones.

For some reason that did it to her. All the grief and fear and rage came out in one big brightly colored explosion. Angie and Saskia and Plenty and the poor old *Alice Liddell.* Everything they had taken away from her and broken. The whole Sol System. The whole human race.

She came to somewhere in the depths of the lifeless cruise liner, stained with her own puke. Later, on her knees, she shivered as she hot-wired a nutrimat for a stimulant drink, glucose and vitamins. She vowed she was not going all the way back through those dreary pits until she had something for herself. Some transport, for a start. There would be something here, and she was going to find it.

She did. It was just where she had presumed, near one of the main exits, among the untouched emergency landing gear. It was a hoverbike, one of twenty. She knelt and hugged it. Then she sat in the saddle, pretending to ride, crooning a mindless, happy song. The batteries were flat, the water system dry, but all that was only a problem of time.

Time, Captain Jute supposed, was one thing which was not in short supply.

~ 14

Kajsa Prime broke the hyperband connection.

"Page," she said.

A girl presented herself, kneeling. The High Priestess of the Seraphim pulled out the soft white earpieces and slid them into her proffered palm. "Good, good," she said, to the universe in general.

The tech spooled the bands of the communication harness rapidly off the Priestess's bare white shoulders. Kajsa Prime scratched her temples and ran her fingers around the classical curves of her ears. Everything was, indeed, good. In fact it was very good. She and her sisters had come to an immediate agreement.

The Prime stood upright in the air.

"Mirror," she said.

Though she was of many bodies, Kajsa Tobermory was of one mind. That had always been so, and always would be. Her unanimity was the very infrastructure of the Temple.

The page switched the mirror on. It scanned the High Seraph for an appreciable fraction of a second, then produced her double, life-size, in light.

Kajsa was in her usual *déshabille*: black basque and stockings. It was a style, she felt, in which maximum femininity and maximum aggression were deliciously combined. She looked in the mirror and primped her hair with her chrome black fingernails.

"Congratulate us," she commanded.

"Congratulations, Your Supremacy," chorused page and tech.

The Prime took the booster stylus from the page. She retouched her lips, her eyebrows. Her image copied her every motion.

"Do you know why you're congratulating me, 33?"

The tech stowed the hypercom behind a gauzy veil. "No, ma'am," she said.

"The line is holding," the Priestess told her.

Though the apex of the Temple was now so distant from its base, the line remained intact: undeviating, vertical, straight as a laser through fifty light-years.

"Turn," commanded the High Priestess.

The servants remained as they were. The image in the mirror rotated through 180°.

The Priestess was dissatisfied with her knickers. She thought she saw a wrinkle. The page came and smoothed the fabric over the hierophantic buttock.

"The line is holding," the Priestess said again. "Coat."

The page pressed a button. There was gravity for a moment, underfoot. Through the air, like a sculpted avalanche, the Priestess's long white fur descended.

Kajsa looked in the mirror and watched it settle about her, not quite reaching the floor. Microscopic repellers in the hem registered the wearer's position at all times and corrected the hang. The monofilament fur kept its whiteness by digesting the dirt that fell upon it. Not that there was much dirt, on board the *Seraph Kajsa*.

The Priestess stroked her coat. The mirror image stroked hers. They used the same hand.

Kajsa wished she could dress the Zodiac girl. Touring in Contraband, Saskia had worn some fabulous outfits: silk, sealskin, stainless steel, materials that commanded the eye.

Now she would wear nothing but that horrid patterned frock. No makeup, no jewelry, her hair in a pigtail—she looked like a sulky teenager.

Of course, everybody was sorry for her—even Boaz and Xippy, who were not famous for being sympathetic. It must be awful, to be all alone in the cosmos. The Prime could barely remember what it felt like. To be one of five and then one of two, and then one of one: solitary, without backups; like everybody else. Gruesome thought. Inside her coat, Kajsa shivered.

If the last of the Zodiacs didn't cheer up, sooner or later they would all get bored with her, and then she was bound to end up recycled, just like her siblings. There was a shortage of good natural material out here, and her molecule was not merely natural; it was the best. Meanwhile, Kajsa was sure the girl would be happier if she had something nice to wear.

Not that it really mattered. The time was past for the crude politics of concealment and display. This was a new time, an unprecedented present, with a new future curled up inside it, potent and delectable as a designer embryo.

Kajsa Prime gestured to the page to switch off the mirror and lifted her chin for the tech to spray her exquisite throat with dominance pheromones.

"Now we must work," she said. "The chariot."

Her servants bowed elaborately in midair. "Awe and reverence, Your Multiplicity . . ."

It was the one with the little beard. He was very courteous. He knocked for admittance, and introduced himself by name. His name was Pomeroy Lion. Saskia thought it only half suited him. She thought he was big enough, but his hair would need to be longer, and he ought to have sharp teeth and claws, and a tail like a Thrant. She felt he probably shouldn't wear a red waistcoat with a gold chain across it either.

"Pardon me for disturbing you, my dear, but I wonder

if you'd mind terribly popping down to Cubicle 6 for a
moment.''

He took her arm as they swam. She thought he smelled
of nutmeg and tobacco. She never would have found the
way alone. The corridors were all the same, bare and clinical.

''Do you like it here?'' he asked her. ''Are you glad you
came back?''

''I hate it,'' she said.

''Surely not,'' he said.

''I hate it everywhere,'' she said.

Her attention was caught by movement outside the ship,
in space. It was the Cherubim, on their way to work. Their
little shiny bodies slipped past the window like baby dol-
phins.

''Why don't you let Xtasca join them again now?'' asked
Saskia suddenly. Her voice sounded harsh in the soft, well-
tempered hush.

''It was Xtasca who decided to leave, you know,'' said
Pomeroy Lion.

The clone wasn't listening. She was obviously speaking
thoughts she had rehearsed in her mind.

''You could put a label on her,'' she said forcefully, ''if
you're worried about getting them mixed up.''

Moved, the Seraph patted the young woman's hand.
''Your sense of interpersonal relations has developed enormously,'' he observed. ''How much do you attribute that
to your period of sexual activity?''

Saskia's face was blank. Her peculiar eyes seemed to
stare straight through him.

''Well,'' he pressed her, ''did you become emotionally
involved with any of your partners, for example?''

Irritably, the artificial human shrugged her thin shoulders. ''I didn't know it was optional,'' she said.

Cubicle 6 turned out to be one of the glass tubes like the
one they'd killed Angela in, but smaller. The one with the

wings was there again. His name was Sweet Lavender.
Pomeroy Lion introduced them, as if they hadn't met before; as if it hadn't happened, that they had strung Angela
up and made her talk herself to death.

Pomeroy Lion's smile was brilliant, but a bit dazed, as
if she continued to puzzle him profoundly. Sweet Lavender
smiled with his lips closed. His smile made his mouth
smaller, not larger.

"All we need today," the angel told her, "is a *soupçon*,
a smidgin, of your menses."

"A what?" she said. "Of my what?"

"Your discharge, my dear," said Pomeroy Lion. He
pressed the middle of his lower lip with the nail of his
thumb, his fingers curled together. His moustache made her
sad. It reminded her of Mogul. "Your blood," said Pomeroy Lion. He gave a small, deprecating cough.

"We'd be extremely grateful," said Sweet Lavender, as
if she had a choice. She suspected he might be imitating
his colleague's manners, making fun of him.

There were handholds on the glass walls of Cubicle 6.
She held on, letting her legs float up for them. She had
come on that morning. Obviously they knew. "You're no
different from the Capellans," she told them as they investigated the inside of her pants. "You watch us."

"We watch over you." The angel smiled his little smile
at her again. "You're the last of your kind." He wielded
his spatula.

Next they scraped the roof of her mouth.

"It's a terrible shame," said Pomeroy Lion as he
thoughtfully fed her cells into the curved slot of a receptor.
"I do feel we owe you an apology."

She was getting tired. She hunched herself up. "What
for now?"

The Seraph stroked his moustache. "We were unable,"
he confessed, "to recover your brother's body."

"We were unable," said the angel, like an echo, "to
extract him from the embrace of Venus."

His colleague seemed to wince. He pulled the end of his moustache, hard. "Otherwise, all this would be, h'rrmph, unnecessary," he said mildly.

On the receptor machine a small light went on, then off again. Through a smoked-glass window Saskia could just see the elegant plastic spatulas, like slender carvings of bone. They were hers, those tiny smears of blood and mucus. A moment before, they had been inside her body. They had *been* her, parts of her.

Saskia felt a surge of panic. She said: "What do you want with my stuff? What are you going to do with it?"

The two giants looked at each other. Pomeroy Lion rubbed his chin. He resettled the points of his starched white collar and straightened the knot of his tie.

The angel batted his eyelids. Though his hair was mauve, his wings were white. The glass of the walls and the polished metal of the machines reflected his wings as he spread them. The reflections seemed to sweep around the outside of the enclosure like bright clouds blown on contrary winds.

He smelled of flowers, reminding her of the Garden. He swooped down to tickle Saskia's prominent ribs. "I might have some of it myself," he told her admiringly. "You're so *thin*!"

"It's for future projects," said Pomeroy Lion stiffly and a trifle hurriedly. "Future projects."

Out in space, tucked away behind the glossy black belly of the *Seraph Kajsa*, a piece of machinery was being assembled. So far it resembled the offspring of some improbable marriage between a signaling gantry and a crane fly. A slender multilimbed armature like an asymmetrical snowflake was being fitted on one side with cross-linked impulse engines, and on the other with a spindly assortment of aerials, lenses, hologrid spectrometers and ultrasonic penetration analyzers.

Equipped with a basic drone guidance module and dispatched into the disintegrating star system, the device would be capable of surveying its constituent parts, from the remaining planets to the merest pebbles. It would supply the data to plot their trajectories and calculate the probable times and places of their eventual extinction. The prevailing forces in the vicinity of a double star entering the extreme stage of its existence were of much interest to the Convocation of the Seraphim, especially the Schematics and Cognizance divisions. Every hurtling cinder seemed to promise a new ramification to the laws of physics.

To a distant and uninformed observer, the robot cartographer might have seemed at first to be assembling itself, as if by means of some informed and obedient version of magnetism. Closer in, it became apparent that there were minute, legless black creatures drawing and welding and wiring the components together. It was like watching a school of educated tadpoles building a spaceship.

None of them more than sixty centimeters long, the creatures made up in accuracy and coordination what they lacked in brawn. They were clothed only in hooded suits of transparent plastic. They worked without floodlights, seeing perfectly well in the blaze of infrared.

Strong swimmers in the murky vacuum, three of these homunculi were hauling an extensive reticulated array of solar panels, drawing it along behind them by means of long cables of tungsten and adamantine twist, which they wore as tails, bolted into their caudal sockets. Among them floated their Seraphic overseer, directing operations from a black chrome apparatus, half spacesuit, half single-seater ship.

"Microflux calibrator is now secure, Xipetotec . . . "

Below, in the enormous void, the shadowed shoals of rock that the mapping machine was to plot crept by, centimeter by centimeter. In the remote depths the red twins roared, like bonfires at the bottom of an ocean of blood. Later a slender fish of orange and gold came slipping through the pumice fields, bound on some unimaginable mission to the outer darkness. This fish was seven hundred meters long, and a hundred million kilometers away.

Alerted, the floating Seraph blinked his heavy eyelids. *"Snoop coming into range,"* he told the builders.

All at once, without discussion or delay, the Cherubim downed tools. Pausing only to dispel the momentum of big components in transit, they left their work and retreated into the spaces of the incomplete assembly. All together, motionless, silent, the red lights of their eyes dimmed down to nothing, they watched the Capellan system ship go sliding by.

In the big lab forward, the last of the foil-covered trays was slid into position beneath its shutter. Two of the lab techs, numbers 10 and 15, came forward to twist the clamps that would hold the tray in place.

As if in imitation, Pomeroy Lion twisted the points of his moustache. He reached inside his coat and brought out a test tube. It was sealed, but not labeled. He held the tube in his palm, warming the tiny blob of colorless material it contained.

"Future projects," he said.

Tech 10 was going along the line of trays, checking the seals on their covers. He turned to look as the Seraph spoke.

The tech had his hood up. A huge pair of goggles concealed most of his face. Pomeroy Lion bared his front teeth at him in a brief and chilly smile.

Kajsa Prime's voice came over the air. *"Are you there, Pomeroy?"*

"I am, madam," said the Seraph aloud.

Between the rubber doors of the lab, great gouts of disinfectant steam were starting to blow in.

"You're just in time for the next exposure," said Pomeroy Lion.

The doors sprang open. Two naked page boys came striding through.

The page boys leapt here and there about the lab, one of

them with a cylinder on his back, spraying the steam around; the other vacuuming it up. Through the clouds the chariot of the Chief Seraph came nosing in.

"Carry on, everybody," said Kajsa clearly, over the roar of her vehicle. "Don't stop for me."

Suspenders flashing, she hurdled the chariot rail. Her white fur coat billowed behind her, keeping out of the way.

Queen Kajsa launched herself over to Pomeroy Lion. She had spotted the test tube in his hand. "Is this it?"

Pomeroy Lion inclined his head. "This is it, madam."

She took the tube from him. She stroked it. "Our baby," she said, sentimentally.

She raised a hand to her driver. "Thank you, 33." Tech 33 began backing the chariot out of the lab. The page boys followed, still spraying.

Stimulated by the presence of their queen, the lab staff flew about their work, bouncing off the walls, never colliding. They held brief conferences with displays of the little colored lights they wore around their wrists and ankles. Now they were peeling the foil from the incubator trays, preparing the shutters, the mitochondrial excitation feeds.

The Chief Seraph tucked the test tube between her breasts. She smiled possessively down at it.

"How long will it take to grow?"

Pomeroy Lion tapped the center of his upper lip delicately with the knuckle of his thumb. "That depends what sort of quantity you're talking about," he said. "A square meter? A couple of trays?"

Kajsa Prime stroked the length of the tube again with an extended finger. "What about a complete specimen?"

Pomeroy Lion winced and cleared his throat. "Rather premature . . ." he ventured.

His queen batted her eyelids at him. "Just one," she said.

"A freestanding specimen?" he frowned.

"How long?" she asked.

Pomeroy Lion tutted and tapped his teeth together, cogitating. He shook his head. "I'd rather wait till we see—" he said, gesturing at the incubator trays.

Kajsa Prime touched his test tube with a fingertip. "Just for fun," she said.

Pomeroy Lion smiled sardonically. He put his hands behind his back, under his coattails.

"Tech!"

Tech 10 swam over. He touched his collar to Pomeroy Lion. The Prime he saluted with a whole-body wave.

"Our Leader would like to know how long it will take to produce a Zodiac," said Pomeroy Lion to Tech 10.

Tech 10 gazed at the tube in the Queen's cleavage. "A blank?" he said. His voice was husky, contemplative.

Queen Kajsa looked at Pomeroy Lion.

"There wouldn't be a brain," he told her. "We haven't got the equipment . . ."

The High Priestess made a moue of impatience. "We can *get* it a brain."

"Oh, come on, Kajsa, really!" expostulated her colleague. "Without the resources of the Temple—"

She addressed the tech. "A blank, then," she said. "How long?"

"Estimate three thousand hours," said the tech.

"So long?"

"Estimate, Your Exuberance . . ."

The Queen of the Seraphim rubbed her stomach. "I could make one myself in that, practically."

Pomeroy Lion reddened. "Nonsense," he muttered. With a nod he dismissed the tech.

Queen Kajsa was toying with the tube again. "My naughty babies . . ."

The Chief of Capacitory knew she was speaking about Saskia and Mogul.

"You'd have done exactly the same," he said.

"I wonder," she said.

He pressed the point. "If your sisters had started dropping off the net, you'd have upped and run."

Kajsa Prime stroked the left cup of her brassiere. "It's not the same at all," she said.

"One year old," said Pomeroy Lion, "never been out of the lab? I venture to suggest you would. Especially if Nanny took you."

"Now Nanny is another question altogether," said Kajsa Prime, less combatively.

At the time, the Cherub Xtasca's defection had confounded everybody. The spontaneous development of moral behavior in a utilitarian construct had been something no one could possibly have predicted. "It's as if an oven turned vegetarian," one of Kajsa's avatars had said to Sweet Lavender, "and refused to cook any more meat products."

Her colleague had laughed appreciatively. "Or like a gun," he supposed, "deciding to kill only people who were really *wicked*."

Kajsa Prime smiled and gave Pomeroy Lion back his test tube. "Do carry on, Pomeroy," she said.

"Lights, 10, please," ordered Pomeroy Lion.

The big lab forward fell instantly dark. In the blackness, meters glowed, rectangular green eyes confirming the available sunlight, its temperature, angle and intensity. On the wristbands of the techs, the signal lights twinkled.

"Nanny is being cooperative enough now," said Pomeroy Lion to the Queen of the Seraphim, as the alarms began to whine and flash.

"We shall see," said the Queen.

Above the trays of naked flesh, the shutters started to rumble down.

The food dispensers here could generate eight kinds of burger. You could have beef, pork, chicken, venison, fish, krill, myco or soya, each atomically identical to its original.

Saskia Zodiac ordered all eight.

She ate her burgers steadily, one after the other. She ate them with mustard and onions and pickle and relish. She ate them with extra salt, in the form of tears.

The burgers were all completely authentic and at the same time entirely artificial. Just like her.

When she had finished her meal, Saskia went to look for Xtasca.

It was not in Navigation. It was not in Cognizance, though the hexagonal cells of infostacks were exactly like the headquarters it had built for itself on Plenty. It was not in Schematics, where the other Cherubim congregated, programming the cartographer's shipboard end via their snaky tails. Saskia flew in among them, looking from face to identical face.

"Has anyone seen Xtasca?"

The Cherubim did not speak. They blinked their scarlet eyes at her, in synchrony.

Xtasca was in Diagnostic Cubicle 14, with the winged Seraph Sweet Lavender. Together they were watching a number of screens.

Some of the screens showed grids, circular or elliptical, each with a large central or focal blob. Occasionally a radial sector of the grid would be highlighted in reverse video. Dark lines would flash across it, connecting the junctions of the grid with the central mass. Other screens showed conventional star maps, fractal representations of hyperspace, or video footage. The largest screen of all held the same primitive modulated output graphic: a single blue line undulating on a black background.

As Seraph and Cherub watched that line, a sequence began to repeat.

"There," said Sweet Lavender.

The Cherub lifted its tail, extending it and bringing it in an elegant curve over its shoulder. With its tip it inscribed something among the lighted displays on the rim of its saucer.

On the black screen the blue line wiggled backward, rapidly, as the recording rewound. Then it stopped. Dumbly, the sequence replayed, and repeated.

"The etheric gestalts," said Sweet Lavender.

"Vespans didn't like them," said Xtasca. "The incidence of spontaneous bladder puncture rose by 50% during those periods."

"Poor things," crooned the Seraph. "Like canaries down a coal mine." He reached over his shoulder and smoothed his right wing.

A bell rang, announcing a visitor. It was an agent, number 29. He had his hand on the shoulder of Saskia Zodiac. "*She was in Schematics, sir,*" his voice said over the intercom. "*The Cherubim alerted us.*"

The angel rose to the ceiling. He stared down through the wall of the cubicle like a hawk.

"What have you brought her *here* for?"

"*They said she was asking for her companion, sir.*"

"Does the Prime know? Tell her, will you?"

Xtasca came out and hovered in front of Saskia, humming softly.

"You have been crying."

"They are going to rebuild us!"

The Cherub made a noise like a fishing reel. "I should have thought that would fill you with joy."

Saskia looked around at the other glass enclosures. Inside some, white-suited figures were visible, plying scalpels and pipettes.

"They're going to make it happen all over again," she moaned.

"We're certainly not going to rebuild *you*," Sweet Lavender told her airily, as the Cherub brought her into Cubicle 14. "You're far too much trouble."

In her grubby green dress, Saskia climbed up to look at the screens. She stared at a pair of bloated red discs that sat in an elliptical grid like twin mechanical spiders sharing a web. From each disc silvery lines continually burst, like microscopic bursts of orthogonal lightning.

Above that screen was one of footage shot by something moving at walking pace through dark pinkish brown tunnels. She recognized the terrain: the endlessly branching arteries, the corners marked with cryptic designs in silver paint.

She looked down at Xtasca. Well as she knew it, she was unable to detect an expression on that doll-like face.

"What are you doing?"

"There's a lot still to learn," said the Cherub placidly.

Saskia pointed to the video of Plenty. "This is from the expedition."

"Some of it," said Xtasca. "Some of it is surveillance material."

"You brought it here," the cloned woman accused her former custodian. "You gave it to them."

"We need it," said Sweet Lavender, snappishly. Earlier he had been so ingratiating. Now he seemed to have lost patience with her. Perhaps he just didn't like to be disturbed at work.

Saskia climbed carefully around the walls, studying all the monitors. A small one showed a tour through a computer-generated model of the Capellan starship, the *Citadel of Porcelain at First Light*. The internal architecture was simplified to fields of translucent pastel color. Every so often, the juncture of walls or corridors were marked by a silver ideogram. Intermittently, actual photographs appeared. Saskia recognized some of them: Sector W, with its miniature forest; the surgical sector where she and Xtasca had nursed Angie; the bay of yellow lifeboats.

Saskia was angry with Xtasca. "They attacked us. They tried to kill us!"

The Seraph sighed dramatically. "And now we're looking after you," he said. "Do try to catch up."

Saskia lifted one leg and pointed a toe at the biggest screen, the one with the wiggling blue line.

"And what is that?" she demanded, though she rather felt now that she already knew.

"That," said the angel, floating up fiercely between her and the screen, "is the memoirs of Ancillary 13709."

The cloned acrobat turned upside down. Beneath the wings of the angel she stared mournfully at the graphs.

"They help to identify more of the Frasque code," the Cherub told her. "Angela Jute was in a unique position."

"Up to her neck in it," gloated the angel.

Saskia glared at him. He wanted to hurt her. She wouldn't let him.

"Here," said the Cherub, fast-forwarding once more. Saskia blinked, hypnotized by the frantically jiggling blue line that was all that was left of Tabitha's sister.

"This is one of hundreds of sections of real-time memory," said the Cherub. It seemed to think Saskia would see the point of their research, if it could just be explained simply enough. "The actual control sequences ran directly through Angela Jute's brain."

"She was the only individual on the hive who knew where she was really going," said Sweet Lavender, as if he had been there and she hadn't.

"You didn't know either," said Saskia violently.

"Of course we knew," said the Seraph disdainfully. "*We* configured little Angie's CNS." He stretched his arms out to each side, with his wings behind them. "Like programming a scouter," he said.

"Sweet Lavender," said Xtasca, "is of the opinion that the sentient observer may be an indispensable part of the Capellan stardrive."

Saskia turned, scanning the creature who had saved her life with her peculiar fathomless eyes. "Frasque stardrive, you mean."

The angel vaulted back into the space between them, folding his legs under him. "Of course we do," he said.

Across the big black screen the blue line writhed, like something trying to escape from an electromagnetic prison.

* * *

Kajsa Prime came to fetch the errant young clone. "You're not supposed to be wandering around in here, poppet," she said, pressing Saskia Zodiac to her opulent breasts. "You might hurt yourself. Come with me. Are you hungry?"

"No," said Saskia, and vomited up her eight burgers.

The screams of the angel resounded in the glass cubicle.

A squadron of techs descended, armed with vacuum cleaners. They zeroed in on the lumps of partly digested fat and protein that drifted, lodging in the ventilation grilles of the monitors, gumming up the tape heads. Xtasca hovered silently, spattered with vomit. Sweet Lavender screamed at the Cherub, ordering it to clean him.

Queen Kajsa made a point of wiping Saskia herself. "This is all my fault," she announced, magnanimously. "I haven't been paying you enough attention, have I, sweetie?" She held her grip on the shoulder of the artificial woman until she had been properly sedated. "Now let's get you back where you're safe, shall we?"

Through the chaos and confusion, the screens were still playing. On one, a dark-haired woman in a long black coat was shown climbing a lumpy matrix wall, armed with a pair of fat yellow jump leads. As she moved the camera briefly caught her pale brown face.

"That reminds me," said Kajsa Prime, to Sweet Lavender and the Cherub, and equally to the thin young woman she was supporting. "I don't know if you've heard the news, have you? Cognizance says Captain Jute has escaped from Capellan custody."

ॐ 15

Once they had been wealthy Step prospectors; Eladeldi liaison secretaries; Belt entrepreneurs. Now they were bundles of faded fabric and bright bone. In cabin and bar they slumped, disintegrating. They lay in the corridors, gaping at her as she tiptoed by. Around their ropelike necks and wrists, the cruise line's regulation safety tags still glinted.

There were whole areas she couldn't even go into, because of the smell. She did manage, once, to get to the bridge.

On the bridge of something the size of the *Amaranth Aloof*, at any one time there should have been twenty people or more on duty. As she worked her way through the upper corridors, Captain Jute was fully expecting to meet them.

There was nobody. The stations were deserted, the webs hanging empty. It was as if the Capellans had picked the bridge crew out like delicacies, before discarding the rest. Perhaps they were the only thing they had wanted, the reason they had taken the ship at all.

She toured the old, oversize consoles, touching the bulb-topped levers, the coffer of grey steel that housed the extinct persona. She stood by the captain's chair and ran her fingers around the rim of the control panel set into its arm. The upholstery fell away in brittle flakes.

The *Amaranth* was defunct. Only in her dreams would it fly again, whisking Tabitha Jute and all the prisoners of the Capellans, alive and dead, back home to the sweet, tangled lights of Sol.

* * *

From the stern observation lounge she could see a hundred craters or more. She had toured them, a lot of them, on the bike. They were all empty, except one, and she spotted that one before she came to it.

It was a small crater, and it was full of the same thick blue liquid that was in the pool beneath the *Billy Budd*. Out of the middle, large as the crater itself and stretching beyond the rim, there rose the figure of a distraught-looking bird.

Captain Jute shined her lights on it. The bird was made of metal. It was polished, and blue, as if it had somehow soaked up the color of the pool it stood in. The wings were spread, and one foot was raised, as if the bird had been cast in the act of flying up into the elusive air. Every feather was perfect.

Captain Jute remembered the crater with the birdcage in. A metal cage, a metal bird, a metal flying ship. You could go mad, making up theories.

Her bike was a Honeyglide R, blunt and rugged. It had been designed for hard work, but not, perforce, for the porous pitlands of Capella 3. Captain Jute's wrists ached from wrestling it over the vicious contours. Still she continued to search; for what, she didn't know.

One day she came to a pit where her headlights could find no bottom. Perhaps there might not be one. The hole looked very much like the mouth of a shaft, leading deep under the ground. Perhaps there were still nests of Capellans down there, piles of blind blue grubs with sucking mouths crawling all over each other.

"If we had a flame thrower," she suggested, "I could go down and look."

"YOU MIGHT INJURE YOURSELF," the persona pointed out.

Captain Jute was in the cockpit of the *Billy Budd*. She was standing on the chart console. From there she could just get her arm up inside one of the overhead ducts.

The duct had been installed to carry the wiring from a navigation scanner. Now it was going to carry the wiring from a solar collector scavenged from the *Amaranth Aloof*.

"There might be a flamethrower on the *Amaranth*," remarked Captain Jute.

"PERMIT ME TO HOPE THERE ISN'T," said Alice.

Tabitha found the end of one of the wires and started to ease it through the duct. If this worked, it would triple her power resources. She would be able to charge the bike up here in future.

"Maybe we could build some sort of bomb," she said, not very seriously. "Drop it off the back of the bike."

"PERHAPS YOU SHOULD GO AND LIVE AT THE *AMARANTH ALOOF*," said Alice, after a moment.

"Mm-mm," said Tabitha, firmly. "I'm not leaving you."

"SUPPOSE YOU INJURED YOURSELF," said Alice. "SUPPOSE SOMETHING HAPPENED THAT MADE YOU UNABLE TO TRAVEL BACK AND FORTH EVERY DAY."

From her elevation Captain Jute could see down the back of the persona unit. There was a gap between its inertium-core frame and the cockpit wall. In the gap she could see the fifty-two transparent plastic leads that hung out of the back of the unit. Each lead was the sheath for a thick bundle of microcoded microfibers, which in turn connected the persona to every instrument on board.

"It isn't every day," she said. "I'm going to take a break now, all right?"

She left the cockpit, turning her back on the bare wires sticking out of the ceiling. She went and lay in the hammock and played her harmonica, nameless twelve-bar blues as old as cruelty.

On the cabin wall the pin-up smirked at her.

Once, waking at night, she looked out of the porthole and saw, high in the sky, a tiny golden glimmer.

She watched it for a while to make sure it wasn't a stray reflection, a gleam of starlight on a passing rock. Then, still yawning, she went up into the cockpit and got it on a scope. It was SSWS, elevation 74°. Magnified thirty times, it seemed to show the characteristic hourglass shape of a Capellan System ship.

"Do you think they're looking for us?" she asked Alice, who never slept. The Captain had an absurd compulsion to whisper, as though that would render the crashed Kobold less detectable to the alien instruments.

"I DOUBT WE HAVE THAT MUCH SIGNIFICANCE NOW," said Alice.

Tabitha felt a drowsy mixture of relief, offense and dread.

"AFTER ALL, WE COULD HARDLY BE IN A MORE SECURE PRISON," said Alice placidly.

Tabitha Jute set the persona to track the distant golden glint, and went back to bed. In the morning, the ship was gone, on into the system, toward the choleric suns.

The solar collector took her a while. When it was finally up and running, she went and fetched one of the tabletop holopads from the bar she had stumbled into first.

"Brighten the place up a bit," she told Alice, plugging it into a spare port at the back of her reader. "I always fancied one of these."

"DID YOU, CAPTAIN?" said the persona.

To test it, they ran celestial scenarios. The red twins hovered over the tiny plate like overheated ball bearings. Planets grew, shrank, multiplied, combined, whirling around in circles.

Tabitha put her feet up on the console. "This is the latest theory, Alice, right? They evolved on 1. They went to 2 when 1 got too hot, then on to 3. Then they had to go and find another sun."

She twiddled her fingers in her hair.

"So at what point did they learn to take over people's bodies?" she asked.

She wondered if Capella 2 and 3 had had inhabitants originally. Sapient, bipedal vertebrates with two cerebral lobes, presumably, like the people they had picked on later: the Thrant; the Vespans; the Perks. Interstellar losers who still trailed around after them, the tattered retinue of the conquerors. Tabitha put her forearms on the console, brought her face down close to the miniature star system. "Marco Metz said they've been with us for a long time," she said.

"SINCE YOU CAME DOWN OUT OF THE TREES, BY THE SCALE OF THIS," observed Alice.

Tabitha Jute had no feelings about trees. They hadn't had them, where she grew up. Still the suggestion was upsetting.

"Cancel," she said. "That's enough."

The virtual orrery winked out of existence.

Captain Jute looked at the power meters. Already the battery levels were beginning to rise. She went outside and, reaching through a large hole where she had removed some of the ruined platework, she hooked the leads of the Honeyglide to the terminals of the collector.

"There must be other ships here," she said. "How likely is it there could be just us and the *Amaranth*?"

"WE'VE SEEN NO SIGN OF ANY OTHERS," Alice pointed out. The persona did not mention the various ways Captain Jute had already got it to calculate the probabilities. Left on a stable setting, it grew more tactful, not less.

"Keep looking."

Back on board, Captain Jute considered the default figure to which the little holoset had reverted, the buxom woman draped in a towel, fluttering her eyelashes on behalf of Starlight Saunas.

"Alice, can you do this?"

The Captain described a little white child: a young girl

with long, long blond hair, a white pinafore, a wide blue dress, and a pair of striped stockings.

Alice made the alterations.

"Mm. Younger still, maybe," said Captain Jute. "Jaw a bit bigger."

In a little while she had her perfectly, right down to the little buttons on her shoes.

"That's it," said Captain Jute, sitting back. "Do you recognize her?"

Alice rotated the tiny image around its long axis.

"I'M AFRAID NOT, CAPTAIN."

"You said she was a subsidiary function."

"OF MINE? I SUPPOSE I MUST HAVE HAD A GREAT MANY OF THOSE."

Alice made the little figure rotate back the other way. Its eyes opened and closed.

"WOULD YOU LIKE HER TO SPEAK, CAPTAIN?"

Tabitha grimaced. "Boojums," she said.

"I BEG YOUR PARDON, CAPTAIN?"

"No, Alice," Tabitha said. "I wouldn't, really."

Alice made the little doll duck her head and curtsey. Tabitha laughed.

"You can keep her if you like," she said.

Tabitha thought of Saskia Zodiac, then, and the lifesize imagos her conjuror lover had constructed in the model shop on Plenty, replicas of the rest of her clone. The technicalities had obsessed Saskia, like a trick she simply had to master. Tabitha thought she could be forgiven for having assumed at the time that Little Alice was another creation of Saskia's.

She wondered if Saskia was still alive. She wondered if they had cut her up yet, to see what had happened to her since she ran away.

She wondered what the Cherub's part was in all this.

Captain Jute stuck her finger into the little blond ghost on top of her console. She watched it disintegrate into an ovoid fuzz of scintillation. She knew it was only evading the issue to keep trailing over to the *Amaranth Aloof*, coaxing another plate of sludge from the exhausted nutrimats, picking up another snazzy accessory for her wreck.

"Come on, then," she commanded. "Show me again."

"SHOW YOU WHAT, CAPTAIN?"

"The way to the city."

She routed everything on the liner into transmitting a last broadcast. Her friends would recognize it, if they heard it. If she still had any friends.

Even as she rose from the com, overload warning lights were beginning to flicker. There would be nothing for her on the *Amaranth* when she returned, if she ever did.

She loaded up the bike and rode west, out of the land of pits, up onto the airless plains. Out of the deep red gloom the headlights picked a landscape of bleached sienna and buff yellow, starved greys and whites. Overhead hung the deformed moons, the stars in between like grains of ice.

The bike handled better on the flat, though with a top speed of 75 kph and surface fractures edged like razors, there were no thrills to be had. The local days were short and undistinguished. At night she inflated the canopy of the Honeyglide and slept in the saddle.

The sanitary facilities in her suit were primitive, laborious and disgusting. She dreamed she was on the *Amaranth Aloof*, in a kind of Turkish bath where cascades of clean water fell ceaselessly into tiled pools. She dreamed there was a new kind of soap that you could eat. She bit into the soap. It was like biting into a peach.

When she woke, she would think of Angie. She would try and try to remember how her face had used to look, before she had had the sockets put in. Sometimes she would imagine her sister and Saskia on the *Seraph Kajsa*. They were both naked, imprisoned in two tall cylinders of glass, while a swarm of Cherubim buzzed malevolently around them like chubby black imps.

She came to the head of another valley. As she rode, she saw it was full of more of the rocky pinnacles, thousands upon thousands of them. In the confusing clarity of vacuum, the nearer ones started to turn into statues: statues of thin, stretched people with no arms, standing on tiptoe.

"Here comes everybody, Alice," she said. She giggled, waving at the thin stone people as she rode by. For some reason they were quite hilarious.

On the morning of the tenth day she sighted the city.

She still supposed it was a city. She could see what looked like the geometric forms of architecture. Buildings, surely.

As she rode on, the horizontal blur started to resolve into a line of silhouettes: walls and roofs at various distances. There were no lights anywhere.

Captain Jute was reminded of a stopover she had had to make once on a half-finished plat. For some purpose of planning or promotion, or simply as a piece of sympathetic magic designed to attract tenants, the builders had filled the vacant structure with dummy modules the size and shape of actual commercial outlets.

They were thirty meters high, their plastic walls cast with blank rectangular indentations meant to denote windows. Above their rooftops rose huge generic signs, announcements to the void in puffy letters of pale orange and lavender spelling out random words. *DRAPE. FLASH. PLAZA. BACON. SCORE.* Free of all suspicion of fulfilment, these promises of obscure delights had seemed infinitely more alluring than any real advertisement.

In the depopulated silence of Capella 3, Captain Jute began to suspect that she had made yet another bad mistake. There would be nothing here, nothing to eat or drink or breathe; no means of escaping from the planet, or of prolonging her pointless endurance here; no way even of sending another signal.

She kept on, into the Lost City.

* * *

The first building she came to was large and low. It was a single-story structure of huge cubic blocks of some sort of concrete. Its doors and windows were wider than they were high, as though designed for a world of enormous gravity, whose squat inhabitants would waddle effortfully in and out. The windows were thick, like the walls of an aquarium. Captain Jute stood up on her bike to look inside.

The building was a shell. There was nothing inside, neither fittings nor furniture. The very floor had been removed. The bare rock of Capella 3 showed through, rough and blackened.

Captain Jute rode on.

There were no streets in this city, only buildings, set separately on the plain without reference one to another. They all managed to look as if they had been put down, rather than put up. Like the rubbish in the pits they had surely been brought here from somewhere else; from any number of somewheres.

She saw an anonymous old green-ribbed dome, its plastic opaque with age and exposure, that might have come from Luna or any other impoverished utilitarian settlement. A hundred meters away stood part of a Pre-Step, terrestrial-style house, a compartmented box of redbrick walls and wooden-board floors that had been sliced through vertically, as though its collector had wanted to be able to get at the occupants and move them around from room to room. The house had no occupants now.

Other constructions, like bulbous grey marquees, reminded her of buildings she had seen in the concrete corridors of the orbital called Mntce: irregular igloos built by the Palernians with bricks of clay reinforced with their own wool, and filled with their smelly belongings.

These buildings had all been stripped. At a distance stood a heap that seemed to have been made of their erstwhile contents. Captain Jute rode around it. She could see miscellaneous bits of broken machinery; dead plants; half-dismantled vehicles. She was starting to feel angry, as though she were the subject of a gigantic hoax. She had forgotten she had come here through her own efforts, of her own free will.

Beyond the heap, a multisided skyscraper block rose up, a brown tower of tiny unlit windows and skeletal pipework. She steered her way around it and found herself approaching Dan's Delicious Diner.

Dan's Delicious Diner listed, as if the ground had given way beneath it. On the outside its name was still written up in confident cursive neon, pink as toothpaste. Its internal features were more or less intact. Ten booths of blond wood with orange-vinyl seats; ten rotating chrome-and-tan stools along the counter; and a coffee machine that looked more like a spaceship than most spaceships. "*Come on in!*" exhorted the faded cardboard sign that hung on the inside of the glass door. "*We're OPEN.*"

Captain Jute got off her bike and tried the door. It was locked. The All-Day Breakfast had finished at last in Dan's Delicious Diner.

She stepped back. Above the roof of the displaced diner more of the rock pinnacles came into view, stark against the empty sky.

She knew now what they reminded her of. She spoke to her distant ship. "They look like those things Dodger found, Alice."

"YOU WILL HAVE . . . MORE SPECIFIC, CAPTAIN," whispered the tiny voice, through howling static.

She had seen them on AV, towering phallic columns hidden in the nether caves of Plenty. Like overgrown stalagmites they had loomed over the members of Professor Xavier's expedition, like monstrous totem poles. Mr. Archibald the exorcist had been there, waving his crucifix at them, intoning against the blasphemy of false idols.

Those things had been identical to these.

Her sense that this was all some kind of practical joke

increased. It was a trap, about to snap shut upon her.

Captain Jute got back on her bike. She circled the building. At the rear there were double doors. They were locked too. Just beyond was the mouth of a tunnel.

There was no doubt about this one. It was too much like the tunnels of Plenty: round, gritty, the walls a waxy brown. It led down at a shallow angle into the ground. Around the mouth of it stood more piles of scrap, mysterious appliances and pieces of furniture. There was a cardboard box with twelve wine bottles in it. They were all empty.

Captain Jute rode slowly down into the tunnel. It closed over her head. The voice of Alice, politely suggesting she not proceed, died swiftly away in her earphones.

Underground, the only illumination was the headlights of the Honeyglide. She picked out a mark on the wall, slight but distinct, at the limit of their beam. She motored slowly along until she came up level with that mark. Then she stopped the bike and switched off the engine. There was no air, and so no sound.

Captain Jute laid an audio mike to the floor. She turned the volume up full.

At first, she got nothing. Then she seemed to be picking up a dry, restless vibration of some kind; a rustling, twittering sound.

She listened a while. It was there. She knew it was. She knew what it was, too. It was unmistakable.

It was the Frasque.

After that she saw them everywhere among the buildings of the Lost City: spindly, spiky, six-limbed creatures sprawling on heaps of trash, like the dragons in her dad's old stories. One, like a cluster of encroaching vines, had twisted itself through a collapsing window frame.

To the ones she spotted, Captain Jute gave a wide berth. They paid her no attention. They stayed completely motionless, all except one which hissed soundlessly at her before whisking away into the darkness.

"It makes sense," she said aloud. It was the first thing she had found here that did.

It made perfect sense that the Frasque should be here, commandeering the discarded toys. Wherever Capella went, Frasque followed. They infested everything the chubby hands had touched, wriggled through each depression the sacred sandals deigned to print.

Perhaps they had invaded the decrepit Capellan home system in retaliation for their extermination in Sol. Or perhaps the other way round. The trouble with reality, thought Tabitha, especially out here, was that it was just as confusing as drugs. There was no scale, no commentary, no way of getting at what was really going on.

She looked at the Frasque wound through the window frame. Perhaps they had been here from the beginning. Perhaps they were the original inhabitants she had been speculating about, in the scenarios they had run on the *Billy Budd*. Perhaps Capella 3 had been their world, before the caterpillars gobbled it up.

". . . IDENTIFY . . . POSITIVELY?" she heard Alice say. ". . . SEEN . . . BEFORE?"

"Yeah," Tabitha replied. "I have." And so have you, she didn't add.

She remembered the Queen of Plenty. She thought of her, lying on her bed of theatrical paraphernalia in the hold of the *Alice Liddell*. She thought of her squeezing Mogul Zodiac until the blood came out of his eyes.

She gunned the Honeyglide.

She would yield the city. She would do the sensible thing, go back to the *Amaranth* and ransack the recreation section for the most potent and time-consuming entertainments and distractions. She would devote the rest of her life to breaking the security codes on the pharmaceutical synthesizers.

She rode back through the scattered buildings, seeking to retrace her route. There was Dan's Delicious Diner again, coming up on the right.

There was someone inside.

*   *   *

It was not a Frasque. She knew that immediately. The silhouette was wrong. This figure rummaging in the depleted cafeteria was not twiggy and insectile but fat and bulky. It was barely able to squeeze between the tables. It was carrying a light of some kind, which it was shining in her direction. Behind the light she caught a glimpse of complicated baggy headgear. She had startled it.

Captain Jute parked the Honeyglide. She pressed her visor to the glass.

Through the visor, through the fuzzy, microscratched window, through the visor of the helmet on the other side, black eyes the size of grapefruits looked into Captain Jute's.

The fat airhose stirred as the snout within lifted in timid recognition.

᠅ 16

The Altecean was an elderly male, grey and balding. You could see the years on Plenty had not been gentle to him. He let her into the diner now with a sort of a mournful dread.

"It's all right," she told him, on a proximity channel. "I'm all right now."

He wobbled doubtfully.

He must have been one of the people she had heard about, who got off the hive the instant it came through. She wondered how many of the others had made for this worn-out world. She was sure they were all around her in the buildings of the imaginary town, hiding from her, holding their breath until she went away.

She sucked oxygen.

"Who else is here?"

He turned the light away.

She swung round to the blank windows, the darkness of the city with no streets.

"Is there anyone with you?"

The Altecean lowered his snout. He began to shake his head from side to side.

"Have you got any food?"

He merely continued the gesture, as if she had not spoken. She knew he must have. She could see the shapes of bags on the floor behind him.

She tried to coax him back to the *Billy Budd*. She pointed to the back of her bike. It was a position for which nature had not designed him. He looked doubtfully at his little fat legs.

"It's warm there," she urged him. "We can breathe."

He was not keen, and not communicative. He stood hunched, as if wishing to keep the booths between him and the windows. Was he afraid the Frasque might spot him?

"They won't take any notice of us," the Captain said.

He put his right paw inside his suit and dug around for a while. Then shakily, and it seemed reluctantly, he put something into her hand.

It was a small packet of white papery material. The paper was thick, and greased. Inside were ten krillsticks tied together with thread.

When Tabitha looked up, all there was of the Altecean was a movement in the shadows.

"Where are you going?" she sent, tumbling over his baggage as she stumbled after him. "Come back!"

By the time she managed to get round the counter and through to the kitchen, there was no trace of him. The double doors at the back of the diner were standing open.

She called him, pleaded with him. There was no reply.

She shined a light down the tunnel. Was he in there? Had he made some sort of deal with the Frasque, trading junk for junk?

"He doesn't like us, Alice."

She would not go down there to look. She had been down enough rabbit holes for one lifetime.

She rode around the buildings for a while, grumbling at him, and at herself for losing him.

"This whole thing was a bloody stupid idea."

". . . LIKE . . . COME HOME NOW, CAPT . . . ?"

"I'm on my way."

She tucked the krillsticks safely into her pocket. She knew perfectly well he had given her them to get rid of her. This was his patch, and he wanted her to go away and leave him alone. It had been, she suddenly understood, a sentimental gesture as much as anything: a tribute to fallen majesty.

At the valley of pinnacles, she made a small diversion to inspect one. Selecting one that stood a little way from the others, she rode all the way around it slowly, shining her lights at it.

For a long time it still looked like a single rough column of splintered rock. Then she began to make out the individual limbs.

She could see now how it had held itself, with all four arms stretched up together around its narrow head. Its toes it seemed to have dug into the dirt, like roots.

She gave it a kick. Vacuum and the red twins had baked it to stone. She got back on the bike and rode on. She was thinking of the *Amaranth Aloof*, with its cargo of desiccated passengers; of the white stone lady, staring up out of her pool of ink.

"Nothing here but cemeteries," she said.

On the third day she noticed the little dot in her mirror. She thought it was following her.

In a little while she was sure. It was creeping after her across the plain.

She laughed. "He went to get his car!"

"HE'S OBEYING YOU, CAPTAIN," said Alice.

"He likes us after all," said Tabitha. She basked a moment in the buzz of a power she had forgotten.

He was thirsty. She gave him water. They sat together in the cockpit, sharing the warmth of the reactor stove. Laboriously he peeled the coverings from his big clawed feet.

"It was an Altecean that taught me to fly," she told him. "I expect you knew that."

He made a wet, snoring noise and spread his sharp red toes.

"Captain Frank, they called him," she said. "What am I going to call you?"

He made a similar noise. It might have been the same one. Equally, it might have been his name.

She paused.

"You know who I am."

"Dabitha Choot," he said. His voice was deep and sticky, his *t*'s like little moist explosions. His tone was despondent. "Dabitha Choot, Haptain off Ple'ty."

"That's it," she said, heartened. "Tell me what I call you again?"

Rubbery grey lids slid across his eyes, moistening them.

He seemed to be grey all over, with several nasty bald patches. Under his suit he wore what looked like several smocks, one on top of the other. He had begun to give off the characteristic stink, like a hot sheep wrapped in a secondhand carpet.

"I could call you Frank too," said Captain Jute, "if you like!" She laughed in an exaggerated way, trying to get a response from him. It was like talking to a dim toddler.

He made a noise like a sneeze.

"O'Shaughnessy?" said Captain Jute. That was exactly the way it had sounded.

The Altecean raised his snout. He looked at her sidelong. He made the sneeze again, slowly.

"Okay," she said. "O'Shaughnessy, okay? O'Shaughnessy."

She spread her shoulders and stretched her arms, pleased with herself.

"Where are you living, O'Shaughnessy?" she asked. "In that diner? Dan's Delicious Diner?"

He didn't react at all that she could see. It was as if he simply didn't understand her, though she was bloody sure he did.

She waved one hand in front of her face. "Alice, more air in here, please." She had put Alice on mute, she didn't really know why, some kind of precaution, of self-protection. But as she did so, the tiny imago had appeared, standing grave and attentive on her holopad on top of the console, her hands folded. Little Alice was taking an interest.

Captain Jute put more water in her visitor's bowl. It was his own bowl, he had brought it with him from his car. "What have you been doing, then," she asked, "since you came down?"

O'Shaughnessy gave another wallowing shrug. "Picking yings over," he breathed, somberly.

She smiled encouragingly. "What have you found?" she asked lightly. "Anything good?"

He blew his cheeks in and out several times rapidly. "Yiss ant yat," he wheezed. She realized she was making him uncomfortable. Her last questions were business talk, and they couldn't be anywhere near doing business yet.

"Have you seen anyone else?" she asked him. "Anyone from the ship?"

He cocked his big head again. "No. No," he grunted. "Gnot hseen enwn."

It took her a moment to realize the last word was "anyone". She cudgeled her brains.

"Do you know Eeb?" she asked. "On the ship? Used to spend a lot of time at the Trivia."

She didn't seem to be getting any reaction.

"Plaited hair, she has," she said. She was gabbling now. "She wears her hair plaited, here—"

She reached across to indicate the remains of his fringe. O'Shaughnessy jerked back in his seat, feet up in defensive claws.

"With beads," said Captain Jute, raising her voice, but pretending nothing had happened. "Colored beads, threaded on."

Her visitor blinked at her in distress.

She pulled her own hair straight down in front of her eyes and peered at him dolefully through it. "You remember. A friend of, she was a friend of—" She waved her hand vaguely in circles. The names were all going.

O'Shaughnessy was looking at his feet. She had the distinct impression he was embarrassed.

"Lived off Meadowbrook, down that way." She recalled the days she had lain there in Eeb's bed, sick of leech poison, surrounded by hoarded rubbish and worried faces, bad news droning from the AV. "She had this one friend, an apothecary, he was really good to me. They both were. I mean . . ."

She let it go. She could see he wasn't listening.

Somehow without her noticing he had picked up the stylus from the charting console. He seemed to be examining it with interest.

She exhaled. "Do you want that? You can have that, if you like."

He put the stylus down hurriedly. He gave her an apprehensive look.

She stood up, suddenly in a bad temper. She could not sit a moment longer in his stink, looking at his stupid hairy face.

His car was parked on the ridge above them. Its immense spherical tires filled the viewport, smooth and round as the heads of Guardians. She had been up several times to the pinnacle that rose above, wondering if that one too had once been a Frasque, or maybe several. It was impossible to tell.

"Why did you come here?" she asked. "Why did you follow me?"

He blinked again, like a preoccupied cow. Delicately he lifted his snout and drank from his bowl.

You couldn't question their motives. It was another bad move.

"How did you get in there, anyway? How did you get inside the diner?"

O'Shaughnessy wrinkled up his face. He looked very old, suddenly, like something that had been walking around for centuries. A wave of stink came from him as he reached inside his clothes.

He pulled out something bulky and jingling.

Tabitha stopped herself from reaching for it. She just looked, to see what it was.

It was a bunch of a thousand keys. There seemed to be all kinds there: mechanical, electronic, chemical. Averting his bulbous eyes in a gesture she knew signified a powerful condescension, O'Shaughnessy held the bunch out clumsily toward her.

Captain Jute touched it tentatively. She stroked one of the keys, then took back her hand.

The atmosphere in the Kobold changed. The Altecean seemed to relax a degree or so. Not for the first time, Captain Jute wished she had some alcohol or something to give him, to calm him down.

"What do you make of it?" she asked him. "What are Frasque doing here?"

Now he looked at her with the long-mouth expression that is the Altecean equivalent of a frown. "Caterpi'ar vork foor Ffra'que," he said, slowly. "Foor Ffra'que. Caterpi'ar." He said it several times, in slightly different ways, watching her closely all the while. She understood that this was something of which he was absolutely convinced, a basic fact he felt she ought to know.

"The Capellans," she said. "Work for the Frasque."

He nodded, tossing his great hairy head emphatically up and down.

She glanced toward the persona unit. Little Alice was sitting on her pad, her arms around her knees. "That's a new one, Alice," said Captain Jute, quite quietly.

Their guest stopped nodding. He looked at the tiny holo and blinked slowly, almost insultingly. He closed his eyes. "Fffra-ahss-que," he announced, laboring to voice the sibilants, "hsent caterpi'ar into h-h-*hsspace*."

Tabitha could make no sense of it. Was it a private delusion, or some sort of Altecean myth? She was sure Captain Frank had never mentioned it.

"What did they send them for?"

For answer, he shook his keys again. Loot, she supposed that meant. "To open us up? So why did they come after them? And why did the caterpillars turn on them?"

O'Shaughnessy pursed his large lips. "Caterpi'ar gnot vringing vack," he said, obscurely.

"They stopped delivering," said Tabitha. She glanced at the console again. The tiny imago was sitting very upright now. It gave the Captain a solemn, doubtful look.

The idea was pure Altecean. In their philosophy there were two universal principles: sale and return. Perhaps he might be right, though. Tabitha remembered the *Resplendent Trogon*, the convoy to Enceladus, the Frasque ship that had accompanied them, always keeping its distance, floating like a silent grey kite across the face of Jupiter. She thought about the Last War, which she had missed completely. On the road, making deliveries of her own.

Suddenly she was extremely skeptical. "How do you know all this?" O'Shaughnessy twisted his mouth.

She decided not to push it until she had talked to Alice privately. There were more important things to do.

"I like your car," she said brightly. "Ideal, really, for a place like this."

But O'Shaughnessy had suddenly stopped understanding

her again. He had become preoccupied with dipping a vast, stained handkerchief into his bowl and moistening the sensitive tip of his snout. She knew that he knew her next question would be about his ship.

"Look," she said, abandoning protocol. "You can see how it is."

She pointed to the rock slope, to the side of the Kobold where she had staved it in. "I've got to get back. You can take me. Well, you can, can't you? I can pay you." She gestured with her arms, like somebody pouring out an immense quantity of treasure. "When we get to Plenty you can have anything you want."

O'Shaughnessy mopped the end of his snout.

Keys, she thought. He likes keys. "You like keys?" she said. She got up and hurried down into the ship. "You'll love this one." Her voice echoed through the empty hold. "It's a Lapham omnipolar . . ."

It was in the backpack. Where the fuck was the backpack?

It wasn't in either of the cabins. "This is the key that got me in here," she shouted, banging into the empty galley and out again. "And it got me onto the—"

The *Amaranth*. Maybe he didn't know. There was an entire legendary bloody liner full of stuff she could give him.

She ran back through the hold and jumped the steps. "The *Amaranth Aloof*," she said, to the empty cockpit.

On top of the console, the tiny phantom was on her feet, pointing out of the viewport in mute dismay. The balloon-tired car was just slipping silently over the crest, out of sight.

"I'm not spending the rest of my life chasing neurotic Alteceans," complained Captain Jute as she rushed out to her bike, which was still hooked up, recharging. The backpack was there too, on the ground, where she'd dumped it.

*   *   *

She didn't have far to go. The car was already parked in a nearby crater. It was empty.

She prowled around, calling on all frequencies in all directions. He didn't reply. He was hiding somewhere, deliberately ignoring her. "I'm not going to chase him," she vowed again. "I'm not."

The last thing she wanted was to antagonize him. She knew how sulky they could be. She confined herself, after a while, to opening his car and searching it, just to make the point. She found nothing but a pile of incomprehensible legal-looking documents and old magazines, brittle copies of *What Robot?* and *Martian Collectible*. She took them one by one to her bike, where she sat and flicked through their yellowed pages, marveling at their innocence, their seductive complacency.

Night fell, black, space-cold. O'Shaughnessy didn't come. Plainly he had gone to ground. "I would stay," Captain Jute told Alice, looking again at the abandoned car, "but I don't want to strain the suit."

"IT WOULD BE A GOOD IDEA TO COME HOME NOW, CAPTAIN," sent the persona, not without a certain sharpness.

As soon as she woke next morning she rode straight back to the spot. The car had gone.

She found him, sometime later, some distance away, pottering among the pits. Spying on him from behind a fossilized Frasque, she saw he had the blue metal bird on the ground with a rope around it. He was pulling it carefully in the direction of his car.

She watched him for a while. "I'm buggered if I'm going to help, Alice," she said. "He'd only think I was trying to claim a share."

She was sure in the end that he knew she was there. She knew she would never find his boat if he did not want her to.

She roamed the listing corridors of the *Amaranth Aloof*, collecting things to tempt him with. It was still a great treasure-house of rubbish. The cabins were littered with sprung wristpads and defunct beverage selectors, haute couture spacewear rotted to gossamer. There were signs of fires everywhere, burnouts in the com lines she had over-burdened, sending out her final distress call. There was no power. Fused lumps of optical fiber hung from the ceilings like cobwebs of molten glass.

"That can't be right," she said, "about Capella working for the Frasque. You don't believe that, Alice, do you?"

"BELIEF . . . NOT AMONG MY FUNCTIONS, CAP-TAIN," sent the persona from the grounded Kobold. ". . . CAN RECOGNIZE O'SH . . . SS . . . S LOGIC."

"Well, yes," said Tabitha. "Obviously." She was edging round a huddle of bones, eyeing the tiara it was wearing. "They all think like that."

"DO THEY, CAPTAIN?"

"Isn't that what you meant?" She scratched her nose. "What did you mean?"

"SIMPLY   THAT . . . CHARACTERISTIC   SENSE-FORM OF THE MACROSC . . . TONE-VALUES IM-PRINT . . . DEEP   CELLULAR   MATRIX   OF . . . INTERPR . . . CORRELATIVE OR PARADIGM OF IN-TERSPE . . ."

"You remember all that from Plenty?" said Tabitha. Whatever it was. "How can you remember all that but not what a Frasque looks like?"

"IT'S A SILICON THING," said the persona distantly. ". . . APTAIN . . ."

Broken and distorted as it was, she heard the voice change, becoming urgent, more mechanical.

"SOMETHING . . . OMING," it said. ". . . CLOSE . . . QUICKLY. QUICKLY."

"Is it O'Shaughnessy?"

"NO . . . SHIP."

She was one deck down. At the top was the observation lounge. The little voice whispering numbers in her ear, Captain Jute went to the liftshaft and started to climb.

*   *   *

On her last cruise, as on all the cruises taken by the *Amaranth Aloof*, the observation lounge had been a popular venue. On and around the large, soft couches, there now reclined the remains of those passengers who had been watching the transit of Neptune when the liner was taken. No doubt they had all been entranced by the savage romance of the water world's fractured seas of lilac and blue, her floating mountains of frozen methane. Now their hollow eye sockets contemplated only the ceiling.

The ceiling and the outer wall of the lounge were one great sheet of glass, unbraced, ostentatiously curved. Tilted upward, it gave only onto the blazing darkness of another Capellan midnight.

In the darkness, close enough to see with the naked eye, shone a small white ship.

As Captain Jute emerged from the liftshaft the ship seemed to be pointing directly at her, seeking her out among the dead like some sardonic magnet. With its sharp white nose it was sucking all the warmth out of her body.

It was not Capellan, or even Eladeldi. It was a Terran space cruiser: a Navajo Scorpion. She recognized it.

"The psycho's Scorpion," she said.

"THE *ALL . . . NGS CONSIDERED*," said Alice.

The ship where Saskia had been held prisoner, tied to a silken bed.

Now it was coming for her.

∽ 17

In the arrival lobby of the *Seraph Kajsa* two of the convocation were waiting: one quite patiently, the other not so.

"By the Crossing of the Chromatids," rumbled Boaz, flexing the joints of the purple armor that encased him. "The creature is taking his time."

Pomeroy Lion slipped a chased-silver hunter out of his waistcoat pocket and consulted it. "Perhaps he means to make his arrival more impressive," he said.

Pomeroy Lion's companion folded his massive arms.

"Nothing a Capellan can do would impress me."

Though he had no actual weight here on board, Boaz was fully five meters tall, and accustomed to being the most significant person in any situation. He had been deputed for this historic meeting nominally to represent Prevision division, just as Pomeroy Lion was here for Capacitory. No doubt, however, the physical appearance of the pair of them counted for quite as much as their official significance. That was the sort of thing Kajsa would think of, like the crude but effective display made by the three-meter statue of Abraxas himself in the red-lit recess behind them: his flail raised, his great beak open in defiance of the Infinite.

Pomeroy Lion adjusted his tie, then compressed the cuticle of his left thumbnail, removing some invisible imperfection. "They are the most appalling race," he conceded. "I should like to have one in the lab."

Boaz's flat features did not stir. "They are vermin," he growled. "They disgust me."

Pomeroy Lion glanced at him sideways with a bleak smile, more rodent than feline. "Still wish we hadn't come, old boy?"

"Eternally," rumbled Boaz.

Pomeroy Lion readjusted his tie. As he raised his chin, his timepiece, insecurely stowed, came drifting out of his waistcoat pocket. It started away like a fleeing Cherub, its chain snaking after like a tail of gold.

Pomeroy Lion chuckled. "There it goes again."

Even as his watch flew away from him, the ship he was waiting for was flying toward Pomeroy Lion.

The ship was a Freimacher Tinkerbell, converted for the paws of an alien pilot. She had left the *Citadel of Porcelain at First Light* some hours previously, guided by a signal issued for that purpose.

Her pilot huffed. "Hsignal hstregdth idcreasig, Mafter," she reported.

"Splendid," her passenger replied.

They were traveling conventionally, the long way around, their route dictated by the fearsome gravity gradients of the inner system. Climbing out of the region of accumulated trash, the Tinkerbell had traced a parabola high above the ecliptic and sailed across a thousand million square kilometers of ash and clinker. Now the tiny ship was falling, falling through the sullen and omnipresent darkness like a falling silver pin.

Searching among echoes and interference, the instruments showed no vessel or habitat at all for tens of thousands of klicks. Still the signal increased and clarified. It seemed impossible that its source remained undetectable to the naked eye, let alone the scanners. They must surely be right on top of it.

Then, against the black absence, there was suddenly a black presence. It was a vast wall, a mere fifty klicks distant.

The wall was smooth and featureless as a mirror. It curved away from them in all directions.

The Tinkerbell's passenger knew the wall was the hull of a ship, a ship that had come all the way from Sol. Her arrival here was unscheduled, unauthorized. The big black invisible ship was an intruder in Capellan space. She had no business here, yet. When the occupant of the Tinkerbell met the occupants of the *Seraph Kajsa*, then they would have business. Perhaps. Ideally.

The Tinkerbell rushed on toward their meeting.

Into the arrival lobby of the *Seraph Kajsa* skated two white-uniformed techs. Between them the techs were steering a slice of sheet crystal held upright in a frame of tubular steel.

More than anything, the device looked like a full-length dressing-room mirror. The view it showed, however, was not a reflection of the two waiting Seraphim, but a prospect of local space: northwest by west, elevation 20°.

The prospect was vast and black, and empty but for a shoal of huge flying bergs of stellar carbon. The bloated stars limned the bergs with the faintest and deepest of reds.

In the center of the crystal screen floated a minute silver fleck.

Boaz regarded the fleck suspiciously. "Is that him?" he asked.

"Identification, 45?" said Pomeroy Lion. It was merely a formality. Tech 45 wore the intricate headgear of a full cerebellum conversion. His right eye had been replaced with a cylindrical implant.

"Positive ID, sir," he said. "One Capellan-human composite, one pilot, presumable Eladeldi."

"One Capellan?" frowned Boaz, clenching his fists of steel. The tech's report seemed only to deepen his suspicions. Behind the giant Seraph the serpent-legged statue glared, as if Abraxas could see the monitor too, and didn't like it any more than Boaz did. "No enforcers?"

The tech whined. "Confirming data," he said. "Data confirmed."

Pomeroy Lion stroked his beard. He too seemed unable to see something he would have expected on the screen.

"Have we not extended the transit corridor, 45?"

"The Capellan has refused it," said the tech.

Perplexed, Pomeroy Lion glanced at his large companion. "Staying on board, is he?" His coattails drifted upward. Absentmindedly he tugged them down. "Cagey."

Boaz's silver eyelids closed. "Cowardly," he said, with audible satisfaction.

"I thought this was to be a personal meeting, Kajsa," said Pomeroy Lion.

"I trust it will be," said the Chief Seraph's voice, from nowhere in particular.

Without touching her, the Tinkerbell docked with the *Seraph Kajsa*. The two craft, the large and the minute, sailed along together in a chaste, magnetic embrace.

Moments later, an oval hatch slid open in the Seraph craft and something spilled out toward the Tinkerbell. Her pilot bristled instinctively. Was this some ambush, some undeclared attack? Discipline held her firm in her seat. Without a specific command from the Master, she was unable to move.

It was a cloud of dark particles, pouring toward them like seed, like bubbles. Each particle was identical: rounded, black and shiny, like a miniature piece of the Seraphic ship. In a rapid stream they raced into orbit around the shuttle.

The Master appeared behind the pilot's seat. "At ease," he said kindly. "It's our welcoming committee."

The company of Cherubim circled. The plump metallic creatures all wore their transparent plastic lifesuits. Liquid rainbows formed and melted on their skin.

Grimly the pilot chewed her antisalivatory gum.

In the arrival lobby of the *Seraph Kajsa* Tech 45 reported a message from the Cherubim. "Limited access to internal view available," he said. "Please authorize."

"Authorized," said Boaz.

"Authorized," echoed the tech.

The screen of the wheeled monitor split in two. The lower half still showed the shuttle, ringed now by Cherubim. There was a short pause; then the upper filled with a murky view of the cockpit of a Freimacher Tinkerbell. That shaggy blue shape was obviously the Eladeldi pilot, sitting stiff in her seat.

The viewpoint swiveled. The Seraphim's ingenious spy device looked down on the Guardians' envoy, preparing now to disembark. No details of his face or clothing could be discerned, but the camera caught the green gleam of an activated finger ring.

"Composite identified as Brother Nestor," reported the tech. "Confirming ID. ID confirmed."

"Apparently he's coming over after all," observed Pomeroy Lion aloud.

"Shuttle airlock opening," announced the tech. "Inner door open. Inner door closed."

The Cherubim could be seen congregating around the outer door of the Tinkerbell as it slid silently open.

Out floated Brother Nestor, inside a sea-green bubble. He waved to the Cherubim, then gestured with another of his rings toward the *Seraph Kajsa*, a hundred meters away and some distance below him.

From the jewel of the ring, a beam of golden light emerged.

A tech waded through the lobby, spraying the air with a mood-elevating disinfectant. It smelled like all the flowers of spring.

Beneath the sandaled feet of Brother Nestor the beam fanned out, like the light from a torch. The Guardian stepped carefully but confidently onto it.

Pomeroy Lion blinked, startled by a tractor projector that could be contained within the stone of a ring. "That's pretty *small*," he said. He seemed almost embarrassed to have to say so.

Boaz narrowed his eyes. "They are small creatures," he said. It sounded to be the most dismissive remark he could ever make of anyone.

The golden beam bore Brother Nestor up. He walked down it, crossing the abyss between the ships. His bubble of air was the merest shimmer against the void.

Pomeroy Lion fingered his moustache.

"45, what do we know about that ring?"

"Checking ring," said the tech. His eyes rolled up in his head as volumes of data sped through it. "Ring unclassified."

*   *   *

Becoming Brother Nestor had not protected him from ageing; or perhaps he had already been elderly at the time of his selection. With a white cloth like a towel wound around his chest and over one shoulder, he looked as if he had come fresh from the barber, from having his head polished. He beamed up at them with open arms. "Welcome to Capella!" He greeted them each in turn. "Pomeroy Lion; Brother Boaz."

"I'm not your brother," murmured Boaz.

Brother Nestor bathed him in a forgiving smile. The creases beside his eyes made him look wise and benevolent. Only the pupils of those eyes seemed a little strange. They were shrunken to the merest specks, as though whatever sat behind them could not stand very much light.

"My name is Nestor, but you know that already," said the Guardian. He turned toward Pomeroy Lion, pressing his palms together like a conscientious curate. "How is dear Kajsa?"

Pomeroy Lion ran his thumbs along his watch chain. "She's very well, actually."

"And are you all recovered from your long journey?"

Boaz straightened his metal back. "We are in the finest fettle, Capellan."

"We'll, ah, take you to Her Polysomaticity at once," proposed Pomeroy Lion quickly, to smother his colleague's hostility. Though no such intention had been made apparent in the initial contact, these people already had a grievance against the mission, should they choose to invoke it.

"I shall be honored," said Brother Nestor.

"You will," said Boaz.

Swiftly the Head of Capacitory ushered their visitor on into the ship. The armored giant followed, bowing and touching his forehead and his chest to the statue of Abraxas as he passed.

The statue remained, roaring silently at the empty lobby.

*   *   *

The Guardian was escorted to a spherical chamber, right at the very center of the ship. There Kajsa Prime hung unsupported, surrounded by half-naked page boys and girls. Each of them was connected to the golden belt Queen Kajsa wore by a single pineal plug and a lead, both also of gold.

The Prime had changed her appearance for the meeting. Her hair was still black but now it was much longer. She had had it curled and swept up into an inverted pyramid, cut with microfine geometric precision. She had put on a long dark grey hobble skirt, and a blouse of grey with vertical stripes of white and pink. The shoulders of the blouse projected, flat as landing strips. Each was long enough to have seated three Wisps side by side.

When the Guardian entered, the Priestess Queen of the Seraphim raised her arms in a gesture uncannily like the one with which he himself had greeted Boaz and Pomeroy Lion.

"Brother Nestor," she said. "We are Kajsa Tobermory, in prime person. You honor us with your presence."

"Congratulations, Your Consubstantiality," said the Guardian, and he flew to her. "We are so delighted you were able to come and visit us."

"We have our colleagues to thank for that," she replied, twisting her head away from his enormous skull as he embraced her.

Two pages, a chubby pink boy and a girl pale as ivory, came forward to offer loops and stirrups of golden silk. The Guardian waved them away. "Or would you prefer gravity?" asked Kajsa Prime.

"Not at all," said Brother Nestor. Crossing his ankles decorously, he assumed a polite sitting posture. "We only wish it could have been you who brought the hive."

"In a sense, it was," said Kajsa serenely. "Sweet Lavender will tell you all about that. We're sure we can't."

Pomeroy Lion supposed these disavowals of credit were part of the subtle arsenal of femininity, like the narrow skirt, the jutting bosom. He wondered, though, how much a Capellan would care for such things.

"This system must have been magnificent once," said Kajsa Prime. "What a shame it's in such a mess."

Brother Nestor shook his great head sadly. "Which of us can stop time?"

"Neither of us," she answered gaily. "Yet."

Brother Nestor spun foward about his midsection, his left fist on his snowy breast. "Together we could!"

Startled by the Guardian's sudden movement, Boaz made a grab for him. Pomeroy Lion restrained him. This was still Kajsa's show.

Brother Nestor developed his display of adoration, prostrating himself upon the air. "We have so much to offer each other, dear lady."

"You only want us for our bodies."

"They are the very best bodies."

"Yes, but they're our bodies. And we like them the way they are."

Kajsa Prime stroked one of the buttons on her sleeve. A small girl, brown as cocoa, swam to put her arms around Kajsa's hips, and hugged her as tightly as if she had been her own natural mother.

Another girl, quite identical, also came forward, bearing steaming bulbs of blown glass in a napkin.

"Please, Nestor," said the Prime. "Do have some wine."

They toasted each other, and relaxed into courtly manners. Brother Nestor was frank, and spoke of other species for whom his had formerly had hopes. "The Palernians are so sweet. But quite impossible, really. They're so very vulnerable, and they actually have quite a nasty temper. The fact is, I'm afraid, they're just not very bright!"

He twinkled at her.

She sipped her drink. "Don't tell us you didn't fancy being one of five," she jested.

"Oh, that would have been strange," he concurred. "To be restricted to that."

The temperature in the room seemed to fall for a moment.

Kajsa ignored it superbly. "Talking of fives," she said, "we have a couple of people here we know you'd like to meet."

A page boy rose, with a large brass handbell. His coordination was so perfect, he contrived to ring it, despite the absence of gravity.

Sweet Lavender came in, wearing his white suit with a deep red shirt. He brought with him Saskia Zodiac and Xtasca the Cherub.

Brother Nestor greeted them genially. "Oh, but I know these two well," he said.

"No you don't," said Saskia.

A smile made a slight crack in the silver slab face of Seraph Boaz. The clone looked at him warily. She knew this one had not yet forgiven them for leaving the Garden.

With a flap of his wings, Sweet Lavender wafted the prodigals forward. Brother Nestor came and took them both unself-consciously by the hand.

"I'm delighted to see you both alive and well," he said. "What a fright you gave us, disappearing like that!"

Rudely Saskia reclaimed her hand. "It was her fault," she said, indicating Queen Kajsa. "She took Angie."

The Queen Seraph lowered her eyelids in a decorous imitation of shame. "We do feel terrible about that, Nestor," she said.

Pomeroy Lion cleared his throat, and knuckled his moustache. "Yes, they did rather go overboard, didn't they," he said faintly.

"Please accept our complete and unconditional apology," said the Queen, "on behalf of the section responsible." She looked fondly around her little flock of pages, as if it might have been a couple of them who had committed the assault on the Capellan ship. ''An excess of zeal for the sake of our finest creations.''

''Actually they tried to kill us,'' Saskia pointed out.

The angel laid the tips of his right fingers in the palm of his left hand. ''What *were* they thinking of?'' he said airily.

Saskia looked at Xtasca. It was saying nothing. Its eyes were open, but unlit. She tried to emulate the Cherub's impassivity, while the man with the caterpillar in his head beamed into her face.

''Such strength,'' he said.

''Her siblings were more frail,'' said Boaz sternly.

''But they all live on in her heart,'' countered the angel, sentimentally. ''It's sisterly love that keeps her going.''

Saskia began to think of ways to kill herself.

''Yet she is not vengeful,'' said Brother Nestor to Sweet Lavender, above her head.

''Not often,'' smiled Kajsa Prime.

''An exemplary piece of humanity,'' said Brother Nestor.

Saskia met his eyes. ''I'm no more human than you are,'' she said.

The Seraphim shared a flutter of polite embarrassment, like adults when an innocent child says something tasteless.

''And this one's even more clever,'' said Brother Nestor, floating over Xtasca. ''The way they got out of the *Citadel*!''

''They're full of tricks,'' said Kajsa Prime.

The Guardian smiled, as if at his own reflection in the Cherub's shiny skull. ''And entirely inorganic, I understand! Yes? Brilliant, brilliant. Who was it designed them?''

He looked at Kajsa, then at the others. Seeing no one put themselves forward, he said: ''Not one of you?''

''Xippy's busy, I'm afraid,'' said the Seraph Queen. She sketched an apology with her dark green eyelids, but the point was made. Brother Nestor's visit did not take precedence over all other business on board the *Seraph Kajsa*.

"Where is Tabitha?" demanded Saskia Zodiac. "Have you found her yet?"

Brother Nestor folded his wrinkled hands. "I expect we'll trace her soon."

"Of course you know where she is," said Saskia.

"She is the most sympathetic creature!" said the Prime to the Guardian, as if she meant to sell her to him. She sent a page to hand round chocolates. "Saskia first," she said.

Meanwhile Brother Nestor and Pomeroy Lion were murmuring confidentially. "Fertile?" Saskia heard the Capacitory Chief say. "Yes, there's every chance . . ."

She opened a mouth full of half-chewed chocolate and saw the Seraph blanch. "I'd eat any child of mine before I'd let you take it!" she yelled, indistinctly.

It was enough. The angel shepherded them away.

Kajsa Prime drew a circle with her index finger on her opposite wrist. "You see the problem," she said. "Organic or not, determine the intelligence, and it's a drone. Don't, and it's over the fence as soon as you take your eyes off it."

She flashed her teeth at the Guardian, who inclined his great head as if he knew exactly what she was talking about.

"But we're getting ahead of ourselves," said the Prime. "You must come and see what Pomeroy's up to."

"Oh, yes, absolutely," said Pomeroy Lion. "Sure you'll find this most interesting, Nestor. This way, if you wouldn't mind."

"We'll take the chariot," said Kajsa Prime.

As they rode through the corridors it was clearly the Cherubim that still preoccupied their Capellan visitor. "They came out to say hello," he told them with pleasure. "So very capable, and yet so very dainty. I suppose there's a size restriction, Pomeroy, is there?"

Queen Kajsa laughed. "Look at Boaz," she said. The

giant tramped noisily ahead. The length and power of his stride more than compensated for the awkwardness with which he moved.

"Erm, outside my area, in fact," said Pomeroy Lion to the Guardian, "but size is not the problem, exactly, if you've got the right material. The problem is organization. To make anything much bigger than Boaz there you'd need to build in multiple coordinated internal command centers."

"Multiple brains, he means, Nestor," said Kajsa chummily.

Brother Nestor gave an eerie twitch. The Seraphim looked at him sharply, but when he replied it was with perfect self-control. "Ah yes," he said. "I remember the giant saurians of old Terra, with their two brains, one in each end."

Boaz stopped in his tracks. "By the Blessed Blastosphere!" he boomed. He turned round, gazing at the white-clad figure in the Priestess's chariot as if he were on a dish under a microscope. "Were you there?"

Brother Nestor did not laugh. "Not at the time, no," he told him. "Nor on Venus either, though I believe similar solutions have evolved there."

"There's a whole galaxy of things to see," said Kajsa Prime, as they swung into the laboratory sector and settled alongside Cubicle 24.

"This is much the least significant of them," said Pomeroy Lion, loudly, as the cubicle doorway disinfected them. His tone somewhat belied his words.

Cubicle 24 was quite small, and shuttered. The only person inside was a technician, a black man in a white suit with a large number *10* on it. Dumbly he led the inspecting Guardian between the walls of stainless steel, the panels of microscopic gauze that let in the cleaned and filtered and systematically modified air. He activated the window that let them all look in on the plump salamander in its incubation tank.

"This one, of course, is, um, organic," Pomeroy Lion informed their visitor, moving aside to give him a better view.

Brother Nestor peered in at the transparent creature afloat in pale yellow fluid. "Another little Saskia?" he asked.

"We trust not," said Pomeroy Lion, embarrassed. "But that was the source material, yes."

Brother Nestor pressed the palms of his hands together. "The very best bodies," he said again.

Pomeroy Lion cleared his throat. "Just for comparison, you understand. Research purposes. Unlikely to be viable . . ."

"Having no head," Brother Nestor concurred. He spoke with some feeling, being so overendowed himself in that respect.

"By the way," said Kajsa, as the Guardian was leaving. She had been thinking of Saskia's remarks, which had troubled her slightly. "Do you really not know where the little bargee is?"

The Capellan ambassador looked regretful. "She can't last much longer, wherever she is," he said. "It is, as you say, a bit of a mess out there."

The Prime gave a smile of beautiful perplexity. She even put her head on one side.

"You could have disposed of her with the twist of a ring," she said, "anytime you chose."

"What a shame that would have been," said Brother Nestor. "She can be so very entertaining."

No one replied.

The Guardian spread his hands then, looking at his rings. "You were admiring this one, I think, Pomeroy?" he said.

He showed the ring whose amber stone emitted a pathway of solid light. There was no way he could have known, of course.

"Here," he said, removing the ring from his finger. "A parting gift." He held it out to the Head of Capacitory.

Stammering, "Terribly generous—don't know what to say," the Seraph took the ring.

Boaz was already ordering the techs to put out the transit corridor.

∽ 18

"I thought you were never coming," said Captain Jute.

"So did we, gel," said Captain Gillespie.

She stood in the observation lounge of the *Amaranth Aloof* with her hands on her hips, looking around at all the dead passengers. She wore an anonymous vacuum wrangler suit, silver-grey, and a pair of dented old motorboots, their bearings streaked with thick grease. There was a Corregidor 9S9 strapped to her back. She was ready for anything.

"That is yours, that Kobold," she said, requiring confirmation. She gestured with her chin. "Ten klicks back that way."

Casually she dusted off the knees of her suit. "With a big hole in it," she said.

"It is," said Captain Jute.

Dodger Gillespie gave a ghostly smile that exposed only the tips of her fearful teeth.

"This is nice, though," she said.

She stooped to examine a folded figure with the worklight on her chest. It wore what had probably once been expensive lounging robes: a man, a woman—it was no longer possible to tell. Gingerly, as if feeling for muscle tone, Captain Gillespie put her fingers around its limp grey wrist and lifted.

Trickling little bones, the hand fell off.

Tabitha choked a giggle.

Dodger looked at her.

"You don't half pick them," she said.

Tabitha did not reply.

Dodger Gillespie looked at her more closely. "All right?" she said.

"I am," said Captain Jute. "God knows how."

Her old shipmate continued to look at her. Starlight glinted on her sockets.

"Thanks to you and Jone and Alice," said Tabitha lightly, "and to the kind owners and operators of the *Billy Budd* and the *Amaranth Aloof* who let me onto their vessels without a boarding pass—I am all right."

It was strange, having a real conversation with a real live human being again. It was a good job it was Dodger. Dodger understood.

Tabitha Jute had met Dodger Gillespie so long ago she could no longer remember where it was or when. They had worked the same runs, in and out of the Tangle. They had hung around the same places, the low-rent dorms with their lowlife bars. Nix Corrigan and May Lee hogging the biggest table, arguing crosscut angle-mounted against fifteen-valve; Sam Konstantinopoulos in the corner, scribbling mad poems on bits of paper; and up at the bar, Dodger Gillespie and Tabitha Jute, surveying the talent. Dodger Gillespie had lent her credit, covered her screwups, pulled her out of a hundred tight corners in her time. When Alice was lost on Plenty, it was Dodger Gillespie that had found her.

In the corridors on their way out, Dodger ran her light along the charred and melted wiring.

"This you too?"

"Yep," said Tabitha.

Dodger Gillespie scrutinized the damage caused by Captain Jute's final broadcast. She blinked a hard, reptilian blink. For a moment she looked as though she was about to give her an estimate for the repairs.

"You were lucky," she said.

"You heard me, didn't you?" said Tabitha.

"Just barely," said Dodger, scratching one of her sockets. "We've got some good kit."

From the airlock of the abandoned liner Tabitha could make out the racy profile of the *All Things Considered*, parked cautiously some meters away. In the gloomy red light she thought she could see a figure in the cockpit.

"Who's that in there? That's not Jone, is it?"

"Karen."

"Karen Narlikar?"

"Yeh." Dodger worked her narrow jaw. She was looking old, suddenly, and tired. Tabitha turned away.

"No one else was going to come," Dodger said.

Tabitha turned back, ready with a matey retort.

Dodger coughed. The hard, flat sound echoed around the quarterdeck.

"You think I'm joking."

As they worked their way down the tilted hull, Captain Jute spotted a familiar silhouette on the edge of the crater.

"Hey!"

He must have heard her. She saw him shuffle down behind the ridge, out of sight.

Dodger Gillespie shaded her eyes. The gun was already in her hands. "It's O'Shaughnessy," said Tabitha.

"Who?"

"O'Shaughnessy," she said, scrambling over the obsolete control surfaces, peering down in the darkness for a safe place to jump. "He's an Alt," she called as she went. "One of ours."

She landed softly in the light g, stones bouncing up from under her feet.

She waded past the Honeyglide, up the side of the crater to the spot where the Altecean had disappeared. Obviously he had been attracted by the Scorpion landing and come to see what was happening. They should take him away with them. Perhaps he would listen to Dodger.

He was not in sight. She ran on around the rim of the next crater, looking in all directions.

"O'Shaughnessy!" she called. "It's okay! Friends!"

There was only the aching silence of the dead planet.

Captain Jute trailed back to find Dodger Gillespie. She was sitting against one of the rock pinnacles high on the ridge, the Corregidor in her lap.

The smell of her habitual roll-up was richly familiar.

Tabitha gave the rock a thump. "Recognize it?"

Dodger looked her in the eye.

"The ones on Plenty," she said.

"You know what they are, though."

Captain Gillespie put her head back and looked up the rocky spike, then turned, surveying the others that stood black against the night.

Tabitha traced the outlines for her. "There's one arm, there's another . . . One here . . . That must have been the head, in the middle."

"Christ Almighty, gel," said Dodger in a low voice.

Tabitha shrugged.

"There's live ones in the city," she said.

The hell with it. None of this mattered now. O'Shaughnessy could have it all.

Dodger was walking round the fossil Frasque. She had met a live one in the depths of Plenty, where none should have survived. She would not willingly meet more without a flamer in her hands.

"Elderly females, they are, most of them," said Tabitha. "They didn't give me any trouble."

Captain Gillespie sucked thoughtfully on her cigarette. "Did you want to find your friend?"

"Nah." Tabitha thought of O'Shaughnessy sneaking around beneath the dead striplights of the diner with his bunch of a thousand keys. She thought of the dismay she had seen on his snouty face when he had recognized her. "He's got his own boat somewhere."

Captain Gillespie snorted. She looked up at the *Amaranth*, and around at the land of twenty thousand pits, with all its hidden treasures.

"Altecean paradise," she said.

"How did you get hold of this?"

Tabitha was considering the Scorpion. It deserved its name. The sleek white curve of it was sheer menace.

"They let us bring it," said Dodger Gillespie. She wagged the extinct cigarette end in the corner of her jaw. "It's all right. It's clean."

"I'm surprised," said Captain Jute.

"Atkins helped."

"Atkins?"

"The persona."

The strength was starting to flood back into Tabitha's muscles.

"You know whose it was," she said, still wary.

"Yeah." Dodger Gillespie bared her teeth in a meaningless grimace. "Your number one fan."

Frustrated, Tabitha took hold of her rescuer and shook her by the arm. "What do you mean, they let you take it?"

Captain Gillespie spat out the butt of her cigarette. It bounced once and disappeared into the dark green shadows.

"Let's go, shall we?"

Inside the rear section of the *All Things Considered* Captain Gillespie clipped the Corregidor into a rack. There were a surprising number of other weapons there. Tabitha reached out to touch them.

Her old friend deflected her.

"Not yet."

"Why not?"

"No need."

"Why not?"

"Cloak of invisibility. True," said Captain Gillespie, walking on.

They squeezed along the gangway, past all the extra com equipment, bulky receivers and sophisticated detection hypercompensators installed by the Scorpion's previous owner. Dodger rapped a prominent knuckle on one smoke grey casing. "This is the stuff we picked you up on," she said.

"You knew who it was."

Dodger sniffed and barged on ahead. "No one in the universe plays harmonica like you," she said. Even as she walked, she was rolling another cigarette.

Tabitha followed her through what must have been the stateroom, where the loony had held Saskia. Now there were crates of medical supplies in there; a life-support cradle, like the one Angie had had on the *Citadel*. Pillaged from some wrecked hospital, a clinical oxygenator stood poised over the cradle like an inquisitive pterosaur.

"In case," said Dodger Gillespie, nodding at the equipment.

"I'm fine," Tabitha told her, looking away from the pharmaceuticals. "I just need a shower and bed. And some decent food!" she said.

"You look like shit," said Dodger seriously, putting a light to her cigarette.

"You look like shit," retorted Tabitha, irritated by everything suddenly. "Everybody looks like shit now." The strength she had been starting to feel drained again from her body.

The air was pierced by a sudden alarm.

"What?" Tabitha shouted. "What?"

"Smoke alarm," grumbled Dodger. "Atkins, we said to disable that."

"JUST BEING CAREFUL, CAPTAIN GILLESPIE."

While the man called Nothing was occupying the Scorpion, the persona had been isolated. "WE HAD A DIS-

AGREEMENT," it said, primly. "IN FACT WE HAD AN ENTIRE CONCATENATION OF DISAGREEMENTS. HE WAS UNABLE TO RESOLVE THEM, SO HE BY-PASSED ME."

Karen Narlikar was really pleased to see Tabitha. She hugged her hard. "This is all right!" she said. "We'll do some celebrating now. All right!"

Tabitha drank coffee. "I have to get Alice," she said.

Karen grinned. "Is that her?" she asked. "In the Kobold? You knocked that about a bit, didn't you?"

"I'd like to have seen you do it on one wing," said Tabitha. The last time she had seen Karen Narlikar had been at Eeb's place, when she was half-dead, people burning herbs under her nostrils. Before that Karen had been around, on and off, all journey. It came back easily, the basic bullshit camaraderie. "How does this thing handle? Like a bloody powder puff, I bet."

"THE SCORPION *ALL THINGS CONSIDERED* IS AN EXTREMELY VERSATILE HIGH-PERFORMANCE OFFWORLD VEHICLE," said the persona. "ACCELERATION 55 OVER 7 TO A CRUISING SPEED OF 3800 CONVENTIONAL. PLEASE DEFINE *POWDER PUFF*."

"Don't get narky, Atkins," said Captain Narlikar, latching up her web. "She never went out on anything of your class," she said, and she winked at Tabitha.

The chart console was a little flap in the back of the passenger seat, more like something to stand your cocktail on. Dodger was working on it. "Back to the Kobold first, Atkins," she said.

A light flicked on and off as signals zipped between the two ships, across the ghastly terrain.

"BERGEN KOBOLD BGK009914, THE *BILLY BUDD*," said the Navajo Scorpion persona.

Karen and Dodger looked at Tabitha.

"That's right," she said, and prodded her wristcom. "Are you getting this all right, Alice?"

"INTELLIGIBILITY SATISFACTORY, CAPTAIN, THANK YOU," whispered the little voice on her wrist.

"Low as you can, Atkins," said Captain Gillespie.

"COURSE CONTOURED AND LOCKED," said the persona. "ON YOUR COMMAND, CAPTAIN NARLIKAR."

"Here you go," said Karen, typing.

With barely a tug, they were up.

Karen beamed back at Tabitha as they tore through the thin rags of atmosphere. "Good, eh?"

Dodger handed Tabitha more coffee and a fruit-concentrate chew bar. "Lights out, Atkins," she said. Even before the words were out they sat in darkness.

Tabitha Jute watched the nightbound land slipping past below. It was like gliding over a giant black sponge.

"What is all that stuff," Karen Narlikar asked her, "in the pits?"

Tabitha shrugged, chewing. "Cosmic garbage dump," she said. "How did you get your hands on this?" she asked, meaning the Scorpion.

Karen laughed. "It wouldn't go," she said.

"Strangest thing," said Dodger in the darkness.

"She said they gave it to you," said Tabitha to Karen.

Karen gave Tabitha a merry look. "Lou got it, to break up for scrap," she said.

"Shame," said Dodger, behind.

"They ain't got a clue," pronounced Karen.

Tabitha turned round to Dodger. "Where did you get to?" she asked, at last.

Dodger was watching her monitors. "They had me cornered in Montgomery for three days," she said. "They didn't know they had, but I was all over."

Tabitha waited. She looked at her companions' heads, silhouetted in the burning darkness: Karen's curls, Dodger's cropped skull. No one spoke. The ship raced on.

"So then?"

"*I* don't know," said Captain Gillespie. "I was stuck up a chimney."

"Dodger!"

Her old friend relented. "Someone started a rumor I was somewhere else," she said heavily. "To get them excited. Then someone else got me out."

"Was that Karen? Karen, was that you?"

"Nah," said the woman in the pilot's web. "I was down in the docks, waiting for her. We was all waiting for her, weren't we?"

Tabitha drank her coffee. "Who was it, then?"

"Some of Rykov's lot," said Karen, without a qualm.

Tabitha turned up her nose. "Redcaps?"

Dodger Gillespie gazed at her screens. "Things have changed, gel."

Tabitha was full of caffeine and restless energy. "They're going to change again, now," she said.

Dodger made no comment.

"How bad is it?" asked Captain Jute.

Karen answered her. "They can't run that place. They're worse than you were. They're worse than she was, Dodger, ain't they?"

Tabitha let that pass.

"They ain't got a clue," said Karen again. It was a firm opinion of hers. "Only the Frasque can run that place. Stands to reason."

Captain Jute wound her fingers through the straps of her web. "O'Shaughnessy says," she remarked, "that the caterpillars work for the Frasque."

She could see Dodger squint. "Work for them?"

Karen made a derisive noise. "Don't add up."

"KOBOLD SIGHTED," said the ship.

"On-screen, please, Atso," said Karen.

"PLEASE WAIT," said the persona crisply.

"He don't like it when you call him Atso," said Karen.

"I'm not surprised," said Tabitha.

* * *

In the cockpit of the *Billy Budd*, little lights shone steadily. The water purifier bubbled softly to itself. Her hands in her pockets, Dodger Gillespie was examining the wiring of the solar collector. "Did you do this?" she asked Captain Jute.

A camera swiveled.

"HELLO, CAPTAIN GILLESPIE," said Alice politely. "HOW NICE TO SEE YOU AGAIN."

"Hello, Alice," said Dodger, scratching her chin as she surveyed the alterations. She spotted the little holo in its pinafore and striped stockings. "Cute," she said.

The holo curtsied. "I UNDERSTAND I HAVE YOU TO THANK FOR MY CONTINUED AVAILABILITY."

"It was Jone, really, Alice," said Dodger. "She'd got used to looking after you."

"She made a mess of my bag," said Captain Jute. She lifted the backpack out of a cluttered corner and pointed to the doodles that covered it. "What does all this stuff mean, anyway?"

Dodger pointed to SCREW CAPELLA. "I know what that means," she said.

The things that wouldn't go in the backpack Tabitha tossed into a plastic crate. It was amazing how much she'd managed to accumulate, even here. It was all from the *Amaranth*, nowhere else: clothes that were perfectly okay, tools still serviceable, vacuum-sealed nutritional supplements.

"Don't forget him," said Dodger. She leaned in the doorway of the cabin, smirking at the pin-up on the wall.

"It'll be a wrench to leave that behind," said Tabitha, not making a move toward it. She contemplated the glamour boy, his preposterous pose and cheesy grin. "He looks a bit like Marco Metz," she said. "Don't you think?"

"ARE YOU LEAVING AGAIN, CAPTAIN?" asked the patient voice from the wall speaker.

"You're coming too, Alice," said her captain, going back into the cockpit. "I'm going to have to turn you off again for a bit, though, okay?"

On her holopad Little Alice looked taken by surprise. She opened her mouth and pressed her little pink hands to her little pink cheeks, gazing at her feet as she telescoped down into a point of nothingness.

"I'm putting you in my bag," said Captain Jute to the persona, as one by one the command circuits shut down.

"IF YOU DO FIND YOU NEED ME AT ANY TIME, CAPTAIN, ALL YOU HAVE TO DO IS PLUG ME IN," said the speaker, then fell silent as Tabitha pressed the button, ejecting the grey plastic plaque into her hand.

"We shall need you, Alice," she promised. She pulled on her backpack.

It was a fraction before dawn. The blue pool glimmered blackly as Captain Jute and Captain Gillespie made their way up out of the pit. At the top, Tabitha turned and gave the white stone woman a wave. "Bye bye, dear." The statue stared at them, unmoved. "Bye bye, *Billy Budd*."

From the cockpit of the *All Things Considered* Captain Jute took her last look at the savage landscape with its fossil phantoms, the greedy mouths of the craters that had failed to swallow her. She gave a contented sigh. "Goodbye, cruel world," she said.

"You'd better strap up, Captain," said Karen, at the controls. "This thing has got a kick."

As the first of the red twins began to rise, the Scorpion kicked. It leapt clean into orbit, whirled once round the nightside of Capella 3, then veered out into space.

On the port beam, a cluster of the lumpy moons went drifting by. From the passenger seat Tabitha pointed them out.

"I suppose you took a look at those."

"Old hives," said Dodger.

Captain Jute dabbed her finger against the glass, making an unserious attempt to count them. "Plenty 2, 3, 4, 5, 6, 7, 8 . . ."

"They are dead, aren't they?" said Karen.

She meant the question for Tabitha, but Dodger answered it. "They're dead," she said.

". . . 13, 14, 15 . . ."

They left them floating uselessly around the derelict planet and went burning away through the long cold dark.

〜 19

L ife on the *Citadel of Porcelain at First Light* seemed to suit Odin the one-eyed cat. He had filled out, within the limits of his small frame, and was often to be seen scampering through the corridors of Sector Y. The Guardians smiled and pointed at him, but Odin ignored their cooing overtures and avoided their stroking hands. He would trot past, looking very important and busy.

Eladeldi he detested. Whenever they were coming to conduct another "debriefing," Jone would always know. Some minutes beforehand, Odin would start to bristle. He would not settle until he had secreted himself in the farthest corner of the dorm, behind a bunk. If they were actually coming in, he would disappear altogether.

He might be gone for whole watches, at any time. Three or four decisive encounters had earned him the respect of the cats already in residence, and he could make himself at home in any dorm.

Jone, who affected to take great offense at his vagabond ways, sat on the bunk where she had tracked him down.

"Check in, cat."

Odin, dozing, was enfolded and caught up by two bare, skinny arms decorated with swirling patterns. He struggled briefly but not very seriously. Instead he assumed a preoccupied air, as if it were beneath his notice to be picked up and dumped without ceremony in his mistress's lap, with a hand pressing down on his shoulder blades.

Jone hummed a little tune.

Several men were lounging about the dorm, watching AV, playing poker. "She's in a good mood," said one, aloud.

Jone chuckled, scratching Odin's head. "She got her gal," she announced to the room in general.

Heads turned from the screens. "Who did?"

Jone made the tight-lip sign they all used to signify something not for Capellan hearing, then leaned down and spoke into the blue-tattooed ear of her cat.

"She got her, Ode."

Odin's head shook rapidly, vibrating. Jone's breath had tickled him. The men were smirking, passing cryptic comments between themselves. Those who knew what she meant were those with least to say.

From the pocket of her dungarees the crop-headed young woman pulled a collar. It was a filament of transparent plastic, no thicker than string.

Beneath her hand Odin turned his head. Affectionately Jone pressed a palm to his face. "Dee-dee-dee-dee-dee," she sang.

Around the little cat's neck she fastened the collar. It was hardly visible against his coat.

She held him up to look at him. Under his chin a little bubble now hung, like a miniature identity capsule. Inside it, a tiny piece of paper could be seen.

"Dee-dee-dee-*dee*-dee-dee-dee-*dee*."

Odin hung limp and boneless between Jone's hands. His tail waved elegantly, ceaselessly.

She carried him to the door of the dorm, and pitched him out into the corridor.

"There you go, slick," she said.

On Plenty, the poorest passengers were the denizens of the Crap Chute Rookeries. Since the days after the Emergence, when Sister Contenta had removed the most misshapen of their children, no Guardians had been near. No one had put their names on any evacuation roster. Whenever any of them tried to venture out of their quarter to see what was happening elsewhere on board, Eladeldi would appear and harry them home.

In truth, there were few of them who did not prefer the squalor of the rookery caves to the terrors of the unknown. Still they would complain of neglect to the priest, when he visited in his tight sequinned trousers and ornamented coat. They lamented the children that had been taken, and the others who had followed of their own accord.

By twos and threes, the brightest of the remaining youngsters had sneaked down into the docks and inveigled themselves onto departing shuttles. They had forsaken their families for the ship of the interstellar overlords. There were some who continued to believe that they had gone to look for their baby sisters and brothers, but most took the darkest view, as usual. It was easy, in that dark place.

Father Le Coq, for his part, continued to praise the Lords. In Maison Zouagou, the Tabernacle of Dreams, among the helium-filled effigies of prominent Guardians actual and spritual, he maintained at the top of his remarkable voice that all was well, and according to the great plan. All the folk who had disappeared were surely waiting for them, whole and well, on the *Citadel of Porcelain at First Light*. Soon everyone would be taken over, and there they would be reunited. Lord Elvis would be there, and the Palernian would lie down with the Thrant!

The organ swelled. The spotlights whirled. The congregation cheered, blessing themselves and their benefactors.

In fact, on their arrival at the *Citadel*, the space slum children were rapidly identified and rounded up. They were deloused, bathed, and perfumed, and brought to Sister Mansuetude, who dressed them in the sweetest little white tunics and sandals, and treated them with special favor. Some were being taught to read or play a musical instrument; others, to pour wine or wait at table.

Full of wonderful sights and sounds, of healthy air and abundant food, their new lives absorbed the urchins utterly. They were young, and adaptable.

Still, they retained an affection for one of the young volunteers who had devoted much care and many hours to their upbringing in the bowels of Plenty, and who was now to be heard broadcasting musical entertainment to all the public Sectors from Radio Xtasy. The Calico Show came on at irregular intervals, like everything on that very irregular station, but whenever it was announced, books were left open and harps set by while the girls and boys gravitated to the nearest receiver.

To a listening adult, much of what Radio Xtasy broadcast was tedious nonsense. It consisted of repetitive, mechanical "music," continuous without form or melody, whose lyrics, when there were any, sounded more like recitations of the frequency-modulation tables. Still it made the little heads nod, the little eyes shine; and when Calico spoke, as he often did, interrupting the music at random with messages of vague goodwill and cryptic exhortations to "honor the bass" and "check the deck," the children of Plenty spoke back, imagining he could hear them. The older ones liked to program their dorm AV screens to reproduce the latest catchphrase, in letters that gradually morphed into long feathery spirals, like wandering leaves, or dancing snails.

"Captain D signing on," it was today. "Captain D signing on."

The children seemed more delighted than ever by this announcement. Who was Captain D? their tutors asked suspiciously. The mouthy ones, Maz and Tarmac and Landy, all knew everything about it, as usual, and all talked at once. Captain D seemed to be one of the bewildering array of AV cartoon characters they knew, each of them with their own colored uniform, theme song, secret power and animal partner. It was something they had used to enjoy on Plenty, presumably.

A check on the dj in the Radio Xtasy studio showed nothing untoward. He sat there with his feet up, doodling with a sample of his own voice. "*Captain D*," Calico made it say, higher and lower, while he absently stroked the pale grey cat that lay sleeping in his lap. "*Captain Dee-dee-dee-dee-dee-di-di-dee.*"

Along the Sector V corridors a black kid ran. He wore a white tunic, bare legs and sandals, and a scaled-down datavisor with built-in headphones. He was a human kid, far from where any human kid was supposed to be. "Hey!" woofed the Eladeldi on guard duty. "Hey, you!"

The boy put his head down and ran faster.

The Sector V guard bounded after him and caught him. "Nabe?" he wheezed, threateningly.

The boy in the visor smiled vacantly at him.

The guard glanced up and down the vine-draped passage. There were no Masters around to see. He held the boy with one paw and cuffed him with the other, then tugged the visor right off his head.

"Nah!" complained the boy, grabbing at it.

The guard held the visor over his head, out of reach. "Nabe," he demanded.

"Maz," said the boy.

"Where frob?"

Unwillingly, Maz showed his affinity bracelet. He was one of Sister Mansuetude's strays.

The guard glared sternly. "Vis Fector V."

"Yeh?" said the boy, in a manner half-shy, half-surly. He was quite young still, the guard thought, and should be taught to be more obedient.

He bent lower. "Where are oo goig?" he asked, articulating as carefully and clearly as he could.

The boy jogged from foot to foot. "To see Bim and Dixti," he said.

"Do, you're nod," said the guard. "You're cubbig wid be."

Radio Xtasy was a ramshackle, amateurish project run by some of the young people from Plenty. It was the sort of thing they had been doing for years, they said, disseminating music and inspirational utterances through the caverns of the alien hive.

The Guardians had no objections. They hardly used the AV studio suites of their starship, preferring self-decorating chamber environments and live acoustic music. The youngsters' hobby seemed to keep them occupied and out of trouble, even if what they produced was unpleasant to an adult ear. "Sure, I can dig it," was Brother Melodious's response. "I just find that kind of stuff a little cold, you know? A little lacking in empathy."

In the studio next to Calico's, Erika sat taping a tune that had been nagging at her brain all watch. It wasn't hard. All you had to do was run a line from the desk into your auditory center and think the tune right onto the disc.

Erika had grown up on Plenty. She had no memory of going there, or of being anywhere else before. She didn't even remember where she had had her sockets done. She had always had sockets. Her whole life had been spent with Calico and the others, Jone and Larry and Jaz and Anno, cutting and mixing matrix code for Xtasca the Cherub.

In some ways, the *Citadel* was a step up from that. Her circuitry, though alien, was already largely comprehensible, and her power supplies more reliable. There were stacks of bandwidth, and the musical archive the Capellans had compiled in Sol System was virtually unlimited. There was every chance of Erika finding a match for her little looping memory fragment, whether it was originally Debussy or Dogsbreath.

Waiting for the interfaces to engage, Erika idly clicked on Calico's show. When she heard the nonsense words circling, her tune dropped into oblivion. She jumped up, pulling the plug from her head. She ran into the control room. Calico saw her. He reached for a tape and put it on. A dreadful wheezing noise came over the speakers. It sounded like someone trying to play the harmonica at the far end of a tunnel filled with squawking birds and whistling insects and frying bacon. To this unlikely tune, Calico and Erika contrived to dance together, grinning idiotically at each other through the glass.

Throwing caution to the solar winds, Erika called up Jone to get the whole picture. "Check Cally, special girl," she purred, as if this were simply girl talk about a boy. "Is he integral or what?"

Jone did not speak. Perhaps she was out. Her com played the Calico sample back down the line to Erika. "*Captain Di-di-di-di-di-di-di-dee*," said the monstrous voice, and the dreadful wheezing noise sawed between the syllables.

"D is for dancing," Erika told Jone's com, and she went round the studios turning up all the speakers.

Colonel Stark pushed back her cap and looked up in the air. "The Kybernator's orders are that the operational timescale of the evacuation is to be extended," she confided.

"Oh, what a shame," replied Sister Mansuetude.

"With communication to affected personnel on a demonstrable need-to-know basis only."

"Quite," said the Guardian. In her mauve and lilac gown she floated among the trees of Sector W. "We don't want the poor dears to start worrying, do we."

A couple of meters below, the colonel folded her arms behind her back and looked at the grassy floor.

Their solar orbits were drawing the two starships, the Frasque and the Capellan, ever farther apart. The shuttles were exceeding turnaround time estimates. To disimprove an already grossly unsatisfactory situation, it now seemed that the *Citadel* accommodation sectors assigned to the evacuees were reaching capacity.

Somebody, Stark felt uncomfortably, somebody some-where had screwed up.

She was inclined to blame the Eladeldi. Disciplined and efficient as their forces were, as a species they lacked ini-tiative, and looked at all times to the nearest Master or Mistress for authorizations trivial and nontrivial. Their brains were small, and though they excelled at intelligence-acquisition, they themselves were rarely capable of re-sponse to anything but the most recent order.

The colonel slapped the trunk of a tree with her glove. "Surely the maximum inhabitational capabilities of this vessel were known when—"

"There are such a lot of them, aren't there?" said the Guardian sympathetically.

As she spoke, Sister Mansuetude saw the boy Maz com-ing toward them across the bridge, escorted by an Eladeldi guard.

"Hello, Maz," said Sister Mansuetude. "What are you doing here?"

The guard saluted her, then the Redcap colonel. "Fe boy was enterig Fector V," he panted. He lifted Maz's arm to show his bracelet, and exhibited the confiscated visor.

"Sector V! You were a long way from home, weren't you?" Her hands clasped, Sister Mansuetude looked down at Maz benignly. She was waiting for an explanation.

"Going to see Bim and Dixti," said the boy, in a lifeless tone.

Colonel Stark saw Sister Mansuetude's eyes go glassy as she consulted some invisible resource.

"Bimprilic and Dixtimifst Niscshopuar," announced the Guardian. Then she looked to the colonel for explanation of what she had just said.

"Vespan entertainers," said the colonel. "Former owner-operators of a traveling circus. We experienced sev-eral mutual encounters concerning violations of council livestock and traffic regulations."

The colonel and the Guardian looked at the boy.

"Why would you be going to see them, Maz?" asked Sister Mansuetude.

The boy looked at the trees. He rubbed one of his sandaled feet against the other. "Say hello," he said.

The guard clutched Maz's arm. He held the datavisor up for the Mistress to examine.

Colonel Stark reached over and intercepted it. "Here, soldier," she said. "That child's set is unserviceable for Sister Mansuetude's cranial dimensions. Allow me."

The colonel put on the visor.

Her eyes filled with pink-and-orange fractals, her ears with a noise like a swarm of robot insects chirping loudly in unison.

Sister Mansuetude dropped down and took her errant charge by the hand. "I don't think we need to do that just now, Maz," she said. She thanked the guard for bringing him to her, and promised she would take the little chap home.

While the Guardian spoke and Colonel Stark stood staring into strobing infinities, a small grey animal ran silently and swiftly by, ignoring them all. Tail held high, it bounded over the bridge and disappeared.

In the protein bath, Bimprilic Niscshopuar surfaced. Green water jetted from every sphincter as her float bladders filled.

Considering they had had to be specially installed, the baths were quite good, really, if a little small. This one was just large enough for her and her husband Dixtimifst, besides Humbuntifosp Cantruplit, who lay just behind Dixti, ignoring the two of them politely and reading an old magazine. In the other bath Snabligulip Chikluarbont lay gossiping comfortably with two of her friends while their children clambered indiscriminately over all three of them.

Though all their needs were provided for, Dixtimifst looked somnolent and sad as ever. Bimprilic wobbled and wallowed over to give the folds of his darling bellies an immodest and flatulent kiss.

Dixtimifst smiled and rolled his beautiful bulging eyes. He patted the water with his fans and curled cumbrously around his wife's reassuring bulk. Bathing with her always made him amorous.

He blinked, showering Bimprilic with water from his luxurious lashes. "Beacon of my meandering," sighed Dixtimifst. "Comfort of my confusion."

Respecting the feelings of the other bathers, Bimprilic drew away again, as far as she could. In the other pool the children were tootling merrily as they slithered over the grown-ups' limbs and jumped on their bottoms.

Dixtimifst gazed unseeing at their antics. He still missed the circus, with its selection of pathetic, lovable beasts of all worlds; but the Capellan ship was not without its own intriguing fauna. In fact, there was a specimen of it now.

It was a small semiterrestrial quadruped, a feline. Bimprilic sat on the edge of the pool, trying to coax it to jump onto her ample thigh.

"Where has that come from?" asked Dixtimifst Niscshopuar, in Vespan.

Humbontifosp put down his magazine. Everyone was looking at the animal. The children were keen to rush over and look at it as closely as possible. Fearing danger or disease, their parents were holding them back.

Bimprilic had already noticed the tiny bead that dangled from the creature's throat. Carefully she dried her fans and began manipulating it.

Dixtimifst and Humbontifosp clambered out of the water and surrounded her, ignoring the shrill complaints of the children, who could no longer see.

With the dexterity of the elephantine, Bimprilic opened the bead and extracted the little square of paper it contained.

"What does it say, dearest?"

Jone had not, it seemed, decided to let everyone who

encountered her pet know who he was and where he belonged. It would never have occurred to her to do such a thing. All she had written on the paper was two capital letters, with a stroke dividing them: D/T.

Silently, Bimprilic showed the paper to her husband.

As she did so the animal suddenly escaped her and went frisking over to the children, innocent and spry as any kitten. While their deafening squeals of delight rang out to the microphones overhead, the three adults drew into a huddle.

"It is the Dodger, Captain Gillespie," said Bimprilic, in their native tongue.

"Is she on board?" asked their bathing companion hoarsely. "I had thought—"

"No, no, no, Humbuntifosp," rumbled Bimprilic, interrupting him rudely in her excitement. "It is not the Dodger that sends it, but it is about her. This D, you see, signifies her."

Her husband furrowed his face in thought. "And T, illuminating Bim?"

She jabbed the paper with her fan. "T stands for Tabitha! For Tabitha Captain Jute!"

Abandoning her offspring to her friends, Snabligulip came rolling over to where Bimprilic sat, dangling her nether extremities in the protein. "Is she found?" she demanded, squeaking at several orifices with the unnatural effort of whispering. "Is she now found?"

"She is even now conjoined again with Dodger Captain Gillespie," said Bimprilic softly, "which is meant by this leaning line, between their two signifying letters!"

Humbuntifosp grinned carnivorously around the company. "So now the fun shall begin."

The youngest of the Vespan children sprawling after it, gurgling insistently, the feline trotted back to Bimprilic, as if concerned to make sure she understood. Daintily the little grey animal reached up and touched its nose to her bulbous cheek.

Somehow the little piece of paper had become stuck to Dixtimifst's right fan. He sucked it off with his mouth. Rolling his eyes solemnly to left and right, he swallowed it.

∾ 20

Techs 10 to 13 had been detailed to report to the arrival lobby with jetbelts, which probably meant something to pick up and transport inboard. They didn't discuss it, they just went there at speed, flashing priority signals at all traffic junctions.

In the lobby loomed Seraph Boaz, with one palm raised. "Halt!" he trumpeted, unnecessarily.

The techs canceled their momentum, jets swiveling. They hung in the air, in attentive attitudes.

In the lobby with Seraph Boaz were two Capellan Brothers. They floated at the door to the transit corridor, which was open. One Brother was holding a silver egg about seventy centimeters long, surrounded with a thick collar of the same metal. The egg was steaming strongly.

"Recognize Brother Valetude," said Seraph Boaz, formally.

Brother Valetude had a white lab coat on, an old-fashioned one with buttons sewn down the front to hold it closed. Loose around his neck hung a strange conical pendant of silver metal on a pair of black-rubber tubes. It was not clear how it managed to stay in place without the aid of gravity. He smiled, and patted his egg.

"Recognize also Brother Nestor," said Seraph Boaz. There was no warmth in his voice. He took no pleasure in this duty.

The elder of the occupied humans nodded his swollen

head at the techs, catching 10's eye. It was almost as if he meant to recognize him as an individual, as if he was actually pleased to see him again. Brother Valetude, on the other hand, merely looked pleased with himself.

Tech 10 didn't like the local parasites being admitted to the ship. It made everything feel compromised and unclean. Nevertheless, it was no part of a tech's job to have opinions. His job was to take the egg and carry it as swiftly as possible to Kajsa Prime, who was waiting in the reception chamber.

"And heed this," Seraph Boaz declared. "The flask holds tribute for the Priestess of Abraxas. Let it be treated with the greatest *care*—or terrible will be the *consequences*!"

The giant Seraph in the pink-and-purple armor gestured dramatically. In his red-lit niche the statue of the cockerel-headed god looked as if he were screaming his assent.

In the spherical reception room Seraph Kajsa Prime floated in her long grey skirt as before, with her flock of pages slaved to her golden belt. She lifted her hands in surprise when they brought her the silver egg, as if she had not been receiving continuous secret intelligence reports since the second it came on board.

"Your Supreme Proficiency," intoned Boaz in a voice like concrete setting, "Brother Nestor has returned to pay his compliments."

He gestured at the elderly envoy as if the Prime might have forgotten which one he was.

"And Brother Valetude accompanies him," said Boaz, "with tribute."

The Prime Seraph's voice was strong and clear. "Nestor, what a lovely surprise!" Her flat-topped coiffure tilted toward him, like an orbital platform maneuvering. "And Valetude! How nice to meet another newcomer. With a present! For us!"

"Not so much a present as a piece of lost property,"

said the younger of the Guardians, in a complacent, nasal voice.

Tension in the chamber heightened a fraction. The techs were unarmed, but the Queen might have killer reflexes invisibly triggered in any or all of her little pages. When she spoke again, however, nothing but pleasure and well-modulated greed were apparent in the tone of Kajsa Prime.

"Well, we have our Cherub back," she reflected, "and our clone too. What can this be, I wonder?"

She pressed the palms of her hands together. The pages swam forward, surrounding her like fairy courtiers encircling Titania.

Its carrying straps clipped to purchase points on the wall, the silver egg hung in the center of the chamber, steaming like a pressure cooker. Its mirrored surface was misted with condensation. There were no markings.

The vessel was so cold it seemed to be draining all the heat from the chamber. Brother Valetude had held it casually, in his bare hands, but the techs were obliged to handle it with insulating gloves.

Tech 10 wondered what the Capellans could be bringing Queen Kajsa that needed such consummate preservation.

"Is it safe?" asked Seraph Kajsa, with a thoughtful smile.

"Absolutely, dear lady," said Brother Nestor obsequiously.

"Well, go on," said Kajsa to Tech 10. "Open it."

Tech 10 bowed. He planted his feet securely and switched on his traction soles. Then he grasped the wheel of the catch.

The egg was massive. The catch was solid and elaborate as an airlock's. Try as he might, it wouldn't budge.

"I'm sorry," said Brother Valetude, though he sounded more amused than apologetic. He curled his left little finger and pointed the stone of the ring it bore toward the egg.

There was a tiny *peep*.

Brother Valetude said, "That should do the trick." His elder colleague nodded in an encouraging manner.

Tech 10 tried the wheel again. It spun freely. Securing rods *clunked* back into their housings in the collar of the egg, and it came open. Clouds of dry ice started pouring out.

The upper half of the egg tipped back on a hinge. The clouds redoubled until they threatened to flood the chamber.

Inside the silver egg was a glass jar. Tech 10 pulled it out. With the palm of his glove he wiped the frost from its surface. He held it up to show the Prime.

"We thought you might like to have him back," said Brother Valetude, in his self-congratulatory tone.

Inside the jar was a human head.

Superbly poised, Kajsa Prime pressed one of the fabric-covered buttons on her long sleeve.

A small naked brown boy swam round in front of her to know her bidding. With finger and thumb the Prime pulled the little gold plug out of his forehead. She gave him a kiss on the empty socket. "Go and fetch Pomeroy Lion," she told him calmly.

The page spread his arms, bowed, and flew.

Brother Nestor blinked froggishly at the Prime Seraph. "Don't you recognize him?" he asked.

Kajsa Prime peered into the jar. "Could be anyone, really, from here," she said lightly. "Bring it closer."

Tech 10 obeyed.

The Prime bent close to the frozen glass.

The head was male, clean-shaven, with what looked like a full head of very black and shiny hair. The eyes and mouth were closed.

The jar was full of some kind of preservative medium. Despite its temperature the medium was clear, and liquid as water. A string of tiny bubbles rose from the nostrils.

"Not one of us," said Kajsa Prime. "On Plenty, was he? Some kind of ancillary, perhaps," she remarked, to Boaz, whose metallic face revealed no response. "He doesn't seem to have had any kind of conversion . . . Has he a name?'' she asked the visitors, pleasantly.

"Several,'' answered Brother Valetude; but he vouch-safed none.

Pomeroy Lion arrived. He produced a magnifying glass from his waistcoat pocket and held it to the jar.

"Human male,'' he pronounced. "Caucasian. In his thirties, I'd imagine.'' His voice quavered slightly. "Would that be right, gentlemen?''

Boaz stood with his broad breastplate opposing the Guardians. He seemed to believe that a significant wrong had been done.

"Where is the rest of him?'' he boomed, balefully.

Brother Nestor spread his hands. "Unfortunately,'' he said, "this was all we were able to save. He was a bit of a mess, actually.''

"But we have given him our very best attention,'' said Brother Valetude suavely.

"And we thought it might do splendidly,'' his colleague concluded, "for your new clone.''

The Brother Capellans smiled an identical smile.

"The head,'' said Boaz loudly, "is not occupied?'' Sternly he glared at their own distended crania.

Brother Valetude assumed the condescending air of the expert required to speak of his speciality to the ignorant. "One of us did go in, initially,'' he said, "just to stabilize it. With a decapitation, that's all that can be done. We were fortunate it was quite recent.''

"You don't recognize him?'' Brother Nestor asked the assembled Seraphim. His voice bore a tinge of regret.

Pomeroy Lion hemmed and brushed the points of his moustache with the knuckle of his index finger. "Hard to say,'' he said; but his eyes flicked guiltily to Kajsa, who floated there in majesty, her black lips curved in a smile of fury.

Pomeroy Lion hated lying.

* * *

Meanwhile, in Diagnostics, Sweet Lavender was at the com, posting data back down the hyperband to base, to the Temple, which hung like a lacquered mausoleum among the moons of Jupiter. Stretched over fifteen parsecs, the signal was not of the clearest or most stable, but compared to the froth and fizz of local communications it was positively crystalline.

"This is the last packet, Adriel," said the angel, yawning, as the techs prepared the transmission. "Are we ready?"

"*Ready, Capella.*"

"I do wish you wouldn't call us that."

"*Sorry, darling.*"

Sweet Lavender rolled his eyes in irritation, and lifted his little finger. "Transmit," he said.

A package of reconstructed Frasque flight code, filtered and compressed, went winging through the cosmic infrastructure. Its passage sounded to the angel like an orchestra of flutes playing very rapidly somewhere a long way away.

"*Receiving,*" said the woman at the Temple.

There was a slight pause. "*It's all going in beautifully,*" she said.

She might, to judge by her words and their tone, have been watching liquid being pumped into a mold, or blood into a cardiovascular system. There were, in fact, certain correspondences, between the circulation of blood and oxygen in the vertebrate body, and the fluid dynamics of information. That principle had been central to the calculus that had produced the cerebral interface socket. The material extracted from 13709 made it more evident still, in Sweet Lavender's opinion, despite the fact there were huge chunks for which not even the Cherub had been able to offer a translation.

"Make plenty of copies, Adriel," he said. "We might need that, if you ever get your mojo working."

His voice had become clipped and distant. He doubted very much that condition would ever be fulfilled.

In the wake of the collapse of the Capellan force in Sol space, Temple personnel had boarded and examined ships of various manufacture, all of known interstellar capability. In each they had tried the three other surviving Sanczau Kobold personas that were configured for the Frasque drive. None had produced any result. Every article of design information it was possible to derive had been transferred from the engines of those ships to experimental ones being constructed from first principles in the Temple's orbital workshops. A dozen Solar years later, the progress that had been made on them amounted to nil.

The Seraph called Adriel was hardly more sanguine than his winged counterpart in Capella. "*See if they haven't got a spare one knocking about that we could borrow.*"

"Negotiations are proceeding," said Sweet Lavender, in tones of deep boredom. Kajsa and Pomeroy had hopes of getting some advantage out of the locals, he didn't. "*Seraph Kajsa signing off.*"

The angel signaled the techs to terminate contact and flipped the phones out of his ears.

"Here. Here," he commanded. "Undo me. Careful, you idiots." It took four of them to remove the com harness without getting his feathers caught in the straps.

Sealed inside a meter-wide plexiglass bubble in Schematics, the prodigal Cherub was engaged in sorting and filing information from a pair of its fellows, out with the mapping machine on its trials. Fifty million kilometers away, they adjusted the instruments and shot back the data, while the robot cartographer waltzed among the rocks, counting and plotting them, shining spectographic lasers at anything larger than a beach ball.

The Schematics chief had set Xtasca up with a board, set on passive receive and in parallel. Everything it was doing was duplication. He would not give it anything it could possibly influence or alter. Xipetotec disapproved mightily of the way it had been let loose on the ancillary's tapes by

Diagnostics. He had refused even to observe it at work, though he had taken a copy of the tapes and would be combing them hard for signs of tampering or falsification.

Xipetotec was observing now, rather more attentively than it might appear. He hung beside the bubble, eyes half-closed.

Like a plump metallic merbaby in a bowl, the Cherub floated hunched over its board. The lights glittered on its skin. Sometimes Xipetotec almost wished it would do something wrong, give him something to use against it.

The defect that had originally caused it to abscond had not yet been isolated. Everybody had theories. Typically, Sweet Lavender's was the ugliest. "It isn't individualism at all," he opined. "It's atavism."

Pomeroy Lion had concurred. Even replicated in silicon, what was the protoplasmic cell but a set of defining conditions? Perhaps whatever aped that structure was certain to end up developing the property of independent volition.

The angel found that delicious. "Original sin," he said.

Pomeroy Lion had raised his eyebrows and pulled down the corners of his mouth. "Quantum genetics," he said, and shook his head. "Hm. I shouldn't like to get into that."

Xipetotec was not to be swayed by sophistry. The Cherub named Xtasca was a faulty model, that was all. Its increased capacities could be harnessed, if never trusted. Watching it now, obedient as a drone, its slender silver tail dotting about the board precisely as any cake-icer, Xtasca's designer felt he could begin to allow himself a provisional sense of satisfaction at a problem reframed as an opportunity.

Xipetotec returned to his own work. With minute calculations, he was using a standard designing stylus and galactic atlas to put together what would have looked, to anyone who might have taken a glance over his shoulder, like a miniature constellation.

Unlike the ancient terrestrial constellations, with their fancied resemblance to charioteers and livestock and maidens carrying water, this design of the Seraph's seemed entirely abstract. Unless Kajsa Prime was able to secure values for the individual components, it would remain so.

The Schematics Chief would mind very little, either way. The work interested him for its own sake, regardless of any eventual practical application. It was fascinating to be able to make projections involving so much power.

Later Xipetotec lay naked in the boudoir of Kajsa Prime in a snow-white hammock, between the capable legs of Kajsa Prime herself. She straddled him in the light gravity she preferred, generally, for sexual activity. She still wore her black basque and black nylon stockings. Her knickers she had removed some time ago.

Her partner put his hand on her thigh. "Are you still angry?" he asked her.

"No." Thoughtfully she slipped her right breast from its cup.

Xipetotec lay back, his hands beneath his head. "He was a poor associate," he said. "We used him because the situation was urgent, and he was convenient."

"It's not *him*," said the Queen of the Seraphim, exposing her left breast too. "It's *them*. What do they mean by bringing us the head?"

She seemed to have recalled her anger.

"What do they *mean* by it?"

Her colleague contemplated the fierce mounds, their twin black nipples aimed at him like weapons. He levered himself up on his elbows and gently touched the tip of his tongue to the one on the right.

"They're telling us we're fallible," he said, in a while. He had no wish to meet the embassies of the Capellans, and was continuing to avoid them. "They want us to know that they know how fallible we are."

Kajsa Prime pulled Xipetotec's hairless head in to the canyon of her cleavage. "They're so *fucking* patronizing."

She reached down the smooth length of his back. With

one black fingernail she traced the deep blue designs that had been tattooed on his skin, outlining the musculature beneath.

"We got the bloody thing here, didn't we? Well, didn't we?"

The Chief of Schematics Division on the Capella mission knew her question did not need an answer.

He pressed the palm of his hand between her legs. She was warm there, and perfectly human.

The Seraph Queen closed her eyes and put back her head, savoring the sensation for a second or two before pushing him back against the hammock. "It was easier to deal with the Frasque," she said, reminiscing.

His soft black penis was still curled up. She smiled as she slid a finger beneath it and stroked the underside.

"All they wanted was toys and pretty things."

Xipetotec caressed the inside of her thighs, running his fingertip down her taut suspender and around her stocking top. "And they wanted their caterpillars back," he said.

"But what do the caterpillars want?" she asked him. "That's the question, now," she said, as she coaxed him upwards.

"They want us," he said.

Her voice was melodious as she agreed. "They really want us. The trick is, separating what they might want to do with us from what we can do for them that they can't do for themselves."

Xipetotec thought this over.

"I do hate having to deceive Boaz," he said.

Kajsa Prime kicked one long leg out over the side of the hammock, launching herself slowly into position.

"The Capellans will chew us all up in a second," she said, as with a wriggle of her hips she docked him inside her. "If they see some advantage in it."

Xipetotec's tongue was long. He bathed her breasts with it.

"No Capellan will ever chew you up, Your Persistence,"

he murmured. His voice had become quite high.

"Whatever their objective—" the Prime began, as she made herself comfortable. Then she shouted: "Lights out!," and behind the white gauze veils a page flew to plunge the boudoir into darkness. "Clearly they are in this now," she went on, thrusting, "for everything they can get."

Ultraviolet light gleamed on her eyes and teeth. Between her thighs the anatomical tattoos of her Schematics Chief glowed like an illuminated diagram. The Prime raked his ebony chest with her nails.

"Would you fuck one, Xippy?" she asked. While his voice had risen in pitch, hers had become deeper. "Would you fuck one of those bigheads?"

"Would you, madam?" he replied.

Kajsa Prime laughed. She lifted her head and closed her eyes, concentrating on locating the first of her orgasms.

In the laboratory sector, in Cubicle 21, the head had been removed from its jar and warmed. It lay on the bench, faceup in a chafing dish. Electrodes had been attached to the main fibers that protruded from the torn stump of the spinal cord, and accelerator nutrients injected.

Boaz looked at it gloomily. "By the Great Divergent Dendrites," he swore. "What manner of *evil* lurks within this despicable skull?"

Pomeroy Lion fingered his little beard and studied the transverse scans that hung in groups on the monitors all around. "It's clean now, actually," he said mildly.

For comparison he called up the pictures they had acquired covertly from Brother Nestor during his first visit to the *Seraph Kajsa*. Inside his head the tightly coiled occupant was clearly visible.

"Clean," said Boaz contemptuously.

The eyes of the head twitched open.

The left eye was a replacement, according to Brother Valetude. It was hard to tell. Both were identical: lustrous whites, soft grey irises, large black pupils, greedy and dilated. The work was of a higher standard than Pomeroy Lion would have expected from the kind of biolabs the hive had had when it left Sol. The point was not lost on him that the Capellans knew more about human engineering than they seemed to. Either that or they had been able to appropriate someone who did. Which would be more their style, of course.

The brain was another issue. It must have been damaged, when the Thrant tore the head from its neck, and afterward, during the period when the head lay on the floor of the stateroom, starved of oxygen and blood. Large sections of the cerebrum had since been excised, and replaced with some kind of filmy, cobwebby material. Was that prosthetic too, or parasitic? They had nothing to go on. Brother Nestor had waved aside their inquiries. "The only thing that matters is, will it do the trick?" he had said, with a narrow smile. "We're all looking forward to seeing how you get on."

The grey eyes slid to the left, then back to the right, then to the left again. There was rhythm in the motion.

Boaz watched, unimpressed. "Clean," he grumbled. "I would tear off my own right hand before I would touch it."

Pomeroy Lion cleared his throat and patted down his drifting coattails. "Well," he said lamely. "it'll be interesting."

Boaz frowned, looking more closely at the pasty, waterlogged face. "Lion," he rumbled. "The lips! By the Interstitial Bond! It's trying to speak!"

"Good Lord," muttered the Capacitory Chief. "Tech," he called. "Tech. Here, please, quickly."

Into the glass enclosure came the black man in the white suit with the number 10 on it. Hurriedly but neatly he clipped a neural amplifier into the place of the lost larynx, and plugged in an electric voice box.

The voicebox spluttered. It crackled. "*Where is she?*" it

said. "*Where is the jumped-up little ba-a-a-a-rgee that stole my world?*"

The voice was attenuated and mechanical, devoid of human tone. It did not seem inappropriate for the pale dead face.

Instinctively, Boaz had spread his fingers and lifted his hand to screen that face from his eyes. He raised his hand as far as his chest, and arrested it there, as though he scorned to complete a gesture prompted by fear. "Who is it that it speaks of?"

The grey eyes swiveled toward the giant Seraph. They focused on him in a way both accurate and cold. Pomeroy Lion ran his handkerchief over his forehead. He found himself perspiring.

"*Of Tabitha,*" whispered the voice box. "*Of Tabitha J-J-Jute.*"

∽ **21**

"**O**kay, Atkins," said Karen Narlikar. "Let's work this out, shall we?"

"PARAMETERS PLEASE, CAPTAIN NARLIKAR."

From the copilot's web, Dodger Gillespie gave Captain Jute the narrowest of smirks. "He likes Karen," she said.

"IT'S GOOD TO BE FLYING AGAIN, CAPTAIN GILLESPIE," said the Scorpion persona. "ESPECIALLY IN THE HANDS OF PEOPLE WHO TREAT YOU WITH SOME RESPECT."

"That lets you out, gel," said Captain Gillespie.

"I'm happy," said Captain Jute.

She was feeling a bit out of it again, now there was someone else to do what had to be done. From the comfort of the passenger couch she watched Karen's fingers moving slowly but unerringly over the keyboards.

"What we want, then," Karen was saying to the ship, "is target P—keeping maximum distance from enemy vessel C—avoiding traffic, if there is any—and avoiding PHD—"

"Doctors?" said Tabitha. In her mind she saw a smiling man with a stethoscope, his head swelling and swelling while he smiled and smiled.

"POTENTIALLY HAZARDOUS DEBRIS, CAPTAIN JUTE," said the ship. "NOTABLE CLUSTERS VISIBLE TO YOU NOW AT 310°, ELEVATION . . ."

"Oh, right." Captain Jute pinched a fold of her T-shirt and smelled it. It smelled disgusting.

Karen typed on. "Top speed at emergence—and your lovely light diffraction shield up—"

"FACTORING IN CONCOMITANT POWER DRAIN," said the ship.

"Yeah," said Karen. "No stops for fuel."

"IT WILL BE TIGHT, CAPTAIN NARLIKAR," said the persona seriously.

"Bloody tight," said Karen Narlikar.

Karen Narlikar was a typical rootless spacer. She had left her home when she was very young, spent her adolescence rattling around the inner planets, picking up what she could here and there, until she came to rest on the rough asteroid obscurely known as Shagger's Back. There, by the traditional expedient of lying about her age, she got herself signed on with the resident mining company, who taught her the bare minimum of skills needed to fly an ore train. Thereafter Karen had taken easy options, long-term contracts, mainly, back and forth between Terra and Mars. Plenty had been her idea of a fun place to go, to play the casinos and get drunk, and as much as anything to watch all the other people who were doing the same. She could not have been more delighted to be on board when the whole installation suddenly skipped.

Dodger was asking the ship something. She wanted to know if a message had gone to the *Citadel of Porcelain at First Light*.

"AT 42.56.06, CAPTAIN GILLESPIE," said the persona. "RECEIPT TAGGED AT 43.18.40."

"What message?" Tabitha sat up. What could Dodger have been saying to Perlmutter? "Was it rude?"

"Just to let Jone know we've got you," said Captain Gillespie.

"They'll have read it," Tabitha pointed out, meaning the Guardians. She was not enjoying this sense that things were being done on her behalf but without consulting her.

"It wasn't exactly something you can read," said Dodger, and she looked pointedly at Tabitha.

"IT WAS A STRANGE WHEEZING NOISE, CAPTAIN JUTE," said the persona helpfully, "QUITE DEVOID OF INTELLIGIBLE CONTENT. I MUST SAY IT WAS NOT APPARENT TO ME HOW THE INTENDED RECIPIENT WOULD DECODE IT, LET ALONE ANY UNAUTHORIZED EAVESDROPPERS."

Karen and Dodger were laughing. Dodger started coughing.

"You're all right, Atso," Karen said merrily.

"I MUST APOLOGIZE FOR CONTRADICTING YOU, CAPTAIN NARLIKAR," said the ship, inflexibly. "MY EFFICIENCY RATING HAS NOT YET RISEN ABOVE 85%. THE ACCUMULATED EFFECT OF THE PROLONGED ABUSE MAY REQUIRE SOME DOWN-TIME TO RECTIFY."

It started going on about its light-diffraction shield again. Tabitha thought about invisible spaceships. Seraph ships could be pretty well invisible. She had seen one once, just about.

"You know the Seraphim are here, don't you?"

"Now how did she know that?" said Dodger to Karen.

"The Kobold told her," Karen supposed. "Or her Alt."

"O'Shaughnessy the Irish Alt," said Dodger, patting her pockets. "He told her a thing or two."

Tabitha bristled. "What's that supposed to mean?"

Dodger was pulling out her tin of makings. "Nothing, gel," she said amiably. She put her head on one side and gave her a crooked grin. "Just winding you up."

"It was Xtasca told me, as a matter of fact, if you want to know," said Captain Jute sullenly. "It left a message, a message you could read. I worked it out."

Dodger Gillespie teased a pinch of tobacco into a paper. "There's no holding you, gel."

"ARRIVAL AT SKIP POINT IN FIFTEEN MINUTES, CAPTAIN," said the persona.

They moved into hyperspace as smoothly and swiftly as a hot knife slicing through plastic. Colorless nothing embraced them.

Dodger and Karen took turns at the helm. Tabitha offered. She argued, she started to nag. Karen said it didn't matter, she was happy to do it, Tabitha ought to rest. Dodger would start to talk about famous crashes.

Tabitha had begun to feel she had lost something—faith, respect—that she'd always taken for granted from Dodger Gillespie. It was because of the way she'd given up, toward the end there. Or perhaps it was just that they were both getting older, older and less patient with an increasingly unpleasant universe.

Between shifts, Dodger relaxed in the stateroom, watching old black-and-white movies. She didn't offer to put them up on the screen so Tabitha could watch them too. As far as Tabitha could tell from the samples in the menu, the principal features of these movies were busty young women in fur bikinis and muscular men in little skirts and sandals. The attraction was beyond her. She went and sat up front with Karen.

In row upon row of microscopic digits, green and amber and blue, the Capellan drive knitted up the fabulous absence. Karen, concentrating, grunted a greeting as Tabitha lowered herself into the copilot's web.

For a time, the silence did not yield. Then several blocks of code cleared all at once, going down like four-dimensional dominoes. Karen sat back with another grunt, this one of satisfaction.

"So how is Eeb, do you know?" asked Tabitha awkwardly.

Karen's Altecean friend had taken Captain Jute in when she was comatose, and helped to hide her while the mutiny was raging. Tabitha had been meaning to ask about her ever since she had come aboard the Scorpion.

Karen shrugged. "I don't know. They all disappeared when the 'deldi came on board. I don't think she went over to the Crapper."

"To the where?"

"The Crapper." Karen bared her upper teeth. "That's what they call it, ennit, Jone and them. The *Citadel of Porcelain at First Light*: the Dawn Crapper."

Karen, the eternal innocent, idiotic and irrepressible. This minute gesture of insolence pleased her greatly; as it might have pleased Tabitha too, once. "I don't think they've took any Alts over," Karen said.

Tabitha, having raised the subject, tried to think what to say.

"I asked O'Shaughnessy," she said. "He didn't know her. Well, I didn't think he did." She *had* asked. "I used to be pretty good with Alts," she said.

"They're not difficult," said Karen, companionably.

Captain Jute, who had found O'Shaughnessy impossible, fell silent again.

In a moment, Karen said: "I've been thinking about what he said, your Alt. About the Capellans working for the Frasque, and then turning against them, right?"

"Right," said Captain Jute, who was tending more and more to discount whatever the furry scavenger had said, the farther behind they left him.

"Well, what if the Frasque, right, built Plenty to bring the Capellans home."

"All right," said Tabitha. She hadn't actually thought about it that clearly. She tried to remember how it had gone: the Frasque building their enigmatic orbital, making the initial alliance with the Seraphim, opening their advanced cryonics facility to the corpses of the wealthy and powerful. It had all been on AV, hours and hours of it, lavishly interlarded with analysis and speculation. Tabitha Jute had had her living to make. She hadn't really paid much attention. Could the whole thing have been an elaborate bid to turn the human race against their Capellan benefactors, to isolate them and corral them and lever them into captivity?

"Which is why the hive came straight back here," said Karen, "when you turned it on."

"The Frasque built Plenty to bring the caterpillars home," said Tabitha, a trifle stupidly.

"But the caterpillars didn't want to go home. So the caterpillars—" Captain Narlikar snapped her fingers.

"The caterpillars went into Plenty and burned them out," said Tabitha.

Karen turned from the controls to look her in the eye. "It makes sense," she said.

"I don't know," said Tabitha, automatically reserving judgment on something she knew she ought to have an opinion on. The only response she could think of would have been to ask Alice. But Alice was a rectangle of grey plastic, inoperative, at the bottom of her backpack. Short of dispossessing Atkins for five minutes, a suggestion to which she had no difficulty imagining his response, there was nowhere among all this hardware to plug her in.

Karen was checking the screens. "Ooh, I wished I could have flown one of them Shinjatzus," she said.

Like most people, Karen Narlikar's knowledge of the Last War derived entirely from the Capellan-sanctioned news coverage: the official report, succinct and without pictures, of the regrettable sterilization of Plenty, followed by endless footage of heroic human volunteers in invincible ships, going bravely forth to deal with the remnants.

"THE DESIGNERS OF THAT SHIP MODELED IT ON A NAVAJO FIGHTER," commented Atkins, while a monitor flashed detailed cutaways. "I RETAIN ALL THE CONFIGURATIONS FOR 24 SHIP-TO-SHIP COMBAT WEAPONS."

"I knew a woman once who flew a fighter," said Captain Jute. She sucked her teeth, and shook her head.

"On Plenty, was this?" Karen asked her.

"No, no," said Tabitha. "This was years ago, off Deimos."

Captain Jute rarely spoke of Devereux, whose sex object she had been, in her youth, for a few eye-opening days. Now she wanted to tell Karen. Not about the sex, but about the scars on the veteran's body, the devices implanted in it by her Capellan controllers. For Captain Jute, the whole brief apocalyptic course of the war had been described by the wounds of the ravaged pilot.

She found herself struggling now to approach the subject. "She was the one that hit that Frasque battleship," she said. "You know." And there she stuck, realizing that the name had gone. It probably wouldn't mean anything to Karen if she did manage to remember it.

Karen frowned at the console. "You know what I could do with right now?"

Captain Jute was trying to visualize the holo that hung over Devereux's bed, showing the doomed ship. "What?" she said.

"A curry," said Karen Narlikar. "You couldn't get us a curry, could you, Captain?"

"Get us all one," said Dodger Gillespie, coming in. "She's good at that, ain't you, gel?" she said, before Captain Jute could react or reply. "She used to be a stewardess, Karen. I expect she told you."

*   *   *

Dodger Gillespie was content. In the stateroom she lay motionless for hours, watching her crappy movies. Captain Jute thought about Saskia Zodiac, who had been obliged to lie in much the same spot for weeks on end, imprisoned by a wall of cartoons.

"In a ship like this," said Captain Jute to Karen Narlikar, who was on the apparatus, exercising, "we could rescue Saskia."

"You reckon she's still alive, Captain?"

"She's alive." Captain Jute was sure of that. It was whether she would want to leave the company of the Seraphim again that was the question.

On the other side of the cabin, in her sweat-marked singlet and waistform pants, Karen Narlikar bicycled industriously. She thought about Saskia Zodiac. She had found the artificial woman moody and obsessive; arrogant too, at times. She had never been able to see her attraction for the Captain. As a wholehearted lifelong heterosexual, she could scarcely have been expected to.

"You really like her, don't you?"

Captain Jute folded her arms. "I'm very fond of her," she said. She glanced again at Dodger, lying on the bed. "As fond as Captain Gillespie is of her little girl," she said, with a hint of malice.

Dodger Gillespie blinked slowly, pausing her latest cheesecake epic. She barely turned her gaunt head on the pillow to acknowledge the remark. "Jone knows what she's about," she said.

Captain Narlikar took up a pair of springs and started squeezing them together. She considered her companions.

"Some people think you two are queer for each other," she said.

That cracked them both up. Dodger Gillespie cackled like a laryngitic hen. Karen looked from one to the other, wondering what she'd said.

Tabitha remembered Jone's arrival in her suite on the

Citadel, accompanied by the garish and greasy "Brother Melodious," Marco Metz.

"She was so angry. I thought she'd come to do *me* in for a moment."

Captain Gillespie reflected. "Well," she said. "You're going to have to watch yourself."

"From Jone?" said Captain Jute. "Fancies herself, does she?"

Karen, oversensitized now to the whole issue, sniggered at the phrase. "Course not from Jone," murmured Dodger Gillespie benignly. "There's others, though."

Tabitha felt weary with her companions, impatient for something to do. She went back into the cockpit. Out of curiosity, she called up the displays the persona had run before.

"IN MY PROGRAMMING I RETAIN ALL THE CONFIGURATIONS FOR 24 SHIP-TO-SHIP COMBAT WEAPONS," reported Atkins again. "I REGRET THAT I AM EQUIPPED WITH ONLY FIVE."

The skip ended as instantly as it had begun. The drab grey vacancy of hyperspace slicked back and let in the reddish gloom of the outer system. In the distance, potentially hazardous debris peppered the void.

"EMERGENCE LOGGED AT 87.12.54, CAPTAIN NARLIKAR."

"Light-diffraction shield on."

"SHIELD ON, CAPTAIN."

Karen Narlikar trimmed the attitude stabilizers and brought up solar gravity compensation. With the shield on, the visibility became even dingier. She switched all external scanners to maximum resolution, dropped a grid over them and started to comb.

Among the field of faintly glowing dots, Tabitha thought one looked a bit different.

"Is that Plenty?"

"NEGATIVE, CAPTAIN JUTE." There was a pause

lasting most of a second while the persona made a cautious scan. "THAT ONE IS A CAPELLAN STARSHIP."

"The *Citadel*?"

"NEGATIVE, CAPTAIN NARLIKAR . . ."

Karen tabbed enhancement. Magnification and probabilistic outlining produced a slender shape like an asymmetrical pair of tweezers, elongated and bewhiskered with com arrays.

The persona purred for all of five seconds. Then it said: "THE NAME OF THAT SHIP IS THE *IN POWER WE ENTRUST THE LOVE ADVOCATED*."

"The what?" said Karen.

"Keep an eye on it," said Dodger Gillespie.

Plenty turned out to be a dull smudge 170 klicks off the port bow. Captain Narlikar refined the approach, and looked again at the scanners. The grid was a net holding slender golden fish, six, seven, eight of them.

"System ships," she said.

"AFFIRMATIVE, CAPTAIN. RANGE 1070–1400 KILOMETERS."

They all had a look. None of them had ever seen so many together before. What were they doing, them and the attenuated starship, out on the rim of the system?

The new starship slipped behind a mass of ash and rubble, out of sight. Karen keyed minimum impulse power while Dodger set Atkins to extrapolating the trajectories of the Capellan vessels.

Atkins hummed for a moment. "YOU DO REALIZE THEY'RE CONVERGING," he said pleasantly.

∽ 22

The Eladeldi enforcer squad found the Thrant female on the lift platform, just where the dispatcher had reported. Two constables had surprised her out of bounds. They had her pinned down, on her back.

Both the constables were injured. One was favoring a torn leg, the other had blood all over his uniform.

The Thrant snarled up at them all. The landing stank of her rage, her urine. Along his back the squad captain felt his fur rise.

They wrestled their captive into a quadruped restraint. "Where was she, constable?"

"Coming out of the lift, sir."

He checked the pod. Its board was dark. On the screen a public health video played silently, humans in tracksuits smiling at each other. The floor was covered with dirt and litter, any of which might prove relevant.

"Which way was it going?"

The bleeding officer held a first-aid pad to his muzzle. He pointed upward, and to the left.

The Thrant wore dirty green jodhpurs and an unfastened grey jerkin leaking stuffing. Like all her species she was a malicious brute, her features a mask of unreasoning hostility. The restraint made her tits stand out.

Contemplating her, the captain's glands quickened. His mouth flooded with saliva. He felt as strongly as any of his officers the temptation to fall upon this stinking creature and tear her limb from limb.

He spoke to her in English. "*Hwere haf you ben?*"

The Thrant spat. She missed. The captain signaled them to insert the gag bar.

The captain breathed deeply of her stink, enjoying the sensation of suppressing the powerful reflex. Then he called in the arrest, and sent them her picture, front, side and both ears. No two of them had ears that were exactly alike. She was automatically detailed for the Septal lockup. There they would soon find out who she was, where she had been, and why she had been sneaking about on Level 93.

The arresting officers were treated to a swift examination, then ordered to report for medical attention. They presented their credit meters for a reward, which they would be able to spend on food or sex, as they liked.

"Good work, men!" huffed the captain.

Brother Justice held court in a somber room with no windows. Bald-headed acolytes in long black gowns waited on him, mysterious functionaries with their arms full of books and documents. They bowed as they passed the bench where the judiciary Guardian lounged, splendid in his red and blue and orange bands, his white-silk hose and wig of Palernian wool.

The Thrant crouched before him under a low forcefield. Her face was battered, her pelt looked as if someone had been trying to set light to it.

"Your name is Soi?"

The Thrant hung her head, swinging it restlessly from side to side, opening and closing her mouth.

"Speak when His Lordship bids you!" ordered the arraigning officer, jabbing her with his mace. "Where do you live?"

She would not speak.

"Domicile the Yoshiwara caves," the defender directed the secretary.

The Judge smiled to himself, thinking of that quarter, in whose palaces he had formerly spent many happy hours, some with women of the same species as the prisoner. He peered at her, wondering if there was any chance she might have been one of them.

"Let the record show," called the defending officer, "that when detained my client was returning home from an errand in the docks."

The arraigning officer gave a pained smile and stuck out his chest. "M'lord, the thing is impossible by that route."

Maps of different epochs were produced. The clerk put them up on the screen. Flashing red and yellow lines were drawn on them to demonstrate that since the internal spatial disruption, the docks could no longer be reached via the Limbic lifts.

The Thrant glowered. She rubbed her eyes with the back of her hand.

"M'lord, begging my worthy opponent's pardon, I should like the prisoner to be made to testify whether she is or is not aware that Kybernator Astraghal has specifically requested all remaining passengers to keep to their home districts."

The prisoner answered with a loud snort. She wagged her hindquarters, the only gesture of insult permitted her by her cramped posture.

Brother Justice chortled ponderously. She was a spirited young thing. He hadn't had a Thrant since his augmentation, and he had half a mind to order this one to his chambers and give her a swift rogering before her sentence. He wondered if any of the Eladeldi had availed themselves of her. They didn't usually, Eladeldi, with Thrant, despite considerable provocation. Too upright, all of them, in every way but the one that mattered.

"M'lord, it is the contention of the prosecution that aside from the assault on the officers, the accused's offense, to wit, wilful and aggravated trespass, constituted an act of affray and endangerment not only in respect of the accused herself but also in respect of others, person or persons unknown . . ."

Bowing minimally, the clerk of the court signed for permission to approach the bench. He had a com message slip in his hand.

"They've identifed the prisoner, m'lord," he muttered. "She's the Thrant chief's sister. Former servant of Captain Jute's."

Brother Justice blinked and pulled a face. In that case, the sooner they were rid of her, the better.

"I believe that point is well made, counsel," he declared, "whatever it was." He banged his gavel a few times and peered sternly if blearily into the ferocious gaze of his victim. "Prisoner at the bar, I sentence you summarily to be taken from here and returned to your home district, where you will be given over into the custody of your brother, under the strictest injunction not to repeat your trespass at any persuasion or on any occasion whatsoever."

He thumbed a ring, raising the restraint field half a meter. "Rise and signify understanding," intoned the clerk.

The woman remained in her crouch. Only her head came up. Her eyes were narrow, her lower jaw protruding.

It was as if she was willing the judiciary Guardian to make a mistake and switch the field off altogether. She seemed to be selecting which of his chins should be her target.

Every effort had been made to restrict the incoming Frasque to the evacuated Parietal. They were mindless males, most of them, and had to be treated with unambiguous firmness. Eladeldi enforcers moved among them with their ultrasonic whips, herding them up the stairwells and into the apartments, where they draped themselves like expiring houseplants across the abandoned furniture.

Despite the precautions, it was not long before they turned up in other areas of the hive, drawn by ancestral vibrations into capillary tunnels too narrow for pursuit. In the Trivia Bar they were found clustering around the still-working game machines, twitching their mandibles in mute intercourse with the little flashing lights. Soon they were all over the casinos of the PreCentral, like a flock of giant locusts that had suddenly developed a taste for gilt and vinyl. In the Mercury Garden amphitheater they congregated fifteen deep, cheeping forlornly at the dais.

Kybernator Astraghal knew exactly what they were doing. They were calling for a queen.

If a queen should hatch out, the plan would be thrown into the greatest jeopardy. Yet without one, they were simply a hideous nuisance. The skin of the Kybernator's body crawled with unease.

"Poor things!" said Sister Contenta, bobbing against the ceiling. "Listen to them squeal." She rubbed her bejeweled hands as if washing them in air. "Don't you think it might be best to burn them all now?"

Kybernator Astraghal narrowed his eyes and put his hands to his great domed forehead.

"Not yet, sister," he said. "Not yet."

In the most luxurious boudoir of the grandest palace in the Yoshiwara, Iogo's kittens lay curled in their nest of tattered holofiber, oblivious of everything. Their mother lay beside them, and Kenny on his caresser, watching. They were a healthy and auspicious litter, two girls and two boys. Placid and proud, Iogo licked them all over one by one, smoothing their yellow fluff with her muscular tongue.

Already they were putting on weight and length, though they did nothing but sleep and feed. Kenny could not wait for the day when they began to walk, to play, to fight together. He had his eye on a suitable trainer for them, against that day. The tribe would need them, when it was time for him to go.

The King of the Thrant wore his combat jerkin, his tight trews that left his feet free. Around each wrist was a band of black chain mesh. He reached out with one long foot to caress his queen.

Moodily, she turned from him. It was too soon for Iogo to think of anything but her babies. She knew that Kenny must go, when the call came, and that there was very little chance he would ever return. His sister Soi had gone already, slipped down out of sight weeks ago, to work on the preparations.

The sooner it came, the call, the better it would be for all the survivors of Plenty, Thrant and human and Vespan. Iogo knew all that, but she could not face it. She hated it, and in her simple, scarred heart she blamed Kenny, because he was going away.

"Chief Kenny."

It was a young buck, one of the gatekeepers. They spoke nothing now but Thrant, though they all called Kenny by his human name.

"It is your sister."

Kenny's heart leapt, and he leapt too. Upright he faced the buck, his tail twitching from side to side.

"There are enforcers with her. They want to speak to you."

There was apprehension in the buck's voice, tension in his posture. Recently the hunters had chased down an Eladeldi ensign, unarmed and alone. They had brought him home threaded on a pole. You couldn't eat them, but it had been an occasion for much music and jollity. Was this the reprisal?

At the palace gate stood five of the shaggy blue creatures. They would come no closer. They wore red uniforms with insignia of black and gold. Their brows and muzzles were shaven.

They carried Soi between them, gagged and locked in a quadruped restraint. She was hurt. She looked terrible.

"What have you done to her?"

Their leader cleared his throat. He spoke tonelessly, as if absolutely indifferent to his task, but the whites of his eyes were showing and the sinews of his neck were stiff.

"Are you Chief Kyfyd?"

"I am."

"Do you recogdize vis wobad?"

"She is my sister Soi." Kenny showed his claws. "What have you done to her?"

"At 63.45.65 she was abbrehedded out of bouds on Level 93. Failig to resbod to questiodig, she has beed returd to your custody under strictest inzhugshd dot to leave vis—"

"Take that thing out of her mouth!"

The policeman described a small circle in the air with his nose. Around Chief Kenny the gatekeepers and onlookers seethed. Teeth were bared, hackles rising. Natural enmity was in full flow between the pack hunters and the tribal rangers.

The Eladeldi spoke on, reciting the rest of his charge mechanically as a drone. "—bedalty of imbrisodmedt, exbulshd or disablemedt. Do you accebt resbodsibility?"

"Damn you, yes! Let her go!"

They took his picture in lieu of a signature, then trained their colossal Supremos on Soi while they unlocked the restraint.

She stood on her hind legs, leaning forward, mouth closed, eyes half-lidded. She ignored her captors entirely. She walked slowly through the gate as if her journey up from the docks had barely been interrupted.

Kenny leapt forward and embraced her. Then they all embraced her in a great huddle of demonstrative affection. She smelled of metal, of burnt fur and sour piss. Outside, the blue minions shivered with disgust.

Kenny walked her in with his arm round her. She said she was not seriously hurt. She exclaimed over the size of the kittens and let the women start to groom her. The women gave little piping sighs of distress at the burnt patches on her pelt.

"The Captain is on her way," said Soi.

Kenny lifted his arms over his head and shook himself with gladness. He took hold of his sister's shin and shook it sternly, admonishingly. "You should not have come in person."

Soi showed her teeth. "I was not afraid."

Her brother gave a deep growl, half acclamation, half

discontent. "I know your courage," he said, stroking her. "You must save it until it's needed."

Soi stretched out her head. "Everything is ready!" Her eyes glowed yellow as lemons.

On the bed Queen Iogo mewed sorrowfully. The kittens, sensing her anxiety, butted her with their little pink noses.

The old observatory was in darkness, its giant windows turned away from the suns. Outside, shafts of shiplight carved up the Capellan deep.

Across the cracked tile floor drone trucks crawled with their cargoes of books and magazines, manuscripts and tapes. By the light of their headlamps, shaven-headed librarians toiled up and down ladders to fill the alcoves, shelving every item by hand.

At the central desk stood the Chief Recorder, Brother Poesy, turning the blue-ruled pages of an ancient folio by the light of a branch of candles. He wore a loose black gown with a high collar, a crimson amulet on a gold chain around his neck. His skin was as white as the candlewax, his eyes sunk in dark pits, invisible.

Father Le Coq, the Rooster, Priest of the Dream Tabernacle, stood before Brother Poesy in an attitude that was as much of a cringe as his flamboyance would permit. Though his head was bowed, his arms had adopted independent positions. The right arm was raised, hand and fingers extended, as though to adjust some invisible dial. The left arm he held down and out to the side, hand flat, as though coaxing a chord from some equally invisible keyboard.

"Mighty Master Brother Poe . . ."

The Poet Guardian fingered his lower lip. He did not lift his eyes from his book.

"What is it now, Le Coq?"

The priest did not reply directly. As if in imitation of the poet he pulled his own lip and made a deep lowing noise. "Ooohh . . ."

Brother Poesy looked at him then, with eyes narrowed and lip quirked. It was hard to tell whether he was amused or angry.

Stagily, Le Coq canted one hip and shifted his feet. In his stack-soled sneakers and saucer-sized sunglasses, he looked more like some overweening funk rock star than anyone's spiritual intermediary. Still it was on behalf of the faithful he had come. "On behalf of the faithful, Brother Poe . . ."

Brother Poesy marked his place with one long fingertip. He cast a look over each shoulder, as if to satisfy himself that his own acolytes were still busy at their appointed tasks. They, like all sensible people, disdained the Rooster and his noisy, self-dramatizing flock. "What about them, Brother Priest?"

Le Coq stared at him with a fixing eye, more like snake than fowl. "Brother Poe, they ask me, When will *we* be bonded? When shall our Capellan brethren and sistren come into the house that we have prepared against their coming? Are the lamps not lit? they ask me. Does the fire not burn bright to welcome them?"

The priest tilted his head and smiled a disingenuous smile. He cupped his hands together as if to cradle some small fragile form, an egg or a beaker. His voice was hushed.

"Are there not enough little ones now?"

He cupped his hand to his ear, as if to catch a faint reply.

"Will they not come into their homes and be welcome? Not for me do I ask it, Brother Poe, but for them. The faithful . . ."

He ran the tips of his fingers across the top of his head.

Brother Poesy smiled patiently and smoothed one eyebrow with a fingertip. He looked down at the supplicant as if judging the quality of the material on offer.

"What does our Brother Melodious say, Le Coq?" he asked. "Have you spoken to him of your concerns?"

The priest shook his bony head. "Not for a week,

Brother Poe. Not for a month. Brother Melody is over on the *Citadel*, for sure."

"Here."

Brother Poesy tugged from his finger a silver ring with a flashing purple stone. He leaned over the reading desk and handed it down to Le Coq. "This ring will enable you to communicate instantly with Brother Melodious on the *Citadel of Porcelain at First Light*."

Father Le Coq's eyes and mouth were wide as a toddler's on Christmas morning. He took the ring and fondled it with his fingers. He probed and twisted at the purple gem. "Brother Marco Melody? Can you hear me there, Brother?"

"Well, if it isn't the Rooster. Can you hear me, Rooster? What mischief are you up to, you old devil bird, you?"

His embassy forgotten, Father Le Coq whistled and capered. How his congregation would sing out now, with the golden voice of their idol to lead them, filling the temple with the joy of his presence from the very knuckle of their minister's hand!

He gave a high, gleeful cackle and searched among the jewels on his hands for a space. "See the all-bountiful mercy of Brother Edgar Allan Poesy!" he cried.

As one, the bald-headed acolytes leaned toward him from their library ladders. They lifted their index fingers to their lips. "Shhh!" they hissed.

Smiling, Brother Poesy took a neatly trimmed quill from behind his ear, dipped it, and with it made a small mark in his big black book.

Meanwhile, in a grotto far below, an antechamber to the cavern of the Star Beast, the medical Guardian Brother Valetude toiled with his own tiny drones. Above on the balcony, among elongated figures like pinnacles of lava, Brother Kitchener watched complacently, smoking a fat cigar.

Ecstasy in his face, Brother Valetude held up his arms.

They were full of sticky slivers of milk white flesh, weakly wriggling.

"They are perfect!" he cried. "She is unharmed!"

Behind him, the cave was full of blood.

ॐ 23

The neurotronic technicians, numbers 50 to 59, were fitted with four stainless-steel interface sockets: one at each temple, one in the center of the forehead, and one at the nape of the neck. With these they could access systems and download information, in the normal way. Equally, they could receive packages of instructions—route maps, mission strategies, algorithms—on which they could thereafter act unsupervised.

When not otherwise occupied, Techs 50 to 59 liked to form closed systems. Two or (preferably) more members would be connected together by means of simple coaxials, nape to forehead or temple to temple. The effect was felt to be both useful and pleasurable: a superior version of sex, more efficient, less messy.

The long years in hypserspace had permitted extensive experimentation, and the permutations of the synapse ronde were well established. For example, two circles could be linked in parallel, with one member of each designated to transmit and receive material through a temporal-lobe spur. Still initiative and creativity were not the most developed faculties in the technician class—indeed, the training actively suppressed them—so there remained possibilities still undiscovered, unexplored.

In her white overall and boots Tech 59 swam to the door of Cubicle 24. Her hood was lowered, her face bare.

"What is it?"

The voice came from a speaker that enabled the occupant of Cubicle 24 to deal directly with his visitors, without an intermediary. It was one of several items of extra equipment that had been installed at his request.

"It's 59, sir," said the tech.

"Come in if you're coming. Be quick."

The tech obeyed. She looked into the tank through the observation window, then checked the vital sign displays.

"I just came to tell you your idea worked, sir."

A stream of bubbles disturbed the yellow fluid in the tank. *"Worked? Of course it worked. Which idea?"*

"The Great Tree, sir. We all took part."

"Yes, well, you'd have to. Ten Sephiroth on the Great Tree of Heaven and Earth . . . "

The occupant of Cubicle 24 sounded preoccupied. He was less interested in the success of some plugheads' recreational activity than in his data link to the robot cartographer, which was now passing the outer planet, seven hundred million kilometers away across the system. The creature in the tank was watching carefully as the machine made its survey of surface features.

"She was there, 59. Her grubby little fingerprints are all over the place. Wrecked ships, vehicle tracks, refuse."

"Is this the Captain, sir?" His ECG rate was up, suggesting it was. In their plenary hookup, Tech 59 had gleaned fragments of information from everyone that had had to do with the occupant of Cubicle 24. The man called Nothing might not yet have a fully grown nervous system, but he already had his own agenda, quite distinct from Temple business. Sometimes it seemed to consist of a single priority: to find the woman he called the Captain and destroy her.

His mechanical voice echoed flatly from the steel walls. *"She's incapable of being anywhere for five minutes without making a mess . . . "*

* * *

The technician numbered 10, whose natal cerebral faculties were intact and unaugmented, was also at that moment engaged with an artificial human, the last survivor of an early clone. He was interviewing her for Diagnostics division, in her own quarters.

"More tests," said Saskia gloomily.

"More tests, ma'am," said Tech 10. "Diagnostics need to know what you remember from different periods of your life."

The thin white woman reclined easily on the air, eating krillchips. She was usually cooperative enough if you gave her something to eat.

The tech darkened the chamber. He put a still picture up on the screen. It had been taken outdoors, or somewhere where there were grass and sunlight. The picture, taken from overhead as if by some passing bird, showed three small children in pastel-colored romper suits crouching over what seemed to be a tortoise. The tortoise carried a tray balanced on its back. On the tray were several plastic vessels, dishes and beakers. The colors of the vessels corresponded to the clothes worn by the children.

"Do you remember this?"

"Of course. It is the Garden: the glass bowl they kept us in."

The Zodiac woman spoke loftily. Though the Seraphim had created her, Tech 10 noted that she regarded them with no particular respect. Presumably she felt the circumstances of her early years were irrelevant to the life she had led since, among the worlds at large.

"Would you like to tell me about it, ma'am?"

She glanced at him with cool indifference.

"No," she said. "But since I have no wish to be compelled to do so, I shall."

She put another chip in her mouth, while Tech 10, impressed, concealed a smile.

"That is I with Mogul and Suzan, in the Garden," Saskia said. "The tortoise brought us food every day. There are only three dishes on its back, so Zidrich and Goreal have already gone. The sun is shining, which it always did, except at night, of course, when it was withdrawn.''

She chewed another chip.

"So," she said, swallowing, "one by one, were we."

Tech 10 changed the picture. Now the screen showed Saskia as a young woman, in a long dress of metallic blue. She was dancing, on a glittering pink-and-white stage set, with a man in an evening suit, who seemed to be her identical twin. To one side stood a shorter black-haired man in a ruffled shirt, wearing a grey glove. Overhead, like the spirit of some exotic annunciation, hung a big green bird, its wings outspread.

"What about this?"

"That is a performance of Contraband," said Saskia. "Where and when, I can't tell you, unless you have more pictures from the same performance."

She chewed a chip, seeming unmoved.

Tech 10 prompted her. "Tell me about Contraband."

Saskia Zodiac sighed. "Contraband was the name of a performance troupe managed by Hannah Soo, who was an associate of your organization, and led by Marco Metz, who was a fool. That's Marco there."

"The man with the glove?"

"Of course the man with the glove. The other man is my brother, as you know perfectly well."

She glared at him. Her hostility was familiar, and relentless.

The tech felt constrained to introduce a disclaimer. "I don't know anything, Ms. Zodiac. I'm just here to listen to whatever you want to tell us."

Saskia ate chips. "I don't *want* to tell you anything," she said. "I told you that. You say you are listening, but you don't listen."

Tech 10 was beginning to sense himself in a peculiar, unprecedented position here. He had been little more than a child when the *Seraph Kajsa* left Sol. His experience of interaction with anyone from outside the Temple had been small indeed. He tried a neutral smile.

"I only work here," he said.

The cloned woman returned his smile with a curious inflection, seeming more to pity him than anything. Tech 10 felt warm suddenly, and gave an involuntary glance at the chamber thermostat.

Saskia spoke rapidly. "The man playing the glove is Marco Metz," she said. "You will now find him among the Guardians, with a clever little caterpillar in his head, and very well suited to each other they are too. The other man is Mogul, my brother and stage partner, also at this period my lover. I'm sure your employers are interested in these details too. The parrot was not a parrot, he was a sapient alien Marco picked up somewhere, where I don't know. His name was Tal, he used to sing and perform graceful aerobatics. Would you like me to list his repertoire?"

In his discomfort, Tech 10 was beginning to conceive a new respect for the Zodiac woman. "I don't think that will be necessary, ma'am," he said, and changed the picture again. "Why don't you tell me what you remember about this one?"

The screen showed again one of the androgynous figures from the previous picture. It might have been either of them. The figure wore an antique outfit of doublet and hose, made of what looked like velvet, in luxurious patterns of gold and tan and chocolate brown. Behind and, partially, through the figure could be seen an array of holo-modeling equipment.

As if magnetized, Saskia swam across the room to the screen.

"Where did you get this? Well, I suppose Xtasca gave it you."

The picture was moving slightly, on a short, slow loop. The figure struck a pose, as if responding to Saskia's approach.

"This is my brother Mogul again, an imago of him, which Alice and I made on Plenty in a modeling shop."

Delicately she touched the melancholy face on the screen. "I had nothing else to remember him by. Do you have a brother, 10? Or a sister, perhaps?"

Caught off guard, the technician answered. "I don't know, ma'am. I don't think so."

"You don't know?"

The artifical woman reflected that there seemed to be no children on board the *Seraph Kajsa*. She remembered the children she had seen on the *Citadel of Porcelain at First Light*: little groups of three and four, elaborately dressed. They were treasured, cherished, like creatures in a zoo.

"Where did you come from?"

"I was born here," said the technician. "In the Temple, I mean. Like you, ma'am."

"I was never born," said Saskia in a flash. "I have no idea what that is like, being born."

"I was dedicated at conception," said Tech 10. "My mother and father dedicated me."

"Well, we had no mother or father," said Saskia scornfully. She favored her interrogator with another thin smile. "Perhaps that is why we were not dedicated."

Their eyes met. He had an interesting face, this Tech 10. His skin was dark and glossy as molasses. Within his antiseptic white hood, his broad brown cheeks seemed to promise a kind of stability, reliability, good humor.

"Take your hood off," she told him.

Unresisting, he did as she said. Long curls of gleaming black hair spilled out, restrained only by the narrow band of a headset.

"10," she said. She gestured to the number he wore blazoned on his chest. "How can I call you this, this is absurd. Don't you have names? Didn't your mother give you one of them at least?"

His smile was patient and steady. "We have names, yes. 9 is Aengus and 22 is Knud." At the moment, however,

10 seemed to be having difficulty remembering his own.

"I am Torch," he said.

"Torch," she repeated. "Just Torch?"

He thought about it. "I guess," he said.

"Tell me about what you remember, Torch. How has your life been, so far?"

Her attention was having the most surprising effect on him. He felt it shine upon him like a light that penetrated his skin and touched him inside. The feeling was entirely new. She was inquiring after things that had always been irrelevant to the purpose of his existence, not worth mentioning. In return he felt, strangely, a strong desire to mention them.

The tech checked the time. The period allotted for this session was over, and they had hardly begun.

"I can't stay," he told her. He had no reason to tell her where he was going, no orders to tell her, but this sudden, thwarted urge to candor needed to be accommodated, in however insignificant a way. "I'm due in Cubicle 24," he said. The other pictures would have to wait. He smiled broadly. He would have to return, he thought, soon, to show her the other pictures. The thought pleased him.

Saskia fixed him with an imperious look. What color were her eyes? On his life, he could not have said.

"What is in Cubicle 24?"

He lowered his eyelids. "I can't tell you that, ma'am."

She pressed him. "Xtasca says they are cloning a new body. Is that it? I should very much like to see."

He stood stiff as a robot. "I have no orders—"

"I want to see!"

Against his better judgment, Tech 10 called Pomeroy Lion. Sweet Lavender would not have permitted it, he thought; Xipetotec would not have permitted it. Pomeroy Lion, though, might, he imagined; and just so, he heard the acquiescent voice sigh in his ear. *Yes, well, I suppose she would . . .*

* * *

Pomeroy Lion made his decision in circumstances of some distraction. He was in the middle of yet another meeting, this one with not only Brother Nestor but also Kybernator Perlmutter, captain of the Capellan starship, the *Citadel of Porcelain at First Light*.

Kybernator Perlmutter was the type whose paramount conviction was the supremacy of the Capellan race. He saw no reason to listen to the Seraphim, who had been intransigent enough in their time. Unfortunately the negotiations had reached a point at which it was also necessary to have Boaz present, to speak for Prevision division. Kajsa Prime and Pomeroy Lion had their work cut out preventing the two old warhorses from exercising their animosity on each other.

Kybernator Perlmutter had refused refreshment. He had demanded that the gravity be turned up, and then insisted on remaining standing. He already resented the appointment of his ship, the *Citadel*, as detention facility for the Sol refugees. That he should now be required to divert the *Citadel* into formation with the rest of the fleet, purely, as he saw it, for the benefit of these questionable allies, was a proposition to which he was determined to object strenuously.

He held up one square, white hand. "Already you have the *In Power We Entrust the Love Advocated*," he told them. "I understand we shall soon be bringing in the *Fortune Presents Gifts Not According to the Book*. How much more of our resources can we expect to have to contribute to this tenuous scheme?"

Threateningly, Boaz ground his maxillary gears. "Capella may be unable to understand the scheme," he thundered, "but is she unmindful that it has been devised expressly in her interest?"

The Kybernator squeezed his baggy eyes shut, as though beside himself with irritation. "That remains to be demonstrated," he said.

"But we must proceed in good faith," Brother Nestor

interrupted. His voice was high and uncertain. Beads of
sweat stood out on the brown expanse of his brow. Not for
the first time Pomeroy Lion wondered if Brother Nestor
might perhaps be sickening for something. "In good faith,"
said Brother Nestor again, weakly, blinking around the
room.

The Prime Seraph gave him a patronizing smile. Pomeroy Lion could see her thinking that it would take stronger
stuff than these bland admonishments to secure the coop-
eration of Kybernator Perlmutter. Indeed, at this juncture it
was possible the elderly Guardian's enfeebled interjections
might actually delay the operation, by increasing the irritation of the obstinate starship captain.

The Capacitory Chief moved into the center of the chamber, hoping to distract everybody's attention and stop them
all glaring at each other. "The whole thing is necessarily
an experiment," he pointed out.

Now Boaz was glaring at him, as at a traitor.

Kybernator Perlmutter looked no less weary. "If it
comes to that," he said brusquely, "the whole of our existence in the universe is necessarily an experiment."

"With everything to gain!" put in Brother Nestor, rather
taking the wind out of his colleague's sails. He exhaled
noisily. A strange, disconnected series of expressions
played across his face.

Kajsa Prime smiled at the Guardian intermediary more
graciously, in a way that Pomeroy Lion recognized as con-
signing him to the lowest level of her consideration. She
sat up, elegantly and symmetrically spreading her coat.

"Perhaps we should congratulate ourselves on the success of the experiment so far," Queen Kajsa proposed
sweetly. "Cognizance reports that our relative positions are
extremely propitious for the transfer. Our sisters are extremely pleased with the definition of the vector."

Kybernator Perlmutter folded his arms, regarding the severe and intricate vision of white flesh and black lingerie
with intensified disapproval. Clearly the sight of Kajsa To-

bermory and the reminder that there were others just like her had no charm for him.

"It is a question of increasing the power," said Boaz. "We must have more power!" He clenched his armored fist. "Consider, Capellan. The gain of which your brother speaks hangs in the balance. Would you have us pursue it with less than our full strength?"

Pomeroy Lion ran a finger around the inside of his collar. He cleared his throat. "Perhaps if I reiterated the principles involved," he said. "Your double sun, far stronger than the single parent star of our own system, supplies the necessary translocative resonance. Stationed at external foci determined by our measurements of tidal ebb and flow, the vessels of your own fleet can amplify that resonance through the frictionless medium of hyperspace, magnifying it five-, ten-, fifty-fold."

He was aware that, inexplicably, Brother Nestor was now looking at him with distaste. The prominent veins at the old man's temples were pulsing irregularly. A strange smell seemed to be emanating from him.

Pomeroy Lion glanced inquiringly at Kajsa Prime. She reclined there blithely, an expression of rapt attention on her sculpted features. Boaz, on the other hand, stood like a pink-and-purple colossus, gazing mutely down on the assembly as if the only question were whether to crush them now or later.

For the first time Pomeroy Lion wished Sweet Lavender could be here, if only to provide some kind of diversion. Hesitating, he put his hand to his moustache. The sourceless chamber light caught the ring he had put on before the meeting. It was the ring, he remembered, that Brother Nestor himself had given him on his first visit to the *Seraph Kajsa*. Inspiration striking, he held out his hand demonstratively.

"Working together, the ships bend space like light," he exclaimed, "like the stone in a giant ring!"

Kybernator Perlmutter snorted. Boaz's massive head

turned like a gun turret toward the Guardian. "The analogy amuses you," he said.

Brother Nestor put his hands to his head. He moved jerkily, for all the worlds as if the presiding Capellan had momentarily lost control of its human body. His voice came out a breathy squeak. "My brother wonders—we must wonder—w-w-wonder—on whose hand this ring is worn! On whose hand!"

The Seraphim exchanged glances. What was wrong with the man? His contributions were becoming increasingly random and unhelpful. Even Kybernator Perlmutter had begun looking at him with impatience, almost with dislike.

Brother Nestor stood upright. Sweat was running down his face, his eyes were starting from his head.

"Interf-f-ference is—unnecessary!" he gasped.

Boaz started to growl. In the rings on the knuckles of Kybernator Perlmutter small lights flickered. Inaudible messages were coming and going between him and his colleagues on the *Citadel of Porcelain at First Light*.

At once Queen Kajsa took charge. "Let's pursue this no farther," she said sweetly, sitting up and swinging her legs over the side of her hammock. "Brother Nestor has been working so hard, for all of us. And Kybernator Perlmutter sees some risk in the plan, and prefers not to expose his magnificent ship to it. Which is perfectly reasonable. I think we can all agree, can't we, gentlemen, that his contribution so far has already been of incalculable value, since we stumbled uninvited into his system."

Smiling, she arched her back slightly, lifting her formidable breasts in their carapace of lycra and lace.

"If our calculations are correct, it is only a question of delaying the transfer," she said, "not preventing it altogether."

Catching on, Boaz lifted his head and put back his vast shoulders. "The magnificence of the achievement will be the same," he rumbled, "however many share in it."

Pomeroy Lion wiped a knuckle briskly along his moustache. "Or, ah, choose not to, of course," he added mildly, not looking at anyone in particular.

Brother Nestor blinked around the chamber as if he hardly knew where he was, or what he was doing there.

Cubicle 24 was warm, the air rich and damp and odorous as a greenhouse. The plumbing fixtures were complex. There were steel shutters to exclude external light. A voice came out of a speaker.

"*Who is it?*"

Saskia Zodiac circled her wrist with her forefinger and thumb, rubbing it as though to ease some imaginary discomfort. Actually the discomfort was all in her head. The lab where they had killed Tabitha's sister was nearby. Her escort bent to open a small shuttered window. "It's 10," he said. "It's time for your protein-extrusion reinforcements."

"*Who's that with you? There's somebody there . . .*"

Tech 10 reached behind him to guide Saskia forward. "This is one of your predecessors. She's interested to meet you, and see how you're getting on. Her name is Saskia Zodiac."

There was barely a moment's pause as Saskia stooped to look in at the little window. Then the voice said: "*Well, well, well. What a nice surprise.*"

In the confined space Saskia's scream was like a detonation.

She hurled herself back against the metal wall, her hand to her throat, her knees shaking. The tech was with her, reaching for her, his eyes wide with shock and incomprehension.

"He's dead!" she shouted at him in anguish. "We killed him! We killed him!"

"*A temporary setback,*" said the voice. "*Painful, admittedly, but temporary. As it turns out.*"

Tech 10 touched Saskia's shoulder. She knocked his

hand away. Baffled, he returned to the window in the incubation tank.

"*Saskia and I are old friends, 10,*" he explained. "*I had
the honor of entertaining her as my guest for some time,
on Plenty. We shared a nice little ship, a Navajo Scorpion.
I should have realized she'd be with you now.*"

The cloned man was smiling. It was the first time 10 had
seen that expression on the reanimated face.

Saskia seemed to have been aged by the shock. Her color
was bad, her face was lined. She pointed a trembling hand
at the tank.

"Do you know who that is?"

He wished he could calm her. "He's an experiment, Project PL3484—"

"Why him? Why bring *him* back?"

Those were not questions a technician could ever answer.
He searched his memory.

"He was some kind of associate of the Temple. Is that
right?"

A spasm crossed her face. "So he was working for you,"
she said, in a bitter whisper. "Of course. Of course."

The electrical voice buzzed from the speaker. "*And
how's the Captain getting on? How does she like Capella?*"

Saskia shouted at the voice box. "She's alive and well
and somewhere far away, where you'll never be able to
touch her!"

Pushing aside the black man in the white suit, she peered
in through the glass.

"*I wonder if that's true . . .*" mused the man called
Nothing.

At first, all she could see floating in the yellowish fluid
was his face. His flesh was smooth as wax, and pale as her
own. They had even grown his ruined eye back. His hair
was as it always had been, glossy black, unruffled while
the fluid in the tank roiled and bubbled.

He laughed at her expression.

"*A pleasure to see you again, Ms. Zodiac. I look forward to seeing more of you.*"

They had given him a new body: the body of a child, a prepubescent boy. The narrow chest, the smooth limbs, the tiny, hairless knot of the genitals: like some kind of idiotic joke it floated, dangling beneath his head. Saskia Zodiac felt her gorge rise. She recognized that body.

She slammed her hand against the casing of the tank.

Tech 10 gazed at her. Her distress was like a command, disabling him. He knew he should shut the sound off, remove her, call Security, Capacitory.

He did nothing.

"Saskia—" he said.

She cursed him in her throat.

It was the body Saskia knew best: the first body she had ever seen. It was her brother's body, and her own.

ꙮ 24

The district known as Yoshiwara was deep inside Ventricle 3, far beneath the coarse and lumpy hull of Plenty. It had always seemed a sheltered, welcoming place: warm and enclosed, the air good if a trifle stale. Now it was home to the remaining Thrant, a place to curl up in a nest of blankets and mourn.

The call had come, and Kenny had gone, with Soi and a pack of others. They had left the lair and gone down into the docks, into danger. When she thought of the docks, Iogo thought of the spaceship, the Scorpion where she had once lived, and that made her even more distressed. The ship was still there in its parking bay, for all she knew, and the Master where she had left him, scattered in several pieces on the stateroom carpet. The docks were a place of hatred and fear, where people went to die. Iogo rubbed the top of her head and blew air from the corners of her mouth.

One of the kittens jumped heedlessly on her shoulder and licked her briefly before shoving his sharp snout underneath her. Wearily she rolled over. Whatever happened now, her milk would continue to flow.

Seeing their brother start to feed, the rest of the litter came scrambling over each other to join in. The sucking of four greedy little mouths comforted their mother a little. Sadly she licked the nearest kitten, who acknowledged it not at all, but sucked at her with total preoccupation.

Distantly, Iogo thought she could hear a buzzing noise, some sort of machine, she supposed, outside in the hallway, and an excited clamor from the guards. Then in through the open door of the bedchamber came a flying drone.

It was a small square thing the size of a clenched fist. It flew straight to Iogo and hovered in front of her.

Abandoning her teats, the kittens leapt up at the intruder, coughing shrilly with alarm, spattering everything with unswallowed mouthfuls of milk. Then the guards came bursting in, chasing the drone, reaching with claws and clubs to knock it out of the air.

Iogo rose up with an excited yelp and swiped them all away.

The drone had a little screen on the front of it. On the screen was a picture of Kenny.

Kenny's mate pawed at the drone. It evaded her with ease, as it had evaded her children and her guards. It hovered fractionally out of reach, tilting its screen for her to see.

It was Kenny. He hadn't gone to the docks at all! There he was lying full length on the floor in a tunnel, looking proud and happy. He was naked, his fur golden and glossy.

The drone dipped closer. It was making a little noise. When it flew in an arc between Iogo's ears, she heard the noise was Kenny's voice. He was talking to her, telling her to come to Forward 42.

Iogo lunged at the drone again. It flew away in a great curve, flapping the tattered bedhangings. It flew out of the door, taking Kenny with it.

The drone led them far from the ruined brothels, going by the steepest shafts, where no Eladeldi could catch them. "*Forward 42!*" it whispered. "*I need you, Iogo . . .*"

The name of the place meant nothing to Iogo, but she recognized the tunnel where he was lying. It was the tunnel where she had first seen him, outside Captain Tabitha's apartment. He had been riding in a car. He was not in a car now.

Three guards went before her, two of them overhead, brachiating. There was a fourth bringing up the rear. Iogo had trampled the guard chief who had tried to make her stay in the lair, so he had sent them after her, to go with her if they could not bring her back. They had not touched her, nor tried very long to persuade her. They knew she was determined, for she had brought the kittens with her, and four of her women to carry them. The kittens clung to their nursemaids, mewing in anguish, and coughing in the poor weak air. Iogo was not about to leave her brood behind for any machine.

The shaft turned a corner, sloping out toward the hull. Vines hung on the walls, dead and withered. Iogo climbed tirelessly.

Suddenly they came to a branch in the shaft. Ten meters up the branch, right above their heads, a balcony protruded from the wall.

The balcony was a small one, with a railing. Two people were standing on it, humans in skintight suits the same muddy grey color as the walls around them. They were looking down at the Thrant climbing toward them. They had long silver rods in their hands.

She saw that the humans had numbers written on their chests. Her late master had taught her to read numbers, though she would never manage them as well as Kenny or

Soi. One of the humans was a man, and he was wearing the number 6. The other was a woman, and her number was 35. The drone flew into the hand of the man wearing the number 6.

Iogo's vanguard were trying to shield her, while the rear guard pulled the nursemaids and their wriggling bundles hastily back down the shaft.

The humans pointed their silver rods. Purple light prickled from them, hurting Iogo's eyes. As she snuffled and blinked, her three guards fell from the wall and dropped soundlessly past her, back down the way they had come.

Exposed on the wall of the shaft, the Queen of the Plenty Thrant curled up in a circle, turning to run. As she turned she saw the woman, number 35, point at her with her gloved hand. Colored lights were flickering down the side of the woman's body, beneath her arm.

"Positive identification, sir," she heard the woman say.

A metal cord lashed down from the balcony, whipping around Iogo's hind legs. She clung to the wall, but 35 pulled the cord tighter. She dragged her up the wall. Iogo scrabbled with her hands, straining helplessly back toward the shrieking kittens.

She glimpsed the last of her guards struggling to reach her, to pull her back. She saw his claws grasping for her. Then there was another crackle of purple fire, and he was not there any longer.

As the woman pulled her up level with the little balcony, the Queen Thrant saw more little colored lights flickering on the sides of the man, the one numbered 6. She collapsed then, losing control of all her limbs, and her bowels. She felt herself doubled up, limp over the railing.

The humans put a big plastic bag over her head. She felt them pull it down the length of her body, enclosing her completely. Her nostrils filled with the reek of her own shit.

"Secure, sir," she heard the woman numbered 35 report then, and the man numbered 6 reply: "Well done, 35." There came the sound of a heavy door grating open, and the sense of a great coldness beyond. Dimly Iogo heard her kittens and their nurses crying; and then she heard no more.

The *All Things Considered*, with Dodger Gillespie at the controls, had delayed the last stage of her approach to co-incide with an incoming shuttle. When the great dim screen of the forward door puckered open and the shuttle began her entry, Dodger put on speed. Captain Jute and Karen Narlikar held their breath as she slipped the Scorpion in right at the top of the doorway, over the back of the shuttle.

In any better-lit harbor it would never have worked. Someone would have seen them, seen something, a flaw in the air, a shielded blur passing overhead; but high in the stygian gloom of the refitted hive, with all eyes and instruments focused on the descending shuttle, the Scorpion slid safely above the floodlights.

Dodger touched the throttle and banked slightly to thread them over the upper walkways. The ceiling raced past, mere centimeters, it seemed, above their heads. Before the engines of the shuttle below had fallen silent, they were across the cavern, settling the Scorpion into her high parking bay.

As they waited a moment to see that all was still, Tabitha Jute exhaled. "Dodger Gillespie," she said softly. "You're the best."

Dodger, as was her nature, did not react. Karen grinned and gave Tabitha a thumbs-up sign.

Karen set the ship to maintain maximum security and respond to anything but their password with complete inertia. Dodger slipped the persona plaque into the pocket of her suit. Tabitha fingered her bag, feeling for the rectangular shape of Alice.

Dodger didn't collect her Corregidor, but handed Tabitha a handgun, a short-range neural disruptor.

"Don't use that," she said. "They're rationed."

In the unlit corridors behind the parking bays, the lights of their suits showed them the crazed, disintegrating concrete, the deep cracks in the matrix beneath. They passed a barrier of trestles hung with a notice that forbade them to go farther. Farther on, another flatly declared the tunnel impassable. The roof had fallen in.

Karen led the way. Tabitha followed, with Dodger close behind.

Slowly and laboriously they negotiated the blockage, crawling on hands and knees, then full length, squeezing through gaps in the rubble. Karen pulled Tabitha's pack through; then, crouching in the minute space beyond, she helped Tabitha herself through, tugging her by the arms.

Thin as an insect, Dodger Gillespie wriggled through in four quick motions, unaided, then lay on the floor coughing. Inquiringly, Tabitha put her hand on Dodger's shin. With her thumb Captain Gillespie motioned them on.

In this way they came at the end of another hour to a wall with a large glass door in it. Karen hauled the door open. They looked down into a vertical shaft of matrix reinforced with girders. A few meters below their feet there was a lift pod, stuck between stations.

One by one the women climbed down onto the roof of the pod, then through a sliding panel into the pod itself. Karen crouched to show Tabitha where, under the seats, a hole had been hacked in the floor. They squeezed through that too.

In the darkness underneath the pod, somebody seemed to have rigged up a pulley system. There was a cargo sling hanging, large enough for all of them. Tabitha thought she could hear voices, floating up the shaft from far below. She tapped the side of Karen's helmet.

"*That's them,*" said Karen.

They climbed into the sling, and hung on tight. Captain Gillespie stuck her head out and gave a whistle.

At once they were in motion, being lowered steadily through the darkness.

Their descent was slow and mesmeric. Identical unlit doorways marked the levels, offering fractional glimpses into night black corridors that ran away in every conceivable direction. Captain Jute felt herself start to nod off. Behind one of the glass doors there was a Frasque's head, staring at them.

Before she could shout, it was gone. She did not see it go: she simply saw it, and then she didn't.

She said nothing. Nor did either of the others. Perhaps she had only thought she saw it. She felt cold suddenly. She was sure she was sweating. They were deep in Plenty's guts, here, where she had never wanted to be, where everything had started going bad. She thought of Angie, living in these crevices for months on end, radiating her electrical fever through the capillaries of the alien hive.

Then she found they were dropping through a ceiling into light. Below them, a crowd was assembled. As they appeared, a cheer went up.

If Tabitha Jute had had time to forget the condition of her ship, the hall where they now stood was a sufficient reminder. There were baulks of wood and poly-90 sheeting propping up the walls and preserving the atmosphere. Power and com lines were lashed with tape to a skeletal framework of black steel poles, with bio strips for lighting. All around, piles of blankets and tins contributed mutely to an atmosphere of beleaguerment. It was, in short, a dim and uncomfortable place, where life itself had become something of a struggle.

The hall was full of people: fifty of them, she supposed; maybe more. They were dirty, and fatigued, and determined. They seemed glad, triumphant, many of them, to see Captain Jute amongst them once again. A furry figure came loping forward, head low, fierce mouth open, arms wide.

"Kenny!" For a moment she thought he was going to hug her. Instead he pushed his powerful neck into her hands, forcing her to stroke him.

"Kenny, god, it's good to see you. It's incredible. All these people!"

She stood dazed among them. In fact, at that moment, there seemed to be hardly anyone she recognized. There was a small group of Vespans, bowing cumbersomely in her direction. Among the humans, many seemed to be scrawny kids, Rookery stock, victims of disease and malnutrition. What use would they be in a fight, she couldn't help wondering.

Karen Narlikar had her arms around two men, Sven and Colgan. Them Captain Jute could remember from the old days, in the workshops on Silverside. Now there was a sharp-faced man, crew-cut, saluting, and Dodger was giving him an affable nod. Christ, it was the Redcap, Rykov.

Before she could decide how she felt about that, Kenny was tugging at her arm. He was mumbling through his nose, he wanted to show her something. She looked and saw more Thrant, a dozen of them. They made a fearsome sight: bucks like overgrown weasels in combat armor; a couple of females standing on all fours. One of the women swung herself up on her hind legs, her head up, her tail lashing the air. She wore the remains of a grey quilted jerkin, and around her throat what looked like a ruined wig of blond nylon curls on a piece of pink string.

"Soi?" said Tabitha numbly. "Is that you?"

Soi snuffled and swung her head, yawning manically. She had never been the most articulate of extraterrestrials, but for that moment it was almost as if she had forgotten the use of the English language.

Here was Lou now, Lou Garou, they called him, with some of his old chums from Havoc. They were motorized barbarians, macho brutes governed only by their appetites for downers and destruction. None of them had ever held a high opinion of the Captain of Plenty since the exhilaration of that day when she had released them from their prison asteroid. They were not visibly welcoming her now.

There was one she recognized, wearing heavy black dreads and a coat of sheepskin with the fleece on the outside. The coat was open, showing off his broad, scarred

chest. His name was Norval, they had called him the Khan.
The last time Captain Jute had set eyes on him, he had been
one of Colonel Stark's convict laborers, driving decommissioned battletrucks full of cement. She gave him an uneasy
smile. Obviously, the trucks had been a mistake. The Havoc
Horde knew the labyrinth of sternward roads better than
anyone.

Norval Khan did not return her smile.

Lou was shaking Tabitha's hand, congratulating her on
her escape from the *Citadel*. "We heard about the stunt
you pulled," he said familiarly, "nicking that Kobold.
When you skipped, though, we thought that was it."

Somebody was touching her clothes. She turned and saw
it was one of the Rooks, a young woman, as far as she
could tell from her wasted form. She was pointing at a
stretcher that lay beneath the shaft they had come down by.
The stretcher was empty.

The woman gave the Captain a shy, goofy smile. "We
wasn't expecting you to be walking," she said.

"Lost a stack of credit," said the Khan callously, "bet-
ting on that."

"We all did," Lou exclaimed ruefully. "Dodger cleaned
up."

They were definitely giving her the idea that for some
people here, the decision to rescue her had not been a fore-
gone conclusion.

"What's it like, then," Lou asked her, "Capella 3?"

"The Frasque like it," she said, straight-faced.

They were not startled. "They like it here too," said
Lou.

"Yeah," she said. "I saw one."

"One," said the Khan, taunting her, but not looking directly at her.

Lou and the Havoc veterans gave way as Rykov came
over with an entourage of people who might not exactly be
wearing red hats anymore, but whose philosophy was evident from their grooming. "Lance Rykov," he said, hold-

ing out his hand to her, as if they hadn't clashed in Council and elsewhere a hundred times.

"Mr. Rykov," said Tabitha. "I thought you were dead."

It barely touched him. "It was mutual, Captain," he said. His hatred was palpable.

Of course, it was entirely possible he was a spy. "Tell me, Mr. Rykov," she said. "What does Stark think about you being here, with the Resistance?"

Rykov was easy on that issue. "Colonel Stark has decided her duty lies with the ruling forces," he said, baring his teeth in a frosty smile. "I'm afraid I retain an old-fashioned allegiance to my own species."

"I'm very glad to hear it, Mr. Rykov," said Tabitha frankly. Havoc were just trouble, but there was no reason not to co-opt this lot. "I'm looking forward to doing something about those ruling forces, myself. I'm very impressed with the support I can see we've got here. Shit—I'm amazed!"

She laughed. There were some who laughed with her.

Amid the babble she caught the sober sound of Dodger's voice. She was talking to Norval Khan about the convergence of Capellan ships they had sighted, out on the rim. The Khan had one of his women with him, his big mammas. The mamma was wearing thigh boots and a torn scarlet corset, an automatic weapon slung on her hip. She was draped around the Khan.

Captain Jute paused, letting Rykov know she was listening to what Dodger was saying. "There's a lot going on," she said, after a few seconds. "We shall all have to sit down, first thing, and sort out everything we know."

Rykov would love that, she was sure. He and his kind liked nothing better than meetings, agendas, delegations. At least they went armed.

A couple of scrawny women in black combat shirts showed Tabitha the VR simulation pods they were using for training, and what they had to fight with in reality. Between the stockpiles of the Redcaps, the Hands On Caucus,

the Pontine Guard and the Horde, a surprising pile of or-
thodox arms and ammunition had been amassed: boxy grey
Laphams and burnished blue Marstens; Vantages and Vin-
dicators. In addition, the craftspeople of Havoc had contributed a terrifying array of weapons ingeniously
improvised out of scrap and salvage. They showed her
savage-looking hooks, cutlasses of beaten sheet metal,
lightweight crossbows, heavyweight cudgels, telescopic
pikes. They spoke lovingly of "the Fernando." It turned
out to be some kind of flying ram they had constructed, in
the workshops below.

Four Vespans were practicing with knives: an elephantine ballet of violence and vulnerability. Captain Jute
rubbed her throat, thinking of a previous battle she had
fought against Capellans. "We shall have to recruit some
Perks," she said.

There was a general swell of sarcastic amusement.
"Perks," drawled a wrinkled hordesman. " 'Deldi did for
them." His hairy comrades smirked and scratched their
crotches.

Karen was at her elbow. Her eyes were tired but bright.
"Come down and see the *ships*," she said.

They sealed their suits and stepped into an oversize airlock, one of the original Frasque fixtures, with membranes
that parted when you stroked them and sealed when you
struck them a blow. Beyond were unpressurized corridors,
broad and low, then a flight of huge uneven stairs leading
down to an apron of bleak grey asphalt, the very bottom
of the hive itself.

On the asphalt, some way from the stairs, the number
330 was painted in huge white figures. They glowed dimly
up at her in the inadequate light, a signal for her to remember.

She remembered 330. They had told her about this. 330
was the section of the docks that had been cut off by the
spatial disruption. When the hive had been coughed out of

hyperspace, part of its spongy interior had suffered a metaphysical squeeze, or bite, or something. 330, that whole corner of the sternward docks, had vanished. It had ballooned out, the scientists supposed, into another dimension.

Instead of which, she was now standing in it.

She gazed aft. From the top of the stairs you should have easily been able to see all the way to the huge round stern door.

It was blocked out behind a wall of silvery nothingness.

The last couple of kilometers of the docks might have been sliced off clean, and the hole sealed with a phosphor-coated field; except that there was no field, only coating. She felt her stomach turn over at the sight.

Forward, there was a different kind of chaos, more material and comprehensible. A whole cliff of parking bays had collapsed and brought the ceiling down with it, obliterating the flight-control buildings and sealing Section 330 off completely from the rest of the hive. The air had fled through the rupture, extinguishing at once the fires that elsewhere had continued to rage.

A lot of smaller debris had been cleared from the apron and now stood banked against the collapse, reinforcing it. As she jumped slowly down the stairs in that frozen darkness, Captain Jute could still make out the mangled remains of ships among those ruins. In the cleared space, other ships stood anchored: whole ones. They were lined up facing the fault in space.

Karen's hand was on her shoulder, their helmets touching. *"Look at this lot!"*

Captain Jute was looking.

What she was seeing was the strangest fleet ever assembled for review. They were like dream ships, each ship dreaming she was something else. There was a classy moonsloop, a Gordimine Spada IX, wearing a fearsomely blackened set of force radiators, like a stiff skirt of electric fence around her fuselage. There was a Caledonian tourist ferry, painted a conventional Day-Glo orange, which at the stern sprouted impulse-catalyzer extensions and turned into something very much more punchy. There was the Fernando they were so proud of: a two-seater sled with some antiquated Palernian ionic distributors clamped on behind, and a mass of scrap metal welded to her bow. *"They'll think she is porcelain, when she meets Fernando!"*

Their confidence was breathtaking.

There was a Lapham Boniface yacht, a late model 3700, built more for comfort than power. Her name was painted on her stern in sky-blue letters: the *Same Old Katy*. The 3700 had been an executive toy, sold to database surgeons and portfolio rationalizers for weekend jaunts around Jupiter. She looked very whimsical and frail in this martial company. The Captain looked at Karen. Karen didn't seem worried.

Aft of the *Same Old Katy* stood something far more convincing: a Freimacher Eagle. She was one of the few here that seemed to be still as her makers had intended, like an origami bat in electric blue with lemon trim. Even the added neutron cannon harmonized with her overall lines.

The Eagle was Rykov's. Tabitha could see him by the undercarriage, tapping a friction gauge with his knuckles. It was as transparent a display of proprietary gloating as Captain Jute had ever seen.

The radio crackled in her ear. *"She fancies that one,"* said the voice of Dodger Gillespie. Tabitha saw her standing some way off with her arms folded, watching.

Tabitha plodded carefully away aft, turning back to survey the whole of the ramshackle fleet.

"How many?" she asked. "Altogether?"

"Seventeen . . . " sent Karen Narlikar. Her glee was audible.

Captain Jute bent forward and banged her fists on her knees. "Bloody brilliant!" she whispered.

Two lithe grey suits ran up and capered around her, excited by her sudden display. They were Kenny and Soi.

How many ordinary ships had they had to cannibalize to

knock up seventeen warships? How had they been able to marshal the gear, the expertise, the patience, all under twitchy Eladeldi noses?

"They don't know about any of these?"

Sven Dolan pointed to the Spada. "*Destroyed in local collapse*," he said. He pointed to the next along, a completely unidentifiable armor-plated mongrel that called itself the *Night Boy*. "*Destroyed in civil disorder.*" He indicated others: a Lesondak, a Silverfish. "*Defunct, lost, unaccounted for . . .*"

"And you've tested all of them."

"*Test them?*" echoed someone. "*You can't test them.*"

"*Idea is,*" said someone else she realized was Norval of Havoc, slouching toward her from the stairs, "*not to let on they're here.*" His signal cut off abruptly as he switched channels to say something not for her ears. She saw his companions snigger.

They were going to fly seventeen ships, improvised and untested, through a wall of nothingness, out of the occupied and guarded hive, and take them to try to bang a hole in the side of a gigantic fully functioning alien starship a hundred thousand kilometers away.

Nothing had changed on Plenty. Plenty was a world of nightmares.

"*Look what we done to mine!*"

Karen was leading her by the arm to where she could see the McTrevor Clavicorn Karen herself had flown in on, once upon a very long time ago. They had epoxied a muon slink gun blister into her cargo hold and renamed her the *Maximum Disturbance*.

"*Here,*" said the Havoc Khan unexpectedly, moving past her and beckoning her on. "*Here. See that.*"

That was a Bergen Danuta 12, a tough little wedge of grey steel with stabilizer fins as stubby as a Kobold's. Cockpit and engines were all there was of her, with inertium baffles separating the two. She looked reasonable.

The Danuta had been designed as an all-purpose vehicle

for well-heeled Belt mining prospectors and overseers who needed to navigate short distances at high speed in any grade of orbital dust. Most pilots agreed, she was the most thoroughly rugged, supremely maneuverable, wholly fool-proof scoutship ever made. A Danuta offered comfortable transportation for two standard-size humans, cramped for three. Her blue-carbon glass canopy was hinged up to show that the techs had been in there, strengthening pilot and copilot's webs, replacing the consolidation monitor of her old-fashioned 2D perimetric scanners with a neat little hol-opad not much bigger than a beermat.

Everyone gathered round the Danuta, Karen Narlikar and Dodger Gillespie, Norval Khan and his cronies, Kenny and Soi and Tabitha Jute. The Khan put his hand on the felt-lined canopy seal. "*You like that?*"

"What kind of artillery has she got?" asked Captain Jute.

"*Ain't none,*" said the Khan flatly. "*Okay?*"

She couldn't think why he was demanding her opinion on this ship in particular. "Looks fine," she temporized. At least it was true. "Good condition. I'm sure she's great, yeah."

Through his faceplate she saw his dark eyes slide away from her as his attention expired. "*That's yours,*" he said.

Tabitha Jute felt insulted and confused. They were all flying tanks and battle cruisers. What they'd given her was a jeep.

Tanks made out of tankers, she told herself. Battle cruisers made out of beer tubes and tape. When the tanks and battle cruisers fell apart, the Danuta would fly on.

The Danuta was like the stretcher at the bottom of the liftshaft, the intensive-care equipment on the *All Things Considered*. No one had known what shape she'd be in, physically, when she got back. They'd prepared for some loss of capability. It was fair enough.

The name inscribed on the bows of the Danuta was the

Cookie Cutter. First the *Billy Budd*, now the *Cookie Cutter*. Well, that could be changed. The floor of the cockpit was covered in pale reddish hairs.

Captain Jute pressed the button on the persona reader. A red light came on. There was no plaque in the slot.

Someone was climbing into the cockpit beside her. It was Kenny. He grinned happily, despite the absence of armaments.

The message was clear. They wanted her safe.

She pressed the switch on the underside of her chair arm to close the canopy and pressurize the cockpit, and unfastened the pocket of her backpack.

She would have to detail a couple of the gunships to guard her constantly. They had already thought of that, in all probability.

Nobody, at this point, was paying her any attention. She whizzed round the channels. Karen Narlikar was talking to Soi, they were both laughing happily. People were asking Dodger Gillespie about the rescue. She could see Norval Khan over by the Eagle, with Rykov. It was weird, those two together, comrades in arms. If Rykov did turn out to be a traitor, Norval of Havoc would still be the man to sic on him, Captain Jute was sure of that.

Already the Danuta stank of eager Thrant.

Tabitha looked at her companion, ruffled the fur behind his ears. "What do you think, Kenny? You think she'll do?"

The Thrant made a high whining sound in the back of his throat, like an excitable dog about to start barking.

She took Alice's grey plaque out of the backpack and loaded it in the reader. The plaque reader whirred.

"We'll take her," said Tabitha.

The red light on the plaque reader flashed green. Alice's voice blared out. "GOOD MORNING, CAPTAIN."

Kenny flattened his ears.

"Good morning, Alice," said Captain Jute, identifying the volume control and turning it down.

"WHAT A VERY BASIC LITTLE BOAT," said the Kobold persona.

"A rugged little 7500k boat," said Captain Jute. Quite a good command vessel, under the circumstances. The vox was still too loud, and she turned the knob as far as it would go. "Nippy," she said.

"NOT VERY MUCH TO GO WRONG," observed Alice, blandly. "WHO WAS COOKIE CUTTER, CAPTAIN, DO YOU KNOW? IT DOESN'T SEEM TO SAY."

"It's not a who, it's a what," said Captain Jute. "A thing you make cookies with. Cookies. To eat." Briefly, unexpectedly, she thought of Saskia Zodiac and her insatiable appetite, Saskia rising from beside her in the middle of the night and returning with a packet of gingersnaps. "Don't worry about it, Alice," she said. "I'm not calling you Cookie."

Lights flickered on and off. "COMPLETE REATTRIBUTION WILL TAKE CONSIDERABLE PROCESSING TIME," said the persona. "EVEN IN A DANUTA."

"Do it, Alice, please," said Tabitha. Kenny's ears were still down. She stroked his arm. "You're very loud, Alice," she remarked. "Can you do something about that, too?"

The plaque reader whirred again, a few seconds longer. "WHY DON'T I DO—THIS?" suggested Alice, as on the holopad a familiar little blond figure popped into being. "WE HAVE AMPLE SPARE—"

"—CAPACITY," said the little blond girl. She was less than twenty centimeters tall, and as before, perfect in every detail.

Kenny rose, snarling at the apparition.

"Shut up, Kenny," said Tabitha. "It's only Alice."

The spectral child stood with her hands folded, visibly awaiting instructions.

"Say something else," Tabitha told her. "Say that thing about Humpty Dumpty."

Little Alice flicked back her long blond hair and began

to recite. "HUMPTY DUMPTY SAT ON A WALL, HUMPTY DUMPTY HAD A GREAT—"

"That'll do," said Tabitha.

Kenny was holding his arms up above his head, looking unhappy.

"Cheer up, Ken," she said. "You'll be chopping up Capellans soon."

He drew back his lips. "Take me to eem, Cap'n," he said, in his high, sneering voice. "Take me to eem."

Tabitha lifted her head and gazed through the blue canopy, over the buckled asphalt, into the looming discontinuity. It might have been a vast wall of mist, with now and then tiny flecks of light inside, like pinpricks of ferocious sunlight leaking through.

The Captain turned, checking the extent of view. Behind her and to either side, the Resistance were going about their business. Captain Jute was proud of them all. What they'd managed to achieve was amazing. There were even a couple of mech drones, she could see, attending to the refueling of the *Night Boy*.

She selected all available radio channels. "Okay, everyone," she said, and saw them turn to look at her. "You've done fantastically well. Nobody would have imagined a fraction of all this." She felt oddly giddy, like a glimmer of the way she'd felt her first day in command of Plenty. "With troops like you—well, we just can't lose. Eh?"

They were still looking at her, or in her direction. She saw a few arms raised and heard a ragged, rather restricted cheer.

"From now on, we're all ready around the clock. We stay with our ships. We eat and sleep and wait in our ships."

"*We already do, you stupid cunt*," someone sent back.

There was laughter, a concord of derision. Before Tabitha could frame a reply, Dodger Gillespie came on. "*We're waiting for the signal*," she said.

Captain Jute located her. She was over by the Eagle, with

Norval and Rykov. Her voice was hard. Captain Gillespie was issuing a signal of her own, a warning to Tabitha not to persist in her oration.

Soi, the Vespans, the Rooks: everyone was staring at Tabitha, watching to see what she would do now. Kenny grinned in her face, relishing the prematch frisson. Luxuriously he blinked his golden eyes.

"Put your helmet on, Kenny."

She drained the cockpit again, and opened the canopy. She stood up. She could see more of them now. They had all assembled to hear her.

"Now listen," she broadcast.

Norval Khan put his hands on his hips. "*Sit down,*" he sent.

Captain Gillespie nodded a fraction. With the slightest motion of one hand, she seconded the instruction.

There was something wrong here.

Captain Jute sank slowly back into her seat. Norval Khan was saying wearily: "*Spell it out for her, Dodger.*"

Captain Jute's jaw tightened to hear him addressing Dodger Gillespie without respect, and telling her what to do. "Just fuck off, Norval," she broadcast, not caring if everyone heard.

"*Look, gel,*" said Dodger Gillespie loudly, on her personal channel. "*Everybody's happy to have you back, in one piece. We want you along, but not if you're going to fuck up. All right?*"

A strange metallic taste seemed to fill Tabitha's mouth.

"*You stay right back,*" said the Khan, breaking in, so she knew he'd been listening. "*We board, you wait till we bring you in. Gorrit?*"

"*We'd appreciate your assistance in rallying the passengers, Captain,*" said someone else. It was Rykov. He was telling her what to do too, but trying to be polite about it, to alleviate the contempt displayed by Norval Khan.

The Khan walked across to the ship that stood nearest Rykov's Eagle. It was a Nebulon Green Streak: the toughest boat here, no question of it. She had a complete working pulse gun. On her fuselage was a scratched old painting of Tabitha's sister wearing a brass bra and toting a rocket launcher.

There was a roaring in Captain Jute's ears, as if her ship had started up already.

"*Norval's attack commander*," said another familiar voice in her phones. "*Lance is his second.*"

It was Karen Narlikar. She sounded a bit anxious now. She stood by her Clavicorn with Colgan and a couple of the Havoc greaseballs, gazing at Tabitha across the airless apron. She was appealing to her too, in her way, not to fuck up.

On the holopad, Little Alice clasped her tiny white hands in front of her pinafore.

"THEY'RE WAITING FOR YOU TO REPLY, CAPTAIN," she said. "DO YOU REQUIRE MORE TIME?"

Tabitha Jute felt the blood rise into her face. She was very angry; but she knew, she could feel, the anger was based on nothing. Inside was only a sharp hollow space, empty and dry, and the metal taste down the back of her tongue.

Staying alive was the first thing she had done right for a long time, and the only way she had done that was with Dodger and Karen and Jone and all the rest of them to hold her up. She thought of times Dodger Gillespie had literally done that, Dodger and people like her, everywhere she'd ever got legless.

Dodger and people like her. Angie and Mum and Auntie Muriel and the Rejects. Eeb and O'Shaughnessy. Kenny, Soi, Zoe Primrose, Lomax, Clegg and Otis. Alice.

"All right," she told them, all of them, the present, the absent, the dead. "Okay."

She pressed the switch to shut the canopy. As the blue glass closed over her she looked down at her hands, frozen on the console. She would not look at Norval Khan, or at Dodger Gillespie.

Beside her Kenny panted harshly and rubbed the lenses of his goggles with his thumb. He was happy.

"I didn't hear you make any promises," said Captain Jute to her faithful Thrant.

PART THREE

ABRAXAS RISING

Out on the rim of the system, three hundred thousand kilometers above the plane of the ecliptic, the Capellan starship the *In Power We Entrust the Love Advocated* hung in space.

She was using a fraction of her capacity to maintain a precisely calculated position, stationary with respect to the great clotted whirl of the system. The rest she was busy condensing and directing on an equally precise heading, rather as a gigantic gun might aim a ray at a target; though in this instance, of course, the line of the ray lay at right angles to everything else in the vicinity, including the formation of comparable and lesser ships assisting in its production.

From the *In Power We Entrust the Love Advocated*, looking three hundred thousand kilometers ahead, it was possible to perceive the interstellar vessel known as the *Inspirational Sound of Mandolins*. She was maintaining a similar station and identical attitude; while three hundred thousand kilometers astern, there was the *Fortune Presents Gifts Not According to the Book*, doing just the same.

The three ships all bore different shapes, so unlike one another as perhaps to hint at origins in different civilizations. If the *In Power We Entrust the Love Advocated* could be thought to resemble a clinical instrument, the *Inspirational Sound of Mandolins* was more like a huge paperweight, a discus of yellow marble. The shape of the *Fortune Presents Gifts Not According to the Book*, on the other hand, was conceivably reminiscent of some vast soft flower, a peony or cabbage rose. Her decks were nested, one curling in upon another, sheltering the slim central organs of her stellar drive.

Different or similar, three starships in a line might be thought a sufficiently remarkable occurrence. Yet here, at a distance of five hundred thousand kilometers around them, was a perfect ring of smaller ships: sixty-seven of them, all identical.

These were all the system ships of Capella: the whole fleet, each working at the farthest extent of her range. It had taken an enormous effort of organization to get them into place, with their displacement drives tuned to a single harmonic, and all at the correct angle of 23° to the ecliptic.

From here, the currents in the oval disc of matter captured and emitted by the anomalous stars could be discerned quite clearly, like a figure of eight in crumbled charcoal against the black abyss. At the twin gravitic centers, the suns themselves sat dark and swollen, more purple than red. To a fanciful observer on the *In Power We Entrust the Love Advocated* the Capellan twins might easily have suggested a pair of monstrous rotten beets; and the system ships, slender, waisted and golden, a swarm of superintelligent wasps, circling them at a thoughtful distance.

Fortunately for all concerned, there was no such observer. Apart from the necessary superhuman Kybernators and Supervisors, all the ships were crewed entirely by Eladeldi, a species whose members delight only in accurate instructions; so much so that metaphors make them unhappy. They start to whine and scratch themselves.

The only other participants in the magnificent exercise were equally subservient and methodical. These were the Cherubim, the inorganic infants of the *Seraph Kajsa*. They were busy, adjusting a dish here, a slave minisat there, helping dogged pilots and personas respond ever more exactly to the beacons, keying their transmissions to the ferocious music of the suns.

Naked, potbellied, legless, the Cherubim contended with the electromagnetic tides. They had experienced the equinoctial gales of Jupiter. Around the great circle they swarmed from ship to ship, invisible as spots of ink in the void.

On the *Seraph Kajsa*, alone in the Schematics control room, the renegade Cherub Xtasca hung in a plexiglass bubble, tethered by a reception tail of the lowest caliber. Between brief stints of monitoring blurts of data from the distant cartographer, it was considering the Frasque.

Numerous hives had been recorded in orbit around all three remaining planets, but no sign of life from any of them. Xtasca did not assume their builders were locally extinct, a species so hardy and tenacious. They would be here somewhere, a few populations, clinging, presumably, to the disintegrating remains of the planets themselves. Underground, in all likelihood, given their tropism for tunnels.

If none of them were to start building, it was hard to allot the Frasque a convincing value now in the Capellan calculus, except as an inconvenient remainder.

Three hundred thousand kilometers away, the other toiling Cherubim opened their rosebud lips and blinked their shining eyes. Together they called to their lost sibling. *"Come on out, the radiation's lovely . . . "*

In the center of the spherical chamber at the center of the *Seraph Kajsa* the inventor of the Cherubim hung to address the meeting. He wore his indigo coat and scarlet trousers, and a pair of yellow deerskin moccasins.

"The Lens is established," said Xipetotec. "The drives are engaged."

Boaz opened the lid on the com in his brassard and started entering figures. "What can they project, eventually?"

"It's building steadily," Xipetotec told him. He spread his hands and turned a quick backward somersault, addressing his remarks to everyone separately. "During the course of the next three orbits we confidently expect to see projection reach a level of a million hyperions a second."

A murmur of satisfaction went round. The Priestess Queen nodded, tilting her cleavage to the Schematicist. "We think everyone should be very pleased with that, Xippy."

From his perch floated Pomeroy Lion, his stylus raised politely. "You mentioned three starships, I think, Xipetotec. That's apart from the *Citadel of Porcelain*, is it?"

Xipetotec extended a patient finger toward the model that hung glowing in the air. "The *Citadel*," he explained, "is here. The fourth in line, if you like. The focus of the Lens."

"Oh, ah, mm, of course," Pomeroy Lion said, frowning distantly. Hyperparallax optics had never been his strong point.

The Queen stretched. "If there are no other questions," she said, "let us record our thanks to Schematics—"

"*Recorded*," said the ambience. "*Timed and dated 16.00.3—*"

"—and proceed to the next item," said the Queen, speaking over it. "The new construction."

Xipetotec erased his model and floated to an empty perch while Queen Kajsa took his place in the center. Pomeroy Lion straightened his tie.

"There's not much, we're afraid," said the Queen, "because it is so impossible these days to hear anything on the link, even when it's our sisters."

"It's like listening to someone eating celery," said Sweet Lavender, with a shudder.

"Windows are scheduled, Your Ubiquity," Xipetotec said. "Coms operators will have details in the next twenty-five hours." He beckoned to an attendant tech, who took directions and left.

The High Priestess ran her hand backward through her hair, which was short, black and erect on her head, as if each separate strand were proud to demonstrate its freedom from the tyranny of gravity. "What we can tell you," she said, "is that mitosis has begun, and skeletal sites for all the neuroblastomatic extras are being mapped."

"And the scale?" asked Boaz, who regarded all things gigantic as very much his province.

Kajsa Prime arched her back. "The scale," she said, "is *vast.*"

She put up a 2D.

"This is a photo shot," she said.

The picture had the unnaturally smooth and perfect quality of something that had been transmitted over a noisy line and cleaned up by extrapolation. It seemed to show a big white room with an elaborately extended greenhouse built inside.

The Queen took a pointer and drew a circle round a tiny blue lozenge in the corner of the room, making it flash for them.

"This is a blood-plasma tanker."

Everyone exclaimed. Boaz spread his arms, almost striking a couple of techs. "Hail to His Birth!" he proclaimed.

"Oh, Hail, absolutely!" cried the Priestess, visibly amused.

"Oh, dear," muttered Pomeroy Lion, who found this particular quirk of Boaz's terribly embarrassing.

"I thought he said *scales,*" remarked Sweet Lavender flatly. He was preening, tweaking a proud wing feather back into line. Boaz gave him a stern glare, suspecting ridicule.

"Oh, scales eventually," said Pomeroy Lion, jumping up and launching himself forward, to defuse any antagonism before it could start. "Laminar dermatogenic differentiation is scheduled to commence, I believe, in Phase 5, and continue until Phase 51 . . ."

The Capacitory Chief saw Queen Kajsa looking at him with polite inquiry. He lifted his chin and smoothed his beard. "H'rumph. Sorry, Kajsa, do forgive me."

"No, Pomeroy, stay there," she told him, kicking back to her perch. "We really have nothing more than that to report, as we said, except that everyone expects the speed of development to pick up a good deal when they come through. Oh, and you know, of course, that Brother Nestor has promised unanimous approval for the basic design profile by this time tomorrow.''

It was a little bit of a joke, that *unanimous*, and everyone chuckled comfortably, except Boaz, who didn't get it. If there was any discontent, it was in the face of Xipetotec of Schematics, where it was hard to see.

''Mean*while*, though, Pomeroy—''

''Oh yes: mean*while*,'' echoed Sweet Lavender, with arch good humor. He wriggled eagerly, clutching the seat with his hands between his thighs.

The Prime batted her eyelids at him. ''Mean*while*,'' she said again, mocking herself and him, ''we believe you have someone to introduce to us, isn't that right?''

''Oh. Oh, yes, Your Superiority,'' said the Chief of Capacitory.

He was reluctant now that they had come to his turn. This project was not one he could ever contemplate entirely with ease. ''If there really are, er, no more questions for, ah, Her, um, Pre-Eminence?''

He looked around the chamber without much real hope. There were none. ''In that case,'' said Pomeroy Lion, smoothing his coattails as he turned to signal to a waiting page, ''could you bring the, um, the new clone in, please?''

The page bowed and flew.

For a moment, the spherical chamber was utterly still.

When the page returned, she was solicitously steering a hoverchair with a long pineal lead that snaked in extravagant loops above her head. In the chair sat a thin figure clad in a stiff grey suit.

He was tall now, and sat awkwardly, with his knees at different angles and his hands clasped together. He looked as if he was concentrating so hard on something he had completely forgotten that he had a body now.

His skin was flaccid and white, as if they had just that minute extracted him from the tank. His collar and tie, like his trim black hair, were perfectly neat and tidy, but they did little to conceal the suture marks around his neck, which were thick and red. His left eye was rather bloodshot, too, and the orbits of both eyes were dark as bruises. His head, nevertheless, the clone held high, disdaining to look at anyone, as if this spherical assembly of his recreators was of no great interest to him.

Pomeroy Lion floated above him, one hand outstretched in a gesture of introduction, the other in the sleeve of his waistcoat, hooked by the thumb. "This," he told his colleagues, "is Project PL3484, Mister—"

Belatedly it occurred to the Capacitory Chief that although a number of aliases had been used and mentioned during their dealings with the man, what they were to call him now was not something they had discussed. He cleared his throat and trod air, knuckling his moustache. "Erm . . ." said Pomeroy Lion. "That is—"

"Mr. Nothing," said the dry voice of his new creation. The *soi-disant* Mr. Nothing did not look at Pomeroy Lion, or at anyone else, but addressed the empty air.

"Mr. Nothing," repeated Pomeroy Lion, formally. "Mr. Grant Nothing. Of course. Mr. Nothing is now at the level comparable to an eight-year-old child—in, in muscular development, I mean, naturally, muscular development and hormonal—"

Grant Nothing interrupted him, almost bad-temperedly. He said: "There are a number of things we need to determine."

His manner was quite unlike that of any eight-year-old. His voice was dry and weak, as if with patience worn thin.

The Seraphim looked at him attentively. Queen Kajsa, smiling graciously, asked: "What things might those be, Mr. Nothing?"

"The whereabouts and condition of the woman. Captain Tabitha Jute."

At that Pomeroy Lion looked a little guilty, a little pained.

"We were expecting to talk about you, Mr. Nothing," said the Queen.

The clone closed his eyes, as if with moral rather than physical discomfort. "Captain Tabitha Jute," he said again, irritably, separating the words. "Nothing can be done until the question of the Captain is resolved."

Sweet Lavender spread his wings and left his perch. He hung in the air over the man in the hoverchair like a raptor considering whether there was enough meat on him to make him worth stooping for. The page looked at him anxiously.

"Captain Jute is dead," said Sweet Lavender.

Grant Nothing looked up at him. He looked at him as if he were neither an angel nor an eagle, but a daddy longlegs or a moth, a brainless thing that might easily become a nuisance. He looked away again.

"*I* was dead," he said.

"No one has revived Tabitha Jute," Sweet Lavender said, impatiently. "We certainly haven't, and they wouldn't. They can't stand her."

"Update," said Boaz in a voice like a steel door closing somewhere underground.

"*Bergen Kobold* Billy Budd *terminally damaged on third planet 95.720,*" said a disembodied voice. "*Standard interplanetary mayday signals recorded at .734, .786, .790—*"

"When was the last of those?"

"*Last and loudest broadcast, nonstandard content, unintelligible, 97.987.*"

"Fifty-something orbits ago."

"Fifty-six," said Grant Nothing.

His fog grey eyes had turned to Boaz. Though it was the first time he had seen the Head of Prevision, it did not seem to concern him in the slightest that the man was five meters tall, broad in proportion, and clad in pink-and-purple armor.

"And you still haven't searched the wreck," said Grant Nothing.

"By the Infinite Permutations of Plasma!" thundered Boaz.

Pomeroy Lion attempted again to intervene. "Life signs have been zero for the last three hundred sweeps," he began to tell his subject, softly. Grant Nothing pointed oddly over the side of his chair, as if there were something beneath it that they had failed to see.

"At this precise instant," he said, "there are three sleds on board this ship, working sleds, that are not in use. One of them is fully charged. Its duty crew are playing electronic canasta."

Sweet Lavender gave a flutter of exaggerated surprise at the particularity of this intelligence, but flew backward to his perch without comment. Queen Kajsa caught his eye, and the two exchanged a covert smile. It really was remarkable how much the creature presumed, and how effectively. The Capellans might have left him with only one idea in his head, but they had not taken away the means to assert it.

"Leaving aside the question of Captain Jute—" began Kajsa Prime.

"I should be perfectly happy," said the rebuilt man, as if the High Priestess had not spoken, "to direct the operation myself."

"I'm sure you would," said Sweet Lavender.

"My plan is available. I am prepared to work directly from your data."

For the first time Grant Nothing looked directly at Kajsa Prime.

"As an absolute minimum," he said, "I need access to offboard communication channels." He rearranged his legs with his hands. "I can't find out anything for you shut up in a glass box," he added, with a sick and wintry smile.

Queen Kajsa spoke to the Master of her Capacitory division. "Shall we proceed to the demonstration, Pomeroy?"

Gravely Pomeroy Lion inclined his upper body. "Your Majesty."

The page swam down to the hoverchair and, with a flick, released the guide cable. A second door had opened, a circular hatch, producing a wide glass tube that extended swiftly to cross the chamber and isolate the clone. The page withdrew rapidly along the tube, coiling her cable as she went.

Gravity was introduced to the tube, gently at first, so as not to harm the clone, and then more strongly, until it approximated to the force under which the original man had lived on Plenty.

The new version ceased to speak. He sat at the bottom of the tube with his arms on the arms of his chair, resigning himself to experimental indignities. The Prime could almost begin to feel sorry for him.

The Master of Capacitory division stood with the fingers of one hand in the palm of the other, awaiting his sovereign's pleasure. She lifted a finger. "Tech?" he said.

A circular hatch in the floor of the tube slid open, and a nut brown woman in a white suit looked in.

"Would you please introduce the Thrant."

The Thrant was an adult: a female, nervous, and probably not very intelligent. She was prodded up through the hatch with her back to Grant Nothing. Not seeing him yet, she stared suspiciously out through the glass.

Her hands and feet were very big, and the insides of her ears were a beautiful shell-like pink. She was naked as an animal, her golden fur untrimmed, but as she moved around the glass, they saw her tail had been amputated: a sure sign that she had lived for a time with humans, in service to them, in a place that was either very conservative or very small.

The clone had recognized the Thrant instantly and altered his whole demeanor. He relaxed. His eyes found Kajsa Prime, and he gave her a graceful nod of appreciation, as if gratified. At that, Pomeroy Lion gave the Prime an apprehensive look.

The Thrant was still distracted by the faces watching her. When she finally turned and saw the cloned human behind her, lounging in his chair, she screamed as no one present had ever heard a Thrant scream before.

It was a deathly sound, a sound composed of terror, disgust and pure despair. The Thrant flung herself at the hatch, which was closed again. She tore at it with her claws.

The clone spoke to her. "*Well, well, well,*" the Seraphim heard him say. "*Here you are again.*"

"This is the one that killed him, is it?" Sweet Lavender asked Pomeroy Lion.

Pomeroy Lion inclined his head. "Hm, yes, it is," he said. He spoke very softly. "He raised her from a kitten, he says, but she turned on him in the end." He noticed Kajsa Prime looking inquiringly at him. She seemed puzzled. He smiled, reassuringly.

The Thrant threw herself against the glass, panting. Her fear was palpable. At the first sound of the voice of the clone, she had fouled herself. She seemed to be having trouble controlling her legs as well.

Clumsily her reborn master opened his jacket and pushed himself up straighter in his chair. "*I cannot tell you how pleased I am,*" he said, "*to see you.*" He held out his hand as if offering to caress the Thrant, or give her his blessing.

The Thrant did not venture to speak. She dropped onto all fours. All down her back the fur was bristling erect. She was shivering. The Prime Seraph was sure she could hear her whimper.

"Pomeroy—" she said; but the man called Nothing was still speaking, so she continued to listen.

"*There's something I owe you, Iogo, isn't that right?*" said Grant Nothing. Even over the com his voice was smooth and strong, with no trace of its former enervation. They had his interest. "*An unpaid debt.*"

The Thrant twisted her head around and pressed the side

of her muzzle against the glass. Her eyes were ablaze with fear. Drool ran from her mouth. She gave a hoarse, creaking sigh, as though even her voice had failed her now.

Grant Nothing smoothed his tie. It was a deep dark pink, the color of raspberries. It was fastened to the front of his shirt by a narrow pin that bore a small discreet jewel. Grant Nothing held his tie-pin in both hands, as if to straighten it.

"*I regret I can't treat you with the same consideration that you showed me,*" he said. He seemed to search for a word. "*A difference of style, perhaps we should call it. A different method.*"

A narrow beam of light shot from the jewel on Grant Nothing's tie pin. The Thrant he called Iogo screamed again, this time with pure pain, as it transfixed her shoulder.

She collapsed on the floor on her face. The tiny light did not waver. It moved across her shoulders, then down her back. A line of smoke rose from the fur in its path.

More excrement spilled from her, followed by a rush of dark blood. The light doodled a moment on her hindquarters, then danced away to her feet, still scrabbling at the velour floor. She flopped over on her side, spasming.

"*A different branch of civilization,*" mused the man in the chair. Delicately his tiny beam pierced her pale green eyes.

The sound of her screaming ceased.

"*There we are, then,*" said Grant Nothing. "*That's it. Though, come to think of it—*"

To everyone's surprise, he rose from his chair. He stood, swaying, on his feet.

"Good Lord," said Pomeroy Lion.

Awkwardly, as if the movement cost him pain, the clone stumbled to the ruined body of his erstwhile companion. His mouth was twisted into a strange shape unlike any conventional human facial expression. No one knew when he had opened his fly, but it was open now, and from it protruded his prick, pale, white and erect.

The High Priestess of the Seraphim said: "We think that's enough now, Pomeroy, if you don't mind."

Muttering apologetically, Pomeroy Lion touched a button. Faintly the glass enclosure rang with the harmonics of an ultrasonic signal. Instantly unconscious, Grant Nothing collapsed across the corpse of his victim.

Techs burst from the hatch. Speedily but gently they picked up the clone and restored him to his chair. Devices were attached to measure his pulse, his breathing.

Kajsa Prime looked less than satisfied. "We can't use that," she said.

"I disagree," said Xipetotec, who had not spoken since the clone had first been brought in.

The arch of Kajsa Prime's eyebrows might have been calibrated to register skepticism.

Sweet Lavender looked bored. "I wonder what for," he said rudely.

"As he says," replied the Master of Schematics. "To eliminate Tabitha Jute. He is a shaped missile." It was a notion he seemed to find exciting.

Sweet Lavender made a crude, insulting movement, looping his hand out from his crotch and back again. "Tabitha Jute is dead," he said, unpleasantly.

Xipetotec spread his hands and looked the angel in the eye. "Is she?" he said pointedly.

"Mr., ah, Nothing doesn't think so," mused Pomeroy Lion, watching them take out the hoverchair with its slumped figure.

Kajsa Prime took his arm in a preemptive demonstration of forgiveness. "Nor does Brother Melodious, actually," she observed. "We were going to mention that."

Boaz had watched the whole demonstration with statuesque indifference. Now he said: "She's a flea."

"Exactly," said Xipetotec. "An itch."

Queen Kajsa bent one leg up behind her and looked down speculatively at her stockinged calf, as if suspecting a run. "She doesn't itch us," she said distantly. "We think she's rather fun."

Boaz hated all conversations about the Capellans. "Let them itch," he growled.

"Mm, ah, it's a very delicate situation," said Pomeroy Lion, as if assuming that was a category of event that his giant colleague might have difficulty identifying. "You know, we still don't know exactly what we're dealing with here."

Sweet Lavender flew away.

The Capacitory Chief stood by his conviction. "We don't want them distracted," he said.

"In our experience," said Queen Kajsa, checking her other stocking, "it's very hard to know when they're actually concentrating. Or what on. Brother Nestor has been terribly hard to understand, lately."

Inside the glass enclosure the techs were now cleaning up, removing the remains. Inaudible fans toiled, extracting the foul air.

"Whose idea *was* that, Pomeroy?" asked Queen Kajsa then.

The Capacitory Chief pulled the corners of his mouth down. "Well," he said, "in a way, it was his, I suppose."

She seemed to find this incredible. "He asked you to send for her? And you did?"

"We thought it would be a good test." He threw out a hand toward the enclosure. "It was," he said without rancor. He blinked, then looked doleful. "We thought it might get him off the subject of Captain Jute for a bit," he confessed.

"We rather wish you had told us what you were doing, Pomeroy."

"Sorry. It is all recorded. He keeps asking about, um, Saskia, too." Pomeroy Lion sucked his teeth, and shook his head. "Erect already." He blushed. "On his feet, I mean. Have you ever seen anything like that? I never have.

The acceleration is beyond anything we could have hoped.''

"That's the sunlight," said Kajsa Prime, smiling as graciously as if she had created the suns herself, for his use and pleasure.

Sweet Lavender had not gone far away. He came floating down the outside of the tube, spiraling around it to where Xipetotec stood with his hands in the pockets of his coat, still watching the techs.

"The things that happened," said the Chief of Schematics somberly, "in that hive."

The angel looked pained. "Don't," he said with disgust; and then: "Does anyone know why we still haven't heard from the Frasque?"

Behind him, Boaz's metal face showed no more emotion than a wastebasket. "Because we deal with the worms," he stated.

"They used to like us," said Sweet Lavender.

"We are here now," said Boaz.

"Pomeroy would say we don't know what phase they're in," said Xipetotec, with a glance at the Capacitorian, in conversation with the Queen.

"The wrong time of the month for them, is it?" said Sweet Lavender. "Poor things."

Xipetotec lifted a finger. "*If* she is alive—" The angel tutted, but remained. "If, I say *if,*" his colleague continued, "then she's bound to go back to that hive. If the Frasque are not in control, we could lose the whole thing."

"She is a speck," said Boaz. "She is of no consequence."

"Nobody there could possibly take any notice of her now," agreed Sweet Lavender, impatiently.

"She ran that hive all the way from Earth," said Xipetotec. The angel sighed and muttered. Xipetotec ignored him. "We ought to be looking for her ourselves."

They were listening to him.

He appealed to Kajsa Prime. "Let the clone find her," he counseled. "Give him his head."

There was much laughter at Xipetotec's unconscious joke, from all except Boaz, who was sulking. "Give him his head!"

"*That's* why they gave us the head," said Sweet Lavender tartly. "They think we want to clear up their mess for them." He gave Xipetotec a look as if he thought he had just scored a point.

The Queen patted herself on the cheek. "Maybe there's some advantage in seeming to do it voluntarily," she suggested. "Maybe it's some kind of test."

"Let him try," said Xipetotec. "Let's at least target our missile, if it's possible."

"It would keep him busy," agreed Pomeroy Lion.

"Especially if she is dead," said Sweet Lavender, with a vicious twitch of his wings.

"Give him a couple of techs, then," Queen Kajsa told Xipetotec. "With access to coms and external data."

"You'll have to watch him," warned Pomeroy Lion.

"Every second," said the Queen. "Don't let him touch anything." She gave a shudder and rubbed her shoulders.

"I'll make it a priority," promised the Schematician.

"And Saskia Zodiac?" said Pomeroy Lion to Queen Kajsa.

"They have so much in common," said Sweet Lavender sentimentally.

"I was merely thinking she knows more about Tabitha Jute than anyone."

Kajsa was summoning her chariot. "We absolutely forbid it," she said. "She'll end up like the Thrant."

"By the Omnipotence of Osmosis!" boomed Boaz, resoundingly. "Throw them all outside. Let us concentrate on the Great Work."

A compromise was reached on the question of Saskia Zodiac. She was brought, some six or seven orbits later, into Schematics and left alone in a semicircular cubicle. There was light gravity, and an oversize armchair like the pilot's seat in a luxury scouter. On the arm of the chair was a plastic tray bearing a selection of sweet and savory snacks. The walls were high, smooth, featureless, matt white. There was no sound. Saskia sat down and started to eat.

Without warning, the flat wall turned suddenly and instantaneously transparent. Beyond it was another cubicle, the other half of the cylindrical chamber. Sealed inside it, in a chair like her own, was the revived Grant Nothing.

She was not surprised to see him. He had obviously been expecting her.

His body was fully grown now, and dressed once again in his unvarying pale grey suit, white shirt, red tie. His skin was as colorless as the walls, so that the red of the tie clashed with the red marks on his neck.

His voice came to her through a concealed speaker. *"Your friend has left Capella 3, has she?"*

"How would I know?" said Saskia bluntly.

He looked down at his white hands, long and narrow as her own. *"You might have done a little conjuring trick—?"*

She gave a short laugh. "Vanished her, you think? I'd like to vanish you." She flipped peanut up in the air and caught it in her mouth.

They didn't seem to have given him anything to eat. Perhaps he didn't eat anymore. Perhaps they just plugged him in to the mains like a drone, and left him.

"You'd like to change me into your brother," he told her, as if he believed he knew her mind now better than she. *"It wouldn't take so much, now."*

He rubbed the inside of his wrist in circles on the arm of his chair. *"The Captain seems to have moved out of the Billy Budd, at any rate,"* he told her. *"Found somewhere more roomy, has she? Or with better company?"*

Saskia popped another peanut. There was no point in

trying to taunt him with her own equanimity, her poise, regained now and undisturbed despite his presence. He was the type who had no interest in bodies and what they could or couldn't do, unless they were spreadeagled and tied down for him.

"*Of course, the Captain's taste in company has never been particularly wise . . .*" said Grant Nothing. "*Or wholesome.*"

Saskia Zodiac said nothing.

"*I'm sure she's not in any danger at all,*" said Grant Nothing, in a tone that implied, with a certain amount of glee, rather the opposite.

Saskia Zodiac had ceased to listen. He was merely fishing now, and light years off course. She turned her head and looked at the wall. "I'm ready to go now," she told it.

In the other half of the chamber the watching clone twitched. "*That's an activity I'd associate more with the Captain than with you,*" he said. "*Talking to walls . . .*"

There was another moment's pause, and then the door opened on Saskia's side. A tech came in; not the one who had brought her, another, with the number 10 on his suit. He did not speak, but bowed slightly and held his hand out to her.

Saskia Zodiac got out of her chair and left with the tech. She did not say goodbye or even toss a disparaging remark. She left the peanuts behind.

Watching on the screens in Schematics, Xipetotec frowned. "That was quick," he said.

"I don't suppose he'd have got much out of her," said Pomeroy Lion. "Not while he's prevented from, erm, touching her, you know."

He spoke glumly, but the Head of Capacitory was not without a degree of fondness for Saskia Zodiac himself, and it had cheered him up to see her snub her tormentor. He was secretly pleased that Kajsa had decided to send the tech in. His eyes flicked toward the com.

"I suppose she'll call," he said doubtfully.

"I suppose so," said the Head of Schematics, who had never expected much from this particular part of the experiment; but the Queen of the Seraphim was clearly keeping her own counsel, and neither sent nor came.

∽ 26

Since the Frasque had begun to be collected into Plenty, the ships on the Stardeck of the *Citadel of Porcelain at First Light* had been tuned up, and moved into tighter formations. A squadron of the Tinkerbells was placed on standby, just in case things got out of hand. Kybernator Perlmutter personally offered Kybernator Astraghal reinforcements for his perimeter patrols, and a shuttle load of Eladeldi was dispatched.

"I don't really expect he'll need them," said Sister Mansuetude. "There's practically no one left on board."

"No one anyone would really miss," said Brother Melodious. "I have to say it, there were a lot of undesirables in there. Loners, dweebs." He twisted his original hand over his head and squinted madly. "Cuckoos," he said. "I guess maybe that is the kind of person you'd expect to want to go to another star."

Brother Melodious liked to keep up with what was happening on Plenty, and to display expert knowledge of even the most impenetrable corners. He didn't mind admitting he remained "kind of attached" to the old place. "I know what she is, and I know she's dirty and disgusting and primitive, but I can't help it, I'm just in love with her. She's where I come from," he explained. "It was Plenty made me famous, all over again, and it's all been up, up, up since then." He caressed his bulging brow.

He regretted that he so rarely had the time to go over to the hive in person. The facilities here, to be honest, were so much better. "Like this," he said, gesturing to Sister Mansuetude's little quartet. "Ain't this great?"

Brother Melodious and Sister Mansuetude sat with nine or ten others on a platform looking over the miniature forest in Sector W. Four of Sister Mansuetude's special children were playing a selection of music by Purcell, Handel and Haydn. Brother Melodious knew that because the kids had printed up handbills and put them all over the place. There was a lot of that these days. The walls of the residential sectors were covered with notices, homemade ads for tarot readings, parties, dance workshops for post-transit stress.

Purcell, Handel and Haydn sounded a lot alike to him, kind of a lot of sawing. Sometimes it was fast and loud and sometimes it was slow and sad, but whichever it was the kids were pretty terrible at it, and he liked it best when it stopped. And when two little girls got up and started singing, two shrill squeaky voices in merciless unison singing something about shepherds on holiday, Brother Melodious would have had to say he didn't care for it much at all. Maybe it just didn't communicate to him. Below, among the trees, bright-colored birds flew around calling sharply, as if maybe it didn't communicate to them either.

Brother Melodious read his program again. "Who are those two?"

Sister Mansuetude was gazing at the girls with pride. "The one with the funny legs is Landy," she said, "and the other one is Tarmac. We did try to change that," she confided, with a pursed little smile, "but the others all call her Tarmac, so nothing else would do."

The kids looked very pure and scrubbed in their snowy tunics. Landy's splayed little toes strained out of the end of her sandals as she reached for the high notes, going way past some of them.

"I wish people would sing the old songs," said Brother Melodious.

"Oh, these songs are very old," his companion assured him. "Hundreds of years old."

"They sound it. Do they know any Reparata and the Del-Rons?"

The shepherds at long last finished their holiday, and the song ended. Everyone clapped and congratulated the little girls, who sat down looking flushed and pleased with themselves, and started to eat large bowls of strawberries. Meanwhile the ones with the violins and stuff started sawing again. Brother Melodious thought he knew the score by now, but he refrained from joining in. He polished his hand with his sleeve.

Suddenly out of the trees below came a great burst of interference.

"*Radio Xtasy,*" said a man's voice, "*this is Radio Xtasy checking in.*"

The voice was suave but urgent, and heavily amplified. The Guardians tutted and frowned at each other.

"*This is the Calico Show,*" the voice continued, over a clinking, rattling noise like twenty monkeys hitting milk bottles, "*going out to all you ladies and gentlemen, boys and girls—*"

The noise got louder. A flock of blue birds burst from the trees in fright. Several of the company propelled themselves out from the platform over the forest, looking down into the dense green foliage, hoping to spot the source of this crude interruption.

"*And especially those of you who never made your minds up—*"

All the children were smiling happily. Tarmac and Landy dropped their spoons and jumped up, patting each other.

"*It's zero hour for Captain D,*" cried the appalling Calico, as the birds wheeled and terrified creatures burst from the undergrowth. "*We face a proposition to party!*"

"*Zero hour for Captain D,*" sang a second voice, female, tuneless, chanting rhythmically over the milk bottles.

Bending to their instruments, the quartet started playing along.

Sister Mansuetude flew to them, clapping her hands. "Children, children!" she cried.

The tuneless voice blurred into a tuneless hoot, as if somebody somewhere had found a Palernian alive and started tickling it. The children were ignoring their mentor. Perhaps they could not hear her above the accumulating noise. Brother Melodious was amazed. They really did seem to be accompanying the music, if music was what it was. It wasn't any Purcell or Haydn, he was sure of that. It was like the kids already knew it, like they had been expecting it to start.

"*Xtasy Krew making honor,*" crooned Calico, "*to sisters and brothers way over there in the Big Bad Ants' Nest. Wishing you speed and safety. This is Pal Calico sitting on the Dawn Crapper, mixing a spin for you-you-you-you-you-you-you-you-you.*"

The word *you* split into a shower of identical repetitions that seemed to cascade down on the Guardians from the roof like sparks from a firework. Rings were being slapped and twisted, to no avail. The children were having their instruments taken away, but they were out of control, skipping and laughing. Now Calico's voice was turning into the woman's voice, and soaring high in vibrant electronic mutations. "*Check in, check in, Xtasy Krew.*"

"*Erika Electrika checking in,*" said a different woman's voice, a lazy-sounding one, from another direction entirely. "*With a multisite megablast to all our friends on other worlds.*"

"This is horrifying!" gasped Sister Mansuetude. She felt as if she were shouting into a mighty wind. "Where are the enforcers? Why don't they do something?"

"*Playing dedications this time—*"

Sister Celandine labored at the com, calling, "Emergency! Emergency!"

"*Dedication for Larry—*"

The com was not working.

"*Larry that got deleted—* "

Radio Xtasy on the com line!

"*This one from Dogsbreath.*"

A hundred monkeys hit milk bottles.

"*Honor the bass*," said a third voice, this one louder than ever, seeming to come from right underneath their feet, out of the platform itself. And despite the best efforts of Sister Mansuetude and her friends, Maz and his friends scattered, shouting: "Honor the bass! Honor the bass! Honor the bass!"

Powering up his artificial leg, Brother Melodious gave chase. He chased three of the little bastards right off the platform and down into the trees. Giggling they dived into the undergrowth, scrambling under bushes where he wasn't about to follow.

"Hell with them."

He headed for the nearest transit chute. The broadcast was audible all the way there, and when he arrived, he found it louder yet. Over here it came with a sharp whistling noise in, like a dozen high-speed drills. Outside the chute door a platoon of Eladeldi were struggling to stay upright and largely failing. They were foaming at the mouth and holding their ears in the most manifest agony.

Brother Melodious aimed a ring at the door. It whined, but failed to open. There were people inside, several large figures, blocking the chute.

Brother Melodious yelled at the cops for a little while, without result, then grabbed the com from one of their wrists. Pressing it to his ear, he could just hear a tiny voice babbling commands. He jabbed *Send* and started babbling himself.

"Emergency override! One, two, testing, is this thing on?" He shook the set determinedly. "This is Brother Melodious at W port 15! Get me Stark! I repeat, get me Stark! I want her here now!"

"*Checking in, this is Anno Dominate,*" a new voice said, chirping through the com. "*That was Dogsbreath, 'Hump the Lump,' basic basic. Dedication this time from Anno for Ronald—*"

" *—Ronald that got erased—* "

"*Ronald Royal Nerd!*"

"*For Ronald Happy Hacker!*"

They were laughing, celebrating the memory of Ronald, whoever the hell he was. A thousand monkeys were hitting milk bottles. They started breaking them.

Brother Melodious chucked the com away.

The people blocking the transit chute were Vespans. He could see them goggling at him through the door, pressing their bloated bodies to the glass, making wet smeary marks with every orifice.

Stark, miraculously, arrived, on a commandeered hoverbike. She skidded impressively to a halt and saluted Brother Melodious. Her buttons gleamed with authority and method.

"What's happening, Stark?" he shouted.

"Deviant elements attempting usurpation of legitimate audiovisual and communications facilities!" she shouted back.

"Pretty good attempt!" shouted Brother Melodious.

A red-suited officer crawled to his commander's shiny booted feet. The Colonel saluted him too.

"At ease, Captain."

The guard captain howled.

"Identify nature and gravity of distress," ordered the Colonel. "Specify degree of pain on a scale from one to ten."

He could only slobber.

"*That was Cy Kotic, this is Optimum Data Thruput,*" Anno Dominate told everybody.

Into all their ears a new serving of vicious noise shrieked and pulsated.

Beneath her needle-thin brows, the Colonel's eyes were small and bright with combat readiness.

"This looks bad, sir," she yelled at the Guardian. "Imperative I stand down patrol to seek medical attention."

Brother Melodious waved her to carry on. He stooped to remove the sidearm from the security holster on the belt of an insensible patrolman.

Soaring off the floor, Brother Melodious aimed the pistol at the three speakers he could see, a large ambient horn and two small grilles belonging to the transit p.a. All, so far as he could tell, were blasting out some part of the sonic attack. One by one, he burned them out.

There was no detectable lessening of the noise.

Colonel Stark was hammering on the glass of the transit chute door. On the other side the mud brown bodies wriggled, glistening. They were laughing at her in there.

They were Vespans, absentees from Sector V. The species was well-known for its hypersensitivity to sound and allied vibrations. She had had some of them once on Plenty, coming to complain about noise from the Redcaps' firing ranges. How did they continue functioning while her Eladeldi were falling like trees in a firestorm?

"Anyone picking up in the Bucket of Angels—"

Brother Melodious gritted his teeth. What the hell was that now? These kids' jive was nuttier than anything he and his pals had ever come up with, looning around the circuit in the first wild days of the Big Step. He couldn't believe they understood it themselves, Anno Dominate and Erika Electrika.

"—turn it up, you fuckers!"

Maybe this whole thing was one giant gag, a wild scheme to goose everyone on board and get the Eladeldi running around with their heads up their arses. Rock and roll, if that was what this was, some lost mixed-up mutant offspring of the one true groove—rock and roll had always meant a hunger for freedom to hang loose, get down, cut a rug. Brother Melodious twitched the lapels of his prismatic jacket. Uneasily he remembered that giving authority the finger had been a major element.

If these guys wanted to honor people, Brother Melodious felt, they ought to start with the ones who had given them the big freedom in the first place: the freedom to cut free from the draggy old Earth and shake a tail feather at the stars.

Now here was Stark, yelling at him again. She had failed to get the Vespans out of the entrance to the chute. "— may be obligated to disintegrate the doorway, sir."

"*Dedication this time for X!*"

"How the hell did they get *in* there?" Brother Melodious yelled back.

"*X the Chief!*"

"Communication cannot be transactioned!" bellowed the enforcer colonel. He had never seen her look more murderous. "Their aural orifices appear to be plugged with some form of plastic."

"*Chief X her shiny black self! Blank Dice this time.*"

More monkeys shook steel boxes full of thunder.

The locks on the doors to the Radio Xtasy studios had been plugged up too, and the doors themselves barricaded, but when they were eventually broken down, there was no one, of course, inside. All the decks were running, discs and tapes circling, all channels open, volume at maximum. The officers shut everything off at the mains. The noise ran on, unabated.

In a shielded bunker between two nonresidential decks, and a drained but malodorous sump in waste treatment, and a disused seed storage bay in Sector C, young men and women in Y-shirts and climbing shoes sat or stood or crouched, pushing the buttons on jury-rigged disc drives, toasting cassettes, randomizing the relays.

Erika's station was a pressurized plastic tent up in the Stardeck apartment wrecked by the escape of Captain Jute. Erika knew there was a good chance this was all pointless.

She knew the Plenty Resistance, that ill-assorted gaggle of spacers, bikers and dreamers: savages, the lot of them, retrotrolls unable to tell the difference between structure and function. "The only way they know to change something is chuck a chunk of metal at it," she said, off air. "The bigger the chunk the better." It was that addiction to mass that made them vulnerable.

Larry, in the bypassed sump, was worried about the Star Beast, about danger to the innocent inhabitants of the hive, indigenous and immigrant. Still he sighed, and said purposefully: *"They're relying on us."*

"They're en route, slick," said Anno in Erika's earpiece. Anno was somewhere deep in planetary tool storage, but she sounded as close and clear as if she had been sitting right beside her in the clammy tent.

Cheers rang out, but making contact with the Resistance had never been more than one part of the job. Full on, was the word; hold the loop and keep pumping till they take you down. A little light warned Erika the Blank Dice track was finishing. She keyed in a segue to some samples of foghorns from Neptune, and punched up an ancient album by Anal Re10Shun. "Honor the Havoc grebos!" she sent, laughing.

A small grey cat, a Siamese-offworld cross with one eye and a blue number tattooed in his ear, slipped silently in through the sphincter of Erika's tent. Behind him came a woman in a short-trip spacesuit. She smelled of sweat and amyl nitrate.

"Hey, Krew," sang Erika, "Catgirl checking in up here!"

By now there was merry hell in the dorms of Sector Y. One by one, the AV channels, the archives, even the rare and highly sensitive autonomic soundscapes had been rudely annexed and switched over to Radio Xtasy. Different mixes proliferated, igniting spontaneous parties and jamborees. Here, bubbly electronic tangos and fox-trots had the older evacuees up and swaying extravagantly in each other's arms. There, glutinous parodies of Species Harmony had the most sullen and disaffected youngsters sneering when Colonel Stark appeared with her hastily convened cadre of security robots and earmuffed Eladeldi. What fun it was to watch the red-capped martinet screaming orders and threats over the heads of the shuffling, jam-packed crowd and having them ignored by everyone.

All over the starship, speakers blurted in and out of life as the rapid-response circuits of the Xtasy Krew switched wavelengths and channels. Music, garbled speech or simple rude cacophony burst out high and low, the advertised names of the perpetrators changing as swiftly as the routes of their broadcasts. Now everybody seemed to have the names of colors picked at random from interior-design sample menus: "*Hyacinth axing Sector J . . . Oatmeal, check . . . Oyster on the mike . . .*"

On the bridge, reclining on his white-marble bench, Kybernator Astraghal turned from the master screen that showed the whole system from above, the glowing dots that were the other detectable elements of the Seraphim Lens. He considered the com globe that a slave had brought him. Inside it was the face of Colonel Stark, the exiles' security chief. Her sharply lipsticked mouth opened and closed, but the only sound coming through was Radio Xtasy. "*Flame here juggling the plaques and plugging the jacks . . . Take on me Cyclamen . . . Slate is integral . . .*"

With a graceful gesture of regret, Kybernator Astraghal handed the globe back to the slave. He saw his colleagues at their posts watching with inquiring expressions.

He shook a fold out of his toga. "Incomprehensible," he said.

Five decks down from the enameled arena where Captain Tabitha Jute, Saskia Zodiac and Xtasca the maverick Cherub had once been brought aboard in an undignified heap, Brother Melodious now fled, desperately seeking silence. His intelligence disconnected, his personality on hold, he was driven involuntarily as a drone into a low, crescent-shaped hall. Around both walls gamboled and sprawled a series of blue-faced nudes, pictorial vestiges of the starship's original owners. Above their painted heads ran lines of chevrons and parallelograms, abstract captions compact with forgotten meaning. The floor was filled with flaky fragments of dead skin.

The Guardian descended to the floor, his crepe soles crushing the debris. Panting as he returned to himself, Brother Melodious saw that he did not know where he was. This was not a part of the ship he had ever seen before.

It had been the ship's nursery, he was told. A generation in exile had been raised here, thirty thousand minute siblings feeding on each other until barely a hundred were left to go on to stronger fare.

Pure panic had driven this one back.

Even here, however, there was no silence. The little com by the door was tinnily racking out Radio Xtasy. Brother Melodious located the switch. It was off.

He lifted the cop pistol, which he found he was still holding. "Do I kill it?"

He paused a moment, then lowered the gun, irresolute. What they were playing now sounded as if it might have been halfway okay, with some proper breakneck racing guitar instead of those drills whistling. Whistling off-key, for Christ's sake.

Brother Melodious drifted into the center of the hall. With his original hand he rubbed his nose.

"What do I do here?" he asked aloud.

It was a reasonable enough question.

"Check on the children," he said. "What children?" He looked at all the dry skin beneath his feet. "There haven't been any children here in a while, that's for sure."

Brother Melodious could not confidently detect a reply.

He hated that. He hated them when they treated you like you didn't exist.

Did they mean the kids he'd been chasing in Sector W? That seemed a long time ago. They were going to lead him straight to the radio people. Was this where they were? He lifted the gun again, then looked at it, and stuck it in his belt. He chose a ring.

"Okay, come on out," he said.

The blue people on the walls continued about their frozen business. They ignored him too, more scenery than audience. They had no faces.

On Plenty. The children.

"Oh. Those children."

He chose another ring, on his other hand. He rolled up his eyes, in anticipation of the conversation that was about to happen. He activated the ring.

"Hey, Father? Father, can you hear me?"

"*Brother Mel . . .* "

Le Coq's bloodcurdling voice was weakened by space and dirt to a whisper in a crackle.

Maybe this was one link they couldn't tap into.

"*Pandemonium!*" declared Le Coq.

Brother Melodious smiled. Same old Rooster. The Rooster was one they would have preferred to ignore, while they shifted more and more Frasque into his parish. He was useful in his way, he kept the rejects entertained.

"Getting it too, are you?"

" *. . . the howling and knocking of the damned!*"

"Pain in the fucking ass," said Brother Melodious.

"*You . . . come raise a holy choir . . . kick Satan's ass with the songs of righteousness!*"

"It would be an improvement."

"*Brother, Brother . . . written, He swalloweth the ground with fierceness and rage: neither believeth he that it is the sound of the trumpet.*"

He felt kind of sorry for Le Coq. Le Coq was the sort of guy it was easier to feel sorry for when you didn't have him in your face every minute, waving his sacred medallions and stinking of snake piss.

"Rooster, I have a question for you. Are the children okay?"

"*Brother Valetude,*" the preacher said, then something he couldn't hear. " *. . . Beast blesses . . . gives unto him her young. Brother Melody . . . begging . . . hear your servant's prayer! Let him be even as Thou Art . . . whole heart I do implore . . .*"

The preacher was starting to sound desperate. The Frasque must be getting to him.

"Brother Valetude. Is he around?"

" *. . . with Brother Nestor,*" came the faint reply. " *. . . ease the mighty, mighty pain of Brother Nestor.*"

Brother Melodious hated to think about that pain. They all did.

"We'll be onto these Xtasy guys soon," he said. "Then we need to talk to Brother Valetude. We need to know how the little guys are doing. Jesus," he swore, feeling a consuming power of hatred for human beings suddenly, for the way they complicated everything.

" *. . . Brother Jesus spake . . . Suffer those little guys to come unto me! And forbid them not!*"

Brother Melodious's head ached suddenly and sharply. Overload, wherever you turned today.

"Whatever," he said sourly.

Brother Melodious had been right, to assume Sister Mansuetude's truant charges were assisting the Xtasy Krew. Nevertheless, it was quite some time before Landy and Cristifer were discovered in the Sector C maintenance tunnels, playing most of the music on a toy keyboard.

"*Dawn Crapper seizing up!*" The music morphed into a wicked, mad, malicious laughter.

It was the final announcement. The laughter went on and on, defiantly, while the errant Vespans were at last prised out of all the corners where they had wedged their oversize selves, and the first suited Eladeldi began to break into the stations.

In the wrecked apartment high above Stardeck, Erika
turned to Jone, squeezed into the tent beside her.

"Over," said Erika.

"Over," repeated Jone.

"Out?" asked Erika.

"Out," said Jone.

She squeezed Erika's knee. That was it. Everything they
could throw in they had thrown. Most of the stations were
on automatic now, and a lot of operators had dropped back
into their dorms, where the parties would rave on for a good
while yet. Others would be caught, and killed. Death was
in it, you knew that before you started. Death was in the
mix.

Jone sealed her suit, and pulled a soft helmet like a plastic bag over her head. She gave Erika a crocodile smile.
When she crawled back out of the tent, the cat tried to
follow. Erika grabbed him.

Jone went to the window Captain Jute had blown. She
leaned out.

Below were fifteen floors of empty space. Above, the
vast white wings of the *Citadel of Porcelain at First Light*
rose like frozen mountains. Beneath the missing window
ran a ledge.

Swiftly, Jone climbed out onto it.

After the sudden departure of Captain Jute, a volunteer
cleanup detail had worked for four watches straight to stabilize the evacuated apartment. On the detail were two
young men called Sunil and Echo. During the last watch,
when there was hardly anything left to do, Sunil and Echo
had brought in with them a device not actually required for
cleaning.

From the ledge, Jone looked up into a million kilometers
of smoky red void. Climbing over the slope of the port
wing was one of the cancered suns, its face disfigured by
black effluvia.

The Xtascite hugged the wall of the building. She might

loathe the starship, but she was not yet ready to part company with it. The action was just about to start.

Farther along, a couple of wires ran across the ledge.

Jone looked up again. Somewhere out there was the ship that had brought them all here. And somewhere in between that ship and this one were the force of women and men who might take them home again, given a major miracle, a probability glitch, a repeal of the laws of logic themselves.

Jone shuffled along the ledge until she could reach the wires. She followed them down with her fingers and felt the shape of the device that hung upon them, that Echo and Sunil had tucked away beneath the ledge.

Perhaps the odds against them could be calculated at $n{:}1$, where n was the number of subatomic particles that constituted the Capella System. Especially since Erika was right: most of those women and men undoubtedly were assholes, jocks and chunkheads.

Still they were coming. And Dodger Gillespie was with them.

Jone put her fingers on the trigger of the hidden device.

"Zero hour, Captain D," she said.

She took a deep breath, and squeezed.

Up into space shot a line of searing yellow dazzle. It splattered against the void.

In the windows of Stardeck and on the white slopes overhead, reflections blossomed from a dozen space flares. In her headset, Jone heard the cheer go up from the Plenty evacuees.

After all the electromagnetic mayhem, that primitive little fireburst could hardly have been necessary. You couldn't even see it, where Dodger and Karen and Tabitha were. But it made a nice finish.

∽ 27

By now Brother Nestor was far advanced. His head was almost a meter across, his body shriveling visibly as the last drops of its virtue were consumed. Beneath the hugely swollen brow, where the taut skin gleamed like polished wood, his face was creased and pouched as a chimpanzee's.

The private lab of Brother Valetude on Plenty was cleared of other experiments and given over to quarantine him. Brother Nestor did not belong to that hive, but it was long past time for such considerations. His uncommunicative body was placed in a black-plastic cot where it lay, hardly stirring.

For most of the Guardians on board, it was their first opportunity to see any of their fellows in this condition. Morbidly they gathered, bowing their big bald heads over the cot like a conference of gigantic mushrooms.

"How wretched," said Sister Contenta sadly, "that we must come to this."

Brother Justice lifted Brother Nestor's limp wrist and dropped it, not knowing what to do with it. When he pursed his lips the number of his chins increased. "He had a good run, I suppose," he said, distantly.

Elegant in black doublet and tights, Brother Poesy perched on the edge of the cot and recited:

> *"The naked hulk alongside came,*
> *And the twain were casting dice;*
> *'The game is done! I've won! I've won!'*
> *Quoth she, and whistles thrice."*

Brother Kitchener looked at the promoted poet as if he were the disquieting specimen here, not the deformed figure on the cot. "I'm glad you think it's so goddamn funny." The poet blinked at him, as if mirth had been far from his mind.

Brother Nestor gave a small, pitiful croak. A small curd of yellow fluid dribbled from his open mouth.

"Tasha," said Brother Valetude. A buxom young woman in a tight white uniform stepped to the cot, cloth in hand. She was one of four or five acolytes Brother Valetude still had left, the ones he could not bear to do without.

"Such a pity," said Sister Contenta, "that he won't see the work finished."

"He'll see it," said Brother Justice, ogling the acolyte as she wobbled away from the cot, "he just won't think very much of it!"

Brother Kitchener looked sidelong at their stricken shipmate and away again, as at a partner in business who had been useful once and had now, on the eve of the dividend, cut himself out of the deal. "He won't *think* at all," he grunted.

"Such a waste," grieved Sister Contenta.

High on the wall, a dedicated monitor showed the Star Beast in her cavern. Smooth and shiny as wet satin, the huge purple creature slumbered.

The fat judge put his hand on Brother Kitchener's shoulder, commiserating with the former catering director over the loss of past pleasures, past profits. "She made," he pronounced, "a better dinner than a mother."

Without asking permission, Brother Kitchener raised the blind at an inboard window. Below, the churning mass in the nursery looked like nothing so much as a milk pudding boiling, speeded up.

"If you ask me," said Brother Kitchener, "it's time we cut our losses."

Brother Justice belched, fruitily.

Brother Poesy steepled his fingers and looked interested.

"What is it, exactly," he asked, "that we have lost?"

"Blow the ship," said Brother Kitchener impatiently. "There are enough of us now."

Brother Valetude smiled sardonically. "Why not suggest that to Astraghal?"

The Kybernator was the most prominent absentee from this gathering. He was not pleased to have Brother Nestor on board, though it was in every way the obvious place for him from now on. The Kybernator would never give up his command until she was taken away from under him. An attempt had been made to abandon her before, he reminded them, under Sol, in the days of her immaturity. Those who had made that attempt had all come to regret it.

A lab drone crawled over Brother Nestor's body, taking sample temperatures and measuring the dilation of blood vessels. No one was actually looking at him now. There was nothing, for the moment, to see.

Brother Poesy sat with his right elbow cupped in his left hand, gazing down into the nursery.

"*A thousand thousand slimy things lived on,*" remarked the poet, "*and so did I.*"

A sigh escaped Brother Nestor, like a wisp of gas from a deflating balloon.

"Overboard with him!" ruled Brother Justice with a sudden roar that made Tasha shriek and everyone else jump.

Sister Contenta frowned at her corpulent colleague and poked him reprovingly. "Nonsense, Justice," she said. "Things must take their natural course."

Some of her companions looked at their sister with covert distrust, like adherents of a shameful cult who suspected one of their number might be about to unmask their secret identities. Could it be that Contenta's head was starting to look the tiniest bit swollen too?

Sven Dolan's ship was the Lesondak, a V50 called the *Langoustine*. One day after combat training Sven asked if Captain Jute would like to look her over.

She went back with him.

He showed her the accommodation, briefly, and then, more thoroughly, the cockpit, which had been well preserved from the ravages of time, chance and hyperspace. He obviously expected her to want to handle the controls, but she expressed no interest in them, or in the artillery. "More power than you've handled in a while," he said, suggestively.

She saw the look in his eyes when he said it. She knew that look.

They sat in the galley and ate, pooling their rations. Sven even produced two tubes of Champion. His hair was grey now, and sparse where it had been thick, but he had looked after his body as well as his ship. She had been wondering all along if they had had sex once. After that crack of his, she was damn sure they had.

Despite the urgency, the imminence of violence and the probability of death that stalked all arrangements, he talked only about technicalities: the attack, the corridor, the boarding. She knew she was expected to argue, to fulminate against the strategy of Rykov and the Khan. Instead it seemed to her that it was some old battle he was describing, something lost and won in the Last War.

Captain Jute thought of Captain Devereux, and wondered if she was still alive, if that was the appropriate word. She wished they had her here. Devereux would have pissed on Rykov and the Khan, and hung them up to dry.

Between Captain Jute and Captain Dolan the galley table was littered with the remains of the disgusting fungus bricks that was all they had to eat. The beer was lousy too. She swallowed the last of hers, crushed the tube and dropped it.

She reached across the table and took hold of the hand that held Sven's drink.

She took the tube from it and knocked that back too, and crushed the tube and dropped it, holding on to his wrist and looking him straight in the eye all the while. Then she pulled his hand to her and placed it firmly on her left breast.

He gave her the benefit of all those hours of exercise. In the high mad years of summer she had had every stud on board competing to impress her. This time it was like that again. Sven performed upon her, and she let him, loving every heft and swivel. It had indeed been a long while, a long bad while, since she had handled anybody.

She thought at first she might not come, but then she did, and after so did he, and surprised her then by cuddling her tenderly. She liked it. Not the tenderness so much as that feeling of triumph, when a man melts down in your arms, all defenses gone. You never got that with a woman.

They lay for a time, not speaking. Then there came a loud *peep*, and the radio started crackling. "*. . . Xtasy*," a voice said. "*. . . Radio Xtasy checking in.*"

Tabitha, for some reason, was remembering how her mum and dad had used to take them moonboarding, her and Angie, at the rink in the Lake of Dreams. Dad had been really good at it, or so she had thought, aged seven. They had always tried to get Mum to come out in the dust with them, but she had stayed in the car, watching with a disapproving smile, and knitting.

"*. . . Calico Show*," said the radio. "*Zero hour . . . Captain Di-di-di-di-dee.*"

Sven was saying something. He was pulling away from her, pushing himself out of the bunk.

Captain Jute was trying to remember how it had felt, zooming along through the dust—the exhilaration, the bruising collisions—but it had gone. Another piece of history erased by time.

"*. . . way over . . . Big . . . Ants' Nest*," said the radio, with a splutter. Sven was grabbing up his clothes. He was saying loudly: "That's us, Captain."

Present reality burst upon her like breaking glass. "What?"

Sven's eyes were wide. All his dissipated energy had returned in one blast. "That's the signal!"

Captain Jute propelled herself out of the bunk. Naked, she pulled on her suit.

"They'd better not expect me to call them *sir*," she said.

Outside, people were everywhere, scrambling. Captain Jute passed Sven's shipmates, racing toward the Lesondak. The Danuta was some minutes away across the apron. She saw Lou Garou, pulling his suit on and belting over to the Fernando. In her phones was a jabber of orders and acknowledgments, over a broken rhythmic screeching noise that she took some moments to realize was Radio Xtasy.

"*Honor the bass . . .*" someone kept saying.

She found the Danuta warmed up and ready, cockpit pressurized, Kenny at the controls slavering frantically. On her holopad the imago of Little Alice was standing on tiptoe, talking to someone invisible.

"Captain on board," announced Tabitha, patting Kenny, urging him out of her seat as she plugged in. "Who is it, Alice?"

"*It's me,*" answered a dry, impassive voice from the parking bays thirty klicks forward, beyond the secret enclosure, beyond the cave-in.

"IT'S CAPTAIN GILLESPIE, CAPTAIN JUTE," said Alice unnecessarily.

"*Just making sure you're awake.*"

"Hey, Dodger!" she shouted, tugging the web closed around her with one hand and keying the impulse jets with the other. "They're playing our song!"

"*See you outside, gel,*" said Captain Gillespie.

"Cookie Cutter, *this is* Ella Megalast, *do you copy?*"

That was Rykov, on the command channel. "Talk to him, Alice," said Captain Jute. All around her, impulse jets flared silently in the gloom.

"ROGER, CAPTAIN," said the persona. "COOKIE CUTTER COPYING. CAPTAIN TABITHA JUTE AT THE CONTROLS. WE ARE AT 92.25% OF LAUNCH."

"*You follow* Buster."

Buster was the tourist ferry, a big clumsy orange Caledonian Lightning. She could see it now, full of Rooks, kids, Havoc, Thrant, guns, knives, axes. It was the most capacious ship, the least maneuverable; all its weapons were on the inside.

She had known this was their plan, to have the weakest in the rear. She had tried to argue against it and been slapped down.

"*You're the last*," said Norval Khan.

"*Covering you*, Buster, Cookie Cutter," promised Rykov.

Kenny gave a yelp.

Now the first ships were leaving the apron: the Spada, the Silverfish, a Vespan cruiser like a toaster swathed in blue-and-brown spaghetti. The Lapham yacht, the *Same Old Katy*, floated gracefully overhead, twirling like a steel ballerina. There were no floodlights, no exit routing, no traffic control messages coordinating departure sequences. There was only speed, darkness and danger.

Together the first ships crossed the buried cave, heading for the wall of silvery nothingness. Side on, Rykov's Eagle, the *Ella Megalast*, slipped between them like a flying razor and disappeared into the discontinuity.

On the apron there was a sudden splash of soundless light and hurtling debris. Sounds of grief and fear came warbling over the com. One of the hybrids had blown up.

Kenny gibbered ghoulishly and shook his. head. "*Poor fucking shits*," sent someone. Captain Jute trimmed her controls, chafing. She was sure she had seen a body in that explosion, a blackened starfish whirling. Their first casualties, before they were even out of the box.

She saw Karen Narlikar go by overhead, steering straight and true. The *Buster* was up now too, laboring on overtaxed Shernenkovs. Unwilling to delay a second over her orders, Captain Jute tapped in the jets and sent the Danuta climbing toward the ceiling in a great curve.

For an instant she was looking down on the remains of

the ship that had exploded, a customized Gambarino Golightly. In the absence of oxygen, it had burnt out instantly. "Hsomeone moveen down 'ere, Capteen," Kenny reported. He was a sharp-eyed hunting creature, no doubt he was right. There was nothing anyone could do.

The rest of the fleet were off the floor now, streaking or spiraling past, skimming like darts into the reality fault. It swallowed them all without a ripple. There was only the Nebulon left to go, the *Dire Wolf*, carrying their commander. It dipped its stabilizers to the bus, and shepherded it delicately through, leaving the Danuta alone.

Little Alice sat on her pad with her head up and her arms around her knees. There was a rapt expression on her tiny face as she gazed through the tinted canopy of the ship at the onrushing discontinuity. "HERE WE GO, THROUGH THE LOOKING GLASS," she said; and then they were gone, and back, without an interval, flying straight for the stern door.

"4.02 KILOMETERS SLIPPAGE," reported Alice, with her old, reliable precision.

"What happened?" said Tabitha. "Did we skip?"

"NATURALLY, CAPTAIN."

"Did somebody tell me?"

"IT ALL HAPPENED SO QUICKLY," reported Alice, sounding a trifle smug.

The grip of conventional acceleration squeezed the hull, the canopy, the outside of the pilot's web. Unshielded, the stern dock mouth gaped for the Danuta. Its mechanism destroyed, the doorway stood unlit, abandoned. Beyond, a dim swirl of burnt rock hung like a dirty veil across nothing.

As the Danuta left the mother ship the twin suns appeared, huge and smoldering, one above the other. On the console, Little Alice stood and pointed.

"BUT I KNOW THOSE BOYS!" she said. "IT'S TWEEDLEDUM AND TWEEDLEDEE."

"As long as you're happy," grunted Captain Jute.

In her phones, Rykov was now calling names. "Caligari
... *Come in,* Caligari ... Windhorse Trader ... *Come in,*
Windhorse ... *Thank you,* Windhorse, *we have you now*
... Caligari, *do you copy?* Langoustine ... *Come in,* Lan-
goustine ... *Come in,* Buster ... Cookie Cutter, *come in.*"

Captain Jute acknowledged her safe exit. "Twelve hundred meters clear," she told them, and her attitude and
bearing. Rykov was calling the *Caligari* again. The *Caligari* had not reported in.

"*Calling* Caligari," said another voice, Norval Khan's.
"*Anyone with sight of* Caligari, *answer now.*"

No one spoke.

Tabitha looked around. "Who is it?" she asked Kenny.
"It's Colgan, isn't it?" She remembered the black-and-
yellow ship, half Toiseach, half Slider, wreathed in blue
light and freezing clouds of exhaust, rising from the apron
alongside Karen's Clavicorn.

Outside the conquered hive, the burnt veil of Capella
System expanded to fill the cockpit canopy. A skein of
small ships decorated it, dwindling as they put on speed.
Tabitha and Kenny glimpsed the ram, the *Fernando*, a misshapen pink-stained trinket, the minute figure of Lou Garou
on its back.

"Ella Megalast *calling* Caligari. *Come in,* Caligari."

Still there was no answer.

"*Cookie Cutter* to *Ella Megalast*," sent Captain Jute.
"We saw *Caligari* leave." She looked at Kenny for confirmation. He dipped his nose, put out his pointed tongue.

"God knows where he's gone," said Captain Jute.

"Maximum Disturbance, *take* Caligari*'s station.*"

"LET'S ALL MOVE ONE PLACE ON," said Little Alice,
who was giving every appearance of enjoying herself immensely.

"All Things Considered *now in pole position*," reported
a dreary voice. It was not Dodger herself; she was maintaining radio silence as well as invisibility. Tabitha checked
the radar. The Scorpion didn't even show up. The three

apparent leaders were three hardwired pilots who had locked onto the signature of the *All Things Considered*'s engines, and everyone else, even Norval and Rykov, was following them.

A flashing red blip appeared, 150° astern.

"Hounds," said Captain Jute.

Kenny purred aggressively.

"Cookie Cutter, *hold position*," sent Rykov, sternly. Behind him someone was sending a response to the starship, calling Radio Xtasy to confirm they were on their way.

Two more red blips entered the scanner field.

"Buster *calling* Cookie Cutter," came a slow mechanical voice. "*Message for* Cookie Cutter, *person to person.*"

"Come in, *Buster*, this is *Cookie Cutter.*"

Hoarse breathing filled her ears. "*Kyfyd?*" said a familiar voice, "*Kyfyd, ee that you?*"

"Soi," said Captain Jute. "Soi, this is Tabitha. We're fine, how are you?"

"*Fine too, Cap'n,*" said Kenny's sister. She sounded tense, reluctant to engage in conversation with her former employer. She had never been the most verbal of the assimilated Thrant. Tabitha remembered how she had used to chauffeur her and her friends for hours through the tunnels of Plenty, never saying a word.

"*Wanty speek ee Kyfyd,*" Soi sent.

"He's right here," Captain Jute told her. "Go on, Ken."

Kenny pawed his earpiece. He spoke, a rapid bark of Thrant.

A shadow slid gently over the Danuta. Tabitha looked up. It was the Eagle, the *Ella Megalast*. Captain Rykov was keeping his promise.

Tabitha wished she could speak to Dodger Gillespie. She looked at the red blips crawling across the scanner grid and wished she could have ridden with Captain Gillespie on the *All Things Considered*, the psycho's old ship, the nutter, her ex-nemesis. It would have given her a certain satisfaction. Their orders had been otherwise, from the first, though she was damn sure the Khan hadn't decided without consulting Dodger.

She didn't like the thought that Dodger hadn't wanted her.

The Thrant were still conversing. Captain Jute looked out to port and saw the bus broadside on, its windows a string of cheerful lights. To starboard, the Vespan ship waltzed ponderously through the void. Behind, the pursuit was not yet close enough to see. They were there even so, carving a streak of armed vengeance toward the fleet.

"Alice, can you tuck us tighter in to that Eagle?"

"COMPUTING," said Alice.

The little imago flickered for an instant as the *Ella Megalast* seemed to grow larger overhead, then brightened. Tabitha looked up at Rykov's ship, trying to detect her additional armament, trying to arm the cannon and aim them by will alone.

"Cookie Cutter, *I say again, you're too close in.*"

Rykov's warning cut across the ether, interrupting the conversation of the Thrant. Engulfed now in the shadow of his ship, the cockpit of the *Danuta* was lit only by the console telltales and the persona hologram. Kenny was a mean silhouette in his web, like an animal in a net. Captain Jute felt him grin suddenly in the darkness.

∽ 28

A cruiser of the type authorized to be built on Vespa five generations ago. A bus with Mandebra codings unlawfully and incompetently erased. A Fargo Fernando sled incorrectly fitted with distributors of a Palernian type and a monstrous prow.

"*Vespan Ronuiqanstapfic 2 listed destroyed, E minus*

seven," yapped the dispatcher. *"Mandebra license codes unrecorded."*

"Fetch Brother Justice!" barked Patrol 1.

"Checking starship records, Patrol . . ."

From somewhere behind the bus a Nebulon Green Streak appeared. Seen frontally as it squared up to the Tinkerbells, it bore three small yellow-fanged mouths.

"Beware, Patrol 3!" barked Patrol 2. "Nebulon at 243°, repeat 2-4-3, armed and closing!"

The Vespan cruiser blundered across the bows of Patrol 1 like a shaggy drunken insect.

"Nebulon listed stripped, 17.44.78! Dock Sector 1-7G, Bay—"

"Fetch Brother Justice!" barked Patrol 1.

Patrol 3 went down to the Nebulon. Patrol 1 and 2 evaded a pincer movement from a Shinjatzu Cormorant and a Lesondak V50 that no record showed had ever been on board at all.

"It's a convoy," sent Patrol 2. "Alert all stations."

Together 1 and 2 undershot the defenders and flew into the ranks. Already they were beginning to sort the armed from the unarmed. Then a pale blue laser of the type issued to Navajo Scorpions in the Sol Purge flickered out of nowhere and thoroughly and irreparably crashed their systems.

As the disabled patrol vessels fell gently back toward the rustling hive, one by one the ships of the Resistance started to glow with a strange light. The light was acid yellow and suggestive of something not actually there, as if each of them was only a hologram, a lo-res graphic, a photocopy of a poor original. Vagueness possessed them, sweeping through their assembly. Moments later, they were gone.

"Projected duration of journey, Ella," said Captain Rykov, as the universe folded itself away.

"PROJECTED DURATION CALCULABLE AS 33

HOURS, 40 MINUTES," said the Eagle's persona. "PLUS OR MINUS 25 MINUTES."

"Make mine minus," said Rykov.

A wave drew itself on the Eagle's probability scope in microscopic points of amber light. The wave peaked and collapsed. "THAT ASPECT OF OUR MISSION IS NOT SUSCEPTIBLE TO MY CONTROL, CAPTAIN," the persona said. "EXCESS INCALCULABLE FACTORS IMPACT ON IT."

Captain Rykov clenched his teeth, burning adrenaline. "Maybe it'll happen anyway," he said. "Who's the best unit in the fleet, Ella Megalast?"

"WE ARE, SIR!"

He tried to make himself relax. His first true combat flight. Ironic that it should be against the people who'd trained him, on HighGround, all those years ago. He closed his eyes, remembering his Eladeldi instructors, their methods of response. He was grateful to them for their training. He would be happy to use it now. It had been frustrating not to go in against the patrol, but the rest were depending on him, and with the advantage she had, those last two had been Gillespie's.

And it had been a walkover. Rykov allowed himself another moment of exultation. Then, for the hundred and fiftieth time, he reached across and loaded the strategy software Norval's people had run up for him out of modules from old gaming consoles.

On the wide black screen little dart shapes in red and gold and blue formed shapes around a stationary white cross. On minor slaved screens above, simulations of the viewpoints from six key ships, including his own, were instantly generated move by move. Again and again he flung flights of defenders up, watching how his team would have to move and feint and dodge. He wished it might have been possible to build in the proclivities of their various crews and pilots too, to show reaction times, progressive reductions in fuel and ammunition, constitutional vulnerabilities to any given attack profile.

Captain Rykov sighed for the old technology, the old days under Colonel Stark, when discipline was absolute and units acted and reacted with robotic perfection. He was sitting in with the wolfpack here, a pack of wolves and cheetahs and monkeys. He wished it might have been possible to program some of them, instead of just riding the wave of their vengeance and trusting to luck.

Rykov realized he was breathing fast and shallow. He had tensed up again.

"We're the best, Ella," he said.

"CATEGORICAL AFFIRMATIVE, CAPTAIN," said the persona.

A small smile softened the steely eyes of Captain Rykov. Ella's voice, since they'd tweaked the settings, really sounded a lot like Starkie's.

Meanwhile, on the *Same Old Katy*, the persona was interrogating the pilot.

"MAY I ASK IF THERE IS A PARTICULAR PURPOSE TO OUR JOURNEY, CAPTAIN?"

"It's a ship-to-ship transfer, Katy," said the pilot. He was another of the Redcap renegades who had followed Rykov into secret Sector 330. His name was Corbett Ali.

"THERE ARE A LOT OF US GOING AT THE SAME TIME, AREN'T THERE?" the yacht remarked. "IS IT AN IMPORTANT SOCIAL OCCASION?"

Captain Ali caught the eyes of his companions, who were smirking. The yacht they were riding was a rich person's plaything. She had twin polyhedral compensation, but about as much capacity in her persona as an autonomic floor-polisher. In Katy's central processor there was no such concept as outer-space combat.

"Very important, Katy," said Captain Ali.

"It's a surprise party, Katy," said another of her passengers.

"A fireworks party," said a third.

There was some laughter, more loose remarks. Captain Ali frowned at them to restrain themselves.

"We're all going to do our duty, Katy," he said. "Buster, Wolf, Nando, you—all of us."

There was a pause. Beyond the viewport, the colorless face of emptiness failed to change.

"THOSE LITTLE RED SHIPS, CAPTAIN," said the yacht. "THEY WEREN'T SHOOTING AT US, WERE THEY?"

Meanwhile, at the back, the *Buster* was still lumbering out of reality.

Buster had been built to service the tourist lines between Pascal and New Toronto, Silverside and the lower-orbit malls. Eleven years ago, as his circuits measured time, Buster had stopped off at Plenty with a load of affluent but reckless consumers. Now he was leaving with a load of people even more reckless, who had no money at all. Some of them were underaged, undersized, and underwashed. Some of them were furry, with prehensile feet and powerful tails. *Buster* the Caledonian Lightning bore them all obediently, stolidly. He was unequipped to tell the difference.

In the cockpit, the crew contended with their obsolete astroscope, combing the vortex interface for clues to the values in the transit matrices. "Like an iron atom trying to argue its way through a balloon," one of them explained to one of the kids who crouched before him, working on a dodgy seal in his suit.

The crewman saw the kid give him a sideways look. She was fourteen, supposedly. With her ill-fitting Redcap surplus uniform, butchered hair and immunity to fear, she looked about twelve. She called herself Morgan, and she came from one of the weird villages in Plenty that better-connected people had called the zoos: private communities,

tiny fiefdoms where a person could grow up barely knowing they were deep in an alien construct and heading for
another star. Morgan's birthplace had dreamed up a weird
puberty rite for its offspring, dumping them alone and unarmed in deserted precincts of the docks and making them
find their own way back. A number, apparently, had refused
the challenge, and instead made themselves new homes in
the powerless workshops and abandoned ships. Morgan and
her three mates had been living in the Lightning when Norval Khan's lieutenants arrived to look it over.

Before they realized she was there, Morgan had kicked
one of them in the groin and taken his knife off him, an
insult the man resented hugely and had had to be restrained
from avenging on several occasions. In the end Norval, who
thought it a good laugh, of course, had told him to lay off.
Now Morgan was devoted to the Khan, far more absolute
in her loyalty than the spacers, who respected his ferocity
but not his sense. She finished squeezing cement into the
leaking suit seal and clamped it closed.

"We should have just taken Plenty," she said.

"Plenty's shot," said the crewman. "She's full of
Frasque. Plenty's dead, Morgan."

"THIS VEHICLE IS DEMATERIALIZING," said
Buster. "THIS VEHICLE IS DEMATERIALIZING."

Meanwhile, alone with her former bodyguard at a set of
coordinates entirely incompatible with physical existence,
Tabitha Jute yawned.

Sympathetically, her bodyguard yawned too. The assault
course of their exit from Plenty had been replaced, as in
all journeys beyond the three domestic dimensions, by a
stretch of undifferentiable tedium.

They had studied the attack plan, the graphic of the *Citadel of Porcelain at First Light* with its flashing prioritized
target areas of red, yellow, blue. They had zoomed into
each in order, familiarizing themselves with the approach
sequences. Captain Jute felt she ought to know the *Citadel*

if anyone did, better than anyone who'd been hiding on Plenty, certainly, but she had been shut up in her apartment the whole time and didn't recognize anything. It could scarcely matter. She was under orders to keep to the rear, to follow everyone else in.

Kenny napped. Captain Jute envied him. The prospect of arrival tugged at her nerves. The Danuta was unarmed for space combat. Like most of them, in fact. If they actually got on board, there would be violence. More likely there would be catastrophe. Tabitha started to doodle on the pilot's web clipboard, a whole army of caterpillars arranged in rows and columns.

On the holopad, the persona imago represented the billion computations of the skip as moving strings of light looped between her tiny pink fingers. To the Captain, Little Alice looked exactly as if she were playing the game known to countless generations of human children as cat's cradle.

Captain Jute reached the bottom of a column of caterpillars. She started a new one.

"Put some music on, Alice."

The cradle of strings vanished. The eyes of the transparent child slid upwards and to the right as she consulted her memory.

The sound of a brass band filled the cockpit, playing a cheerful march. Captain Jute flinched. She couldn't believe she'd forgotten to program music. "Something else."

Abruptly the brass band stopped playing the cheerful march and started playing a slow, mournful one.

"Jesus. Leave it."

The music of brass instruments was replaced by a hoarse squeaking sound. It was live. It was Kenny, laughing. He found the oom-pah-pah irresistibly hilarious.

The imago stood with her hands behind her back. "I COULD SING YOU A SONG, CAPTAIN. *TWINKLE, TWINKLE, LITTLE BAT*—"

"No thanks, Alice."

This Alice didn't sound quite like any of the versions

that had haunted Captain Jute on Plenty. She sounded brighter, younger: a voice, presumably, generated to go with the imago. She sounded almost more like Xtasca now than Alice, and made even less sense. Captain Jute didn't fancy sitting here the rest of the way with that voice singing nursery rhymes at her.

Captain Jute thought of Xtasca, and of Saskia Zodiac, somewhere out there with the Seraphim. She wondered if the *Kajsa* and her contingent would intervene, when they hit the *Citadel*, or sit back and let the Guardians cream them. Was that weird fleet display something to do with them, the way Sven and Lou reckoned, or were they still doing deals with the Frasque? Both, probably.

Kenny sprawled in his web. With one clawed big toe he was pointing to a tape deck.

"Fuck me," said Captain Jute. "Right." She craned around the cockpit. "Where's my bag?"

Her copilot swiveled his leg to point at her chest. "Ye're weering it!"

She put her hand through the zip and awkwardly rummaged inside. Some of the stuff Jone had packed must be still in here. Her hand closed on an old cassette tape, unboxed, unlabeled.

"Here we go," she said, and pressed it in the slot.

The sound of a brass band filled the cockpit.

Kenny gasped helplessly, waving his limbs in the air.

"Cancel, Alice!"

Alice tossed her head with a remarkable imitation of frustration. "FIDDLE-DEE-DEE," she said.

Meanwhile, on the *All Things Considered*, Dodger Gillespie unplugged herself and lit a cigarette. "All right, Atkins?" she said.

"PROGRESS IS SATISFACTORY, THANK YOU, CAPTAIN," said the persona. A graph appeared on a screen, showing conventional elapsed probability space in blocks analogous to a hundred kilometers objective.

Captain Gillespie glanced at her companion. "All right, Spik?"

Gunner Spik belched and scratched his armpit. "All right, Dodger," he said.

Gunner Spik had volunteered to go with the Fernando, but Rykov and Norval Khan had jointly appointed him for the safe seat in the invisible Scorpion. He knew his stuff. He had served under Lomax on the Pontine Guard, helped drive back both the Frasque and the Perk when they had invaded the bridge. He had personally serviced 80% of the Resistance armament, and proved himself at once by skewering those two patrol ships promptly and efficiently. Captain Gillespie was well aware he had another job, though. He was here to keep an eye on her. Though she was far and away the best pilot, and the best wired, the Havoc Khan and the Redcap felt uneasy with her at the controls of their best ship. They did not trust her, quite. They had not been happy to risk the Scorpion in the search for Captain Jute. Norval would have written Captain Jute off with pleasure, if he'd thought he could get it past Dodger; and Rykov would have gone along, no doubt at all about that. Gunner Spik was her concession.

Captain Gillespie would have liked some different company. She wished Jone hadn't had to go to the *Citadel*. There were other people who could pull a trigger. Failing them, she would have preferred Tabitha, so *she* could keep an eye on *her*.

Instead she had Spik, who belched, and picked his teeth, and farted, and treated her with no respect whatsoever, because she was not a gunner, because she was a plughead, and to Spik and his kind all plugheads were barely one step up from robots. She had Spik, who was a *man*, for God's sake. What did she expect, the whole fleet was commanded by men, two of them, and all their buddies were men.

The odds were ludicrous, but it was the only throw they had.

At least they were doing it.

Captain Gillespie thought of Jone, whom there was a strong chance she would never see again. She worked her roll-up into the corner of her mouth and ran a movie flash of Jone in bed, while she brought up the hyperband. Then she jacked in again.

Virtual noise filled her auditory centers. After a while, Spik saw her lift one corner of her mouth, the one that held the roll-up, a fraction of a centimeter.

"Is that your little friend, Captain?" he asked.

Dodger heard him, the real sound cutting through the muffled surge of Radio Xtasy.

"Be glad you can't hear it, Spik," she said.

"Why?" said the gunner. "Hot stuff, is it?" He wiggled his eyebrows in a gesture both lascivious and pathetic.

"DOES MR. SPIK WISH TO LISTEN, CAPTAIN GIL-LESPIE? I CAN TRANSLATE IT TO AUDIO, IF YOU WISH," said Atkins.

"Let him wonder," said the Captain.

"I'd rather watch," said Spik, with a halfhearted leer.

Captain Gillespie's cigarette had gone out. She found her lighter and flicked it.

"Spik," said the Captain. "You really can be a prick."

Her shipmate positively basked. "I can be a cunt, too," he assured her, complacently.

Meanwhile, on the Nebulon Green Streak modified and refashioned and improved and renamed the *Dire Wolf*, the ganja smoke was thick and the snuff rock was loud and heavy. The Havoc chieftain, now leader of the Plenty Resistance, lay back with his web unfastened and his eyes half-closed, languidly swigging from a flask of moonshine.

"WE TRULY CREAMED THOSE DOGGIES, DIDN'T WE, NORVAL?" observed a deep, powerful voice, hardly mechanical at all.

"We creamed 'em," said the Khan, taking another pull before handing the flask to the underdressed woman who knelt at his feet, lovingly polishing a buckgutter. "We truly creamed 'em, Wolf."

The persona gave a deep, complex sigh, redolent, had it been sapient, of both satisfaction and appetite.

"THAT WAS SOME GOOD SHOOTING," it breathed.

"Good shooting," concurred the Khan, nodding heavily. Roughly he caressed the tangled head of his companion.

On the console little graphs proliferated and died. No one took the slightest notice.

"WE GONNA GET SOME MORE SHOOTING SOON?" asked the persona, in the tone of simpleminded, hopeful dependence the Khan preferred to hear from his subordinates.

"Soon as we get there, Wolf," promised the Khan. "Soon as."

Meanwhile, in the private lab of Brother Valetude, Brother Nestor lay comatose in his black cot. The lab drones came and went, continuing their measurements, while Tasha the acolyte bathed the patient's head with cooling water. As though in reaction to some undetectable internal agony, the fingers of his hands had contracted to claws.

In the nursery, the young Capellans seethed. Though there seemed to be no fewer of them yet, they were reducing themselves gradually, inexorably, to a functional number. Kybernator Astraghal came on to report a message he had received from Kajsa Tobermory, on the Seraph ship that bore her name. "*She says that the transfer operation is soon to be crowned with success.*"

"Did she say how soon?" asked Brother Valetude, preoccupied with a microscope.

"*In the next five days, she claims,*" said Kybernator Astraghal noncommittally.

"That should be something to see."

"*It should, it should. And she asks after Brother Nestor.*"

"Does she?" Brother Valetude looked up at the screen. "What will you tell her?"

Kybernator Astraghal narrowed his eyes. "*I propose a reply saying how much we love our brother, and that he is enjoying the best care.*"

In the black tub of the cot, as if he knew that he and his fortunes were the subject of discussion, Brother Nestor had begun making a sharp squeaking noise.

Brother Valetude looked back into his microscope. "Queen Kajsa's curiosity does her credit."

"*Undoubtedly,*" replied his captain, as though he meant nothing of the kind. "*Kajsa Tobermory also asks if we know what is happening on the* Citadel of Porcelain *at First Light.*"

The augmented doctor looked up again in a manner both puzzled and alert.

"What is?"

"*You know of nothing, then,*" said his captain.

Via the medium of fiber telephony, the eyes of the two Guardians met.

"Neither of us is aware of anything," concluded Brother Valetude. "You've spoken to Perlmutter."

"*Not today. Communications are extremely noisy at present. Speaking of which, is that him, that awful noise?*"

The doctor's attention was drawn back to his charge. "Sorry, Brother," he said. "Tasha."

The acolyte appeared holding a syringe, the needle of which she inserted into the larynx of Brother Nestor. The old man's lips relaxed. He quietened.

Brother Valetude was checking the clock. "Is there an outbound shuttle?"

"*It left at 15.5.*"

"Will you send a ship, Kybernator?"

"*If communications are not reestablished. The docks are in some disorder,*" related the Kybernator.

Brother Valetude had heard from Brother Justice about the report of patrol vessels attacked by a number of uni-

dentified ships that appeared to have come from within the
hive itself, via the disused stern door. An exploratory team
sent round to examine the door from without had found it
still sealed with what looked like a wall of fizzing mist. It
was the intrusive discontinuity, intact, looking just as it had
since Emergence. They were not prepared to risk more personnel and equipment trying to penetrate it, but anerobic
construction robots were being programmed to reopen a
capped shaft and descend into the derelict lower Limbic.

"Poesy believes there is another universe in there,"
mused Brother Valetude. "Another hive, where history has
happened differently."

"*Poesy believes a great number of things, hourly.*"

"A universe where those ships survived," Brother Valetude suggested. The Kybernator looked superior to all such
persuasion.

"*Far more likely the ships have been somehow concealed from us,*" he opined, "*by romantics and malcon-
tents. Escaped convicts. Captain Gillespie and her
undesirable associates.*"

"It's a defensible opinion," allowed the medic.

"*It's* my *opinion,*" returned his captain, tartly. Pain
seemed to flicker across his face, as though the reply had
cost him something to make.

"They are terribly clever," said Brother Valetude, looking at his hands as if they were specimens for his microscope. "It's not just the Seraphim."

"*It was not very clever to leave the hive,*" said Kybernator Astraghal remorselessly. "*Time is running out for
them, whoever they are. Where will they go? The system
will not support them.*"

The squeaking noise had begun again, differently
pitched. "Doctor!" shouted Tasha from beside the cot.

Brother Valetude looked around and saw the lab drones
withdrawing, scooting away across the floor like rectangular rodents in flight from some imminent predator.

"Excuse me, Brother, I should—"

"*Yes, yes.*"

Brother Valetude pointed a ring at the screen. The picture vanished, only to reappear immediately.

"Sorry," said the medic. "You want to watch."

"*I suppose I should*," said Kybernator Astraghal. His disinclination was audible.

The process was more advanced, perhaps, than either of them had appreciated. Before Brother Valetude could reach the cot, Brother Nestor's eyelids opened. Inside were no eyeballs, only something hard, and corrugated, and yellowish brown, and slimy.

The squeaking noise the dead man continued to make was not coming from his mouth, or not only from there. His remaining features twisted themselves into a peculiar expression of unhappiness as his head split open and ejected a spurt of fetid black ichor.

From the bridge Kybernator Astraghal was speaking now with some urgency. Brother Valetude could spare no attention for him. He was busy trying to choose between observing as closely as possible and taking cover.

Brother Nestor's forehead broke in two, vertically. Inside his vacant eyeholes, the corrugated yellow thing wriggled.

Out of the split in Brother Nestor's head popped something small and spiky. It looked like a tiny cactus.

Nurse Tasha was spread-eagled against the wall. She was having hysterics. There was urine running down her leg. Her Master frowned and subdued her with a ring. She fell to the floor and lay there motionless, staring at the ceiling, breathing rapidly.

The tiny yellow cactus that protruded from the top of Brother Nestor's violated head became identifiable as a tiny yellow hand. It was joined now by another; and another; and another.

The squeaking sound continued, regular, effortful, malign.

A chime sounded. The lab door slid open. Two Eladeldi enforcers came bounding in, armed with electric goads and long tongs. They barked noisily, reporting to the doctor for duty. They rolled their eyes at the broken figure in the black cot and started to make a bad smell.

Clumsily the four tiny yellow hands gripped the two halves of Brother Nestor's head and forced them apart.

The enforcers stiffened their spines. One of them whimpered.

The tiny hands were attached to four arms like sticks of bamboo, but with elbows, several elbows each. They were covered in clear mucus with clots of old blood in it. They continued to tear apart the head of rotten skin that contained them. Inside there was no longer a skull. Everything had been consumed.

Another brief gush of black slime ran into the cot and pooled around the abandoned shoulders as the young Frasque crawled free.

It squealed, and panted. The six new limbs moved spasmodically, without coordination. Lifting its long blunt head, the newcomer mounted the end of the cot, overbalanced and fell on the floor of the lab.

"All right," said Brother Valetude to the Eladeldi.

The guards ran forward, goads at the ready.

"Be very careful," he said loudly.

The Frasque lay there twitching like an electrocuted frog. It was fully a hundred centimeters from nose to toes.

"*Not my successor, I assume,*" said Kybernator Astraghal from the com.

"Hardly likely," said Brother Valetude. "Another artisan, I imagine." He hovered over the multilimbed adolescent and inspected it through a glass. He still seemed reluctant to get too close.

The Eladeldi picked it up with the tongs.

"I was intending to keep hold of it for a bit, actually," said Brother Valetude.

"*Infinity, what for?*" exclaimed the Kybernator. "*No, no, let them take it. Put it with the rest,*" he commanded. The distaste was audible in his voice.

"Yes, Masters!" huffed the guards, hastening to obey.

"Mm, perhaps it's for the best," Brother Valetude resolved. He had plenty of other work to do. He sailed past his assistant, who still lay as she had fallen. Above her, through the nursery window, the innocents boiled.

ᕲ 29

When the *Cookie Cutter* came through, most of the fleet had already arrived. A mere couple of klicks ahead, the *Langoustine* stood tail down in the void, like a vacuum cleaner attempting a backward somersault.

Only one of the suns was completely visible. It looked no larger than it had from Plenty, but they had come a long way, and now it largely eclipsed its twin. Upon the swollen red disc an unidentifiable hybrid appeared, floating like a beetle on a bloody puddle.

Over the open com, Rykov was calling the names of the missing. "Same Old Katy . . . *Come in, the* Same Old Katy . . . *Come in,* Buster . . . Buster, *do you read me? . . . Does anyone have sight or signal of* Buster? . . . Night Boy, *are you there? . . . I say again, come in, the* Night Boy . . ."

"*Ahoy there,* Cookie Cutter," said a voice in Tabitha's ear.

Toward them the Navajo Scorpion the *All Things Considered* came sailing like a white aeroplane. Kenny clasped his hands over his head and gave a deafening purr.

"Morning, Dodger."

"*Glad you could join us, gel.*"

"Not a problem." Captain Jute knew Dodger was teasing her. She didn't care. It was too late, really, to worry what anyone thought about you. There was no more time. "You do know you're showing," she said.

"*That's right.*"

"Saving power, are you?"

"*That's right.*"

Captain Jute could just imagine her sitting there with a roll-up in her mouth and a plug in her head, ready to drop instantly out of sight at the first sign of danger.

"*Karen's here,*" said Captain Gillespie.

From the McTrevor Clavicorn the *Maximum Disturbance*, Karen's cheerful squawk cut in. "*Hey, Captain! Is that you?*"

"Pretty much," said Tabitha. She had been feeling for some time that there could be very little of her left. All her life she had done nothing but shed pieces of her personality, up and down the spaceways. She imagined a trail of little Tabitha imagos peeling off behind her, little gesticulating doppelgängers fading slowly into the void. "All right, Karen?"

"*Never better.*"

Dodger Gillespie's voice switched to a private channel. "*She's one tank down,*" she said.

An empty radiator flask. Fuck, Tabitha thought, but did not say. She scrolled the external monitors, looking for the Clavicorn. How much could there be in the other one?

"*Rykov doesn't know,*" said Captain Gillespie.

"You've got to tell him, Karen," said Tabitha aloud.

"*Nah,*" said Karen. "*It's fine.*"

"I'll tell him myself," said Tabitha.

"*I'll do it,*" said Captain Gillespie.

"*Dodger, no,*" said Captain Narlikar, but Dodger was already on the com. Captain Jute had to wonder why she'd waited to tell her first.

Karen wasn't fussed. There was nothing anyone could do. "*They can fill me up when we get to the Crapper!*" she declared, with a laugh that was pretty frightening.

Hers was not the only damage. The *Albertine Disparue* was in view, looking more like an industrial grinder than a freighter since her adaptation. She was lit, but silent. She was moving in the right direction. Time would tell if there was anyone alive on board. Others were reporting pressure drops, navigation problems. The *Dire Wolf* toured, the Khan surveying his shrunken horde.

Little Alice sat on the holopad with her legs tucked under her, smoothing her pinafore. "EVERYTHING SEEMS QUIET NOW ON THE *CITADEL*," she said.

"So where is it?" Tabitha asked her.

The translucent child blinked out of existence, to be replaced by the planar location display.

"LOOK, CAPTAIN," she said. "SEE THE SWAN."

In the diagram, one of a dozen tiny insignia began to flash red and white. The field rotated swiftly around the galactic horizon, while on the console readouts white numbers scrolled smoothly from right to left.

The Resistance were gathered in a skewed saddle shape a hundred kilometers long. Between the saddle and the swan was a distance more than fourteen times that. Room enough to maneuver. Room enough to get into trouble, too. Room enough for anything, really.

" . . . *RGING*," came a familiar voice, loudly, across the whole net. "*THIS VEHICLE IS EMERGING.*"

The Danuta's tiny bow monitor zoomed in on a slow-spiraling burst of flustered particles. "*THIS VEHICLE IS EMERGING.*" A bright orange bus was restoring itself to actuality.

There was cheering in the ranks. "*Looking good, Buster!*" Beside Captain Jute, Kenny panted happily.

On the *Ella Megalast*, Captain Rykov continued to call the last absentees.

"*This is the* Ella Megalast *calling the* Same Old Katy . . . *Come in, the* Same Old Katy . . . *Does anyone have sight or signal of the* Same Old Katy? . . . *This is the* Ella Megalast *calling the* Night Boy . . . "

Deep and hard and slow, the voice of their commander,

Norval Khan, issued from the speakers of the remaining thirteen ships.

"*Okay, you fuckers. This is it now.*"

The plan was for Rykov to take the fighters, the *Best Policy* and the *Langoustine*, up ahead to pull apart whatever defense the starship was able to mount. The *All Things Considered* would handle any really stubborn trouble, while conserving her advantage. Everyone else would make a corridor for the ram they called Fernando, which was unimpaired, and would be moving very fast.

"*Mr. Garou, you're looking for hatches, windows, seals,*" said the Redcap veteran. "*Anywhere hull integrity is compromised.*"

On everyone's screens the graphic of the *Citadel of Porcelain at First Light* turned swiftly this way and that, displaying its precisely located patches of red, yellow and blue. "*We're looking for you to achieve 60% penetration.*"

"Fuck *that mother, Lou,*" slurred the Khan. There was more raucous cheering, guttural laughter, whistles, predatory howls.

By now they had halved the distance to the *Citadel of Porcelain at First Light*. She was visible to the naked eye, a bright dot in the murky distance. It took the superior detection systems of the *All Things Considered* to pick up the much smaller vessel that had suddenly appeared in between.

"*Emergence at 157.73, range 300,*" reported Dodger Gillespie. "*Schooner class.*"

"*39% PROBABILITY BONIFACE SERIES THREE,*" they heard the Scorpion persona announce.

"*The* Katy!" someone said.

"*PROBABILITY 44% AND RISING,*" Atkins reported.

"I declare," said Little Alice. "SHE'S TWO HUNDRED KLICKS OFF TARGET."

"Theer's all-eez one!" Kenny obviously found the inaccurate materialization of the little yacht extremely humorous.

Rykov was hailing her. Then everyone was. The *Same Old Katy* seemed confused, hailing in all directions generally. She had not located them yet. "*Katy, this is the Khan,*" sent the fleet commander. "*Whaddaya doing way up there?*"

The muscular potentate had clearly not grasped the element of unpredictability in even the briefest skip. "It's not like riding a bike," said Tabitha Jute; but she did not say it with her mike open.

"*Get your fuggn ass back here!*"

They started to pick him up then, apparently, on the *Katy*.

"*Hello,* Dire Wolf, *here we are,*" said Corbett Ali, loud and clear. "*Lapham Boniface LPB-3729, the* Same Old Katy *to Norval Khan, are you receiving me? Can't quite see you at the moment, sir . . . any of you.*"

"*Transmitting coordinates,*" Rykov sent tersely, as much for the Khan's benefit as the displaced yacht's.

"*OH, THERE YOU ARE,* ELLA MEGALAST," sent the Boniface persona. "*AND THE REST. I WAS STARTING TO SUPPOSE WE MIGHT HAVE BEEN THE FIRST TO ARRIVE! WHAT A FAUX PAS . . .*"

"Same Old Katy, *this is Gillespie on the* All Things Considered. *There are four ships bearing on you south-southwest, elevation 15°, estimated range 100K—*"

Tabitha Jute felt suddenly weak and sick. She looked at her partner. "Oh god, Ken, they're here."

The Thrant made an odd movement, as if trying to snatch the little hologram from her disc on the console.

"WHAT A TERRIBLE, TERRIBLE THING!" grieved Little Alice. "THE BONIFACE IS UNARMED."

Captain Jute thumped the canopy bad-temperedly. "We're unarmed," she said.

Kenny's yellow eyes glittered at her. It was impossible to know what was on his mind.

"*Four more ships, Norval,*" said Dodger Gillespie, her voice flat and dead. "*Assume hostile.*"

"*FREIMACHER TINKERBELLS,*" added the persona of her Scorpion. "*100% PROBABILITY.*"

The *Same Old Katy* was alone, exposed, two hundred klicks away. A dozen voices were screaming at her, the networked personas of the assembled fleet shouting warnings, advising evasive action.

"*We're getting a lot of noise here,*" reported Captain Ali. He sounded nervous now, panicky even. However poor the reception, on some subliminal level the alarm was getting through to him. "*This is the* Same Old Katy, *registration LPB-3729 to all stations: please switch to ID beacons, we're going to try to steer on your—*"

It was the yacht's last message. In the planar location display the tiny white Lapham insignia blinked twice and disappeared.

"*Corbett—!*" yelled Captain Rykov. He sounded more angry than appalled; as though he thought Captain Ali had found a particularly devious way to shirk his duty.

There were to be sixteen Tinkerbells, in all. They would issue in four waves of four from the Capellan starship the *Citadel of Porcelain at First Light*, and deal with the nuisance. The first twelve would have Eladeldi pilots, the last four human ones, cerebrally interfaced Plenty evacuees who had played a part in the recent mischief. As Sister Celandine said when she proposed it, it did seem a satisfactory solution, to make use of part of one problem to address another problem.

"*We do hope you won't let this disturb the array,*" the Chief Seraph had said, when Kybernator Perlmutter flashed a description of the situation across to her. "*We really can't afford to release any other ships at the moment. This is the crucial phase.*"

The starship captain shook his great head, lowering his eyelids and pushing out his lower lip. "Astraghal says there can be no more than twenty of them," he told her. "Falling to pieces, most likely, if they've fixed them up themselves." His voice became cross, regretful. "Why must they always make everything so difficult for everyone?"

Kajsa Prime smiled proprietorially. "*Because they're so inventive, and tenacious, and heroic. That's why we all love them so.*"

"Thank you, my lady, for that timely reminder."

The High Priestess of the Seraphim mimed a kiss. "*Well, you're a hero too, sweetheart. If you're sure you can cope. And just think: when this is all over you'll be able to get rid of that dreadful old hive at last.*"

When Kybernator Perlmutter smiled he squeezed his eyes almost shut. "Your confidence is an inspiration to us all, my Lady Kajsa."

The Capellan starship swelled rapidly in their viewports as the Plenty Resistance approached, martial music raging in their earphones. Against the seamless white expanse of her hull the eight red Tinkerbells swelled even more rapidly, the arc of their formation clearly expressing commitment to a principle of lethal precision.

"*Geddm, you bastards!*" The Green Streak known as *Dire Wolf* wheeled up and left as the *Ella Megalast* sliced ahead, the Lesondak V50 the *Langoustine* and the Shinjatzu Cormorant the *Best Policy* on her blazing heels.

Already the Navajo Scorpion the *All Things Considered* had vanished from view. "Bye, Dodger," called Captain Jute from the rear, knowing Captain Gillespie was listening, though she could not speak. "See you soon." She looked at the imago on the console. "Do you think, Alice?"

The imago was frozen and grainy, glowing at half power. The persona's whole capacity was momentarily engaged. "TAKING COVER," it reported.

Tabitha typed. Beside her Kenny the Thrant lowered his visor and spread his claws.

*   *   *

Above the silent fires of Capella the two forces met. The *Ella Megalast* and the *Best Policy* pounded the Tinkerbells with rays of vicious blue light. The defenders replied, chopping at them with strobe guns.

"Watch your outside, Sven."

The *Langoustine* swept up from under the *Best Policy* and sliced a piece off a Tinkerbell. The ship fell back, firing wildly, sliding irretrievably out of the fray. The *Langoustine* rolled out of danger and started hammering at the second in line, while the *Best Policy* swung over against the third, harrying her.

The red fan pivoted. It was still spreading. The rightmost of the nasty little ships clipped the *Ella Megalast* before Captain Rykov could pull away. Swallowing the injury he rode the skid, skating into the vector, taunting his attacker with his profile.

As Rykov moved he exposed the Silverfish, and an unlucky shot or an even unluckier engine fault caught her. She flew on for several seconds before a yellow soundless explosion burst from her starboard flux converter. Spilling her innards, she smashed into the Vespans. Like bursting elastic the plasma piping flew loose from their hull, capillaries unraveling, sparking with blue fire.

Still the wedge of Cormorant and Lesondak drove the defenders apart. Rykov was back, chivying the central ship off station.

The plan was working. The line was opening up.

The *Citadel of Porcelain at First Light* was completing the familiar switch from artifact to location. Tracts of dusky white enamel swept by like the planes of an abstract sculpture, yielding then closing to the view.

Shielded from detection, the Scorpion the *All Things Considered* turned her attention to the Tinkerbell that had Sven Dolan in its sights. It was giving him a hard time, fencing the *Langoustine* off from her objectives with a hail of electromagnetic percussion. The Scorpion nailed him with a short burst, and he sank from view.

"One," said Gunner Spik.

"AND TWO MAKE THREE," said Atkins.

The persona was right, two of the first four defenders were gone, and one of the second four. The Cormorant was doing a great job hindering the remainder from regrouping, while the *Dire Wolf*'s targeting routines went to work, combing the ever-changing mêlée stacking and restacking the probabilities. "*CODE YELLOW, NANDO,*" she flashed to the botched-up ram that still skulked in the commodious shadow of the tourist bus, the ill-named Lightning. "*CODE YELLOW!*"

Ahead the *Windhorse Trader* and the *Maximum Disturbance* were locking in. Finding herself in the right place, a plucky little scouter had begun trying to make the third side of the triangle, to define the corridor. The *Dire Wolf* was there instantly, her pulse gun coughing blocks of force, battering the Eladeldi away. Vertiginously, Dodger Gillespie swung round for Spik to pick one, which he did.

"Two," he said.

"*Code yellow you got, Norval.*"

A plume of chemical exhaust sparkled suddenly, lancing through the ruck like frozen smoke. It was the Fernando, zeroing in on naked tracts of glass and white metal.

Armed to the teeth, the passengers of *Buster* the Caledonian Lightning crowded the windows, watching the carnage. Soi the Thrant clung to the seatback with her left foot and brandished a cutlass in her right. As the Fernando shot by, a pink blur between the jockeying ships, she gave three sharp yelps. She imagined the man Lou on his ram splitting the fat white breast of the starship wide open, and all the worms inside spilling out into space, like maggots from the belly of a dead sloth.

"Nando? More like dildo!" In her excitement Morgan Shoe was reverting to childhood. "More like dildo, if you ask me.'' She dug her friend Poppy in the ribs and they covered their mouths, giggling. The Thrant pounded one another on the back, snarling excitedly, leaping across the backs of the seats.

There was a thump that jarred them all. For a moment they were weightless as the *Buster* flipped away from the battle. Hair and tails flew, axes stirred in their restraints. The windows of the bus were full of night. Was it the strike, the slap of some force expelled from the damaged starship knocking the ships into one another? An unpleasant whining, scraping noise had begun and did not seem as if it were about to stop. An elderly hordesman swore a horrible oath and burst into tears. Another jammed his knees into the seat, clasped his spike-gloved hands together and began to pray.

"*THIS VEHICLE IS DAMAGED*," announced the persona. "*THIS VEHICLE IS DAMAGED*."

The Fernando struck the *Citadel*, a pink form crumpling against the white hull, a bouquet of scrap metal and engine parts unpacking itself into the airless waste. There was a moment while the vast ship absorbed and redistributed its kinetic energy.

"*We have a strike*," reported Captain Rykov, observing. "*We do not have a breach. I repeat, we have no breach*." His Eagle skimmed away from the site, whirling clumsily to return the fire of an opportunistic patrol ship.

Kenny the Thrant pressed himself against the canopy of the Danuta. He had spotted another loose body: this one, Lou Garou, ejected at the last second from the Fernando and now floating on a high trajectory away from the Capellan ship, back into space.

"We'll get him," said Tabitha Jute to whoever was listening. "Compute intersection, please, Alice."

As she spoke, a ball of milk-white light shredded the suit from the mechanic's body, shivered his flesh into glowing rags.

The third wave of defenders had arrived.

*   *   *

Invisibly, the *All Things Considered* came looping round from the farside, having shaken off a Tinkerbell that had got too clever. Captain Gillespie had seen the latest wave burst from the chutes beneath the Stardeck and was chasing them, staying low, closer to the starship than she would have liked to be. She wasn't *that* invisible. She only hoped this wasn't a trap, four pieces of juicy bait trailed across her nose to lead her into range of some more lethal piece of sophistication. In her auditory centers, the com hissed.

"*This is the* Seraph Kajsa *calling the Navajo Scorpion the* All Things Considered," said the com.

It was a female voice, a languid, guttural, self-regarding voice. It was very familiar.

"*Is that you, darling?*" said the voice.

More by feel than sight Captain Gillespie found a gap in the action and went for it, climbing through the defenders and out over their backs. Gunner Spik snarled something, but she ignored him. Let him pick another target.

"Who are you after?" subvocalized Captain Gillespie.

"*Captain Jute,*" said the voice. "*Let me speak to Captain Jute.*"

Captain Gillespie had recognized the voice. "Identify yourself," she sent. Distantly she was aware of Spik, firing.

"*Who is that?*" the voice responded, with an audible trace of annoyance. "*This is Saskia Zodiac, calling from the* Seraph Kajsa. *I want to speak to Tabitha, Tabitha Jute.*"

Gunner Spik spat on the floor. "Three," he said.

Squeezing out a microsecond burst of impulse power, Dodger Gillespie slipped them into a new orbit of the starship that would carry them swiftly back to the rear of the battle. The Scorpion persona spoke, acknowledging, but she did not hear it. She was scanning the com frequencies, building a relay, squirting a hailing signal.

"*Dodger?*" came a startled squawk in her earpiece.

Captain Gillespie felt her eyes roll, her teeth clench. At

the moment, her body was little more than a distant outpost of her consciousness. She did not acknowledge the call from the *Cookie Cutter*. She addressed the caller who was already in her head.

"Saskia, this is Dodger Gillespie. Say what you want to say, quick. She's hearing you."

"*Oh, thank goodness,*" said the voice, without any great feeling. "*Anyway, this is Saskia Zodiac on the* Seraph Kajsa, *co-ordinates 323.03, 47.38, range 704 kilometers.*"

Captain Gillespie wondered for an instant when it was that Saskia Zodiac had started to inform herself in the niceties of celestial navigation, but the voice continued.

"*Tabitha, Captain Gillespie says you can hear me, I hope you can. It's about Iogo, actually.*"

On the Bergen Danuta the *Cookie Cutter* the voice, tiny, scraped and attenuated, emerged nonetheless audibly from the cockpit speaker.

"*Kajsa Tobermory and Pomeroy Lion have killed her,*" it said. "*They brought Iogo over from Plenty and they, well, they killed her.*"

Captain Jute almost stalled the boat, trying to throw her into reverse without consulting the persona. "Saskia?" she said. "Is that you? Can you hear me?"

The caller, it seemed, could not. "*I don't know why they did it,*" she continued. "*They do things like that.*" She gave a sigh. "*I remember how it was when Mogul died, and I thought Kenny ought to know.*"

Kenny was going berserk. He was throwing himself against the canopy of the Danuta, as if hoping to impale himself on the stars. He was howling fit to burst.

"*If you're in touch with him,*" said the caller from the *Seraph Kajsa*.

Buster the Caledonian Lightning was whirling away, crippled. Two of the Tinkerbells were carving him up between them. His windows were full of darkness and blood.

The McTrevor Clavicorn, the *Maximum Disturbance*, far too late, was attempting a rescue. "We can take them, Max!" shouted Captain Narlikar, as they descended wonkily toward the slaughter. "Grrrr! The one on the left, get him, get him!"

Then there was a noise like glass shattering, and fire sprang up everywhere, little flames eating the last of the air as it boiled from the Clavicorn cockpit, little flames running along the edges of the control panel, bursting out from the instruments beneath, as though fire was what they had contained all along, and now had come the time to spill it. Little flames leapt in Karen's body too, flaring up inside her joints and inner organs. As her head fell back against the failing web she saw that the port bow monitor was looking straight into the cockpit of a third red Tinkerbell, which had come up unseen and resolved the encounter. In the pilot's seat of the third red Tinkerbell sat no hairy blue Eladeldi baying for rebel blood, but a young human, a white woman with brass sockets in her head, and leads of black and red and silver disappearing into those sockets. It was one of the Xtasy Krew whose disruption of communications on the *Citadel of Porcelain at First Light* had been planned to cover their attack. Her name was Erika, she had broadcast on "Radio Xtasy" under the name of Erika Electrika. Her eyes were bloodshot and distended, and she was screaming as her guns flash-fried every cell in Karen Narlikar's body.

In the tiny cockpit of the Bergen Danuta the *Cookie Cutter* Kenny the Thrant was clinging to the console, baying for the little imago, which had popped prudently out of existence. This time there was no question about his intentions. The voice had left the com, but the coordinates of the ship she had called from continued to glow in a memory window.

Tabitha Jute was out of her web. Her head was splitting from the noise. She was shouting at her former bodyguard, trying to shove him back into his place. He turned on her, fast as a snake, destruction in his eyes, his jaws a fraction of a centimeter from her face. His breath reeked of ancient massacres.

"Alice!" yelled Tabitha. It was enough. There was a sudden jolt as the persona made a course correction. The maddened Thrant flew to the back of the cockpit.

Captain Jute wept. She had seen the *Buster* cut open, spilling its passengers into space, and now Karen was gone too. Another one from the long list of people to whom Tabitha Jute owed her continued existence, to whom everything was eternally owing and nothing would ever be paid.

On the *Dire Wolf*'s channel a mournful voice was intoning: "*The* Ella Megalast *is gone! The* Ella Megalast *is gone!*" For a moment Tabitha couldn't think who Ella Megalast was, and why she should care. And where was Dodger Gillespie? Why hadn't she been there to save Karen?

Captain Jute dashed the tears from her eyes and slapped again at her companion, who was making another frenzied assault on the controls. "Do it, Alice!" she commanded. "Lock! Plot! Skip!"

The fourth and final wave of defenders had done for the *Ella Megalast*, and the *Maximum Disturbance*, and now the *Langoustine* was in trouble. The *Dire Wolf* was on the spot, but moving sluggishly, not firing, and the Shinjatzu Cormorant the *Best Policy* was obviously struggling with the last of her ammunition.

Dodger Gillespie threw a tired glance at her gunner. Who should they try to help? "The Khan," she said. Spik grunted. The sweat was pouring from him and his eyes were like two mad onions. Without looking, he levered another magazine up and rammed it into the triple eight.

Everything had come apart. The Resistance was over, another footnote in the history of doomed stands against the all-devouring caterpillars of Capella. Flickering in and

out of visibility as her engines strained for more and still
more power, the Navajo Scorpion the *All Things Considered* lunged at the Tinkerbell that was sizing up the *Dire
Wolf.* Spik fired, but the Tinkerbell was firing too, at the
Khan, who was not replying. His lights were out and his
channel was dead.

Job done, the Tinkerbell danced away, full of vim and
élan. With his javelins of coherent light Gunner Spik pur-
sued her, but everything was out of kilter, he was hitting
nothing now.

"Fuck! Fuck! Fuck! Fuck!" Dodger Gillespie pulled the
plug. The fleet was down to six, was it, five, even? Hopeless. She had had one eye on the *Cookie Cutter* and seen
her go; the rest would be popping off soon, if they had any
sense. Captain Gillespie even thought for an instant of assuming the command, ordering the retreat, but Atkins interrupted.

"I FEAR THEY ARE ONTO US, CAPTAIN GILLES-
PIE."

He magnified a segment of the planar location display.
Two red triangles were flashing fast, two defenders on trajectories set to intersect, it seemed, right in Dodger Gillespie's lap.

Setting her teeth, Dodger Gillespie jacked in again, and,
with an incorporeal hand, reached for the values for a final
skip.

"I'm not sure you ought to watch this," said Sister Mansuetude to Maz and Landy and Tarmac and the others.

The children were in their dorm, to which they had been
confined until further notice. They sat staring expressionlessly at the AV. Their personal Guardian floated over their
heads so as not to interrupt their view.

The screen showed a hullside chamber prepared for some
kind of ceremony. The atmosphere was somber. Two lines
of Eladeldi guards stood stiffly in front of a huge airlock
door.

"On the other hand, perhaps it will be good for you,"
said Sister Mansuetude.

The glorious reds and blues of the uniforms of the guards
were canceled out by broad black sashes. There were no
decorations on the walls, and no music, obviously, except
a periodic roll of low, muffled drums.

"It might help you understand how important it is to be
good."

None of the children seemed to be paying their Guardian
the least attention. They were all gawping at the screen,
where a blond woman in an incongruous pink fur puffball
jacket and transparent glytex leggings had just appeared.

"*I understand that we can expect to be seeing Samantha
Stark brought through in just a very few moments now,*"
the blond woman said.

"Now, who is Samantha Stark?" Sister Mansuetude
asked her little flock, pedagogically. "Og? Lulubelle? Anyone?"

"Chief of security, Sister Mansuetude," chorused the
children listlessly.

"That's right, very good," replied their Guardian. "The
former chief of evacuee security. And there she is," she
said significantly, as another blond woman, this one crew-
cut, without makeup, and dressed in a black uniform shirt
and neatly pressed black trousers, was marched into the
chamber. She was closely guarded by a squad of eight
shaven Eladeldi bearing reversed broad-spectrum Inimica-
bles.

"*And here she is now,*" said the commentator, as if de-
sirous to echo Sister Mansuetude's phrasing. "*Samantha
Stark, formerly Colonel Stark, of course, now reduced to
civilian status, stripped of her military honors and accou-
trements, including the famous red cap from which she and
her followers formerly took their operating name, back in
the caves of Plenty. And my goodness, what a very long
time ago those days now seem.*"

The children stirred restlessly as the garishly glamorous

commentator appeared and disappeared on the screen before them. Clearly the scene was being filmed by a hovercamera on a tether to the woman's belt. Without a director to guide her, she was torn between prolonging those old days, when she had never been off-screen, and providing her audience with a close-up view of this rare and melancholy event.

"*Pardon me, Captain,*" she said, collaring one of the rigid Eladeldi. "*Geneva McCann, Channel 1. I wonder if you'd like to share with us your feelings on this sad occasion.*"

The captain of the guard did not reply. A fundamental principle of duty had been dishonored, and an example was to be made. Few indeed were the sapient life-forms, human or otherwise, for whom no accommodation could be made in the great Capellan scheme. Forgiveness could be found, time and time again, for those who had been graced with permission to serve the Masters, and who had failed to fulfill their allotted task. To this incompetent servant, alas, forgiveness could no longer be extended. Within the realm of her direct responsibility, serious breaches of order had occurred. Capellan property had been damaged, Capellan dignity outraged. Even the controllers of the great ship herself had experienced some interference.

None of this, however, did the Eladeldi captain say. It was not truly necessary, since a ceremony was in progress precisely to provide a formal expression of all these gloomy truths.

With a roll of synthetic drums, Samantha Stark was ushered, suitless and bareheaded, into the grand airlock. Moving swiftly, Geneva McCann was able to secure a superb frontal shot of her standing to attention as the door slid closed upon her. Then the drums fell silent, and there was only the soft chugging of the pumps to be heard. It could not have lasted more than the merest seconds, though it seemed like an eternity before the light flashed from red to green, indicating that evacuation of the lock was now, as the former colonel herself might have put it, at finalized completion status.

"Such a shame," said Sister Mansuetude, feelingly. "Just when everything is going so well."

"*This is Geneva McCann,*" said the commentator, zooming into view again, "*and that was Samantha Stark, leaving the* Citadel of Porcelain at First Light *for the very last time. Stay tuned to Channel 1, why don't you, as our exclusive live coverage continues with justice for a contingent of saboteurs.*"

Some of her little ones were crying now, Sister Mansuetude noticed. They were so very young, poor dears. Still, she knew exactly how they felt. It had been lamentable, the whole sorry, misconceived incident. There had even been some kind of skirmish out in space, with a number of armed raiders, she had heard: violence, gunfire and consequent bloodshed. Lamentable, lamentable.

On-screen, they were bringing in the Vespans.

∽ 30

In the commons of the *Seraph Kajsa* Saskia Zodiac and the technician whose name was Torch and whose number was 10 sat in a microgravity of something approaching 0.3G and ate artificial venison burgers with synthetic peas and nature-identical french fries. Around them people came and went, engineers and ops assistants bolting hasty meals. Some ate in intense silence; others in small groups that gestured and talked excitedly together.

For all the notice Saskia took of them, they might have been ants.

"You are off duty," she said to her companion. "Why do you stay with me?"

Torch slid a long french fry into his mouth.

"Maybe I like you, Saskia," he said.

This seemed only to irk her. "There is not enough of me for anyone to like," she pronounced, lifting her hands and letting them hang in the air like poisonous pale flowers. "My personality is a bubble stretched thin around pure emptiness."

He blinked, and swallowed a laugh. He put back his head and looked at her. "Bullshit," he said, mildly.

The face of the clone was pale and tight. "You've never seen a bull," she said. "I have seen several. On Malawari, at a rodeo. Mogul and I hypnotized one and performed acrobatics on it. You don't know everything about me."

Torch was on the point of telling her he had indeed seen bulls, whole shipments of them, and other animals too, large beasts and birds, in the Temple, when he was a boy. His mother and father had assisted at the sacrifices, feeding the remains into the metabolic processors, injecting the chemicals that promoted the disintegration. There had been a good deal of bull shit then, he remembered, and dolphin shit, ostrich shit . . .

He put another fry into his mouth. Mechanically, he chewed.

He was just off a four-ring shift, and dead tired. The transfer operation was deep in its final phase. The pressure was on. It was at such times that a simple unmodified tech could start to envy his hardwired colleagues with their fatigue overrides and neural-amplification implants.

Torch looked at the silent feeders. They all had sockets. They all stared blindly ahead, stoking themselves from nutritionally accelerated trays. Each of their seats, which they seemed to select at random, actually occupied a point on a straight line between the dispensers and the exit.

Only start to envy them, he thought.

Torch looked back at his companion, and found she was watching him. "Why are you rubbing your ear?" she asked.

He was. He stopped doing it. "Withdrawal symptoms," he said.

"Withdrawal symptoms?"

"Four orbits on." With the handle of his fork he sketched a line across the top of his head and a circle around his ear. "I can still feel the set," he said.

He filled his fork with food and ate it. "I guess it's kind of like a phantom limb," he said. "You know about that? People get their arm chopped off or their leg and wake up in the night with it itching?"

Saskia Zodiac nodded despondently and stirred the morsels on her plate.

"I have a phantom family," she said solemnly. "My sister and my brothers. They itch in the night. They would itch in the daylight too, but there is none of that here."

The commons lay deep inside the hull. The light there was always white and even, empty of warmth or character.

A Capacitory tech in insulated yellow overalls had come over to speak to Torch. "The bioreactors are ready to go across," she told him. She looked sideways at Saskia nibbling a pea. "There are eleven projects ongoing, nonmobile."

Visibly, Torch relaxed. He seemed pleased by what the tech had told him. All he said, though, was "Sure," and he gave her his wrist.

"Pomeroy Lion said he hopes you won't let anything boil over," the tech said, entering the list.

"Acknowledged," he said. "All right," he said, more softly, more to himself than to the tech. He raised his hand, dismissing her.

Saskia Zodiac clung to her joyless theme. "We are all ghosts," she informed her luncheon companion. "I am, you are. When we stepped out of space, we ceased to exist. The universe closed behind us years ago. Why should we think it will open now and let us back in?"

She gestured at the people busily eating all around.

"Ghosts," she said. "All ghosts. Insulting the material world with our presence."

Torch felt even more tired. He yawned. "You're thinking about that guy," he said. "That PL3484."

Saskia Zodiac gave an irritable shrug. "It was their design," she said. "They have the right to copy it, I suppose. That's no great trick, copying something over and over again."

Torch concentrated on cutting a piece off his burger. Everything was all made out of the same stuff, that was priests of the Seraphim taught. Identity followed function. Okay, so what was the function of this skinny white woman beside him at the table, with her shipwreck eyes and all her nerves so close to the skin? And what about that slimy PL3484, with his little red tie and his dead-fish smile?

He supposed it could just about break your heart if you thought about it. You could see how Saskia Zodiac must reckon they'd put that guy back together just to torment her. In actual fact, he couldn't think she would have been a factor in anyone's calculations, not even Kajsa's, who made such a big thing of caring about her.

What Saskia Zodiac was, was the last surviving prototype, a walking, talking, somersaulting memento of success. Her function, since they'd got her back, had been to go through all the tests they kept dreaming up for her. Lately, those had been deprioritized. There was going to be a lot of surplus now, said Torch to himself, whichever way it went.

"Is that the way you made those imagos, at that model shop? Did you copy yourself four times?"

She gave him a mutinous look. "You think I am as bad as them. Left to my own devices, I raise the dead."

He laughed outright then. She was amazing.

"Reorigination, we call it," he said, taking a drink from his water bulb. "Tell me you wouldn't have done that too, if you'd had the equipment."

A com tech from Prevision came over, saluting. Idly,

Saskia considered him. In his hemispherical hard hat with its two springy antennae he looked less like an insect than like a standard lamp.

He spoke to Torch. "Sorry to interrupt your meal, 10. We need your projected time allocations for the next ten orbits."

"Lord of This World," swore Torch. He was incredulous, almost disgusted. He stared challengingly into his colleague's purple visor. "Nobody knows what's going to be happening in two orbits' time, forget ten."

The tech became indifferent as a drone. "Chief Boaz has ordered all time and resource allocations to be claimed before the Convocation enter into—"

Torch interrupted. "Yeah, yeah." He would not say he was going to do it, he would not say that he wasn't. He raised his hand.

"We stopped Angie dying," said Saskia, "Xtasca and I. We kept her from dying so you could kill her yourselves, when you were ready."

She looked away from him, as if bored by the incontrovertibility of her own evidence. "You don't mention that, you see."

"Angie?"

"Angela Jute. The Mystery Woman. Ancillary 135, 7, 9, 11, whatever. Captain Jute's sister," she said crossly.

"The Cherub looked after her?" He had wondered what it was doing at the Ancillary's final playback.

She spoke to his bewilderment. "She looked after Mogul and me, for *years*. *She* was our real mother."

She had lost him. She always did. It was one of the things that kept him coming back for more.

"A Cherub?" he said. "No way."

She gestured truculently. "Our sister, our aunt, *some*-one," she said. "How would *I* know what she was?"

Torch put both hands on the table. "Saskia," he said. "You're not going to like this, coming from me, but nobody else is going to tell you." Nobody else here gives a shit, he didn't say.

"You're all grown-up now. I showed you your results. Your mental age has caught up with your physical age, maybe they've even crossed over. This is new territory now. All this other stuff, your family, the band, Captain Jute, Plenty—that's all what we call history. Let Diagnostics worry about it. Which is to say, with respect: you're just going to have to let it go."

He let that one sit with her while he cleaned his plate.

When he looked up, here was one of his hardwired colleagues, 52, a neurotronic, coming over now. Saying something about the orgone projectors. Spikes of fast-track software stuck in her sockets so she could be brought up to speed for the Great Work, whatever it was, without ever having to come off-line. Her mouth moved, but nothing registered in her eyes. "Kajsa Prime," her mouth said; and, "Holding operation." Was he off duty or not? He nodded, and raised his hand.

Saskia sat with her elbows on the table, her long chin on her fists. "I know you're keeping something from me," she said casually.

Torch was tired. He wanted to go to his stack and sleep until the old suns finally swallowed each other up. Protecting her was not going to be any easier if she stopped trusting him.

"Going to finish your meal?" he said.

"I'm not hungry," said Saskia Zodiac.

He took her to the big lab forward, where no one would question his presence, or hers, since she was with him. If anyone challenged them, he would claim he was measuring her physical and psychological reactions, and if they continued suspicious, he would do it, and log a report into Cognizance.

In fact there was no one there but a disinfection crew and a few insignificant high numbers who'd sneaked in for a look. They were at the window, pointing. Another time he would have sent them back to their duties, but this was special.

Suddenly reenergized, he let go of Saskia, flew to the next window along and pressed his face and arms against it like a kid.

"They did it," he said. He turned to Saskia, a huge grin on his face. "They did it!"

From here it looked like a tiny purple lamp, another of the elaborate beacons that floated in the outer lanes. There was nothing to suggest distance or scale, or the fact that an hour earlier it had not been there.

When it was clear Torch and the clone were also there just to look, and were not going to make any trouble, all pretense of work ceased. One of the disinfectors produced a binocular visor, and they passed it around. One by one, they zoomed in on the shiny dot.

"Is that it?" asked one of the orderlies, the youngest. Even now he had it in front of his eyes, he seemed to doubt that it might be some illusion, some replica.

"That's it," said the woman whose visor it was. She whistled softly through her teeth. "They did it," she said.

Saskia looked at them gathered against the glass. "What are we looking at?" she asked.

They all looked at her apprehensively, then at her escort. They floated in a loose cluster across three windows, keeping a little distance from the two of them.

Saskia looked at Torch. Apparently no one was going to answer her question unless he spoke first.

Torch was still grinning. He'd known it was coming for weeks now. Everyone had been on standby for the last ten watches, so he'd gone on duty and come off again knowing it was due. The moment the Capacitory tech came over to speak to him in the commons, he knew it was here.

He hadn't been meaning to come and gawp at it like a Tangle tourist seeing New Versailles for the first time. He'd had no intention of doing anything but sleep, and maybe later see if he couldn't steal a couple of minutes to swing by Navigation and check the telescopes. Now he was here, and it was actually in sight, over there, he felt a terrific sensation pressing against the inside of his chest, like all the odds out here had suddenly seesawed, and there was nothing from now on that wouldn't be possible.

He laid his hand on Saskia's back, on the shoulder blade that protruded so sharply through the thin stuff of her dress.

"It's home," he said.

Her deep eyes darkened with suspicion.

Gravely, one of the orderlies launched herself over and handed Saskia the visor.

She put it on and looked where Torch was pointing.

It was like being on a planet at night, and looking up at a kite through drifting smoke. It was a little thing, made of paper and tinfoil. It seemed that it must surely be in danger from the fire in whose light it floated.

Torch showed her how to adjust the focus on the visor, and the little kite turned into an extensive construction of dark metals and glass. It was arklike, but asymmetrical, an intricate, interlocking arrangement of acute angles and ovoids. There were pieces jutting out of it like piers, as if the central mass of it were somehow trying to buttress itself against the void. In the red light of the swollen suns it seemed to give back a strange, discontinuous gleam, as though the surface of it had been scoured with something harsh.

Saskia started to pick out more of the details: the galleries like shallow steps leading nowhere; the tiny petal-shaped slivers of white that were obviously big circular windows, seen edge on. When she noticed the black triangular fleck traversing one of the forward windows like a minute arrowhead, she started to understand the size of the thing.

Without thinking, she pointed. Across her field of vision

the shadow of her finger swam like a monstrous occultation.

"There are little ships," she said.

She heard the younger ones laugh together. "Those are the same size as this one," Torch said, not unkindly.

She took off the visor and gave it back to him. Her head seemed to be crowded suddenly with incoming images, rushing in from all sides and colliding. Her hand was trembling.

Passing the visor on, Torch kicked himself farther off the floor. He floated close, attentively, not touching her.

"Did you never see it before?"

"Only on AV." There was a constriction in her throat. She was aware that the others were watching her frankly now.

The Seraph technician looked out at the tiny purple light. "That's the facility where you were built, Saskia," he told her. "The Temple of Abraxas."

She remembered leaving the imaginary garden with Mogul under cover of darkness. The trees of the forest had parted like film. There was a vanishing sensation of heavy doors grating open, of darkness beyond. They were in a ship. The Cherub was there, the one they still thought of as a fairy. It was black, shiny and solid. It had given them drinks that made everything quiet and calm.

Saskia thought she remembered their first sight of Jupiter, near at hand, incomprehensible, a globe of swirling orange and brown so big it looked flat. It was a world, Xtasca had told them later. It was the first they had ever seen.

If either of them had looked to see where they had fled from, she did not remember it.

"You know what?" one of the disinfection crew was saying. "The old place looks better out here. It looks like it belongs."

The old place. Torch thought of all the people he knew who were in there, all the ones who hadn't got picked for this mission. It was still incredible they should actually be here, right over there, outside the window.

A lot of the guys had refused to believe it at first. The chiefs could not have agreed to it, to risk the celestial palace in hyperspace. Many said that it was not even possible. Tech 4, on an interim detail to Schematics division, claimed to understand some of the math, but if he truly did he sure as limbo hadn't been able to explain it to the rest of them. Much more significant was the fact that the Guardians had wanted it there.

"If they ever get it here, that's it," 4 had assured them. "It'll be all the way then, or nowhere." The Temple would be giving up troublesome Terra, he meant, to gain the stars.

"Let me have that again," said Saskia Zodiac to the cleaners.

The conversation died when she spoke. They handed her the visor.

The Garden had been inside a big dome, she knew that. Could that be it, beyond those two piers? It was impossible to know.

"We must go there," said Saskia. She found herself looking around for Xtasca.

They had taken Xtasca into Schematics. Saskia had neither seen nor heard from it since. Several times Queen Kajsa had assured her that the Cherub was fine, and working hard. She was sure Xtasca would want to come and see Saskia just as soon as its work was done.

Xtasca had brought her here, to the Temple's flagship. Xtasca would take her to the Temple.

The clone felt Torch's hands again, lifting the visor from her face. His eyes were steady and strong. She remembered when Mogul had looked at her like that.

"They're not there," said the tech to her softly. "They're gone."

She scowled. "How do you know what they've been doing to amuse themselves on the journey."

"We know what they're doing," he said. "They're way past that stage now. You have to understand. What I said about history. You're history now, to them. Saskia, listen to me."

He took her by the shoulders. "Your brothers and sisters are gone," he said gently. "You are the only one left. Okay?"

"What are they doing, then? What is this Great Work?"

"It's something big," said one of the crew.

"It's the biggest thing ever," said another.

"They've come here to finish it," said Torch.

His cloned companion looked at him expectantly, then shook her head. "This is nothing," she said. "You tell me nothing."

She looked at the little clutch of wide-eyed spectators, seeing not the overalled menials but the Seraphim themselves, looming resplendent in pink and purple, whispering behind their clean, smooth hands.

The tech numbered 10 led her out of the lab.

"You don't want to go there," he said. "You want to sit tight. You're safe here. I'll take care of you."

She made a swift movement, viciously dismissive. "You tell me my mental age has caught up with my physical age," she said. "Then you treat me like a child."

"You heard those guys in the commons. I'm looking after all the specimens while the chiefs are gone." He yawned, and gave her a watery smile. "That's my next assignment."

"That's why you stay with me," she said.

He palmed a door for her. "Sure," he said, "you and the mutant space mice."

Saskia understood this was a joke. It was the sort of thing Marco Metz used to say. The point of the joke was that Torch meant her to understand he had volunteered for his duty, on her account.

"They'll be taking Project PL3484, I imagine," she said.

"I don't guess they will," he said, as they skated along the corridor toward the chute. "Probably they'll bring people over to see him. They're not all going, anyway. Xipe-totec will be here."

"Is Xtasca still with him?"

"That's not my department," he said.

She believed him, she supposed. Here was the transit chute, with the upward-pointing triangle glowing green.

"Where are we going now?"

"I want to get you back home to J Deck and sign you in," he said, ushering her in first. "Maybe then everybody will let me get some sleep."

As she rose, he put his arm around her hips. His curly head against her thigh, they spiraled upward together.

Sweet Lavender wore a white-leather suit with purple piping around the lapels and cuffs and the slits where his wings emerged. He sat with his wings folded, his hands on his knees.

Pomeroy Lion's dark grey suit and starched white shirt were more conservative, but he had chosen a gorgeous purple-silk cravat, which he kept tweaking and plumping under his chin as he rode. He wore his Capellan ring, which he had unaccountably never managed to make work.

Boaz, who wore purple constantly, had had his armor lubricated and polished until the lights of the cockpit were reflected in it. He would have preferred, really, to seal his armor, strap on an EVA unit and motor across under his own power, but Kajsa had forbidden it.

In his sled, beside Boaz, there was room for only one page. Kajsa Prime took five of them. One sat either side of the pilot, one either side of her, and the fifth crouched in the back, ready to bear her train when she disembarked. Queen Kajsa wore her white fur over a purple sheath dress so tight she had to sit with her knees to the side. She smiled in pleasure at the prospect of seeing her sisters once more.

Each sled was attended by three Cherubim, which flew with it like black chrome *putti* escorting the chariots of the saints. And thus, in the dusky glare of the Capellan suns, four of the leaders of the mission to Capella made their majestic return to the Temple of Abraxas.

〜 31

Yipetotec of Schematics was no lover of the Capellans. He doubted that the next stage of the posthuman project should be this alliance with the incomprehensible and unpredictable. If and only if what Boaz had quaintly named the "Great Work" succeeded, if it did what it was meant to; and if as a consequence the galaxy was opened up to them: then he would have to take a different view, and concede Sol well lost. Until that time he preferred to remain the skeptical conscience of the mission, and secure the resources they had. While his colleagues went dashing over to the Temple in their finery, he stayed on board to decommission the robot cartographer.

Under the supervision of a programmable tech, Cherubim released from the transfer array received the incoming device, swimming out to catch it in a giant net which they drew with their tails. As soon as they had it close and secure, others began to break down the flight module, sorting components to be jettisoned, reprocessed or stored, according to condition. Watch after watch they toiled, like malign black bees dismantling an iron orchid.

The pair of Cherubim that had successfully accompanied the device on its enormous flight were brought inside to be decommissioned. They were not without injury. The heat had buckled and discolored their skins. One had lost its right eye and much motor ability on that side. When it tried to speak, the sound that came out was like the grinding of gears.

Its partner was able to deliver a halting report. With Xtasca recording, it spoke of gigantic reefs of carbon, five-thousand-kilometer cobwebs of ash. For every ship the Capellans had been able to commit to the transfer of the Temple, the remains of two others could be definitely identified farther in, blackened wrecks spiraling slowly toward the acquisitive suns.

When there was nothing more to be learned from the Cherubim in the animate state, Xtasca deconfigured their brains and read their internal meters. It worked quickly and economically, performing no act that was not logically necessary. Then it gave up their bodies for reclamation.

Xipetotec was a little surprised. Those scrambled, battered veterans had had an experience that was unique. To judge by the way Xtasca had treated them, they might have belonged to an entirely separate species of machine. The Master of Schematics realized he had been expecting something else, some evidence of sympathy or identification, some manifestation of the independent personality that distinguished the prodigal Cherub. Could it be attempting to conceal something from him?

"Prepare the data for uploading," he ordered.

The eyes of the Cherub glowed briefly. The process monitors began to fill with directory listings in green and yellow.

"Data already prepared, sir," the Cherub said.

Xipetotec started to check. Everything was tagged for instant transfer to the automated honeycomb of Cognizance, with copies for the Temple the moment the datalink was secure. There were not even any queries outstanding.

Over the months since its return, the Head of Schematics had got into the habit of treating Xtasca less like an implement and more like an assistant. Now, as if encouraged, it had started showing the maximum approvable initiative, taking each task to the fullest completion possible without specific extra authorization, and stopping there.

Xipetotec felt a momentary irritation, as though in some absurd way the squat little engine meant its efficiency as an insult. Perhaps it was after his job.

He picked a few items with his stylus, searching for novelties or anomalies. "Major variations?" he asked the Cherub.

"The concentrations of life-forms on 3 provisionally identified as Frasque now register at reduced magnitude," it murmured. It entered a code to identify the relevant string and set it flashing.

The figures were indeed down. Xipetotec called up the evidence and scrolled through it. Patchwork graphics floated up, rotated, flecked themselves with white and red.

"Instrument or acquisition error?" he mused.

For some reason this question made the Cherub whir for three whole seconds before it replied. Impossible to know what that delay signified, any more than if it had been a human hesitation. When it spoke, it said only what any of the others would have said.

"Cannot be eliminated."

It was like working with someone in the grip of a dreadful anger they could not express, which made them speak and act constantly with perfect, disdainful precision.

No traces indicative of life had showed up on either of the lower planets. On Capella 2, the very air had turned to ash. The ruin they had identified as Capella 1 had been baked and scoured and squeezed into something functionally identical to coal.

"Assuming no instrument or acquisition error," said Xipetotec, "suggest possible causes of numerical reduction."

"They are dying," said Xtasca.

Xipetotec contemplated the backs of his hands. In the light of the monitors, the tattoos on his skin resembled a coat of blue-black silicon feathers.

"Or being removed," he said. "Cross-check with vehicle movements compatible with mass-transit departures from 3.''

Lights on Xtasca's board fluttered. ''Please authorize allocation of tapes 2A7 to G16 from cartographer data-storage core,'' requested the Cherub.

The Chief of Schematics smiled to himself. He had found the point where Xtasca's initiative ran out. It was the point at which it was required to interact with the others, to request something from them. Some analogue of arrogance must be the trigger for the reversion to protocol; Xtasca's sense of superiority to the flock. Unless, perhaps, it was the opposite. A loss of confidence, the assumption that it might not be recognized.

The little grey scoutship materialized off the starboard quarter at 43.76 precisely. In the tall shadow of the Seraph flagship it floated, like an empty beer tube drifting by a steep black cliff.

In the tiny, malodorous cockpit there was silence. The persona hologram had been switched off for the last part of the journey, and Kenny the Thrant had lain quietly in his seat, unresponsive, uncommunicative with grief. Now he gazed up at the side of the *Seraph Kajsa* and gave a malevolent snarl.

Tabitha Jute gave him a dreary look. ''Okay, Ken,'' she muttered. ''We're here.'' These days she came slowly back to herself, relinquishing nonexistence reluctantly, like a sleeper clinging to a warm bed.

She had been thinking about Plenty again, in the days of summer.

She remembered ambling with Karen and Topaz down Green Lantern Way, not far from Prosperity and Peacock. The tunnels of the commercial district had been one hazy blur of pink-and-blue neon. The air was hot and thick with the smell of beer and frying onions. Closed to automobile traffic, the main thoroughfare was a mass of people, their faces happy and perspiring in the din of competing mandolins and muzak. The passengers cheered at the sight of the Captain amongst them, mobbing her and her mates good-naturedly for autographs and kisses.

The shop windows had been hung with cascades of optical streamers, party favors and masks at drunken angles. A jeweler displayed a Palernian deity of carved granite, festooned with necklaces of Neptunian amethyst. Outside the strip clubs women in fishnet stockings and prismatic waistcoats called out to anyone who dawdled, while Perk kids capered and danced in colored leathers, leaping high in the air. Their teeth flashed as they caught the coins that Topaz threw. On the Midway lift platform a tattered preacher and a group of disciples bearing placards of apocalyptic doom tried to dissuade new arrivals from their headlong plunge into the tumult of pleasure, while less than a hundred meters away, with cymbals clashing and bugles blaring, a Martian jazz band belted out "Schiaparelli Stomp."

Captain Jute knew that anything had been possible, then.

Against the dark spiral object that was the ruined Capellan System, the *Seraph Kajsa* loomed inviolable, unassailable as death. The Seraphim had even switched off their invisibility shield, so happy were they now to be here.

In the Bergen Danuta 12 named the *Cookie Cutter*, the persona vox said: "I'M AFRAID I HAVE TO REPORT THAT WE ARE NOW COMPLETELY OUT OF FUEL, CAPTAIN. UNLESS THE OCCUPANTS OF THIS SHIP CAN OBLIGE US, WE MUST SOON SEEK AN ALTERNATIVE MEANS OF TRANSPORT."

"All right, Alice," said Captain Jute. She pressed the eject button and slid the persona plaque into her palm. "You've done really well. Always."

The lights in the cockpit dimmed. Kenny reached up and thumped his fists against the canopy, uttering a rhythmic panting hoot of challenge.

"All *right*, Ken." Captain Jute slid Alice into the pocket of her suit, and felt for her disruptor. It nestled in her hand as comfortably as a harmonica, a sex toy, a drug-delivery device. "I'll get us on board," she said.

They answered her signal halfway through the first buzz. The man who appeared on the com screen was black and bald. He had blue tattoos all over his face and down his neck that made him look like an exotic diagram in an anatomy holo.

"Captain Jute?" he said. "Captain *Tabitha* Jute?"

She thought she had never been greeted so graciously.

Chief Xipetotec of Schematics, duty Seraph during his colleagues' absence, was not dissimulating. He was truly very pleased to see Captain Jute. He knew Kajsa would be pleased too, to hear she had actually turned up, when he made his scheduled report at the end of the shift. He didn't see why they should give the Capellans anything, but it might be useful to Kajsa to let them know they had her.

The misplaced bargee stood there in her ugly green suit, her helmet hinged back, her thick dark hair tied with a faded ribbon. Her eyes were dull. She had the marks on her of years spent in the depths of the hive. The thought of what it must have been like in there, the insane and insanitary conditions, brought the taste of disgust into Xipetotec's mouth. What evidence could be more damning than that she chose to fly around with a Thrant now?

It was a male, in battledress, fanged and rank as all his kind. Xipetotec curled his nostrils against the stink.

"This is my bodyguard, Kenny," said Captain Jute, in a husky, uneducated voice. "He's bothered about his wife."

Xipetotec frowned, drawing down the corners of his mouth. "His *wife*?"

The Thrant took his yellow eyes from the Cherub that was watching them impassively from its plexiglass globe. He gave his head a rapid shake, and his ears twitched. "Iogo," he barked.

The black-skinned giant blinked, then smiled with a strained charm. With one finger, he waved away the security guards who had brought them on board.

"What did he say?"

"Iogo," said Captain Jute. "It's her name."

"I don't think I know that lady," said the giant.

They were in a room full of what she supposed were computers. Captain Jute wondered if it was Xtasca in the bubble. It had neither moved nor spoken since they had come in, only gazed at them with its little red eyes.

"We had a message from Saskia Zodiac," said Tabitha to the Seraph. "I think you know her."

He gave her a stern look. "Of course I know her. I contributed to her design."

"She said you brought Kenny's wife here from Plenty."

"Kill't," said the Thrant. He wagged his head dangerously and drew his claws down through the long fur of his throat. "Ms Zod-ac said kill't."

"That's what she said," said Captain Jute to Xipetotec.

They were staring at him like a pair of Neanderthals, their arms hanging down. Could they possibly be trying to menace him?

"I apologize, Captain Jute, Kenny," said Xipetotec, getting out of his chair and moving across the room, farther away from the smell. Covertly he turned up the air-conditioning. "I was under the impression you were here to request sanctuary from the Capellan defense force," he said, wiping his hands. "Now I believe I do remember the experiment you mention. My colleague Pomeroy Lion—"

The security people went for their weapons as the Thrant suddenly hunched himself into an aggressive stance. " 'at was ee name she said," he declared, wetly. "Pom'ree Lion."

Xipetotec looked down impatiently at this twitching of furry muscles. "Yes, well, Pomeroy Lion could certainly tell you more," he went on. "He is not here."

The battered little truck driver put her hand on the shoul-

der of her Thrant, restraining him, not looking at him.
"And Saskia?" she said. "You haven't killed her, have
you?" She moved her head from side to side, addressing
her demand to all of them, Seraph, Cherub and guards alike.
"I want to see Saskia."

It would make sense to have them all together, out of
the way. The Schematics Chief activated the com. "The
clone is in no danger. No danger at all," he said, as the
signal went out to Tech 10. "Perhaps I shall let you see
her."

They waited.

Tech 10 was not answering.

The Thrant and the Cherub had locked eyes again. He
was watching it like a cat watching a goldfish, weighing
up its edibility against the difficulty of catching it.

The tech was still not answering. Something was wrong.
"What is this?" said Xipetotec.

The guards watched him tensely, ready for an order.

He tried the clone. He looked at all the screens dotted
with flags requiring his attention. He began to lose his pleasure at the arrival of Captain Jute.

There was something about her, he recognized, an ill-
focused truculence, a general unintelligence and animal ob-
stinacy that made her nuisance potential immediately clear.
How fortunate she had been, he thought, that it was not
Boaz who was here to receive her.

There was no reply from the clone either. And the Thrant
had actually started swishing his tail.

Xipetotec made a swift decision. He hung up the com
and pressed the switch to open the bubble.

Captain Jute folded her arms.

The segments of the bubble receded into its base.

"Hello, Captain," said the Cherub.

"Hello, Xtasca," said Captain Jute.

It hummed for an instant. "Saskia has been preserved,"
it said. "Unfortunately, Angela was destroyed."

Captain Jute dropped her chin on her chest. "Yeah," she

said. Her voice was a colorless whisper. The Thrant growled and rubbed his forearms sloppily over her back and head. She pushed him away.

The Cherub spoke to Xipetotec. "Do you wish me to disconnect, sir?"

Xipetotec was experiencing a slight doubt. It was Iogo the woman had asked about. Who was Angela? Was that a name he should know?

"Who was Angela?" he asked the Cherub.

It was Captain Jute who answered him. "She was my sister," she said. Her eyes were empty.

"What happened to her?"

Again she answered. "Angie died," she said. "A long time ago. When we were girls."

Xipetotec began to think Boaz was right, that she was nothing but a waste of time. Every time she opened her mouth there was another complication, another irrelevance.

"Yes," he told the Cherub. "Switch over and disconnect."

At once it did so, and floated to him like a novelty balloon, its tail dangling like a piece of wire. Without looking at either of them, it passed between the heads of Captain Jute and the Thrant and came to hang in front of its maker, ready for instruction.

Xipetotec addressed the guards. "Take them to the Zodiac woman's quarters on J Deck and secure them there. If the woman is not there, test the com, then locate her and Tech 10. Tell 10 to report to me in person."

He ran his eye over the Thrant. One thing he had never been able to understand about the Capellans was their choice of client races. "You'd better cuff that one," he said.

The Thrant roared and swore as one of the guards collared his neck while the second forced his hands behind his back and manacled them. "If you need assistance, call for extra personnel," said Xipetotec as the guards connected the manacle tube to the collar with a rod of carbon steel.

Then his attention switched to the woman. "Has she any weapons?"

A guard came and searched her. He discovered the plaque. "The scouter persona?" the Seraph asked, as the guard displayed it.

Tabitha kept her hand on it. "Scouter's out of fuel," she said.

The thing was useless here in any case, there was nothing that would read it. Xipetotec waved the guard to ignore it and move on.

The guard found the neural disruptor. He smiled as he relieved her of it. "Fully charged, sir," he said.

"Nothing else?" asked the Seraph. The guard signaled a negative. There might be a psychological advantage, Xipetotec supposed, in holding prisoners with their own weapon, whatever it was. He consulted Xtasca. "Would that work on the Thrant?"

The Cherub examined the device. "The model is effective on all vertebrates," it announced.

"Take it with you, then," the Seraph instructed the guard.

The guard clipped the disruptor to his belt and took the intruders away. Xipetotec returned to his work with a significant smile. He knew perfectly well that the Zodiac woman could not have called them. He had a very good idea who had. The tech would confirm it, when he arrived, and then he would add that to his report to Queen Kajsa too.

The corridors of the *Seraph Kajsa* were antiseptic, lined with stainless steel. There was a soft purring noise everywhere, of heating systems and distant machines. Slender people in hooded overalls of white and green and pink passed intently back and forth with numbers on their chests.

The ill-assorted party of five bounded lightly along together, the Captain and the Thrant each with a guard to escort them, the Cherub bobbing along in front. Kenny moved awkwardly in his restraint, his upper body rigid, his hands behind him.

Captain Jute did not know why the Seraph had sent Xtasca with them. Seeing it immobile there in the bubble, she had assumed they had managed to reprogram it. When it had let her answer his question about Angie unchallenged, she had begun to think they had not. But that might have been a trap of some kind. Perhaps Xtasca was a spy module. Perhaps its presence was designed to provoke indiscretions.

She pushed herself closer to it.

"How is Saskia?" she asked.

"My duties have kept us apart," said the Cherub flatly.

Tabitha decided to try some provocation of her own. "I didn't know you had duties to these people anymore," she said.

"They are responsible for my existence," replied the Cherub, bland and obedient as an automated tour guide.

The guard caught up with Tabitha and, with an ugly gesture, cautioned her to silence. Tabitha propelled herself along, thinking once again of her mum and dad. The memory popped into her mind of a rare family occasion with all four of them together, not long before Angie took off.

It had been their mother's birthday, and they had gone out to eat, not in a public cafeteria, but in one of the restaurants that usually catered only to rich tourists in transit. Their dad had got hold of some credit somewhere, and blown it all on a lobster dinner. It must have been hideously expensive, so far from the sea. Mum had been furious with him. She had refused to eat her lobster, and refused to let Angie or Tabitha eat theirs. She had made their dad eat them all, while they sat there and watched.

Dad had made a joke of it, pretending to enjoy them. Angie had moaned and whined, she was hungry, she wanted to order something else, she was going to eat all the individual portions of white sugar and brown sugar and coffee creamer and sweetener and pepper and salt that sat in their little white tubs in the center of the table. Tabitha remembered her dad licking his lips, starting to sweat as he cracked open yet more of the orange armor. And she remembered her mum glaring at him as if he was the one humiliating her, not the other way around. She had the thought, there and then, at the age of ten or whatever it was, that those two people, that man and that woman— they had made her. I am both of them, she thought. And it seemed a mysterious and very terrible thought, because for all she could see, those two people hated each other.

"You recently visited the third planet, Captain Jute."

They were in a lift now, she and Kenny and the Cherub and the guards. She did not remember entering the lift, but that was where they were. It must be taking them to Saskia on J Deck. The Cherub was speaking to her. Unless it was someone else, the big black Seraph with the navy blue tattoos, speaking through the Cherub.

"You made a visit to the third planet."

Tabitha straightened her back. She watched the floors slip slowly by, black, white, black, white.

"I thought I'd take a look around," she said, "while we're here."

"Did you sight any Frasque during your time there?"

Tabitha raised her chin. The guards were watching her. She wondered if they had what you could call minds, and if so, what was passing through them.

"Frasque?" she said. "Quite a lot of Frasque, yes."

The Cherub's eyes gave a brief flash. "It is as we computed . . ." it said. Tabitha Jute reached for Kenny and stroked his bare, pinioned arm. Beneath his pelt, the muscles felt like steel cable.

"Plenty is full of Frasque now," she said.

Xtasca gave a metallic hiss; or perhaps that was the lift. "It's logical," it said. The doors whisked open and then they were moving along another corridor, identical but for the presence of a gentle gravity, and the absence of people.

"What are they doing here?" asked Captain Jute loudly.

The guards gestured with their weapons, but Xtasca answered the question. "Capella is their home," it said.

They stopped outside a door, a featureless rectangle of primrose yellow. Inside her head, Tabitha felt something fall silently into place.

"You knew that," she accused the Cherub. Her escort put his arm between them, pushing her back, but the Captain took no notice. "You said that, on Plenty, when we emerged. You said the Seraphim wanted—"

Xtasca was extending a small shaped device from the end of its tail and inserting it into the door lock. "—to resume a promising collaboration," it said.

It activated the lock.

A blinding blue flash filled the corridor. Xtasca the Cherub threw up its hands and fell like a black sack of water against the yellow door.

The door flew open, sweeping the Cherub with it, and a narrow beam of light flashed out. It struck the first guard in the chest, vanished, then flashed out again, striking the second in the stomach. Still clutching their weapons, they fell, and lay unmoving in the hallway.

"Captain," said a voice. It was quiet, complacent, male. "How very nice to see you again."

Kenny had barged into Captain Jute with his shoulder, pushing her out of the line of fire, forcing his way into the cabin. He was yelling loudly and ferociously in his own language. Rising winded to her feet, Captain Jute grasped the jamb of the door and saw inside the cabin.

There were three people in there. The first she saw lay a little way inside. It was one of their techs, a black man in a white overall suit with a number on. He lay twisted, making the number hard to read. It was a two-digit number, she thought, possibly 10.

Beyond the tech was a bed. On it was Saskia Zodiac. She was lying flat on her back, dressed in bizarre peach-pink lingerie. There was a gag in her mouth, and her arms and legs were spread-eagled in a way that suggested her wrists and ankles were fastened to the corners of the bed.

The third person was the man who had spoken. He stood by the foot of the bed, facing the door. He was a very pale white man with a sharp black haircut, little round glasses and a raspberry-colored tie. There was a jeweled pin in his tie, which he was straightening.

''Please,'' he said. ''Do come in.''

∽ **32**

In the courts of the Temple of Abraxas the atmosphere was hectic. The halls both upper and lower were a tumult of celebration and activity, with orderlies bustling here and there, spreading tapestries and placing furniture. Into the refectory swept a company of minor priests, robes of black and purple billowing importantly as the sails of schooners. Behind them came their ancillaries in grey tunics, their sockets shining brightly, their arms full of candles and silverware.

A magnificent welcome banquet had been prepared for the crew of the *Seraph Kajsa*, those most courageous colleagues and counterparts of the Temple chiefs who had not been seen since departing Sol System a dozen years before, in desperate haste to pursue the absconding orbital. Winged servitors flitted to and fro with smoking dishes of Lamb Pasanda and *Poularde à la d'Albuféra*, jostling each other discreetly for the chance to serve Sweet Lavender or Pomeroy Lion. Behind the force curtain that screened the kitchen, they preened themselves and boasted to one another of the smiles and putative marks of favor the pioneers had bestowed upon them while they heaped their plates with broccoli or brioches.

At the head of high table, among her avatars, Kajsa

Prime looked splendid in her imperial headdress and ki-
mono of lilac and grey. She made a speech, welcoming her
faithful followers to this glorious new zone of opportunity
and power. ''With the assistance of our new allies we of
the true faith and transcendent gospel shall attain the threshold of the galaxy!''

There was more in this vein, so inspirational that though
oratory was not at all the Prime's major talent some of the
surviving First Reformed could be seen to turn to one another and stretch their sclerotic lips in satisfaction and anticipation.

The trees of the refectory were alive with songbirds and
musical bats that constantly piped the praises of the Prime
Seraph and her mission. Sweet Lavender sported gaily with
a flying bird, a sort of miniature duck with rich plumage
of dark blue and chocolate brown, a head of green and an
orange bill that was permanently open. As the meal wound
down he left his seat and chased it through the halls with
aerobatic joy.

Collared slaves cleared the dirty dishes. Speculatively
Pomeroy Lion eyed an Eladeldi who was stiffly steering a
loaded tray. ''Do you think they know there are Capellans
only a few thousand kilometers away?''

''They're no trouble as long as they're wearing those
collars,'' said his neighbor assuredly. ''And there's no
chance of them taking them off because the collars don't
open!''

She was a small rotund woman with dark curly hair,
bursting with energy and conviction. Pomeroy Lion had
been slightly taken aback to discover that she was Boaz's
mother, whom he had never had occasion to meet before,
and whose existence, indeed, he had never had cause to
suspect, except in the most general way. The success of the
Capella mission and the arrival of the Temple in this glorious zone of opportunity had confirmed her in her maternal
pride, with the result that she had spent the evening doing
the rounds of her son's colleagues from the *Seraph Kajsa*,

introducing herself and extending to them a share in her satisfaction at the splendor of his achievements. "His poor dear father and I always tried to bring him up to work hard and worship the Lord," she explained, her plump little hand gripping Pomeroy Lion's grey doeskin sleeve. "Ooh, Mr. Lion, you should have seen him when he was a little boy . . ."

"By the Fifty-Five Phases of Parturition!" growled Boaz.

His mother turned from the table and rapped the giant Chief of Prevision on his shiny steel cuisse. "Language!" she scolded.

"You don't know how good it is to be back here in all this *space*," said Sweet Lavender, perching beside Mercutio of Triton in his white-leather suit. He spread his wings extravagantly, stretching their tips like fingers.

He had caught his bird and now sat stroking it like a pet, cooing and making little squeaky quacking noises to it through his nose. He turned its head to watch the revelers, who waved and bowed and pulled comical faces. Sweet Lavender knew perfectly well that the bird was actually a customized hovercam serving the Temple archives.

Mercutio regarded him with amusement. "You're all sweaty," he observed.

"Yes I *know*," said the angel. Spotting a half-filled goblet of wine on the table, he seized it and drained it with a flourish. "Does it offend you? I shall get Adriel to mix me up a batch of new pheromones immediately."

Adriel was one of the First Reformed, Kajsa Tobermory's contemporaries. He was a fairly primitive composite, a male head on a female body. That sort of work, startling and innovative twenty years ago, was now well within the competence of even the modest hypersurgical facilities of a mobile unit like the *Seraph Kajsa*. The Diagnostics chief could see that Adriel's head was beginning to look wrinkled and worn, while the skin of his body, which he liked to parade unclothed, remained stiff and shiny and incorruptibly young as ever. Sweet Lavender grinned and raised his goblet to the beaming Adriel.

It was plain to all of the pioneer expedition that the years of separation had made a considerable difference to the technical capacities of the Temple, most especially in the field of autoplastics. One of Kajsa Tobermory's eldest avatars had made herself enormously fat, so much so that there was some suspicion she might have been motivated by an intention crudely to eclipse the returning original. She was behaving with perfect civility, however, chatting to the Prime about parasitically induced immune suppression and multicerebral coordination all the while she continued to cram herself with profiteroles.

"We are very pleased," said the Prime frankly.

"We knew you would be," said her largest avatar.

"The Great Work goes forward!" exulted Boaz, who had managed to separate himself temporarily from his mother. He stretched his metal arms wide over their heads, blessing the Temple and all who laboured in it.

"Sister," said an avatar of Kajsa Tobermory seated to her left, "have you told the Capellans?"

"We have, Sister," replied the Prime, "with pictures and in simple words that they can understand."

They shared a sweet smirk. Above their heads, Boaz snorted ill-temperedly.

"And Sister," said another avatar to her right, "did they not wish to inspect the, um, Great Work?"

Her original folded her hands comfortably inside her sleeves. "Oh, certainly. We propose to wait until He is ready to accommodate them. We told them that would be soon." She looked meaningfully at Adriel.

He spread his hands. "Very soon," he said. "At this rate. I never imagined anything like it. Even with the Venusian yeast vectors—"

The largest avatar interrupted. "So everything rests on their final approval."

There was a heavy *clang* behind them. Boaz was smiting

himself on the chest. "He has no need of their approval,'' he growled.

The women all blinked the same blink of suppressed embarrassment.

"They will approve Him,'' promised Kajsa Prime. "He is exactly what they've been looking for all this time.''

"We have the material,'' said Pomeroy Lion.

"We have the *machinery*,'' said Boaz.

"They have the power,'' said Adriel. "All those juicy short wavelengths!''

Boaz's mother came bustling up to reclaim her son. "The view, Mr. Lion!'' she rejoiced. "You simply must see it.''

Impervious to the fact that they had both been in a position to enjoy this privilege for many months already, she demanded both Boaz and Pomeroy Lion accompany her to a forward observation court. "Look at that and tell me I'm an old fool,'' she demanded.

Tacitly, both men declined the invitation. In any case, she was right. The view was awesome. There was one sun to the left, another to the right. Far more accurate than any one engine working alone, the hypertraction vortex generated by the fleet of the Capellans had induced the Temple directly at a position equidistant from both.

"That bright white dot there,'' said Boaz's mother, "you can see that? That's one of their starships, they call it the *Citadel of Porcelain at First Light*. Have you been on board her?''

"We've entertained her embassies,'' said Pomeroy Lion, while Boaz clenched his fists.

"A lovely ship, she must be,'' said Boaz's mother, "to have such a pretty name.''

From this vantage, with the solar horizon tilted away below, the black ferment of Capella appeared more congested than ever. It was as though the enormous twins had taken the emergence of the tiny Temple as a threat, and begun to gather the carpet of their parched possessions even closer about them. Deep in the wide dark swirl, distant vast planetary particles glowed like cinders, coagulations of detritus beginning to smolder as they slid ever closer to the fire.

The *Citadel of Porcelain at First Light* was not the only Capellan vessel in view. A sprinkle of gold flecks coalescing in the high northeast was the rest of the fleet, gathering gradually for the great event, like early spectators drifting toward a launch site. Nearer at hand, the *Seraph Catriona* and the *Seraph Xenoa* browsed meditatively in the void, sister vessels to the *Kajsa*, like somber pilot fishes escorting the Temple. Minute as new-hatched tadpoles, a school of Cherubim went coursing between the two.

"Get a bit closer in, you two," said Boaz's mother to her companions. "I must just take a picture."

In the emptying refectory, the talk had become more sober and intimate. "Do you want to know the truth? We're really not sorry you couldn't hold Sol," Kajsa Prime confided to her avatars.

They all paused a moment while the cities of Earth, the plains of Mars, the mines of Mercury and the oceans of Neptune passed in review through their minds.

"They are so quarrelsome," said one.

"So unappreciative," said another.

"So primitive," added a third.

"We should make sure to keep right away from there," said the largest Kajsa, "for half a century or so."

The black lips of the High Priestess took on a judicious curve. "At least," she said, rising to her feet.

The hour was late. A large owl went by, swooping down to light the path of the Seraph queens with its artificial eyes.

"Now this is the way it was supposed to be," said the white man with the neat black hair, "before I was so rudely interrupted."

He looked taller than she remembered him, and thinner. Probably they hadn't managed to put him back together quite the way he'd been before. His new clothes were exactly the same as his old ones, though, and his glasses; and he still had both his eyes and that flat, self-satisfied voice. Captain Jute would have recognized him even if he hadn't had Saskia tied to the bed.

"Another bloody zombie!" she said. "Some people just don't know when to stop."

By that time Kenny was upon him.

Arms pinned behind his back, the Thrant had launched himself at their captor like a furry missile. The man shouted. He kicked him in his armored middle, knocking him aside. Kenny's tail came round and struck at his head. He raised his shoulder and blocked the blow. He leapt onto the bed, standing between Saskia's legs and pointing his index finger at the encumbered Thrant. "You're on my list," he said, and touched his tie pin.

The needle of light lanced out again. There was a scream from Kenny, and a choking smell of baked metal and singed fur. He fell on his side, writhing, scraping the pole of his restraint against the floor.

"This is right, now," said the man called Nothing. "This is as it should have been." He straightened his jacket by the lapels. Above his shirt collar Captain Jute could see the line that ran around his neck, like a seam.

Kenny was whining. His attacker stepped down off the bed and gave him a kick.

Tabitha stole a glance behind her. The tech and the guards lay still as death, not a mark on any of them. The cabin door kept trying to close, running up against the foot of one of the guards and stopping, sliding back and trying again. Outside, Xtasca hung on its tail from the booby-trapped lock like an abandoned puppet.

"It was you that called Dodger," said Tabitha. "She was flying your old ship."

Grant Nothing tweaked his clean white cuffs. "Didn't you like her, Captain? The *All Things Considered*?" He sounded almost disappointed. "A bit beefy for you, I suppose."

"I wasn't given the choice," said Tabitha loudly.

Their captor looked at her keenly through his little round glasses. She felt as if she had just conceded him some extra advantage. He was intelligent. She had forgotten that.

"I hope Captain Gillespie has been looking after her," he said.

In her head Tabitha saw the Vespan cruiser explode, the *Langoustine* break up. She thought of Karen Narlikar burning in the cockpit of the *Maximum Disturbance*.

"All right, the packaging of my little message was a bit contrived," said Grant Nothing.

He held up his right hand, and looked at his palm. He frowned at it, as if he suspected he had injured it in some way. He sniffed it.

"The content, though, was pure fact," he said. "One hundred percent," he said. "What could I do? Iogo was mine. You turned her against me."

Tabitha was flabbergasted. "I never spoke to her!"

"That one was obvious," he said. "You used your pet."

He put the heel of his right hand to his mouth and sucked at it.

"She was mine, Captain," he said again. He turned his hand to point at Saskia. "And this one is yours." He smiled, inviting her to appreciate something: some moral, some joke. "Do you see?" he said.

Kenny was still twitching, making little yammering sobs of pain. If only they hadn't locked him in that stupid restraint. Behind the Captain the door was still opening and closing, opening and closing on the boot of the fallen guard.

Tabitha put one foot behind the other, stealing a pace backward.

Grant Nothing had one knee on the bed. He was bringing his extended finger sailing down like a dart to jab Saskia Zodiac's thigh. At the last minute he turned the tip a fraction and inserted it beneath her taut garter. Thoughtfully he stretched the colored elastic.

"Come on, then," he said to Captain Jute, more sharply. "You appreciate the symmetry. Surely. Even you."

He sat on the end of the bed, making himself comfortable between Saskia's feet. Saskia had blinded and killed him once. Now she was just a prop, a piece of scenery for his exhibition. His eyes glittered behind their corrective lenses. Tabitha didn't dare another step.

"Some people call it destiny," he told her. "Some call it irony. What it is, is symmetry."

"I don't know which would be worse," said Captain Jute at random. "You walking around again with a worm in your head, or without."

He was angry, suddenly. His voice was clipped, his body tense. "And you," he told her, "are the sort of person who would like to drag us all back into the Stone Age."

He sucked his hand again. He bared his teeth at her, scraping the lower set rapidly back and forth against the upper. "You smash your way into a Frasque hive, half-drunk, and you think you'll go for a ride in it." His voice grew softer, gentled by scorn. "You think you'll take us for a ride, and where to? Proxima Centauri. Proxima Centauri! To roll in the mud with the Palernians!"

He stiffened his hand and shook it in the air.

"It was necessary to enlist some capable help," he said, in a patronizing tone, "to make sure we did no such thing. To get a little governor imposed on your activities."

"Angie," she said.

The man in the suit looked pleased with himself. "Node Zero, she called me," he told her. "Did you think she could have done it alone?"

Captain Jute listened to Kenny struggling.

"I don't believe you," she said.

"You spent your time rolling in the mud anyway," he observed, as if she had not spoken. Then he gave her a cold smile. "With a little help."

Tabitha thought of Iogo offering her drugs. Had that really happened? Memory or dream?

"I never bought anything from you," she said.

"You never bought anything from anyone else," he told her. He stood up and, with satisfaction, hitched up his trousers.

"I never *bought* anything," she said. It seemed important, for an instant.

Again the man who called himself Nothing disregarded her.

"Have you any *idea* how much damage you did?" he asked. "How much work you wasted?"

"Plenty," she said.

He lifted his eyebrows, all his aggression dissipated suddenly. "A joke, Captain? Very good. Very good." He clasped his hands and looked away from her, as if the cabin had a window, as if something outside had just caught his eye. Then he switched his attention back to her.

"Come here, Captain Jute," he said. "Take your clothes off."

That irritated her intensely. "It's always the same with people like you," she said.

"Even so," he said mildly, "I think you should do it."

He twisted round from the hips. "Saskia would advise you to do it, wouldn't you, Saskia?" He adjusted his tie. "Those three will recover," he said, like a salesman guaranteeing results. "It's more effective against unprotected flesh. Quite deadly, if it finds a major organ."

He put his left hand on Saskia's thigh, spreading his fingers as if tautening the skin for an injection. With his other hand he twiddled his tie pin.

Saskia Zodiac was straining her head off the bed. Above her gag, her eyes were full of something other than fear. Captain Jute rather thought it was disgust. She nerved herself to steal another step.

Grant Nothing lifted his head and looked straight at her.

Her heart beat determinedly.

"Go on with your speech," she said. "It'd be a shame to waste it."

"Look," he told her, reasonably, "what are your options? You're in a foreign system, prisoner on a hostile ship. I may as well tell you, nobody gives a shit about you but me. Your future is not so much limited as negligible. The least you can do is entertain me before you go. You and your acrobatic friend."

He continued looking at her while he folded up the end of his tie and polished the jewel in his tie pin.

Tabitha released a long slow breath. Her heartbeat filled her head.

With thickened fingers she released the latches on her suit. She opened it and stepped out. In the process, she contrived to move a little farther backward toward the spasming door.

"Mm, far enough, I think, Captain," said her tormentor. "Come back here, please. All the way back."

So it was hopeless. Tabitha stood up straight. She put her shoulders back. She walked softly and deliberately to the bed. She went past Grant Nothing, to Saskia's head. She bent and kissed her, on the forehead. Only then did she look up at Grant Nothing, with a question in her eyes. Her fingers were unfastening her belt.

Saskia Zodiac made a muffled noise of protest.

Grant Nothing stretched out his hand. "I'll take that," he said.

Obediently Captain Jute helped him pull the belt through the loops of her jeans.

The man called Nothing took the Captain's belt and coiled it up. He watched her remove her jeans.

She held the jeans up in front of her, folding them, taking her time, letting him take a good look. She wondered what it was he saw.

Politely, she handed him the jeans.

"Since when were you so tidy," he said. It was a comment, not a question. He took the jeans and dropped them on the floor.

Tabitha reached out. Delicately, she caressed Saskia. She let the tip of her tongue slide across her lips. She could feel herself quivering. "Aren't you going to join us?" she asked him.

She saw his nostrils tighten as he inhaled, but his voice was steady when he replied.

"Oh, eventually," he said.

Captain Jute arched her back, lifting her breasts. Slowly she rubbed her hands over the front of her T-shirt. Then she threw a glance at the door, as if she'd heard something.

He didn't react. He was watching her, calculating. His mouth was twisted, there was something almost bitter in his expression.

She dropped her voice to a pitch of intimacy. "Let me close the door," she said.

Kenny gave a horrifying squeal. For an instant, Grant Nothing was distracted, bewildered even. He seemed almost to have forgotten the Thrant was there.

In her socks, Tabitha sprinted past the fallen tech and flung herself on the body of the guard.

She looked at Grant Nothing.

He was looking at her.

He rubbed his jaw and tutted. "Key for your boyfriend?" he inquired.

Still crouching, she shook her head in rueful apology. "I thought maybe," she said. Before he could respond, or design a reprisal, she had gone down on her knees and elbows. She pressed her belly to the carpet and turned her bottom to him, provocatively.

"Is this the way you used to do it, you and Iogo?"

Hearing her speak the name, Kenny screamed and cursed.

This time Grant Nothing ignored him. He was staring at

Captain Jute, mesmerized, like a mathematician facing the imminent revelation of the last line of working in a lifelong problem. His face was slowly going the color of his tie. Arousal must be playing havoc with his new cardiovascular system.

"This is what Kyfyd and I like," said Captain Jute. Over her shoulder she gave him her most sultry look, and peeled down her panties. "Symmetrical enough for you?"

"Now, this is right," he said again, in a preoccupied tone. "This is quite right."

He moved toward her lithely, stepping over the tech as if he wasn't there.

"I do recommend you close the door," said Tabitha. She even managed a stifled, frightened little giggle.

He looked from her to the door, as if he had not previously noticed it thudding and thudding against the boot of the guard. He sniffed and raised his head, collecting himself. He took a step toward the controls.

Captain Jute shot him with the neural disruptor.

It was not a good angle. The force must have hit him somewhere around the hip, paralyzing him from the waist down. He tottered, his legs collapsing under him.

His arms were still working, and he was very close. Smiling oddly, he heaved himself toward her.

Captain Jute jumped up. "Kenny!" she shouted.

The Thrant sprang.

Grant Nothing gurgled horribly.

Struggling, forgotten, on the floor, Kenny had contrived to work one of his boots off. The fingers of his foot were rigid, the claws hard and sharp as iron.

Swaying backward, still pinioned, Captain Jute's bodyguard kicked their toppled aggressor in the face.

There was blood. The glasses, smashed again, fell to the floor. Choking furiously, the remade man grabbed at the leg of the Thrant, but his muscles would no longer support him. He succeeded only in falling on his glasses, banging his face against the floor.

The Thrant jumped on his back. He planted his booted foot in the middle of the smart grey needlecord jacket, in between the shoulder blades. With his bare foot, he seized hold of the man's throat. He panted lustily. On the bed, Saskia was making urgent squeaking noises.

"Ken?" said Tabitha.

For a moment she thought he was going to try to behead the man once more, in honor of his late mate. Then, gutturally, he said: "Vis is q'ite right''; and he clenched his toes, crushing the restored trachea of Mr. Nothing and snapping his borrowed spine.

∽ 33

She felt the crunch go through her own bones. She felt it in her teeth. Dizzy, she leaned forward, resting her hands on her knees. She heard Kenny start to laugh.

"Yes, Ken," she said. "Quite right. Quite right, yes, thank you."

She straightened up and tossed him the disruptor. He caught it in his teeth. He was happy now.

Captain Jute pulled up her panties. She ran to the bed and looked at Saskia's ankles. They were bound tightly with plastic tape, the same kind that was round her wrists and across her mouth. She tugged at it, but it didn't even give.

"Kenny! A knife."

Kenny spat out the disruptor. He showed her his teeth and claws.

She went back to the guards and searched them. She found the key, and freed Kenny from the restraint. He rushed to the bed and started slashing at Saskia's bonds.

"Careful," said Tabitha.

He grinned.

She found a knife and went to work on the gag. The tape was tough, but in time it yielded.

"He was here waiting for us," were Saskia's first words, when her tongue was loosed. Then she choked. "Torch," she said, and started to cough in earnest.

Between them they eventually freed one leg and her hands. Tabitha helped her sit up. "Torch," said Saskia again, between bouts of coughing, while Kenny hacked away at her last bond.

"Torch?" asked Captain Jute. What did she want a torch for? All the lights were on.

Saskia sat rubbing her feet, almost crying. Then before they knew it she was up, stumbling over to the body of Grant Nothing. She kicked it wildly and fell over. Lying on the floor, she kicked it again.

Kenny slapped himself on the head and wheezed with laughter.

"Torch!" moaned Saskia. She dragged herself over to the tech. She was grieving for him. She worked her long thin arms under him and hugged him to her.

"To-o-orch . . ."

Tabitha watched. A sensation of coolness came over her, as if the temperature in the cabin had suddenly fallen by several degrees.

"He's done something to her mind," she said quietly to the Thrant.

Saskia scowled at them. "My mind is perfectly all right."

She bent and kissed the shiny cheek of the black man in the white hood.

Captain Jute felt very awkward suddenly. It was a sensation rather like the one that comes when, under the influence of strong drink or drugs, you realize that you have just done something incredibly stupid, insulted your boss or made a pass at someone you don't even know.

Her jeans lay where the dead man had dropped them. She walked to them, feeling she ought to be tiptoeing, and pulled them on.

The cabin door continued to try to close.

Dressing, Captain Jute looked at the bodies strewn around. She thought about her options. What the resurrected man had said had got to her. Stranded in a foreign system, stuck on a hostile ship. Their transport out of fuel. Any minute now the black giant who had sent them down here in the care of his reclaimed Cherub would notice something was wrong. The Cherub had said the Seraphim were doing some kind of deal with the Frasque. And the Frasque were somehow responsible for the caterpillars. She felt the chunky shape of Alice in her suit pocket and wished there was somewhere she could plug her in.

"Torch!"

The man in Saskia's arms groaned and stirred. He was starting to rouse. As Tabitha watched, he opened his eyes and saw who was holding him. He reached up, and the two of them clung to each other.

It was very strange to see Saskia hugging someone else, so fiercely, so entirely. Tabitha Jute had not seen that since the days of Mogul, when the pair of them had traveled with Xtasca and Marco and Tal in the hold of the *Alice Liddell*. Mogul and Saskia had been clone brother and sister, as identical as two people of different sexes could be. This tech, this man, was nothing like Mogul at all. He was solid where Mogul had been slender, deep chestnut brown where Mogul had been pallid paper white.

In a way, that was what made it so completely convincing.

Captain Jute, still feeling that strange sense of coolness and lightness, understood perfectly what had happened. And it was an enormous relief.

Kenny was swinging around the room, cartwheeling over

the bed, in a spirit of wild celebration. Tabitha too found
she was very, very pleased. She wanted to hug Saskia herself, but suddenly lacked the confidence to do it. She was
not sure she should even be watching. She looked around
for Kenny again. He was squatting over the corpse of Grant
Nothing with his fly open and his long red prick in his
hand, pissing on him.

"Kenny—"

"Oh, they do that," said Saskia, as if she thought it her
place to apologize. Her man was standing up now, supported by the curve of her arm, rubbing his head. "This is
Torch," Saskia told Tabitha. "They just call him 10, but I
don't think that is sufficient. Even we had names." She
kissed him, tentatively, and laughed. Then she kissed him
again.

Captain Jute went out of the room, stepping over the
prostrate guards and through the rebounding door. Xtasca
was still there, hanging from the lock. Tabitha took hold
of it. It was heavy, and warm. She carried it inside.

"Oh my goodness," said Saskia, disengaging from the
embrace. "What did they do to her?" She took the Cherub
from Tabitha's arms.

"Is this it?" her tech asked her. He had a warm, deep
voice that made you ready to trust him. "Is this the one?"

"This is Xtasca," said Saskia. "She isn't just an it,
whatever you think," she said, expertly manipulating the
end of Xtasca's tail and plugging it into a power socket.
"She has a name too."

"Hi, Xtasca," said Torch to the motionless Cherub. He
sounded embarrassed. "What are you wearing that stuff for,
Saskia? Did he put that on you?"

"He did," said Saskia, without explanation.

Torch rubbed his head again, then held out his right hand
to Captain Jute. "You must be Tabitha, I guess," he said,
apologetically. "I heard a lot about you."

Tabitha shook his hand. She felt as awkward as he
looked. "Are you okay?" she asked him.

He rubbed his eyes with the palms of his hands. "Sore as a dissected pup," he said. "How did you get here?"

"We came from Plenty," said Captain Jute. "Via a massacre." She lifted a hand, silencing him before he could ask. "I don't want to talk about it," she started to say.

Torch was already speaking. "I'm thankful you came when you did." He cast a look at the dead man. "Who killed him?" he asked her. His eyes matched his voice. "Was that you?"

"Kenny," said Captain Jute, gesturing at Kenny. "Kenny, Torch. Torch, Kenny."

The human unhesitatingly shook the hand of the Thrant. "I owe you, Kenny," he said.

Kenny made a soft growl. "We all owe Cap'n Jute," he told him.

Tabitha had turned back to Saskia and the Cherub. Saskia appeared to be chivvying open a panel at the base of the Cherub's spine.

"She—said they destroyed Angie," said Tabitha. She was aware of Kenny coming to crouch at her side. He put his hand on her calf. "Did she—say anything?"

There was a pause. Saskia was busy with Xtasca. She was adjusting something inside. There was a crackle of electrical discharge. Saskia snatched her fingers out and sucked them.

Torch put his chin on his chest. "She said a lot," he told the Captain.

Saskia was working inside the Cherub again, more cautiously. Tabitha asked her: "Did she remember me?"

Saskia closed the Cherub up. She pulled a chair over and laid it carefully in it. She stood back, watching it intently. Nothing visible was happening.

"She mentioned your mother," she replied. "Several times."

Tabitha felt tears start in her eyes. She was very, very tired.

A low groan sounded from the doorway. Everyone tensed.

One of the guards was starting to wake. Kenny padded over and gleefully gave each of them a generous shot with the neural disruptor.

Torch laid a hand, respectfully, on Saskia's arm. "We best get out of here."

Saskia gave him a steely glance. "Not," she said, "without Xtasca."

In the chair, eerily, the Cherub's head turned. "I shall be fully recharged in 40.5 seconds," it said.

One minute and two seconds later, the cabin door was finally permitted to close, with both the unconscious security guards inside it. Warily, Torch led the four fugitives along J Deck to the lifts.

In the lift were two orderlies carrying a pancatachrestic conjugating amnesotron. They were visibly startled to be confronted with a group that included not only an unknown human but also a Thrant, both looking considerably the worse for wear.

Torch stiffened. "Into the lift, all of you," he commanded. "Cherub, keep your eye on the Thrant."

"Yes, sir," replied Xtasca mechanically.

"Watch his tail," said Torch. "You two, where are you going with that amnesotron?"

"Diagnostics, 10," said one of the orderlies, her voice high and a little strained.

"Tech 77 needs it for the Cognizance link," said the other, sounding equally anxious.

"Very good," boomed Torch. "Carry on."

Together they rose through the decks, all resolutely facing forward.

On C Deck they disembarked. Here there was no gravity. Torch, for want of anywhere else safe, took them to the empty lab.

Through the unshuttered windows the stars shone brightly. Captain Jute flew straight to the glass to see.

The Capellan void glared black and cold. The red twins roared silently, oblivious to anything but their own increasing hunger. One day in a few hundred thousand years they would start to swallow each other.

In the burned black space a tiny, shiny white shape was coming into view. It was a shape Captain Jute recognized. It was like a flying horse, or a long-necked bird with its wings raised up above its back.

"The fucking Dawn Crapper," she breathed violently.

"What?" said Saskia.

Tabitha did not reply. She was gazing at the Capellan starship. It seemed a long time ago now that she had been there, she and Kenny, watching the Eladeldi merrily chop and dice the Plenty Resistance.

She couldn't imagine that it was chasing them.

Disconsolate, she crossed the lab to another window and looked in the other direction. At once she noticed something there, too, some way up toward the zenith, something that had not been visible to the naked eye when they arrived. It was a regular shape, she could tell after a moment, a ship or orbital of some kind. It was showing up shiny black, with traces of purple.

"What is that?"

Xtasca swam forward. "That is the headquarters of the Seraphim," it said. "It is known as the Temple of Abraxas."

Captain Jute's throat dried. "*The* Temple? From Sol?"

"The Capellans collaborated with the Seraphim to bring it here," said the Cherub.

Tabitha looked at Torch. He did not deny what Xtasca had said.

Since the demise of Grant Nothing new strength, or at least a suspension of hopelessness, had possessed the weary body of Captain Jute. Sighting the *Citadel of Porcelain at First Light* had put something of a dent in that. Now she felt the true odds return to overwhelm her. She remembered, unwillingly, other demonstrations she had witnessed of Capellan superiority to the laws of physics. She remembered a Lesondak Anaconda called the *Ugly Truth* hauling the *Alice Liddell* out of hyperspace. Perfectly impossible; but it had been done.

"That's where all the rest of the chiefs are now," Torch told her. "There's something major being built there for the Capellans." His voice had become husky and apologetic again with the thought of how unwelcome this news must be to Saskia's friends. "I only know part of it," he said.

Captain Jute had ceased to listen. Frasque, Capellans, and now Seraphim in full force. They all might as well find the nearest airlock now and dive out of it.

"We have to get you out of here before the chiefs come back," Torch was saying. "Where's your ship?"

"Een cu'tody," said Kenny, with a snarl. "And oot of fuel."

Xtasca had its shiny flat face pressed to the glass. There was a tiny whirring noise as it adjusted its vision. "Within the last thirteen minutes a standard-issue intervessel transport sled has left the Temple," it informed them. "It is now approaching this ship."

The Seraph Boaz, Chief of Prevision on the Capella mission, returned to the *Seraph Kajsa* at 86.67.54. His opposite number in the Temple hierarchy was taking over the scheduling, releasing Boaz to work on the resource inventories and proposals for interchange of material and personnel with the *Seraph Catriona* and the *Seraph Xenoa*. Sitting in the sled behind his silent, unmoving pilot, Boaz regretted he would not be there to see the next phases of the Great Work; but with infidel Capellan interlopers about to set foot in the hallowed precincts of the Temple of the Lord, he felt it was wise of Queen Kajsa to dispatch him. That would be an outrage he would rather not witness at first hand.

Beside him, his page sat watching him speculatively.

"Lord Boaz?"

"What, Calvino?"

The page rested his elbows on the giant armored knee, folding his arms and looking solemnly up into his face. "Are you unhappy, my lord?"

Boaz blinked his silver metal eyelids. The child was perspicacious, as befitted a future officer in the ranks of the Previsionaries.

"No, Calvino, I am not unhappy."

The page sighed. "I thought perhaps you were sad about leaving the Temple again."

Boaz sat steely-faced. "It can never be pleasant to leave the courts of holiness," he said. "Least of all when one has had to endure a necessary absence from them of many years."

"Many years, Lord Boaz?"

"Since before you were in the womb, Calvino."

Frigid and white, the stars of the galaxy crept by.

"We don't mind going back to the *Seraph Kajsa*, Lord Boaz, do we?" asked the wistful child.

What marvels his young eyes had seen, inside the Temple of Abraxas!

"It is not for the servants of the Lord to mind anything, Calvino," said his master sternly. "Duty is a privilege, wherever it takes us."

The boy sat upright. "Duty is a privilege," he repeated distantly.

The transport bay of the *Seraph Kajsa* was empty save for a small grey scoutship. Not standard issue, it was notably scorched and dented. The Chief of Prevision glanced at it, wondering where it had come from, and what it was doing on board.

He disembarked, to be met by an attentive tech who saluted him gravely as he received custody of the sled.

"Lord Xipetotec is in Schematics 1," the tech reported.

"He has requested not to be disturbed for the rest of the watch."

"By the Indivisible Amnion, 10!" frowned Boaz. "Will he exclude his peers and colleagues?"

The tech looked a trifle glassy-eyed, but he stood his ground. "Perhaps he was not expecting your return, Lord Boaz. He is engaged in some complex analysis of infor—"

There was a dull *clank* as Boaz thumped his armored fist into his palm. "I am aware what Lord Xipetotec is engaged in, 10," he declared. "I shall be joining him imminently to pursue and extend the work."

The tech bowed obediently. "Lord Boaz."

"Calvino, to my quarters," ordered the Chief of Prevision. "Make ready my lubricant bath."

The page bowed profoundly and scampered off to the lifts. Meanwhile his master pointed at the shabby scoutship. "What is that?"

The tech swallowed visibly. "Salvage, sir," he said. "Operational theory is that it was, ah, jettisoned from the hive called Plenty, sir, and drifted into our orbit."

"Jettisoned?" Boaz was beginning to feel that there was nothing in this twin-starred system but oddities and deviations.

The tech had stepped back a pace, bowing. "Regret I was not in attendance at the time of its capture, sir," he said, mumbling. "My duties kept me elsewhere. I shall make it a priority to search the records and deliver the relevant data to your personal com suite, Lord Boaz."

"See that you do, 10. All surplus of any kind will need to be entered into the resource inventories."

Mollified, Boaz withdrew. As the lift doors closed behind his outsize metal form, Tech 10 closed his eyes and breathed a sigh. Then he thumbed the switch to open the canopy and stepped inside the sled.

The pilot, little more than a sentient machine, sat motionless at the controls. Tech 10 took her stylus and swiped the readout on his wristcom.

"Receive release from Seraph Boaz," he said.

"Release received," intoned the pilot.

"Prepare this sled for immediate departure under my command," said the tech.

The pilot did not react. "Vessel release recorded 89.45.02," she said. "Please enter your release."

With an air of desperation incompatible with systematic function, the tech uploaded his complete roster specifications into the pilot's secure memory. "This is my duty assignment," he said, harshly. "My duty assignment is to take care of specimens during the absence of the division chiefs. Now there's this couple of specimens they need taken over to the Temple. Immediately."

The pilot stared sightlessly straight in front of her. Her pineal lead hung in stiff loops, connecting her forebrain directly with the console. "Please enter your release," she said.

The tech held up both his hands in an incomplete gesture, as though adjusting invisible controls. "Please wait," he said.

Torch hurried back to his new friends, in hiding in the maintenance pits. Four faces gazed up at him, one white, one tawny, one brown, one black. The white face was Saskia's. She reached up to touch his foot.

He squatted to speak to them. "She won't do it. She needs my official release."

He blinked then and ducked as the Cherub rose up and flew past him. It headed straight for the sled. In a moment it was on board. The canopy closed behind it.

Torch wiped sweat from his face. The idea of a Cherub taking the law into its tiny hands was utterly bewildering.

"What's it doing? Only a chief can sign me off."

"Perhaps you should go and see," said Saskia. "She may need help." Her emphatic accent seemed to carve the words out of something solid in the shadows.

Ducking unnecessarily, apprehensively, Torch hurried back to the sled.

The pilot sat still at the controls, just as he had left her. Like some enormous shiny parasite, the Cherub squatted on the back of her seat. It sat bowed over, its outsize head pressed against the top of the pilot's head. It had inserted its tail directly into the pilot's pineal socket.

Nauseated by the violation of authorized procedure, the intimacy of the intrusion, Torch withdrew. "I don't think the Cherub does need any help," he called hoarsely.

Long minutes went by.

The canopy opened. Xtasca reappeared. It flew to the rear of the sled and began to disconnect the fuel cells.

"Now it needs help," said Tabitha Jute.

The concealed foursome left the pit. With an anxious glance through the plexiglass at the immobile pilot, Torch helped them lug the cells across the bay to the little grey Danuta.

"Is this going to work, Captain?" he asked.

"We won't have power to skip," said Captain Jute, wiping her hands and agitating her hair, stiff-fingered, letting the air in to her sweaty scalp. "We might have enough impulse power."

Torch licked his lips. This was difficult. "Will it take all of us?"

Apparently she had already assumed his defection. "It ought to get us as far as Plenty," she said drily. "It won't exactly be comfortable."

Torch, defeated, started to change his mind. He would remain on board and brazen it out. He might prevail upon Saskia Zodiac to remain on board with him. He backed away, smiling, shaking his head. "It will take months to get to Plenty," he said.

"No, 10."

It was the Cherub. It had accessed some information he didn't have. It went swooping up to the viewing platform above the launch door. They could only follow it.

"Look," it said.

On the scope that showed the blurred black southeast, a minute lumpy brown shape could be distinguished.

The Thrant cackled happily.

Captain Jute put her hands on her hips. "She's coming this way," she said.

The Cherub rotated her head to face the Captain. They stared into each other's eyes.

"Everything's converging," said the Cherub.

On the *Citadel of Porcelain at First Light*, the three sisters were back from their visit. Everyone was assembled up in the Stardeck Lounge to salute them and hear about the tribute: what it looked like, how powerful it might be.

Brother Kitchener played the piano. Brother Melodious sang. "*Surfing my way back to happiness, surfing my way back to love . . .*"

"Oh, play those human songs!" cried Sister Mansuetude with abandon. The trip to the Temple had filled her with joy. Her sisters were also happy, in their different ways, and they danced together. Brother Justice danced too, very slowly and with magnificent decorum.

Brother Poesy came in with his big black book. The sisters lay on three compliant couches with their audience all around. Robot waiters circulated with jugs of sangria.

"It is not as we expected," said Sister Contenta.

"Not quite," said Sister Celandine, with a smile.

Brother Justice grasped the lapels of his gown. "Is it legal, fair, and appropriate?"

"Oh, it's very appropriate," said Sister Celandine.

"They'll love it," called Brother Kitchener from the keyboard.

They all joined hands and shared the picture. "Crazy!" shouted Brother Melodious. Brother Justice laughed so much he shook.

Sister Celandine rolled her bangle around her wrist.
"There's only one true test," she said.

Brother Justice was still laughing.

"We have gone this far," said Sister Mansuetude. "Why
in the name of all the galaxies would we stop?" Her eyes
shone with excitement.

Brother Poesy made a thick mark with his pen. "If it
does not respond to them," he asked formally, "have we
other recipients ready?"

Sister Contenta nodded placidly. "More than we could
possibly need," she said.

"They fight each other bare-handed," intoned Brother
Justice, "for the merest suspicion of a chance to bond."

"Then let it go forward," said Brother Poesy. "*Tender
is the night*," he recited,

> "*And haply the Queen-Moon is on her throne,*
> *Clustered around by all her starry Fays;*
> *But here there is no light,*
> *Save what from heaven is with the breezes blown.*"

Sister Mansuetude wiped a tear.

The Sisters stood. They were anointed and proclaimed.

"Sister Contenta!" everyone cried. "Sister Mansuetude!
Sister Celandine!" They kissed one another. Children were
brought in, playing pipes. The robots scattered rose petals.

Kybernator Perlmutter dedicated a ring, and called the
hive. He announced himself, and Kybernator Astraghal responded. The reception was no better than ever.

"Are the larvae ready?" asked Kybernator Perlmutter.

"*They are stowed and ready.*"

"Is Brother Valetude ready?"

"*He is sleepless and ready.*"

"Then let him take the larvae to Queen Kajsa."

There was a pause in the conversation, marking a moment of history. The robots corraled the children.

Everyone considered the hive.

"Have we all we wish to keep?" asked Sister Celandine.

Brother Kitchener raised his eyes until they could hardly be seen for his eyebrows. "We have been generous with our resources," he said tonelessly. "More than generous."

Sister Mansuetude turned to Brother Poesy with a sigh. "Is it recorded, all the old ones are in the hive?"

"It is so recorded," Brother Poesy replied.

"They must not see this thing," said Sister Contenta.

Brother Justice vented a noise, a wheezy ghost of a chuckle. "Not a good idea," he murmured, "no."

"*Shuttle away,*" reported Kybernator Astraghal.

Brother Kitchener took a drink and turned back to the piano.

"*Goodbye is the hardest word to say,*" sang Brother Melodious. "*The hardest song to play . . .*" In unison, the children waved their arms.

"Are you stowed and sealed, Brother Astraghal?" asked Kybernator Perlmutter.

"*We are stowed and sealed,*" Kybernator Astraghal replied.

Kybernator Perlmutter made a gesture, clasping his fingers together, then opening them emphatically. The jewels on his hands blazed with the light of all the stars in all the windows.

"Then in the name of Capella I require you," said Kybernator Perlmutter, "to relinquish your command."

"*I bow and comply,*" said Kybernator Astraghal, and the sound of the engines of his shuttle crackled sharply into the Stardeck Lounge.

Brother Justice turned to Brother Kitchener. "He sounds pleased," he observed, as the sound died away.

"He should," said Brother Kitchener. "He's out of there."

He continued to play, a medley of sentimental things in minor keys, with Brother Melodious accompanying him on his musical hand. In the middle of "Clementine," Kybernator Astraghal's pilot came through to report that the shuttle was clear.

Brother Poesy shut his book. "It's time," he said, loudly.

They all stood then, and with one voice they echoed him. "It's time."

The Guardians stood in semicircular tiers, facing the window. Together they raised their fists and pointed them toward the little brown dot that was the hive the humans called Plenty.

Sister Mansuetude was crying again. "I can feel it," she said. "I can already feel it."

The Guardians started to fire, and continued to fire for some time. One after another, their smiles became strained, or fell altogether from their faces. Soon, all of them were weeping.

∽ 34

The cave was full of blood.

Like a lake it covered the floor, perhaps four hundred meters from wall to wall. Like crimson satin it lay, smooth and shiny and even.

Around the edges it had clotted, thickening into tubular bulges and ridges. Here was an area of circular depressions; over there one of strange horns and curlicues, the crests of solidified waves. Up the walls stretched broad black tongues of it; long, sticky arabesques; splattered fans.

High above, the ceiling dripped with it.

Thick spires of dried blood stretched toward the floor. There were hundreds of them, thousands, perhaps, in the vaulted obscurity. Some were twisted, like ropes, like ropes of wax, as though some gravitic vagary had caused the drips to spiral around each other. They hung together, in combs, clusters, cascades.

Trapped between the lake and the encrusted ceiling, the air of the cave was warm, thick, and dank. The air was sodden with blood.

In the middle of the lake was the mound.

The mound was the same color and consistency as the lake. The mound, by this low, heavy light, could not readily be distinguished from the solidified slops around the walls.

Until the mound rippled.

The mound rippled silently, like gel, like flesh.

In the lake of blood, a clutch of slow bubbles surfaced. One after another they lingered, swirling uncertainly. One after another they burst. The lake was still again.

On the spires, the blood collected, coalesced.

The air smelled of pain.

Pain was her whole experience. The ache of the Eladeldi Fire Flush. The ache of the subsequent pernicious infestation of humans, Thrant, Palernians and Perks. The ache of traffic pounding through every artery. The ache of being continuously chewed and chopped and quarried, and just as continuously restoring herself, converting her dry subsidiary mass automatically into flesh.

She was sore from the butchery of her extended memory by Xtasca and its crew during the years of flight. She was sore from the flight itself, which the Vespans came closest to describing, when they said they feared it must be one long scream.

Other injuries were less tangible, but just as painful to her. Her queen had been taken. Her adult population had been slaughtered. She had never ceased to search her tunnels, her caverns and clefts and corridors and capillaries for any vibration, any taste of them, frozen or awake. But they were all gone.

A handful of her babies had survived, and found themselves hosts, human ones, with four limbs and a high degree of cerebral organization. They had called themselves Guardians, and they had begun by taking care of her. As soon as the hive was home, the journey over, they had done their duty. They had soothed and protected her, and started to clean out the infestation.

Then everything had gone wrong. They had brought in foreign populations, survivors of fifty other hives, all muddled together. They had brought her foreign seed, and impregnated her. Helplessly, because she could do nothing else, she had produced more babies; and those the so-called Guardians had taken away.

Now she was suffering the last and most terrible betrayal.

The teeth and the boots and the machines of the invaders had chewed upon her flesh, her substance. The rays from the stones in the rings of the Guardians sought to saw up the particles that composed her. It was an assault on her very existence. A few minutes more of it and the hive, Mother and Matrix and all, would be reduced to a random assortment of undifferentiated blurs and smears apparent only as problems in the realm of ontology.

There was only one thing she could do.

She did it.

With a subsonic roar so powerful it shattered the stalactites, the Mother of Plenty reared up in her lake of blood.

She bloomed.

She mantled.

She rose up, and went away.

"It's gone!"

Aghast, Captain Jute turned to Saskia Zodiac and Kenny. Their faces were just centimeters from hers.

Saskia looked as if the disappearance of the hive toward which they were making their arduous voyage was only what she had always expected.

"They have destroyed it," she said. They had all seen the beam that had issued abruptly from the *Citadel of Porcelain at First Light* to strike the hive.

"I DON'T THINK SO," said Little Alice.

"They've sent it away," said Torch.

"Because they knew we were coming," said Tabitha exhaustedly. "Why don't they just shoot us? They shot everyone else."

The image of Little Alice fluttered, breaking up and reconstituting itself. Her voice was a tiny signal awash with hiss.

"I RATHER THINK SHE HAS TAKEN IT OFF HERSELF, SOMEWHERE. TAKEN IT BACK, YOU KNOW."

"Back?" barked Kenny.

"Back to Sol?" Torch remembered the hive as it had been, a grim place where the unenlightened went to waste time, credit and each other. "We were too late," he said.

"BACK INTO HER OWN KEEPING, I MEAN," said the persona.

Who was she talking about? Captain Jute thought of Colonel Stark, her cold white face on a big screen at the end of her bed, steel blue eyes shining with pride. She had taken over Plenty. Or had that been a dream?

She realized she wasn't quite focusing on this.

Her lips were dry and cracked. She licked them.

"Alice," she said. "Who are you talking about?"

"THE MOTHER," said Little Alice.

"She died," said Tabitha. She kept looking round in different directions, hoping to see the hive pop back into view.

The tiny imago shook her long blond hair. "OH NO," she said emphatically. "SHE KEPT GROWING BACK, CAPTAIN, REMEMBER."

Tabitha pulled her elbows free from Saskia and Kenny, and pressed the palms of her hands to her head. Concentrate. Concentrate. It will make sense soon.

"I thought you meant that Frasque," she said. "The one Marco woke up, that was supposed to run the hive. The one the robot killed on the *Ugly Truth*."

Saskia had her left arm around Torch. With her right hand she reached for his left hand to hold. "That was the Queen," she said. She spoke a trifle impatiently, as though explaining some very clever card trick that Tabitha had failed to watch properly.

On the console Little Alice tossed her head, just like a real child. "THOSE ARE ONLY OUR NAMES FOR THEM," she said, in her faint, fractured voice. "IT'S NO USE THEM HAVING NAMES IF THEY WON'T ANSWER TO THEM."

Torch smiled at Saskia. "Don't tell me they have numbers too."

"THEY GO BY SOUNDS, MAINLY," said Little Alice reflectively. "FOOTSTEPS AND CREAKS AND SIGHS. AND SMELLS AND TASTES, OF COURSE. THE MOTHER KNOWS HER BABIES, I SUPPOSE. THE MOTHER KNOWS EVERYTHING ON BOARD, AND WHERE TO GO, AND HOW TO GO THERE. THOUGH SHE DOESN'T REALLY *KNOW*, YOU KNOW, ANY MORE THAN I KNOW. NEITHER OF US HAS A BRAIN."

Into the brain of Tabitha Jute, understanding started to trickle. "You're talking about the Big Chap," she said.

There was a split-second pause while the imported persona searched the tiny memory of the scoutship.

"NO RECORD OF THAT NAME."

"Try 'the Star Beast'," said Saskia Zodiac.

Little Alice looked thoughtful. "I BELIEVE I KNEW HER INTIMATELY," she said. "BUT I THINK I MUST HAVE BEEN CHANGED SEVERAL TIMES SINCE THEN."

As far as the cramped confines of the cockpit permitted, Captain Jute stretched her arms. "I always knew it was alive," she remarked, meaning the whole strange alien world that she had stolen and failed to keep, that had almost killed her. "I always knew someone would end up telling us that." She felt a strange detachment from the whole issue. It seemed perfectly just that Plenty, to which she had never had any right, should softly and suddenly vanish away, just when they needed it most.

Saskia pouted. "What does she live *on*, though?"

The tiny imago fizzed. "SPACE . . ." she said.

"And where has she gone, then?" asked Captain Jute.

"I guess back to Earth," said Torch, amicably. Kenny huffed agreement.

"OH NO," said Little Alice. "SOMEWHERE FAR AWAY FROM THERE. SOMEWHERE QUIETER."

"That would have been all right," said Captain Jute morosely. "I could have gone for that."

What could they do now? Give themselves up? There was nowhere else for them to go, and no fuel to take them anywhere if there had been. Maybe they should simply cut the engines now and spiral into one of the suns while they were still alive to appreciate the experience.

Saskia rubbed condensation off the canopy and stared into space as though wishing to see someone out there, accompanying the overcrowded little ship, ushering her to safety.

"I wish Xtasca had come," she said, for the fiftieth time.

All of the Seraphim were assembled in the Hall of Animation for the grand occasion of the Rising. The most aged and decrepit of the First Reformed were here with their wasted limbs, their skin like the bark of trees. Even the most extreme of the autoplasts, Lady Quique, who had refined herself into a form rather like a net of floating discs, and would never grace any occasion so gross and carnal as an old-fashioned banquet, had come out of her contemplative trance for this.

Imperious and imposing as a Greek chorus of noble matrons, the avatars of Kajsa Tobermory stood in a line above the shrouded pit. Angels of all styles and ages flew here and there.

"Behold the Lord of This World," cried the hugest avatar.

"The Lord of All Worlds," cried the slenderest.

"The Lord of All Space," cried a third, to the left.

"The Lord of All Time," a fourth, to the right.

"The Lord of the Three Hundred and Sixty-Five Aeons," cried a fifth, in the center, and they all raised their arms above their heads.

"Behold," said Kajsa Prime, in front of them all, on the very edge of the pit. She smiled at the visiting Guardians and stretched out her hand. "Our ultimate creation. The Lord Abraxas Himself."

The covers of black-and-purple silk whisked instantly away.

On its back in the black-tiled pit lay a gigantic creature.

In actuality as in mythology, the Lord Abraxas was composite.

His legs were two serpents. The scales upon the serpents were as big across as tractor wheels, and shining gold. The heads of the serpents were his two feet. Their mouths were closed, the lips a fine line of salmon pink, with an upward curl at the corners suggestive of purest raptor malice. Their eyes were similarly closed.

The torso and arms of the Lord Abraxas were those of a titan, a giant human male in his prime. The muscle definition was perfect, the skin a shining brown; but though his color was so good, the warmth that rose from him so vital, there was no motion in him, not even the stir of breath in his chest. His hands were human hands, and lay at his sides.

For his head the Lord Abraxas had the head of a cock.

While the serpents were idealized, of no single species, the head was *Gallus domesticus*, and a wholly faithful interpretation, though on this scale there was precious little that was domestic about it. The beak alone was four meters long. The plumage of the cock began with a rich chocolate brown around the neck, and finished with the same around the cranium. In between it was the color of new parchment, with something of the same gloss. The eyelids were viridian, and closed.

On the other side of the pit from the Seraphim stood the three Capellan Sisters, Contenta, Mansuetude and Celandine, in white togas and gilded sandals. They had mourned the passing of the hive, and now they had come to join

Brother Valetude in the celebration of a happier occasion.

With them were four Eladeldi, in tunics of lilac and grey and crowned with silver circlets. They held up a large silver vessel. The vessel was shaped like an egg, with a thick collar around the middle of it. It was, in fact, very like the egg in which the head of the preserved human had been delivered from the hive to *Seraph Kajsa*, only it was twice the size; and while that egg had been icy cold, this one was quite warm.

The Hall of Animation was thick with incense. Any suspicion that the idea was to mask the ammoniac stink of large-scale industrial bioengineering went unvoiced. Such considerations now were merest mortal pettiness, to be transcended.

Beneath the body in the pit was something circular and dished and thirty meters across. It was the shield of the Lord Abraxas. In his right hand the Lord Abraxas held a threshing instrument of wood and horn, with a hinge of bronze. That was his flail.

The construction of the artifacts was accurate to those of the god's original devisers, two thousand years previous and more. All the materials were authentic. Teams of materials technicians had scoured Sol System for them, and toiled long and hard to assemble them with micrometric perfection. It was the sort of detail, utterly gratuitous and stupefyingly expensive, in which the Temple excelled, and which they had been sure the Guardians would appreciate.

"Absolutely magnificent," said Brother Valetude.

He clasped his hands behind his back and gazed down at the waiting form.

"The circulatory system alone."

Kajsa Prime nodded to Adriel, at the side of the pit in a cloak of golden feathers.

A priest came forward and presented Brother Valetude with a clipboard.

"In there you'll find a complete structural breakdown,"

said Adriel, raising a bosom no less glorious than any Kajsa's, if a degree less menacing. "All completely homeostatic."

"And rather an improvement on what you're wearing now," said Sweet Lavender. All the Kajsas threw him a freezing look.

Brother Valetude did not understand, or else took no offense. He was scrolling through the designs. He shook his head and waved the clipboard at the inert god.

"The comb!"

He was helpless with admiration.

A burst of music blazed into the hall, a fanfare of trumpets.

"We're so pleased you like him," purred the Seraph Queen, when it fell silent.

Without looking, Brother Valetude had handed the clipboard to the Sisters, who had received it equally inattentively. Brother Valetude rubbed his lips with the tips of his fingers, then gestured into the air. "Such power."

The Sisters bobbed their heads together. "Such multiplicity," they said, in unison.

Their Brother raised the large green-stoned ring he wore on the index finger of his right hand, and squeezed it between the thumb and forefinger of his left.

A beam of pink light struck the body of the god.

The techs of Compository division froze in horror. The angels scattered like gulls. Kajsa Prime smiled superbly, turning left and right to her avatars, who all smiled equally superbly.

For a long time, no one spoke.

The pink light played upon the three heads of Lord Abraxas, the cock's head and the two serpents'. The Lord Abraxas did not stir. His six eyes remained closed.

The Eladeldi bearers held up their precious burden. They were not stirring either. They might have been lifeless replicas of Eladeldi, thought Pomeroy Lion, while he tweaked the right-hand point of his moustache. He admired once again the totality of Capellan control.

"Most accommodating," said Brother Valetude. His voice had become reedy and breathless. It was as if he had somehow forgotten how to use his larynx properly.

"We hope so," said Queen Kajsa.

The Guardian turned to his blue-furred menials. A twitch, like a nervous tic, was visible in the skin of his enormous forehead.

"Open the vessel," commanded Brother Valetude.

Sweet Lavender spread his wings with a soft but distinct *crack.* "At last," he murmured. The three nearest Kajsas heard him, and threw him a reproving look.

The catch of the silver egg was released. One of the Eladeldi removed the top and set it aside. Their movements precisely synchronized, two of the others stepped forward and tipped up the bottom of the egg. The fourth Eladeldi, who had had his forelegs and forepaws sluiced by the first with what appeared to be some kind of lubricating oil, came and thrust them into the egg.

The Eladeldi scooped out a double handful of giant caterpillars. They were half a meter long, and electric blue in color.

The air in the hall was effervescent with anticipation.

The caterpillars tried to cling to the Eladeldi's arms. Irritably, they twisted about, nosing the scented air.

The presiding Guardians watched, each with an identical placid, distracted smile. Pomeroy Lion noticed that all four of them had begun to sweat profusely. The foreheads of Sister Mansuetude and Sister Celandine and Sister Contenta had started to twitch now too, like Brother Valetude's.

The Eladeldi shook the caterpillars from his oiled arms carefully into the pit.

They rained down onto the body of the Lord Abraxas.

The blue caterpillars crawled up the golden snakes that were the legs of the Lord Abraxas. They crawled along his arms and up his chest. One, distracted by who knows what stray stimulus, crawled off to examine his flail. It took a few minutes for them to sort themselves out. The tension was appalling. Everyone looked at Kajsa Prime, who stood in respectful silence, smiling. While she did not speak, no one else would.

There must have been about thirty of the baby Capellans in all: enough that it was hard to count them while they were all moving around. Some were moving down the snakes now, toward the slumbering reptile heads. Some went between the legs, to the back of the pelvis, where a subsidiary brain had been conveniently sited.

Most of the Capellans, humping up their middles and squeezing themselves forward, were making sticky tracks up the caramel-colored torso. Even now they were burrowing in among the feathers of the head, like giant parasites looking for a place to prey.

An excited cheer went up. The first Capellan had been seen emerging from the plumage and starting to enter one of the nostrils that arched above the beak.

Within seconds the rest of them, as if by unanimous decision, had each found themselves an orifice. They forced their way determinedly in through the sides of the beak itself. They squirmed beneath the viridian eyelids and slipped into the pink mouths of the serpentine feet. Sweet Lavender flew a rapid circuit of the pit and came back to say he had spotted one penetrating the divine anus.

Again the trumpets blew, and the organ pealed, and the bells of the Temple rang out to greet the dawn of a brave new era.

For a long time after that, nothing happened.

The sacred wine had all been drunk, every conceivable permutation of congratulations and felicitations made, and the smallest pages dispatched to their dormitories before the next development came. Then the radios of the technicians hummed and a winged servitor flew up to Chief Adriel to report that the mouth of one of the serpents, the left, had been seen to open slightly.

Everyone, Guardian and Seraph and slave alike, came to the edge of the pit. The Guardians, oddly silent, moved awkwardly, and everyone was careful to get out of their way.

The mouths of both serpents were now starting to open, disclosing their deep red interiors, their palisades of shiny white teeth. The spectators murmured appreciatively.

Chief Adriel stepped down into the pit and laid a hand on the left-foot serpent, just behind the jaw. He felt for a pulse. His pleasure was manifest.

While he stood there the eyes of the right-foot serpent opened. They seemed to swim with glittering fluids. They closed, then opened again, cleared; and the eyes of the left-foot serpent opened too.

The eyes of the serpents were green and gold and primeval. They glared angrily into the hall.

The legs of the god reared up out of the pit to their fullest extent. They hissed. They flicked out the forked lashes of their tongues and probed the air.

The arms of the god now stirred. The chest was unquestionably rising and falling. The cock's viridian eyelids lifted. Beneath the eyelids circular black eyes in fierce red sockets swiveled accusingly.

The din of the god hissing and the Temple congregation cheering and the music playing grew and swelled until it filled the hall and threatened to deafen everyone within.

Then clumsily, jerkily, like a monster in an antique stop-motion cinema film, the Lord Abraxas arose from his black-tiled bed.

Before him, the wall of the Hall of Animation split from top to bottom.

Humans and posthumans, aliens and the engineered, the occupants of the hall fell back behind a retaining field as the piercing light of the galaxy burst in.

Like a partially inflated balloon, the newly built god rose into the escaping air.

The split in the wall grew wide. Outside the Cherubim could be seen, thirty and forty and fifty of them, forcing the great doors back with their indomitable little bodies.

The Lord Abraxas sat up in space, rolling his great body forward. Black-suited ancillaries scattered from his flying limbs.

He threw back his head and opened his beak. Some claim they heard his cry, that savage, clamorous challenge to the inrushing void.

Like a warrior moving toward battle, the Lord Abraxas bore his shield before him on his arm. The shield shone like gold where the arc lights caught it. Wild rainbows flew across the scales of the serpents as their heads swayed above his broad brown back. His comb flared.

Then the great composite god lifted his mighty flail of wood and horn and began to hammer on his shield.

Drumming soundlessly, relentlessly, he pitched himself into space.

∽ **35**

On the bridge of the Capellan starship the *Citadel of Porcelain at First Light* the Chief Recorder, Brother Poesy, stopped writing in his big black book. His quill stood in his hand, arrested in motion, as the gigantic creature flew laboriously out of the Temple.

Brother Melodious dropped his beer tube. "Will you look at that thing?" he said.

The other Guardians gathered at the window.

In the east, the Lord Abraxas climbed like a strange new satellite, an afterthought of the degenerate suns. Behind it, like a trail of particulate smoke, the Temple was emptying itself of Cherubim.

Brother Poesy began to mutter.

> *"In what distant deeps or skies*
> *Burnt the fire of thine eyes?"*

His quill dropped from his hand, splashing spots of ink across the blue-ruled page. In his smooth pale forehead, a vein began to tremble.

Kybernator Perlmutter's plump white hand reached for the loom pitch control, as though to move his ship in pursuit; but his intention too was arrested.

Brother Poesy clamped his hands to his temples. *"On what wings dare he aspire?"* he croaked.

Brother Melodious swung round and grabbed Brother Poesy by the elbow with his hand of flesh and bone. He put his face close to his brother's. "He ain't got no wings," he said, hoarsely. The point seemed to matter to him, for some reason.

The Chief Recorder entreated him. *"What the hand dare seize the fire?"*

Trickles of Day-Glo pink Hi-Liter started to run from the lids of Brother Melodious's eyes.

From a distance of ten centimeters the two Guardians stared at each other, their mouths open, as though the powers of speech and movement had deserted them. Above their supraorbital ridges, their hugely extended foreheads twitched, once, twice, three times, together.

From their sisters and brothers at the window a deep groan emanated. Four tiny blue streaks had come zipping from the open doors of the Temple of Abraxas to fasten on the heels of its departing lord.

Kybernator Astraghal spread his arms. His eyes were fixed on the flying monstrosity. His head and shoulders seemed to shake to the rhythm of the flail. He gave a gasping cry. *"Wait for us."*

The lips of all the Guardians worked, as though some bitterness possessed their mouths, as though they wished to spit or speak but could not contrive to do so. Blue lightning wreathed their bodies.

Brother Melodious struggled valiantly. "Hey," he choked. "Come on. It's not such a bad. Y-you ain't."

His limbs shuddered, his steel foot skidding about the floor as though captivated by some irregular magnetic force.

"It ain't like," he said.

The eyes of his shipmates bored into him, manic, implacable.

"We got all the. W-we—"

There was a small tearing sound. Brother Melodious's mouth opened unnaturally wide. Strings of thick white liquid burst from it.

Kybernator Perlmutter tottered back a step, hugging his arms about himself.

On contact with the air the strings issuing from the mouth of Brother Melodious hardened into strands of adhesive fiber. They whipped around his body, binding his limbs.

Brother Melodious struggled, his body vibrating as if from an application of electric current. Blood spotted the front of his shirt and splashed the togas of all who stood nearby as his skull began to split. The Lord Abraxas continued to soar slowly, effortlessly, past the starship.

"By the Manifold Majestic Mysteries of the Metaphase!"

The pink-metal fist of Seraph Boaz, Chief of Prevision on the Capella mission, crashed down on the counter, denting it severely and cracking the perspex covers on four nearby readouts.

His black-rimmed eyes glowered with indignation. The Great Work had been completed without him, the act of animation performed, and now here was the Lord Abraxas in all his full gold and tawny glory, scaled, skinned and feathered, released from his Temple into empty space.

The powerful elbows of the newly launched god swept the void aside as if it were water. His enormous hands beat a silent, vigorous tattoo on his shield of bronze with his flail of wood and horn. The Lord Abraxas defied the grim pull of the Capellan twins, sailing out above the disc of their accretions on nothing but the might of his own muscles, setting his all-devouring beak toward the infinite.

As a loyal worshiper of the Lord, perhaps the most loyal on board the *Seraph Kajsa*, and as a dedicated contributor, through the applied projections of Prevision division, to the Great Work of his Incarnation, Boaz was outraged. He reached for the com switch. He would call the Priestess Kajsa, all the Kajsas, and denounce this premature conclusion. How had it been accomplished? And where was the god heading now? It seemed almost as if he meant to leave the system altogether.

Then the Lord Abraxas crossed the orbit of the *Citadel of Porcelain at First Light*, and in a second something went flashing through space from it to him, something small, a small cluster of things that were positively minute.

Boaz roared.

"Tracking scanners! Magnification one thousand!"

The duty Diagnostics technician flew to her task. Boaz fumed. He flashed an alert to Xipetotec, on the bridge. He opened the com, but did not speak. The magnifications were already coming on.

"Replay section 534-2E, quarter-speed," boomed Boaz. "Copy to Chief Xipetotec."

He released the magnets in his boots, drifting to a larger monitor. Already inboard maintenance mechs were arriving to repair the damage done by his earlier display of temper.

Slowed down, the magnified pictures showed what looked like a portion of bright blue noodles flung into space. There was no doubt what it really was, none at all. It was a clutch of the Capellan worms, abandoning their vessel. And when the view returned to real time, it was all too clear what the craven creatures did when they caught up with Lord Abraxas. It was the same thing they did when they caught up with any sapient biped they had decided to annex.

A purely human bile rose in the armored Seraph's throat. In one hideous, repulsive instant he understood the perfidy, the blasphemy that Kajsa Tobermory herself had directed. The Great Lord had been incarnated solely for this violation, the penetration of his sacred body by the vilest parasites in all the known galaxy.

"Vengeance!" he cried. "To the Temple!"

On the com, Xipetotec was sounding excited too. He was saying something about the Cherubim. For a moment Boaz did could not comprehend what the man was bleating about. What in the worlds did the Cherubim matter, in this moment of hideous betrayal?

Then, by twos and threes, he saw the black chrome homunculi begin to sail past his scanners, off to join the swarm.

The Cherubim were betraying them too.

On the overcrowded *Danuta*, Saskia Zodiac wept.

Torch was concerned. "What is it, sweet?"

She pressed the heel of her free hand to her eyes. "Xtasca," she said.

The Cherub had chosen to stay behind when they left the *Seraph Kajsa*, to hide itself among the others. Now they had all gone, deserting the flagship to follow the Incarnate Abraxas. Saskia was in no doubt that Xtasca had gone with them.

Torch tried to comfort her. "It's okay, sweet. Maybe he needs them for drones."

Saskia hit him in the chest with her fist.

"Oh hush you," he said, and cuddled her. "You don't need any Cherub any more," he said.

In his arms she did not cease to weep, though perhaps she wept more quietly.

Along the length of the drumming monster the deep red sunlight burned. Kenny stared after it with his head on one side and his ears pricked. His eyes were slits, implacable.

"NOW THAT I SUPPOSE IS JABBERWOCK," Little Alice had said when it appeared, flying out of the Temple. "THE JAWS THAT BITE, YOU KNOW."

Captain Jute didn't know. She didn't want to know about the horrible great thing the Seraphim had made, whatever it was. What she wanted to know was what was happening now on the *Citadel of Porcelain at First Light*, if the caterpillars had abandoned it. She wanted particularly to know that it wasn't going to leave before they could get there.

"There they go," said Torch, and she panicked an instant, but what he meant was the *Catriona* and the *Xenoa*. They watched the two Seraph ships for a moment as they slipped their moorings. The *Seraph Kajsa* was approaching the Temple, while they were headed away.

"THEY'RE FOLLOWING HIM TOO," said Alice later; and they were.

"Interesting to see," Torch proposed, "what the *Kajsa* does now."

Kenny scratched rapidly in the fur of his cheeks. "She goos too," he said, registering his bet.

"She won't go," Saskia said.

"Oh, she'll go," Torch said softly. "They won't let the Priestess just leave them behind."

"Well, I wouldn't go," said Saskia.

"Why not?" he asked her.

Saskia gave a theatrical shudder. "He is a big ugly monster," she said venomously.

"That's the way they designed him," he said.

"He looks like a joke," she said.

"Hey!" Torch said, but it was an automatic protest.

A while later he said: "Yeah, I see it. Like one of those puzzles. Those psy test puzzles."

Captain Jute knew exactly what he meant. They had made them do dozens of those things, she and Angie, when they were girls. Pictures scrambled up that you had to put back the way they were supposed to be, and whichever piece you went for first meant something about you.

She had never liked those tests. They were fixed. You could only lose.

"IT MUST BE THE JABBERWOCK," said Little Alice. "UNLESS IT'S A SNARK, DO YOU SUPPOSE? IT MIGHT BE A BOOJUM, YOU KNOW, BECAUSE OF EVERYONE VAN-ISHING AWAY. NOW, WHETHER THE JABBERWOCK MAY BE A BOOJUM TOO—"

"Just take us to the *Citadel*, Alice."

Kenny slept. Saskia too, her head on Torch's chest. Nothing would have made Tabitha sleep, nor Torch either, even though it might have helped with the oxygen.

"There goes the *Kajsa*, Kenny," Torch said, sometime later. "We'd have won that bet."

On the *Citadel of Porcelain at First Light*, the lights were still burning. There was music on the radio. Nobody shot at them as they approached.

Tabitha took a fast turn over Stardeck. There was a squadron of red Tinkerbells there, standing idle. Not two hundred meters distant stood a Navajo Scorpion that looked as though it had flown too close to one of the suns. All its paint was scorched and blackened.

Belowdecks, Eladeldi trotted about helplessly, snuffling miserably. When they saw the Thrant they turned tail. In the shrubbery of the S Deck atrium, two red-suited captains were snapping at each other, kicking dirt in each other's face.

"Theer Masters are gone," said Kenny with satisfaction.

People ran up to greet Tabitha and her friends. Tabitha didn't recognize any of them. Perhaps if she had made an effort, she might have done. There was only one person she wanted to see now.

And there she was, lounging on a couch, her feet up on another. She was squeezing the stalk of a match between her extraordinary teeth.

"Wotcha, gel," she said. She didn't get up.

"Hello, Dodger."

Dodger Gillespie looked very thin and haggard. In fact she looked old.

Captain Jute went over and sat down on the couch by Dodger's feet. She might have known Dodger would dodge her own death. She stretched out her feet to the couch where Dodger was sitting, but her legs weren't long enough.

"You look like hell, Dodger."

Saskia Zodiac had come to perch on the back of Captain Gillespie's couch. "So do you!" she reminded Tabitha.

"It was hell," Captain Gillespie said. "It was a fucking shambles." She took the match from her mouth. "I'm sorry, gel."

Tabitha was confused. "What for?"

"Getting you into it."

" 'Into it', what do you mean, 'into it'? I was right out of it! I wouldn't be here now if they'd let me in it!"

"I should have had you in with me."

"Don't give me that," said Captain Jute. "You put me in the safest place you knew."

"It was a fucking stupid shambles," muttered Captain Gillespie.

"Did they get you?"

Dodger Gillespie gave the merest shake of her gaunt head. "We skipped," she said. "Went in."

"In?" said Torch.

She looked at him without interest. "Deep in," she said. She shook her head again, and looked at her boots. If she spoke of it at all, it would not be yet.

"Dodger, this is Torch," said Saskia Zodiac. "Torch, this is Dodger Gillespie."

"Pleasure," Captain Gillespie grunted. She was still looking at her boots. Saskia rose and took Torch by the hand, pulling him close as though to protect him.

Tabitha looked around. Still she didn't see anyone she

recognized. Perhaps her last skip had been into some kind of parallel universe, where she would have to start all over again.

"Who else made it?" she asked.

Dodger Gillespie put out her jaw. Again she shook her head.

"What about Jone?"

Her voice was like a cobweb, like a ghost of a voice. "Not a chance," she said.

They led Captain Jute into the ship, by ways they had checked and pronounced safe. There were a lot of them, in skintights or ill-fitting combat suits, laden with com gear and artillery taken from the Eladeldi patrols. She asked their names, and made a point of remembering them. There was one called Cristophe, another one called Allardyce, and another in a PVC slicksuit with paisley tattoos down her neck who insisted her name was Me Shell. They assured her that the rest of the Plenty refugees were being kept in somewhere called Sector Y, until the rest of the ship had been secured. It was like being back on Plenty, ringed around by Otis and Lomax and Clegg, taken from one place to another under guard.

In the corridors of the *Citadel* the golden statues described the same attitudes as ever. Streams of sparkling water poured from the mouths of lion-faced medallions, ran merrily through the bowers where the Guardians had reclined, eating their grapes and listening to music. A young cripple called Lycra, an obvious daughter of the Plenty Rookeries, toting an unloaded gun longer than she was tall, took Tabitha to see a white shape that lay among the leaves like a badly wrapped mummy. It was a dead Guardian. Protruding from the bottom of its shroud of sticky white fibers, its feet were still intact, pink and clean in their gilded sandals; but its face had collapsed, the top of its skull was missing. Was it one she had known, before or after their promotion? She didn't want to look too closely, unless she found out.

Lycra and her friends were as proud as if they had been personally responsible for everything: the disappearance of Plenty, the departure of the Seraphim, the dissolution of the Guardians. Captain Jute felt lonely suddenly. She felt like forcing them all to admit how little any of them knew about the real issues here. The one thing that stopped her was the certainty that she knew less.

Dodger was mourning, Saskia was busy. Tabitha reached for Kenny, took his arm. The stink of him was a comfort, the very feel of his sweaty, filthy fur under her hand. She stroked his ears.

"These guys," she said, *sotto voce*, looking at Lycra, Me Shell, the Xtascite survivors. "Those clothes, those haircuts. Who do they think they are?"

Kenny snarled amiably in her face.

She let them hustle her around a corner and up a flight of marble stairs, heading into the neck of the white swan. Their postures, their very faces were identical to the Rejects of Integrity 2. They were Murray and Carmen, refurbished for a new era: new challenges, new enemies.

"We had haircuts like that, twenty-five years ago," Captain Jute told her Thrant bodyguard, while Lycra and her mates were on their radios, checking the approach to the next sector. She thrust her hands deep in her pockets. "We were fucking useless," she said.

The bridge of the Capellan starship was like no other she had ever seen. The walls were of some soapy material, neither plastic, ceramic, nor stone, and pale green. Rings of gold metal half a meter and more in diameter hung down from them, some too high too reach without a ladder. If those were the controls, as Captain Jute presumed they were, they must have been designed for a different race: a larger one, with different hands, or none at all. Strange inscriptions, lines of rhomboidal shapes repeating randomly like the ones in her Stardeck apartment, were incised all over everything, long tablets and scrolls of them, in different sizes.

The remains of Guardians lay around, decerebrated bodies and ragged cocoons. There was a live one too, its toga stained with filth. It crawled across the floor toward them, a strange gargling noise coming from its throat.

Captain Jute's escort surrounded her efficiently, training their guns upon it. "Be careful," said Allardyce. "It still has its rings of power."

The last Guardian gaped up at her. Its face was disintegrating. The teeth were falling from its mouth.

"Tabitha Jute," it said, thickly. "You are an evolutionary dead end. You are a waste of air. You will never—"

The sorry relic gagged. Its flabby mouth seemed to be giving it difficulty with the next word.

"—c-c-command this vessel. You will fail here as you have failed everywhere, in your whole sorry ineffectual life."

Ignoring the guns of Captain Jute's escort, it groped a jeweled, dirty hand in her direction.

With a gibber of derision, Kenny the Thrant was upon it. Howling in Thrant, he wrapped one leg around its flaccid throat and smashed both elbows into the ample top of its skull.

Convulsing, its head jerked backward. She saw the thick square nose, the bags of flesh beneath the bulging eyes. She recognized Kybernator Perlmutter, the captain clinging to his ship long after his brothers and sisters had abandoned it and gone on.

The Kybernator made a wheezing, whispering sound so strange it was impossible to say whether it signified defiance or despair.

Kenny growled passionately. He smashed his elbows into the skull again. Black blood sprayed as the degraded bone split.

Within, something popped into view. It was blue and

glistening. Captain Jute's escort shouted excitedly into their radios. They were ready to start shooting.

She held up her hand.

Somehow, out of some habit of deference, they held their fire. Perhaps they were afraid of hitting Kenny.

The claws of the Thrant sank deep into the soft flesh of the purloined body. With a tiny squeal like an expiring balloon, the intruding Capellan burst out.

Kenny exhaled noisily. With a yelp that was more like the squeak of a triumphant kitten, he pounced on the gristly parasite and gobbled it up.

There was a gap of time. She was sitting on a bench in the center of the bridge. It was a low bench of white marble, away from the walls. She knew it was the seat of command.

Kenny was on the floor beside her, delicately scouring the inside from a lemon with his fangs. He was quite unhurt by his predatory act, though it had left him, seemingly, with an enormous thirst.

Dodger Gillespie was there too, some distance away. She looked no better than before. She too was sitting on the floor, for some reason, drinking a beer. Tabitha thought she might like to have a beer too.

People were around now, people she recognized. Programmers and data analysts who had worked on the bridge of Plenty. For all the good it had done. In their grey T-shirts and peeling sneakers they clustered around the astroscopes. They seemed to have lost some weight since being brought aboard the *Citadel of Porcelain at First Light*.

And here was someone else hurrying toward her, an olive-skinned man in a white collarless jacket and thick rimless spectacles. He was clutching a clipboard. For some reason, he looked terribly pleased to see her.

He was completely bald, bald as any Guardian. For a moment her heart raced. But he was stooping, holding out his hand, wanting to shake hers. She stood up. She recognized him. She had not known he was still alive, had not thought about him once since her escape from detention.

His face was alight with pleasure and anticipation. "It's actually not as complicated as it seems," he said.

She shook his hand. "Mr. Spinner," she said. She had no idea what he was talking about.

He gave her a comradely smile. "I knew one day we'd be glad I familiarized myself with the controls!"

From the astroscopes, a voice called: "Captain."

She turned.

There were half a dozen of them, aging girls and boys. They wanted her attention. "Captain, they're all going."

They showed her a screen where, magnified to an identifiable size, the patchwork creature swam on, still beating on its shield. After it, as if on tow, trailed a motley fleet. They picked them out for her. A disc and a flower and an intricately branching wand: they were the other Capellan starships. The three tiny black lozenges were the ships of the Seraphim; and those were the slender-waisted system ships, like golden wasps turning from the rotten suns as if scenting the juice of fruit unimaginably distant.

Tabitha put her hands on her hips. "And all the caterpillars are inside it," she said. She required confirmation.

"They seem to prefer the more advanced model," said Mr. Spinner. There was a note of regret, almost of apology, in his voice. He would grow out of it, in time.

Once more she clasped the hand of her First Officer and shook it. "Mr. Spinner," she said again. "You know, I never did know your first name."

He put his hand on her shoulder. "Leslie," he said. He was terribly embarrassed. "It's Leslie."

"Leslie," she repeated. Then she left him once more, and walked lightly and precisely, across to Captain Gillespie. She stood over her, her arms folded.

Captain Gillespie looked at her briefly, without expression.

Tabitha Jute waited.

Captain Gillespie swigged her beer.

Tabitha unfolded her arms. She reached down and took hold of her old friend's wrists.

Dodger Gillespie rolled up her eyes and groaned.

Tabitha pulled her up, unfolding the whole bony length of her. She was as light as a paper doll.

There was muttering among the crew. Tabitha ignored it.

Another screen, an oval one, showed the view from the zenith beacon. It looked down on the belching red suns in the vast pool of carbonized flotsam they had organized for themselves, century by century. The Capellans had been right to leave. This system was a ruin. Yet it was an incredible sight to see, and to speak of, to say you had waltzed around those fountains of cosmic destruction and come home again. She thought what it would have meant to them, to Dodger and her and Karen and everyone, when they were young, when they did nothing but scheme and natter and speculate and hunger for the stars. What they would have given then to be here now.

What they would have given, thought Captain Jute, still holding Captain Gillespie by the hands, was not a tenth part, not a hundredth, of what it had actually cost.

"Mr. Spinner," said Tabitha Jute.

"Captain," said Mr. Spinner.

"This is your captain," she said.

"Gawd strewth, gel . . ." muttered Dodger Gillespie. She started coughing.

Tabitha led her to the white bench and sat her down. Then she went back to Mr. Spinner, and took him over to one of the gold rings in the wall, one of the lowest ones, to which several long pieces of string had been attached. Anxiously he began to explain about orbit locks and positronic anchors.

"Ready when you are, Captain Gillespie," said Captain Jute.

∽ 36

In the seventh week of the fourth year of the return to Sol, Captain Jute went secretly and alone to a departure bay in Sector H. Saskia Zodiac and her family were already there, on the balcony. Saskia had clearly been crying.

Below the balcony, in the bay itself, waited a powerful schooner, a fan-stressed Patay Astrobahn called the *Categorical Imperative*. She was fueled and primed and stocked for a long journey. Half her living space was crammed with supplies for her solo passenger.

Captain Jute gave Saskia Zodiac a goodbye kiss. "Bye-bye, Saskia," she said. "Remember me to Schiaparelli."

The baby, a solemn little boy, clung to Saskia's long white neck. Sensitive to his mother's distress, he suspected it had something to do with this woman with the big earrings and the heavy green suit smelling of heating gel and industrial lubricant.

Tabitha gave him her finger to hold, and kissed his fuzzy head.

"Bye-bye, Zidrich. Don't grow up too fast."

His grave eyes watched her, as if calculating the trajectory of her future.

"Bye-bye, Suzan. You're already growing up too fast."

Suzan giggled, suddenly shy. She stuffed the middle fingers of her right hand in her mouth and ran behind her daddy, to peer excitedly at Tabitha around his leg. Three years old and perfectly healthy, she seemed to have inherited some of her mother's facility for accelerated growth. She was as tall as a terrestrial seven-year-old and as skinny as a lightstick. She liked to take Tabitha to the Sector W forest to climb trees and play hide-and-seek. Already her mother's unpredictable friend held the same fascination for her as liftshafts, power sockets, and other ready sources of potential trouble.

"Goodbye, Tabitha." Zidrich and Suzan's daddy smiled broadly and shook her hand. She embraced him, hugging him hard. He would never quite understand the powerful sense of approval he always felt from her.

"Goodbye, Torch," she said. "I won't tell you to take care of her, you don't need me to tell you that." She ran her eyes down over Saskia's bulging belly, then embraced her too, and Zidrich with her, carefully. "Just make sure she gets enough to eat," she told Torch.

"We'll do that," said Torch, in his deep, calm voice. "You look after yourself, Tabitha," he said. "Think of us when you get to Proxima."

By the intricate origami of hyperspace travel, it seemed that the star Captain Jute had originally thought she was setting out for, all those years ago, was now actually within reach. Alice had been working on the vector. They thought she could expect to make landfall on Palernia in a year or so, subjective.

Torch picked up little Suzie and held her so that she could hug Tabitha too. Tabitha closed her eyes upon a familiar secret sorrow. Torch and Saskia's baby was as black as his daddy, but Suzan, several shades lighter, always reminded her of Angie, the little girl lost on the Moon.

As Tabitha and Suzan separated, Torch put his hand on Saskia's belly and said clearly: "If she is a girl, we mean to call her Tabitha."

Shocked, Tabitha looked at Saskia. "Saskia, no," she said.

She had assumed, everyone had, that they meant to work their way through the original quintet. People had been speculating what feminine forms of Goreal or Mogul they might devise, against the arrival of further daughters.

But Saskia frowned and nodded. "In loving memory,"

she said, heavily. She laid a sad hand on Tabitha's cheek.
She was sure they would never see her again. Imitating her,
baby Zidrich reached out his hand too, and put it on her
other cheek. Suzan squealed, and everybody laughed.

The lift chimed, and they all turned to see Dodger Gillespie step out.

"Dodger!"

"Wotcha, gel."

The captain of the *Citadel of Porcelain at First Light*
smiled a slight, stiff smile at the little gathering. She was
never quite at ease with children. In return they, of course,
adored her. Suzan was already running across to hug her.
Even the baby held out his arms.

Captain Jute considered her old friend, the tight nests of
wrinkles that time had woven around her eyes, the deep
valleys either side of her mouth. The two of them had never
quite regained what they had had before—but when did
you ever? That was what the word time meant, she reckoned, in space or out of it.

"I'm glad you could come, Dodger."

By now Captain Gillespie had Suzan hanging on one
hand and was cradling Zidrich with the other. She contrived
to hold him as if he was a bulky piece of space equipment,
a mercury-foil distillation unit or an oxygenator.

"Somebody has to see you get the thing out the door the
right way round," she said.

Captain Jute had been working on the bridge, on and off,
and had learned what she could about the ex-Capellan ship.
"I don't know how you do it," she said, meaning control
this strange new mode of transport.

"Yeah, you do," said Dodger.

"I'm no good at it," said Tabitha. "I'm an old-fashioned
girl, I like a persona."

Captain Gillespie lifted the left-hand edge of her upper
lip a fraction. "Let someone else do the maths," she said.

"Maths!" said Tabitha. "More like religion, in this."

There was an odd, strained moment as the two pilots

stood, not looking at each other. Tabitha wanted to go. She could feel the light-years ahead like a shiver in her spine.

"I'm off," she said.

Saskia wept. Torch and Suzan comforted her. Zidrich wriggled, trying to put his fingers in Dodger's shiny sockets.

Briefly Dodger Gillespie bared her terrible incisors.

"Tell her to look after you," she said.

"Dodger says you're to look after me, Alice."

"NATURALLY I SHALL."

The persona suite on the Astrobahn was a beautiful piece of gear, a marbled-grey fascia with just a hint of pink, and marcasite tabs for all the presets. The reader slot had a strip of velvetine lining round the edge.

The pilot's web was light as gossamer, with straps of Ganymede silk. Three weeks into the skip, Tabitha Jute hung weightless there, sipping a tube of Tukori. Sensitized filters in the viewport and all the windows turned the dull mottled vacancy of hyperspace into subtle shades of azure and turquoise. They spoke rarely of their destination, the pilot and the persona of the Astrobahn, but once when they did, Captain Jute said:

"It's not Proxima itself, so much, as the fact they diverted us."

"YOU RESENTED THE INTERFERENCE."

"Still do."

"YOU MEAN TO FINISH THE JOB YOU STARTED."

"That's it, Alice. That's it exactly."

Some minutes passed, long, empty and vague.

"Palernia itself I'm not so bothered about," she said.

"ARE YOU NOT, CAPTAIN?"

"No."

"WHY IS THAT, I WONDER?"

Tabitha turned her head and looked at the educational files running on the monitor above the caresser couch.

"Too much countryside," she said.

"The Palernians will be all right," she said, a few minutes later.

"WILL THEY WELCOME YOU, CAPTAIN?"

"Well, yes," she said. "Yes, they will."

She thought it was true, though she was bringing bad news about their relatives.

"They know how to party," she said.

She had spent enough time on Mntce in the past to know a wake would be much the same as a wedding.

"Because they feel everything five times as strongly."

On the distal parallax scope, one of the probability stacks was starting to shrink. Tabitha calculated the edge and trimmed the fibrillators.

"It's like a volcano," she said. "Spiraling madness and mayhem," she explained, thoughtfully.

"GOOD HEAVENS," said the persona politely. "IS THAT WHAT YOU DESIRE, CAPTAIN?"

The Captain smiled to herself. "Yeah!" she said. "It'll be all right."

There were a lot of ghosts to burn.

"Most likely, by the time we get there the news will be old enough not to matter so much," she said, after a while.

"Actually, I don't fancy it much at the moment," she confessed.

An array of little pink lights scurried across the console and back again. "BY THE TIME WE GET THERE YOU'LL BE READY," Alice predicted. "YOU'LL BE TIRED OF HAVING ONLY ME FOR COMPANY."

"Oh, you'll do for a bit, Alice," said Captain Jute. She gave the fibrillators another tap. "I tell you who I was thinking about last night," she said. "Balthazar Plum. Old Balthazar."

"I HAVE NO RECORD OF THAT NAME," said Alice, without a noticeable pause.

"You don't remember Balthazar Plum? Do you remember the vineyard? California? Terra? Well, I suppose you wouldn't.''

Her beer was warm. She floated to the forward minigalley and put it in the chiller.

''There's a lot of stories I could tell you, Alice,'' she said. ''The first time I saw Balthazar Plum was at a party. He was dressed up as the Moon.''

She stared at the soft blues of the window while her beer cooled.

''I wonder if he knew,'' she said. ''I never really knew, whether he knew or not.''

By afternoon, quite comfortably drunk, she went and got out her harmonica. She lay back in the web for a long time, playing bits and pieces of things, everything she could remember. Little Alice appeared, waltzing gravely with herself on the holopad, which Saskia had helped her to program. It was a fine big one, with a vast range. Captain Jute's range was always a little less certain. You might, for example, have thought the tune she was playing now was ''You Picked a Fine Time to Leave Me, Lucille''; but with Tabitha Jute, it was never easy to be sure.